HATRED DAY

A HATRED DAY NOVEL

T. S. PETTIBONE

CHRYSANTHALIX PRESS

Copyright © 2016 Chrysanthalix Press

ISBN-13: 978-0997202915
ISBN-10: 0997202912

Library of Congress Control Number: 2016930254
Chrysanthalix Press, Gilroy, California

Cover design by Firnadi Iqbal
Formatting by Polgarus Studio

10 9 8 7 6 5 4 3 2 1

For those who daringly dare

Contents

PART I

To Buy a Girl

The Gehenna slum, Oregon
November 1, 2052

Neko was prepared to die. His hands trembled on the steering wheel of his Wrangler jeep as he neared the looming entrance of the Gehenna slum: he told himself not to be afraid. It didn't matter that in Gehenna he might be strung up by a gang or have his organs cut out and sold at the nearest black market stall for a few coppers. It also didn't matter that he was risking his life on a wild guess. All that mattered was *her*.

"I doubt my sister's in Gehenna, Neko," the young man in the passenger seat said. "The last place we know she went is the forest. I still think she's lost in there."

"Your assumptions don't concern me at this point, Desya," Neko replied. "We've already searched the forest—all that's left is Gehenna."

"Then maybe we should search Red Cross and Cell City again, because Snofrid's definitely *not* in the slum." Desya raked a hand over his high-and-tight buzz cut. "She'd break her own leg before going in there alone."

"Perhaps she didn't enter by choice."

"Look who's making assumptions now." Desya's eyes, deep-set above his half-face gasmask, hardened on the red laser gate ahead. He sat silently a while before saying, "Fine, we'll have a look in Gehenna. But we should swing by the slave auction before we check in with any of the gangs."

"How much time until the auction begins?"

"Thirty minutes."

Neko would have to drive fast. After deactivating the red laser gate using his identification tag, he accelerated onto the Infernal Highway, toward the entrance of Gehenna. Trash and clods of dry sewage clung to the highway like a railing; the stench was as foul-smelling as the slum's mass graves and as polluted as Earth's atmosphere.

By most, Gehenna was thought to be a war refugee slum just outside of *Hollowstone City*, but, being a doctor who'd once worked within its walls, Neko knew the truth—that only a fraction of the slum was populated by refugees. The rest were armed ex-military and thugs.

With each festering carcass Neko passed on the wayside, he accepted that death was as much a reality as his morning commute to work. He didn't know where in Gehenna he expected to find Snofrid, but, more than anything else, he hoped she wasn't hurt. He'd always considered her to be intelligent, yet wandering off and getting lost was the mistake of a child.

He rode the highway into the mouth of a dank tunnel, Gehenna's only gateway, and switched on his headlights; the beams illuminated a message scrawled in red paint on the wall of the tunnel: *Abandon all hope beyond this point*. His last string of optimism snapped, only his concern for Snofrid fueled him onward. He would've told her how he felt about her if his life was different. If the world was different.

"Speed up," Desya advised, eyeing the rearview mirror. "There's a gun truck on our tail."

"Shoot out its tires, then," Neko told him, who was already driving eighty-five. "When you lay down, you make yourself a carpet."

"I'd rather be a carpet than a corpse rolled up in one."

When Neko didn't budge, Desya massaged his eyes, as he always did when reevaluating his strategy. "Alright, look at it this way—if those guys pin us down on our way out of the slum, we'll risk getting Snofrid out safely. Just speed up or pull over."

"The day I pull over will be the day my dead body steers this car off the road," Neko declared. He stepped on the gas pedal until he'd dusted off the gun truck. He doubted a day would come when his species of Inborn saw eye-to-eye with Desya's. They were like lightning and rain, existing together, but clashing in their very natures.

The tunnel eventually branched into nine separate tunnels. Neko veered into the second tunnel, descending deeper into the belly of Gehenna. He hadn't driven a hundred feet when the stench forced a hot sprig of vomit up his throat. Swallowing, he wound a black scarf over his gasmask filter cartridge. The morass of rank odors—urine, vomit and open sewers— singed his eyes, blurring his view of the dusty road.

"No wonder so many people drive into ditches down here," he croaked. "I can't see through the blasted windshield."

"No one down here gives two cats' asses," Desya said, also wrapping a scarf around his mouthpiece. "Just watch out for spike strips."

Neko coughed. "Why me? You're the one with super vision. If we hit a spike strip, you're replacing my tires, and whatever else might get damaged." He coughed again and the oxygen enflamed his lungs in spite of his filter. But the noise was worse, like a maniacal orchestra. Death metal rattled the walls of the tunnel, echoed by working machinery and a chorus of human languages.

"All right. Run through the plan," he wheezed, as he slowed his jeep on a dirt plain scattered with armored Growler cars and cargo trucks.

"You're the buyer and I'm your bodyguard."

"And if the auction goes bad?"

"Then we put on Concealing Spells and squat on the upper levels." Desya fed his rifle a cartridge and shrugged into a flak jacket. "Lycidius will swing by at 0700 hours with backup."

Neko hoped they wouldn't need backup. He dug a box from his jacket pocket and removed a pair of optical lenses, equipped with facial recognition. "We'll keep contact until I make the buy," he said, fitting the contacts over his eyes. He blinked until his vision colored green. "I'll stream you a feed of the auction, along with the private information of each buyer. If anyone looks questionable, send me his records."

"Yep." Desya grabbed his computer bag off the console. "Let's go. The doors close in thirteen minutes."

Neko grunted. "Thirteen minutes is the earliest I've ever been in my life."

"Come on, man," Desya grumbled. "For once help me out without forcing me to pay for it." Slinging his rifle over one shoulder, he jogged toward the row of cage elevators at the furthest end of the plain. Neko slammed the car door and ignored the stain of guilt that had run across his conscience.

During the descent to Stratum 23, Neko tuned out of their environs. The rotting bodies strung up on the rafters didn't bother him, though the same couldn't be said for Desya, whose eyes filled with pity when he glanced at the labyrinth of stacked shacks and sweatshops below. This was something Neko would never understand about Desya. He pitied everyone, even took compassion on suffering strangers that might club him to death after he'd tossed them a coin. Neko could only guess it was because Desya and Snofrid had once lived in Gehenna and, for some reason, Desya still counted himself as part of this world.

"Which street is the Oubliette Hotel on?" he asked, once the elevator rattled onto ground level.

"Rock Spider Street." Desya yanked open the cage door and waded into the heaps of trash that carpeted the ground. "The slaveholder's name is Master Mookjai. He's the top Inborn trafficker in Gehenna, and he only holds his auctions once a month, so there's no chance she was already sold. We'll definitely have to pay up, though."

Neko scoffed. "Lycidius gave us fifty-thousand silvers. If Mookjai asks for more, all he's going to receive is my foot in his rear."

"I've never paid much attention to the slave business, so I don't know what he's gonna ask for. Just be cool. If he finds out we have no idea what the hell we're doing, he'll think we're rat jackets and toss us in the meat grinders." Desya booted a dead rat from his path. "If it comes down to it, I'll call Lycidius and ask him to transfer more silvers."

Neko pulled on a pair of gloves with two violent tugs. Knowing that Inborns were being peddled to humans as either pleasure slaves, organ donors, surrogates or laborers made him hate humanity even more. Some would claim that all humans weren't such villains, but a great many businessmen used the *Inhuman War*—the twenty-two-year conflict between humanity and Inborns—as a means of exploiting refugees. Even though it was widely known that the Oubliette Hotel facilitated the illegal Inborn trafficking ring, not a badge had stepped in. After all, another dead Inborn, another human smile.

Leaving the elevators, they walked down an alley that meandered through the sweatshops. Neko picked up on the aura of misery as if it were a stinking gas cloud. Here and there, black X's had been slopped on doors, broadcasting to all that disease had killed the inhabitants; half-naked children sprinted down the steel drainage pipes, so skinny that their skin cleaved to their skulls, and child soldiers patrolled the streets without fear or inhibition; women with black rashes on their faces hastily rinsed tunics in muddy gutters, averting their eyes from the armed street soldiers urinating in the dirt.

Neko stared at his shoes as he walked, avoiding the animal carcasses bloating in the sewage rivulets. He'd always detested the sight of poverty; it reminded him of his home planet, which had been rich in natural resources but had been plunged into desolation in the last years before the Inborns had abandoned it. The memories of its decay were torturous, so painful that he'd considered extracting them more than once. At this point in the Inhuman War, Earth was seeing a similar decay. Filth. Everywhere was filth, and not just externally. Man at his core was rotting.

"The Oubliette Hotel is just up that ramp," Desya said, pointing to a dirt ramp that twisted up the left side of the alley. "We have four minutes."

Neko made the climb after Desya, disliking that his back was exposed, before stepping onto a rusted platform. One look at the Oubliette Hotel and he was amazed that it was standing. He'd never seen such a lopsided pile of stitched up lumber in his life. However, it *was* a high class establishment in comparison to its neighbors, which didn't even have electricity or running water.

The mob of attendees fanned Neko's impatience; buyers of all nationalities poured through the splayed doors of the windowless hotel lobby. He hadn't expected the competition to be so high and knew it risked their chances of a successful purchase.

"Here's our number," Desya said, tossing him a bidding stick. "It's pretty jammed, but I saw some room at the back." He checked the platform's edge, where the buyers' bodyguards had assembled, and cocked the bolt handle of his rifle. "Personal security details aren't allowed inside, so I'll wait for you out here."

"Stay out of sight," Neko cautioned. Gathering his courage, he fastened the top button on his jacket and then followed the buyers into the warehouse. He'd never attended a slave auction, but the layout was self-explanatory. Sweat-stained cushions ran a ring around a broad center stage area. Most of the buyers were already lounging on the cushions being served vodka by Inborn slaves in black tunics, who crawled on all fours and carried the alcohol on their backs. The place buzzed like a hive, roiling with the tumult of conversation and laughter as men and women discussed their preferred slave type, the worst species to purchase, or their most recent conquest.

Neko melted into the crowd at the back of the warehouse, just as Desya's voice echoed in his earpiece. "Incoming," he said. "Three o'clock."

Neko noticed a slave girl crawling toward him like a mutt.

"Vodka, master?" she asked, staring up at him from the tops of her eyes.

"No."

"As you please, master." She inched toward the next couch. Neko eyed the jangling chains on her ankles and a sick feeling bucked in his gut.

Suddenly, the fantasy of dragging Master Mookjai into the alley and forcing him to drink from the sewage rivulets shot to the front of his mind. His fingers itched as he imagined the man gurgling in his hands. No one would care that one less bounder worked the street. But he'd do nothing until he'd confirmed Snofrid wasn't in the slave lineup.

"Do a sweep," Desya instructed. "I need the buyers behind you, too."

Neko scanned the crowd and his optical lenses identified the buyers through their Tags—wrist implants that verified they were human.

"Most of these guys are dead-heads," Desya told him. "Two of them are from Hollowstone City, so they might pay more, but other than that, we don't have to sweat. I doubt most of the others will cough up more than a couple hundred coppers a slave."

"That's both reassuring and insulting," Neko muttered.

"Welcome, great masters, to Oubliette," a shrill voice with a Thai accent called from the center stage. "Let's make some winners!"

Neko checked out the announcer and recoiled in disgust. The man looked like a toad, except he had facial piercings in place of warts. Ornamental chains, stitched to the skin by safety pins, were strung from his earlobes to his mouth like a bridle. He reclined on a plywood litter with his neck turned toward the audience, for he was too heavy to hold his head upright, and oozed a lazy indifference belied by the calculating sheen in his eyes. A floral robe sheathed his sagging gut, but dipped at the neck to reveal his bald chest. Fruit flies whirred around his infected chin piercings.

"For those of you who don't already know, I'm Master Mookjai," he continued. His voice was hoarse as he puffed on a glass bong. "I see new masters, so I'll run through the rules for their benefit. Most importantly, all sales are final! Done! Finished! If you're dissatisfied by your slave in the days to come, I won't repurchase her. From the moment she leaves the Oubliette, she'll be yours to do with what you choose." He took a cracked coconut from one of the slaves and sipped the milk. "Following the auction, you'll pay for your property here and then take possession of it at the back of the warehouse. Any buyer who fails to pay the coin he's bided will pay in blood.

"This evening, I bring for your pleasure eighteen slaves," he declared, picking at a scab on his chin. "Taken from the forests, rivers, cities and mountains of Oregon, the girls I bring to you are among its finest Inborn treasures. Groomed by my best masters, they'll submit to whatever you desire. We begin with a Necromancer of nineteen years." He rang a bell that was looped around his pointer finger. A trapdoor slid open in the floor and two street soldiers hustled a sobbing girl onto the stage.

The crowd erupted into laughter. Quick as a clicking dial, Neko realized his error in thinking he could stand calmly aloof. The sparkling green power source, or *Halo*, on the girl's right bicep indicated that she really was a Necromancer Inborn, like *him*. Her bruised body quaked under the coos of the onlookers. Dressed in a silk tunic, her brunette hair was wound in copper wire, and half of her Halo was burnt by nitric acid, ensuring that she couldn't fight back.

"We begin the bid at 20 coppers," Master Mookjai said.

One by one, buyers raised their bidding sticks; after an inner struggle, Neko held off from joining in: he knew that one less silver might decide the difference between saving Snofrid and watching her be sold to another buyer. Staring at the wall, his posture rigid, he ignored the girl's cries, and muttered, "The bastard should be beaten to death with his coconut."

"He's a slime bag," Desya agreed, his voice quiet, "but if someone wanted to pop every criminal down here, they might as well burn down the slum."

"I'm considering it."

"Sold at 62 coppers," Master Mookjai concluded, burping out a cloud of smoke.

When the girl had been hauled out the back door of the warehouse, another took the stage. She appeared oddly composed. Standing with her ankles crossed, she picked at the beads in her hair with the red claws that jutted from her fingertips. From the scorched red Halo on her left palm, Neko identified her as a Hematic Inborn, like Desya.

"The second product is a Hematic flower of fourteen years," Master Mookjai announced. "We begin the bid at 30 coppers."

Neko did another survey of the crowd. Most of the girls were being sold at offensively cheap prices, but only because the wealthier citizens had turned up their noses at the girls displayed thus far. He assumed that the 'best' of the selection were being saved for the end.

As he continued to probe the ranks, one of the second-level buyers snagged his attention a moment longer than the others. He stuck out like a wolf in a den of hyenas, standing at the rear of the warehouse with his hands locked behind his back. He observed the proceedings with the patience of one who awaits something he knows will happen shortly. His lava-red gasmask, cast in the shape of a bull's head, boasted a set of polished horns, and the black cassock he wore billowed about his ankles, even though the only draft in that stuffy arena was courtesy of an elderly man sneezing near the stage. With each Inborn slave sold, he clicked together the seven-inch raptor claw gloves strapped over his hands.

"This is the first I've seen of this guy," Desya said. "It doesn't look like he's got a Tag."

"Then he's not human," Neko deduced, curious that one of his kind would enter a human settlement without a forged Tag.

"Oh my hell," Desya cursed. "Neko, look at his ring."

Using his optical lenses, Neko zeroed in on the man's ring and his brain short-circuited in confusion: the ring's seal was embossed with the sovereign flower, indicating he was an Inborn *Commander*. "Why in blazes would a Commander want to buy a slave?"

"We'll find out soon enough," Desya replied. "In the meantime, keep an eye on him."

Nodding, Neko divided his focus between the Commander and the auction. The auction progressed, selling off Skinwalkers, Necromancers and Hematics. The prettier girls, particularly the younger ones, grossed the highest. This put a spark in Master Mookjai's eyes. Still sipping on his coconut, he regarded the girls' misery like a kind of spectator's sport, while the audience played the role of a sadistic cheerleading squad.

Finally, the auction drew to a close.

By the time Master Mookjai had summoned the sixteenth slave to the floor, his eyelids sagged and a string of drool glistened on his chin; his coconut now lay discarded on the floor, leaking milk into the dirt. "The next product I bring to you is a Mystish flower of eighteen, who has the ability to heal herself at will."

A wave of 'oohs' passed through the crowd. Neko heard Desya's astonished words in his earpiece. "Did he say she can *heal*?"

"He did," Neko confirmed, his heart thudding in alarm. Snofrid was also a Mystish, who, coincidentally enough, had the power to regenerate her body. Mystish rarely shared the same abilities, so Neko felt certain that the next slave would be her. At this thought, hope flickered inside him for the first time in the fifteen dark days since she'd been missing.

All the filth, discomfort and anger he'd felt washed away when Master Mookjai concluded his introduction with the words: "The Mystish hasn't been fully groomed. But I'm sure her new master will see to her needs." He rang his finger bell and a girl with tangled black hair was jostled onto the stage.

Neko rocked on his heels, recognizing Snofrid in an instant. He couldn't mistake her petite build or her skin, which was still utterly perfect. It had no scars, no sun damage, and no rashes from air poisoning, merely a seashell-like pallor. He glanced at the blue Halo shimmering on her right bicep and felt his muscles go slack in relief. It wasn't burned, but he knew this didn't mean she hadn't been tortured.

"I'm coming inside," Desya burst out.

"No," Neko said firmly. "*Follow* the plan. And keep your voice down, or the entire assembly will know we're communicating."

Footsteps drummed in the earpiece. "Fine, I'm heading to the drop point. Make the buy."

Neko hoped the buy would go as smoothly as Desya made it sound. "I doubt we'll need more silvers, but keep Lycidius on hold in case."

"I'm dialing him now," Desya said.

Neko trained his focus on Snofrid and willed her to look at him. If she saw him, she'd know he was here to take her away from this human toilet. But she didn't lift her gaze. Staring stubbornly at the ground, she bared all the resentment and degradation of a caged animal in her expression. The thought that she'd been abused pulsed in the front of his mind, making his fists clench in rage.

"We begin the bid at 60 coppers," Master Mookjai called.

To Neko's horror, the Commander raised his bidding stick.

"80 Coppers?" Master Mookjai tried. Neko flipped up his number. With a thin, but pleased smile, the slaveholder proceeded to test the waters. "130 coppers?"

"100 silvers," Neko blurted, too impatient to haggle. Hopefully, he wouldn't be punished for challenging a Commander. If he explained his connection to Snofrid, the Commander might understand.

Master Mookjai's eyes popped open and he sputtered, "*Silvers?*"

"That's what I said. Silvers."

Murmurs rippled through the ranks. Buyers stole suspicious or intrigued glances over their shoulders at Neko.

"500 silvers," the Commander bided, clicking his raptor-claws together.

Neko struggled to reign in his irritation. The fact that the Commander's raptor claws were pure silver made his wealth obvious. How high was he willing to bid for Snofrid? And what could he possibly want with her?

"1000 silvers," Neko sneered; it was echoed by a delighted squeal from Master Mookjai and a gasp from the crowd.

"2,000 silvers," the Commander countered calmly.

"5,000 silvers."

"7,000 silvers."

"10,000 silvers."

Master Mookjai sat upright on his litter, his arms quivering under his weight, and looked back and forth between the bidders with the frenzied excitement of a child.

"15,000 silvers," the Commander called.

"20,000 silvers," Neko said louder.

"I don't like this," Desya broke in. "I've got a neurotoxin dart. I'm gonna put him down."

"Are you crippled in the mind?" Neko hissed. "Assaulting a Commander is suicide."

"I won't have a choice if he outbids us. Commander or not, there's no way I'm letting him get away with my sister."

"He won't," Neko promised. "I'll do what's necessary to help Snofrid."

"30,000 silvers," the Commander challenged.

"35,000 silvers," Neko fired back.

"40,000 silvers."

"45,000 silvers."

"Damn," Desya barked. "5,000 more and we're out!"

"Call Lycidius," Neko ground out. "Have him transfer the funds."

"There's too much bloody interference. I can't get a connection."

"50,000 silvers," the Commander said.

"55,000 silvers." Neko upped him swiftly, and then told Desya, "Use the satellite phone!"

Master Mookjai, who'd all the while been flopping about like a fish, beamed in euphoria. The bell tied to his finger jingled wildly and he broke into hysterical pants. Snofrid, who'd stopped gazing at the floor, braved a glance at the Commander. Her face flushed hot with anger, though she showed no fear, even if she felt it. Neko stood up tall, trying to get her attention, but she continued to stare at the Commander intently, as if letting him know that she wouldn't go with him willingly. At this, Neko swished his jacket and pushed through the crowd.

The Commander held Snofrid's stare, and said, "60,000 silvers."

"65,000 silvers," Neko growled.

"70,000 silvers."

Neko, shoving a buyer out of his path, bellowed, "75,000 silvers!" He turned on the Commander and discreetly raised three of his fingers—a sign that he was an Inborn war hero—with the hope the Commander would stop bidding. The man locked his raptor-claws behind his back and made no move to continue. Gradually, silence swooped in across the warehouse.

"Did we win?" Desya asked.

"I don't know," Neko panted. "Standby."

After several sluggish seconds, Master Mookjai licked his lips and spoke. "Will you offer 80,000 silvers?" he asked the Commander, his voice an airy whisper.

The Commander again glanced at Snofrid, clicking his raptor-claws together, and decided, "No."

Neko exhaled a long, ragged breath. *75,000 silvers*. The slum would be talking about the buy for weeks to come. His gasmask covered his head fully, so his identity was secure, but not Snofrid's. He needed to make sure that no one ever got ahold of her real identity. "Did you reach Lycidius?" he asked Desya.

"Yeah." Desya cleared his throat. "Yeah, he's gonna make the transfer."

"Where is he now?"

"Uh…he was searching North Crestvania. He's on his way back and should be in tonight." Scuffles sounded in the earpiece. "Make the buy. I'll grab Snofrid. We've got about an hour before close-up."

"I only need five minutes." Neko approached Master Mookjai as Snofrid was led through the back door of the warehouse.

The slaveholder raised his neck, clearly with great effort, and grinned. "Great master," he began. "We have two slaves, beautiful and seductive slaves, left to auction. Would you like a private showing?"

"No," Neko retorted, wanting nothing more than to be free of this filth hole. "I only want what's mine and I want her now."

"Of course." Master Mookjai rang his bell, summoning his accountant. Neko made the purchase with saintly patience; he used the alias Guillaume Admiraal to transfer the money from his Necromancer friend, Lycidius Heidrun's, secure offshore account to the Oubliette Trust Fund. The buy progressed without issue and when it was finished, he searched once more for the Commander. The man's spot was empty. He'd probably left the moment he'd been defeated, yet his very presence troubled Neko. He'd been willing to pay seventy-thousand silvers for a stranger, which meant he'd likely come looking for them.

Leaving Master Mookjai to his new fortune, Neko ducked outside. He made quick strides to the back of the warehouse where ten street soldiers stood before a slave cage. One of the soldiers lay unconscious on the ground, his nose a bloody mess; Desya stood over him, holding Snofrid in one arm and his rifle in the other.

"What happened?" Neko demanded, upon seeing that Snofrid was out cold.

"The bastard hit her. He's lucky I didn't break more of him."

Neko took Snofrid into his arms, his fingers digging into her skin in fury. "If you want to get out of here alive, Desya, be quiet and cover me."

Desya nodded. "I've got it. Go."

Neko hiked down the ramp and into the alley of sweatshops. His feet itched to run, but he kept an even pace, aware that betraying he was in a hurry would attract trouble.

Snofrid's body remained limp in his arms. The spot where she'd been struck had healed, but her face was rigid with tension. In the ten years he'd known her, he'd never seen her look so helpless and it woke emotions in him he seldom experienced—pity and a desire to comfort. Being detached in character, he felt little empathy when people came to him with their problems, but Snofrid was different. She was like an amplifier, intensifying his emotions to the point where he hardly knew how to react. His concern was bursting at the seams, so much so that his body broke out in a sweat.

"Do you think they did anything to her?" Desya panted, falling into step beside him.

Neko stiffened. "If they touched her, I doubt she'd tell us. But we should let her rest before asking those questions. All she needs to hear right now is that she's safe."

At the jeep, Desya opened the back door. Neko gently laid Snofrid on the seat. "Get the smelling salts."

Desya tossed him a white box from the medical kit in the trunk. "That's all we got," he said.

"She's small. It will do." Neko tore open the box. He waved an ammonia tablet under her nose, until her nostrils flared and she choked out a gasp. Eyes flying open, she sat upright in a fit of hoarse coughing. Neko quickly removed his gasmask to show her his face, but she thrashed at him with her bare feet.

"Get away from me!" she shouted, her frail body seeking refuge near the door. "Touch me and I'll bite your nose off like the other guy."

"Move." Desya shoved past Neko and climbed onto the seat. "Sno." He held out a hand, trying to calm her down. "Sno, it's alright. It's Desya."

"Get away from me." She cocked her foot back in preparation to strike, breathing hard. "I told you, don't touch me!"

Desya passed Neko a confused look. "Is she in shock?"

"Give me a minute." Neko lowered onto the seat and moved his hand toward her. She tensed, before scooting further against the door. "Snofrid, this is your brother, Desya," he said in a quiet, soothing tone. "Do you remember him?"

She eyed Desya briefly and answered, "No."

Desya's face paled faster than a dying soldier. "Wait, what? What do you mean, she doesn't…?" His voice cracked. "Neko, what the hell is going on?"

Neko worked his mouth to form a reply, but found he couldn't speak. He checked her head for injuries and her pupils for signs of shock. After turning up with nothing, he trembled under a petrifying realization: the only person in the world he loved didn't recognize him.

A Shot of Treason

Black rain was streaking the windshield by the time Neko, Desya, and Snofrid left Gehenna in their taillights. Neko watched Snofrid in the rearview mirror as Desya showed her photos on his phone, trying to remind her of her family. The hope in her expression didn't surprise him: after what she'd suffered in Gehenna, she probably felt desperate to belong somewhere.

Now and then, she met his gaze in the mirror. Although she smiled, he couldn't bear the eyes that stared back at him. Their glimmer was gone. She was just as much a stranger to him as he was to her, like two people standing shoulder to shoulder, yet for all their closeness could've been a universe apart. Initially shocking, this thought now made him furious. He felt cheated. Robbed. His mind fumed with confusion and rage, but, most of all, with the need to get revenge.

"She seems to have calmed down," Desya said in Russian. He carefully climbed into the passenger seat. "I think the photos helped."

"The photos are good," Neko agreed, replying in the same language. "But don't overwhelm her with stories from the past. She shouldn't be made to remember. She'll remember when her mind is ready."

Desya nodded. "You're a doctor. What do you think caused this?"

"Due to her regenerative abilities, the memory loss couldn't have been caused by brain damage or trauma," Neko mused. "I believe the cause is magic. If she can tell us everything that happened the day she went missing, perhaps I'll find a more definite explanation."

"She told me the first thing she remembers is waking up in the woods."

"What else did she tell you?" Neko glanced at Snofrid; he'd ask her himself, but he didn't want to make her relive what she'd undergone.

"She said all her stuff was swiped by scavengers," Desya answered. "After a few hours in the woods, she headed for the slum to find food. She didn't remember she has a Tag, so she tried to get a human alias from a company that fronts Mookjai's trafficking ring. That's how she ended up getting nabbed." Desya paused, as if a realization had just dawned on him. "If you're right about the magic, you should be able to fix her amnesia. Spells can be lifted."

"Not *all* spells," Neko countered. "Lifting the spell would depend upon its magnitude. I'll know more after I do an examination of her mind."

"When?"

"As soon as we reach your house."

Desya sat back and took a long drink from his canteen. Then he exhaled loudly, and said, "They didn't touch her. I asked."

The knots in Neko's gut unwound and he checked Snofrid in the mirror. Her attention was fixed on the holographic photos on Desya's phone. "Did she mention the Commander who tried to purchase her?"

"Yeah. I asked her about him, but she told me she'd never seen him before today."

Neko considered. "I'll make inquiries. We should be prepared to see him again." He tapped on his gasmask. "There's also the question of Snofrid's identity."

19

"I know. But Master Mookjai doesn't have her real name, only a photo of her on file. I'll hack in tonight and wipe it. As for the auction attendees who saw her face, I'll figure that out with Lycidius when he gets back."

"The two of you can stop talking about me as if I'm not here now," Snofrid interrupted. Her Egyptian blue eyes looked up from the phone. "Also, I'm not so traumatized that I can't answer questions about my amnesia. I can tell you right now that my memory loss isn't normal because I still remember a lot of things, like this jeep," she pointed around the vehicle, "it's mainly just people I've forgotten. Oh, and by the way...I haven't forgotten how to speak Russian either."

Neko's cheeks went hot.

"Sorry, Sno," Desya said, facing her. "We didn't mean to cut you out, we're just not sure how many questions you can handle right now."

"I can handle as many as you can ask."

In the darkness of his gasmask, Neko let out a small smile; Snofrid had just shown a flicker of her old self. Still, he didn't trust that she was as unaffected as she let on. Her captivity in Gehenna couldn't have been anything short of hellish.

"Someone just sent a message," Snofrid said, passing the phone to Desya. "The ID says Lycidius."

Desya skimmed the screen and sighed.

"What is it now?" Neko demanded.

"I told Lycidius about Sno's memory loss."

"That was the backside of foolish. What's he done?"

Desya slid the phone onto the console. "You know Cid. He's gonna blow holes in the city until we figure out what happened to Snofrid and fix it."

Neko scrunched his brows, foreseeing much unnecessary stress. "I was under the impression that he'd stopped throwing fits."

"It's not as bad as it was."

Neko grunted. "That's highly fortunate." Turning his tail to Black Butte Mountain, he accelerated toward Hollowstone, a grossly wealthy megacity erected over the Deschutes Forest. The city itself soared above the tree canopy, over all except the tallest Redwoods, which broke the skyline and shaded the streets like umbrellas.

Scenarios of Snofrid's captivity pulsed through his head as he mingled with the columns of traffic on *Albanus Bridge*, a famous bowstring-arch bridge that led into Warburton, the humblest borough of Hollowstone. The ten-lane highway brimmed with electric cars, military tanks and tactical vehicles, all swerving, braking and honking as they fought to enter the west city gate. Armored skyline vessels sped toward aero-stations to unload passengers from confederate cities, and drones marshaled the skies, defending against Inborn airstrikes. Neko noticed three search and rescue helicopters darting in and out of the clouds and frowned. Since yesterday, authorities had been searching for the Chancellor of Hollowstone's son, Remus. Apparently, he'd gone missing. But while the entire city made a fuss about it, Neko utterly disregarded the situation. Based on Remus's track record, he was probably passed out from intoxication in some back alley.

By the time the west gate emerged from the smog, Neko had worn himself ragged from foul imaginings of how Snofrid had been treated. Briefly, he debated making a wild U-turn and killing every man employed by the Oubliette Hotel. His military training helped him establish how he'd do it, what were his most strategic escape routes, and which gangs would come after him in retaliation. But his plans dissolved with the arrival of common sense. Gehenna wasn't just a gaping hole of trash in the earth; it was a business investment for some very powerful humans.

"Shades down," Neko muttered. He guided the jeep into a checkpoint booth near the outer wall and shifted into park. Green light diffused through the glass, scanning the forged Tags on their wrists and identifying them as humans. Then an automated voice broadcasted from the sound system:

Name: NEKO GRIMACE ABERTHOL
Age: 33
Occupation: FORENSIC PATHOLOGIST

Residence: 123 GNOMON STREET
Borough: WESTERBRIDGE / SECOND RING OF
    HOLLOWSTONE
Clearance Level: 5

Name: SNOFRID LORNA YAGAMI
Age: 18
Occupation: WAR LOBBY EMPLOYEE / STUDENT
Residence: 4018 SUN PROMENADE PLAZA
Borough: VANCASTLE / SECOND RING OF
    HOLLOWSTONE
Clearance Level: 2

Name: DESYA KEO YAGAMI
Age: 21
Occupation: EIGHTH STAR BLUECOAT
Residence: 4018 SUN PROMENADE PLAZA
Borough: VANCASTLE / SECOND RING OF
    HOLLOWSTONE
Clearance Level: 6

Neko's heart raced when Snofrid suddenly brushed his shoulder. She had leaned over the console, her face colored with curiosity. "Why are you a policeman?" she asked Desya. "For humans, I mean."

"I do it for the intel. I'm a spy for the Hematic Cell in Hollowstone."

"Is being a spy as risky as it sounds?"

"Yeah," he granted. "But it's worth it. And we all take risks."

"Some more than others," Neko corrected. He hurled an accusing look at Desya. The downside to his bluecoat position was that it aimed the eye of the human law in their direction.

Ignoring him, Desya offered Snofrid his canteen. "Don't worry about it," he said to her. "You'll see that it's not so bad after a while."

"Don't let him reassure you of things he can't promise, Snofrid," Neko said.

Desya jerked his chin at the road. "Not everyone's a skeptic, Neko. Just drive."

"My skepticism is what's kept me alive this long." Crackling with irritation, he accelerated up a ramp and through a gleaming glass tunnel suspended above the city.

Finally, they departed Warburton and entered Vancastle, the richest borough of Hollowstone City after the Golden Circle. For all of its beauty, Neko had few fond memories of it—though Snofrid seemed to have a different opinion. She stared out the window with a mixture of awe and relief. The booming metropolis appeared to strike her as familiar; either this, or she was merely happy to find that it didn't resemble the slum.

Stretching into the horizon, Vancastle's buildings were a rare feat of modern majesty. The lead crystal domes, floating platforms, glass towers, ecological skyscrapers and green high-rises reflected the red glow of the sunset like a field of compact mirrors. In their midst lay thriving meadows and ecosystem gardens that nurtured curative plants and precious trees native to the West Coast. There were zoos with rainforest-like biospheres, all dedicated to protecting endangered animal species, and beautiful forested parks, blooming across floating arenas beneath the clouds. Higher up, freight crafts touched down on air stations where they unloaded cargo from overseas, and even higher up still, bullet trains raced across magnetized tracks, transporting civilians from office blocks to quiet suburbs; far outside the city limits, the environmental waste incinerators puffed smoke into the sky.

"This is Sun Promenade Plaza," Desya said, as they drove down a winding street framed by department stores. "It's one of the most expensive shopping centers in Hollowstone, but it still gets a ton of business."

When Neko turned into a spacious flagstone courtyard fenced by mansions, Desya pointed to one: a two-story mansion with tiled roofs and broad eaves; an *engawa* corridor wrapped around the exterior wall like a porch, lavish with a hill-and-pond garden.

Snofrid leaned over the console again, this time with a gasp. "*That's* our house? How much does your informant job pay you?"

"Not much," Desya admitted. "Our friend, Lycidius, is actually the one who owns the house. He was looking for you up north, so you'll see him in the morning."

She nodded, but Neko recognized the hesitation in her bearing as plainly as he'd recognize his surgical instruments: she was wondering why Lycidius allowed them to live with him, and possibly, what kind of friend he was. Neko was surprised to find himself actually pitying Lycidius, but only for an instant. If he failed to restore Snofrid's memories, no previous relationship she'd ever had would be the same—especially the friendship, perilous though it was, that she'd had with Lycidius Heidrun. However, instead of tossing a few scraps to her curiosity, he decided it would be better to let her figure things out.

Desya pointed to a hut beside the mansion with a sign that read: *The War Lobby*. "That's our store. Well actually, you're the one who runs it," he explained. "But don't worry about any of that right now. We're just gonna focus on getting you better."

Snofrid faced Neko, her eyes painfully hopeful. "Do you really think you can fix my amnesia?"

"I won't know until I examine you," he replied, his confidence swelling at the full comprehension of how much he was needed. Due to Snofrid's healing ability, she'd never required a doctor before—more specifically, she'd never required *him* before. He sped into the mansion's center garage and swiftly cut the engine, eager to begin. Just as he reached for the door handle, his beeper went off.

"Tell me that's not a first responder's call," Desya said.

"I'll need a second to verify," Neko informed, and checked his beeper screen.

Casualties: 7
Priority: Blue, Red and Black.
Location: 313 Willow Street, Eastwick

"Damnation," Neko muttered. While his first occupation was an Inborn trauma surgeon, he day-lighted as a human forensic pathologist. "I must leave."

Desya cracked his door. "It's fine. You gotta go. Just swing by later."

"I don't foresee that happening." Neko's eyes found Snofrid and darted away. He hated the regret in her face. "It would be better if you rested now anyway," he advised. "I'll examine you tomorrow evening."

"Don't worry about it," she said, climbing from the jeep. "Thank you for everything. I'll see you tomorrow."

Neko wanted nothing more than to stay and see her now. He felt an ember of warmth and attacked the feeling, dowsing it with cold indifference. Then, as was customary between parting Inborns, he said, "May we meet again."

You don't have a choice anymore, slave. My will is yours and you'll submit to it."

Snofrid, standing under the garage skylight, had resisted this command with her entire being—the first one uttered to her by Master Mookjai. The code had been her miserable, two-week life's compass: obey or be subdued. The bruises she'd earned for resisting had long since faded, though she still felt the hot, needling pain of being smacked for each time she'd spit in Master Mookjai's face, kicked her muddy water bowl at the door guards, or refused to obey the slave groomers.

All of that was over now.

Energetic and confident, she found reassurance in everything that she saw—the dusty tarp-covered cars, the paint-chipped yellow work lights, and the glistening metal shelves stacked with red toolboxes, racing gear, and oily car parts. The garage was cleaner and far more spacious than the basement she'd squatted in for the past two weeks. There was no hard dirt floor, insect-infested walls, moldy straw, stinking open sewers, or rusted chains. Without a doubt, she'd rather sleep beside a car engine here than return to that basement, not simply because of its distance from the slum, but because here, she hadn't been forced to do anything.

In the pocket of her tunic, she fisted a rock shard and rolled it around her palm, letting the notched edges scrape her skin until a blister had formed. She'd dug the rock from the basement wall and squeezed it like this many times before. The slight prick of pain grounded her in the moment, honed her focus and convinced her that the things she was experiencing were real. But she was careful to believe that she was truly free; if she embraced freedom too carelessly, it might disappear, and she'd wake once more in Oubliette. Her brother and the Inborn doctor seemed *too* kind. The way she'd been treated the past few days had been nothing short of savage. To suddenly be treated with kindness left her cautious.

The Wrangler jeep backed suddenly from the garage, its engine rumbling like a factory, and its wheels skidded on the icy drive. Snofrid waved farewell to Neko, who gave her a curt nod before speeding from the house. She moved to help Desya close the garage when a grumbling sound stopped her. She cupped her stomach, suddenly dizzy with hunger, and her mouth watered at the thought of a giant bowl of miso ramen. Master Mookjai had only fed her potato peels. She waited until Desya had shut the garage before asking, "Would you mind if I made myself some food?"

"Why don't you let me make something for you, Sno," he said. "You've been through enough and should take it easy." He engaged the air-purifiers and then guided her across the garage.

Snofrid, at first startled by his touch, gradually found herself at ease. He was so tall she felt like a child, though this wasn't exactly unusual. All Hematics were giants. As she knew it, cold weather made them sluggish and moody. Along with telescopic vision, tremendous sprinting ability and contractile red claws, Hematics also had retractable fangs—an upper and lower set—packed with a deadly neurotoxin.

Desya scanned his Tag on a titanium door at the edge of the garage and they passed into a *genkan* entry area with a smooth parquet floor and a sloshing bamboo fountain. Here, he took off his gasmask for the first time. He looked nothing like her. In fact, two people couldn't have looked more unrelated.

The olive tone of his skin was in stark contrast to her fair complexion. He had a full, sensuous mouth, the appeal of which made up for the thin white scars casing his jawline and neck, and well-defined cheekbones, which looked like they'd met with one too many knuckles. There was a softness in his otherwise spirited eyes, one that seemed present only when looking at her. His brown high-and-tight buzz cut seemed to be a requirement of his bluecoat position, and the way he stood, with his shoulders square and his chest open, projected confidence. A button was missing on his Henley shirt, even though it still bore the crisp look of new clothing, and grease stains spotted his jeans. Unlike his bedraggled clothes, his fingernails were trimmed, his chin was clean-shaven and his teeth were white.

"Still don't recognize me, do you?"

"No," she said, trading her muddy shoes for a pair of house slippers. The slippers were spotless and so soft that she had to resist the urge to push her hands into them. "But I recognized the city. Like I said, I'm pretty sure it's just people I've forgotten."

"Yeah, I remember. I just figured you might have found something about me familiar." As he stepped into a pair of scuffed house slippers, his face twitched. She sensed he was acting a lot calmer than he felt. "Come on," he said. "Let's eat."

"Wait, Desya—" She paused, surprised at how naturally his name rolled off her tongue. "You said we lived with a friend, Lycidius. Where are our parents?"

Desya's manner grew cautious. "Neko told me I shouldn't dump too much on you too soon, but..." He stopped to consider his response. "We're not blood related," he finally told her. "We were both adopted by a man named Ryuki Yagami. Our Inborn parents died a while back, so he became our stepdad."

She frowned, not seeing how this made sense. "Our Houses didn't come forward to claim us?"

"No. My parents were executed for treason, so obviously no one wanted me after they were condemned. But after your parents died, you didn't have family to go to."

She suddenly felt more unwanted than the dust on the floorboards. On her way to hang up her gasmask, she hurried to change the subject. "Ryuki Yagami sounds Japanese."

"It is. He was a Trojan Mortal. Do you remember the Trojans?"

"I remember they want to help us. They think we can coexist and have been trying to persuade world leaders to negotiate peace." She caught a flicker of cynicism in his face that reeled in her interest. "You don't think peace is possible?"

"I think peace is *possible*. Just not in this century."

She wanted to believe differently, but imagined her brother would think she was naïve. The crossing through the portal from their world, *Armador*, had transformed Earth's atmosphere, mutating all the living organisms, and this was something the humans couldn't forgive; it was why humans called the day that Inborns had arrived on earth, *Hatred Day*. "I remember we left Armador twenty-two years ago, but I can't remember why," she admitted. "Did we leave our world by choice?"

"It's a long story and it's more to chew through. I'll tell you about it later." He shifted on his feet, then crossed his arms. "I know I asked you this before, but I want to make sure you're not keeping quiet cause you don't trust us…or even because you're embarrassed. Did Mookjai's guys hurt you, Snofrid?"

"They punished us if we disobeyed, but that was all," she assured.

He uncrossed his arms, seeming convinced. "All right, let's go." He strode through a sliding, louvered door and into the drafty kitchen. "Heater on; lights on," he called.

Pendant lights floodlit the hardwood floors. When Snofrid stepped into the kitchen, her eyes prodded every fixture, hoping to unlock even the smallest glimmer of a memory.

The mansion was styled in the Japanese fashion, complete with *tatami mats*, a soft-lit *washitsu* room, a *zen garden* basement, an *irori* hearth for cooking and an indoor courtyard. Everything registered as slightly familiar—like a blurry picture that wouldn't come into focus—but, to her frustration, she felt no connection to any of it. The low *chabudai* table was furnished with *zabuton* cushions in place of chairs; it abutted a long counter, overhung with rows of mahogany cabinetry. On the walls hung ornate glass lanterns, decorative Japanese scrolls and *Katana* swords.

While the house was picturesque and serene, Snofrid felt a tangible emptiness. Something was missing. Exactly what she couldn't say; maybe it was a person.

"That's your room," Desya said, pointing to a loft adjacent to the fireplace; a ladder led to the door with a plaque above it that read: *Snofrid's Tower.* She hadn't imagined she'd live somewhere so fancy, and the extravagance loaded her down with guilt after having just come from Gehenna. Due to the loft's placement, she got the impression that it was built outside of the mansion's original design. That someone might've built it for her gave her a warm feeling.

Desya served her a bowl of miso ramen and she scarfed it down. When the bowl was empty, her attention stalled on a holographic calendar above the genkan. The date read: *November 1ˢᵗ, 2052.*

"Shoot," she breathed. "*Tomorrow* is the anniversary of Hatred Day."

"Yeah," he called from the refrigerator.

"Hatred Day hasn't changed since the crossing?"

"No. It's uh…it's worse now than before actually. But don't worry about it right now, Sno. We usually just stay indoors." He shut the refrigerator, then headed toward the loft ladder, like he wanted to change the subject. "I'll show you your room so you don't have to spend an hour looking for your toothpaste."

Leaving her bowl on the table, she waited until his back was turned, before snatching a knife from the counter. Then she tailed him up the ladder, sliding the blade into her sleeve.

"This isn't all mine, is it?" she asked, looking around the bedroom in wonder. Strangely enough, it was the only room in the house that wasn't the slightest bit familiar. Her emotions tugged back and forth, stretching her to the edge of tears. She'd never even dreamt that she could belong in a place like this.

"Well it sure as heck isn't mine," Desya replied.

The room was an intimidating kind of nice, so much that she didn't want to touch anything for fear of breaking it. Soft tatami mats were rolled across the floors and Japanese lanterns cast elegant shadows on the walls.

Fascinating treasures were tucked in the corner cubbies—apothecary chests, a floral *uchiwa* hand fan, a clay cross, pots of bamboo and bonsai, jars stuffed with colorful feathers, and a slew of red *Daruma* dolls, which were traditional amulets of good luck. A vase of orange lilies on the nightstand provided a splash of color to the muted shades; they matched a holographic television idle display above a lacquered desk.

"Just a heads up," Desya said. "Everything's voice automated, so just tell things to shut up, or turn on and they will. Also, the window doesn't open." He nodded to a glass bay window above the bed. "It doesn't have a filter screen. It's just for looks."

"I won't break it open," she promised. "But…you're *sure* all this stuff is mine?"

He gave her a small smile. "I'm sure." He pointed at a bathroom next to the desk. "If you need to shower or anything that's your bathroom. The water's like dragon spit, so turn it warm if you want it hot."

"I'll need it hot to wash off the slum."

He waved a hand at her hair, his nose wrinkling. "Yeah, you've got some goo or something stuck in your hair."

"I don't know what it is; it was all over me when I woke up in the woods." She patted her hair and winced upon finding a crusty patch. The slime had congealed too much to be rinsed out with sewer water, which was all Master Mookjai had allowed her.

"If you want to have a shower, we can look at more photos after."

She nodded. "I'll need to burn my clothes after, too. I had to lift them off a body." She paused at the desk computer. The background displayed a photo of Desya and a stunning exotic girl with rich black hair.

Desya seemed to notice what she was staring at. He touched a chain around his neck, then quickly crossed his arms. "Her name's Parisa Namdar. She was your friend and my…uh…my girlfriend until she became one of the Chancellor's mistresses earlier last year."

Snofrid almost let the knife fall from her sleeve. "You *dated* her?"

"Yeah." His expression remained so composed that she suspected he was hiding something. But he definitely had reason to: coupling with a human was a *Level Three Offense*. Even though Desya already bore the shame of his parent's treason, this was a personal stain on his name. *Human worshipers*, as they were infamously called, were officially titled *vagrants*. This thought left her petrified, for if what her brother had done was ever made public, he'd undergo severe corporal punishment and then be expelled from Inborn society.

"You should clean up," he suggested. "I'll wipe your photo from Mookjai's database while I wait."

"Before you leave, I want to thank you," she said.

"Don't. We always watched out for each other, Sno. It's nothing that even needs thanking for." He gave her a reassuring glance. "Even though we were adopted, I always thought of you as my real sister."

In the bathroom, Snofrid caught a glimpse of herself in the mirror. Apart from a pair of large slanted eyes, the face that stared back at her was familiar. She assumed the eye-slant was due to mutation.

Planting her back to the mirror, she shook the knife from her sleeve. The glass reflected the brand mark, *M*, that had been tattooed on her nape by Master Mookjai's slave groomers.

She bit down on her lip, bracing herself, before scraping off the brand with the blade. Blood dripped onto her tunic. Squeezing her eyes shut, she set her teeth as the scalding pain pulsated through her neck. The blood trickled along her spine, slowing as it reached her tailbone. Suddenly it stopped and reversed, retreating along its path and surging back into the cut. The torn skin stitched together, leaving her neck pure. Spotless.

She exhaled a shaky, relieved breath.

The King of Terrors

A nightmare wrenched Snofrid from sleep. She kicked the damp blankets from her body, hands fisting the mattress, and took long, deep breaths through her nose. When her heart calmed, she rolled onto her side and stared blankly at the vase of orange lilies on her nightstand. Her body trembled as she contemplated her nightmare. It had forced her to relive the final day of her imprisonment at Oubliette. Although the day had begun uneventfully, it had taken a violent turn when Master Mookjai had ordered one of his slave groomers to interrogate her until she surrendered the *secret* of her healing. Snofrid winced as she recalled the biting lashes of the slave groomer's belt. Since there was no secret to Mystish abilities—it was simply genetics—the interrogation hadn't been brief.

For over an hour she laid still, struggling to find peace in the knock of the rain against the window. She longed to forget most of the memories she still possessed. They floated across her mind like fiendish ghosts, taunting her. She detested Master Mookjai; she hated what his groomers had done to her. A part of her yearned for justice, wanted Master Mookjai to get his due; but a larger part reminded her that in war, there was rarely justice.

Unable to sleep, she rose and searched the kitchen for something sugary. The *mochi* ice cream she found brought her little comfort.

Setting down her bowl, she touched the spot on her nape that had once been marked by a slave tattoo. The spot felt clammy, silky with hair. The Commander who'd tried to purchase her hadn't strayed far from her mind; his bull-head gasmask grinned at her when she shut her eyes and it snarled at her when she opened them. What could a Commander, a man who presided over armies, want with her? She was a mere Inborn civilian. She wondered if perhaps they'd met before. Almost immediately, she dropped the idea. Desya and Neko hadn't recognized him either.

After putting away the ice cream, she returned to her bedroom and rummaged through her belongings in search of clues about her past life. The drawers creaked like rickety floorboards and she cupped the sides, trying to keep quiet. Desya was still asleep.

The drawers held nothing but clothes, so she combed the bookcase beside her dresser. In vain she tried to locate at least one familiar book. The titles ranged from biology, archeology, and religion to fairytales and historical novels, to proper speech and etiquette. Clearly, she'd valued education after moving out of Gehenna. Out of pride or real interest in these subjects, she wasn't sure. Perhaps she'd merely wanted to fit in with the fashionable people of Vancastle.

Selecting a sketchbook from the bottom shelf, she found it empty except for a drawing of an upside-down black tree on the first page. She frowned, thinking the drawing strange. An upside-down black tree was the Inborn symbol of death.

As she traced her fingers across the boughs, an image popped into her mind of a young man with bright red hair. He was laughing, and on his neck was a tattoo of the same upside-down black tree. Her hand flew to her head in surprise, and she fumbled with the sketchbook. When she finally registered that the image was a memory, she gasped. Then she latched onto it, treasuring it protectively.

With a rush of excitement, she eyed the door, debating if she should call Neko or wake up Desya and tell him. Whoever the red-haired man was, he was the one person in all the world she remembered. Maybe because he was important to her. In that case, surely Desya knew who he was.

Snofrid snapped the sketchbook shut and hurried downstairs. With each step, her spirits rose from anticipation. If she was already beginning to recall things, she had hope that Neko could restore her past fully. He'd promised to examine her that evening, though now it felt like the moment would never come.

The door to her brother's room was cracked. Peering through the opening, she found him asleep on a low platform bed beside the television. She was midway through the doorway, when the sight of his pale face stopped her. He'd been searching for her for days and probably hadn't even slept since she'd gone missing. She sighed. The sun would rise in less than two hours. Waiting wouldn't be too onerous.

A short while later, in the aftermath of the storm, the sun rose gloriously. Snofrid lingered at her window, rolling the rock shard from the Oubliette around in her palm as she watched a few courageous citizens climb into their cars and drive to work; the rest were hiding in their homes, unwilling to venture into the city on Hatred Day.

As she went to dress, the television switched on and she spun around in alarm. Annoyed at herself, she quickly regained composure. She needed to get a grip and stop imagining that the Commander was coming after her.

On the *Coast to Coast News* station, an android fashioned after a woman stood proudly before a podium stamped with four interconnecting circles—the emblem of humanity's one-world government, the *New Global Union*. The android's steel exoskeleton, glossy visor, and erect posture gave it an influential flare.

"This is Tera X, reporting the will of the New Global Union," it began. "New Global Union citizens are expected to follow the proper *Hatred Day* safety procedures. Authorities will not be held responsible for tragedies that occur in disregard of these guidelines. If medical assistance is needed, citizens are advised to call the emergency codes which their district area has provided." Snofrid skimmed the map of the New Global Union that appeared on a hologram screen behind the robot announcer and found many areas were red zones. "Police aid will not be provided to those who reside outside of green zones," the robot continued. "If citizens wish to pray, spiritual gatherings will be held in local centers until midnight." The android propped up a metal hand in warning. "Rioters and looters will not be tolerated. Citizens who show violence to their fellow man will be shot by authorities on sight."

"Television off," Snofrid said. She checked the clock on her nightstand: 5:44 a.m. The details of previous Hatred Days were a blur, but she knew the anniversary of the Inborn crossing brought about more violence than usual.

Crossing the room, she drew back the closet doors. Hanging in neat rows was an assortment of silk and lace dresses, silver fox and sheared rabbit fur coats, hiking gear and a medley of cashmere sweaters. "Stone me," she gasped. The clothing must have cost a fortune, for it contained brands such as *Carter and Roke*, *Armani*, *Louve*, *Valentino* and *Imperial Black*.

She unhooked a men's white suit jacket from the rack. Its scent of oakmoss and laurel was familiar. Stitched into the collar were the initials *A.B.F.* She guessed the jacket belonged to one of her friends.

"Sorry man, you're gonna have to be the one to tell Sno about our decision." Desya's voice echoed from the kitchen. "The Chief wouldn't take the Gurkha. I'm on duty until 6:30."

"I'll tell her," a man promised. It was a new voice. Perhaps it belonged to Lycidius.

"Awesome. Uh…and if she asks about her past, try not to drown her in info."

"She's probably already drowning in info."

A sound like skateboard wheels pricked Snofrid's ears. Looking out the loft window, she saw a young man coasting around the kitchen on a beat-up skateboard. Immediately, she recognized him as the man from her memory, and pressed toward the window in eagerness. He had the same black tattoo on his neck—an upside-down tree, barren of leaves—and the same sterling red crew cut. It gleamed like ruby satin under the kitchen lights and clashed with the orange jackal-head emblazoned on the back of his scuffed bomber jacket. There was only one confusing difference: unlike the man from her memory, this one emanated brute hostility. His bearing was aggressive, as if a network of invisible cords was hitched to his shoulders and he was trying to break free of them.

She noted the streams of magic rushing from his mouth and cocked her head in surprise; he was a Necromancer Inborn. She was curious how he and Desya had managed to become friends: generally, Necromancers and Hematics detested one another.

When she got a good look at his face, she found it difficult to turn away. Masculine and intimidating, Lycidius's features drew her in like a pair of forceful hands, pulling her toward him despite resistance. She edged away from the window, suddenly worried, for her compulsion toward him wasn't a shallow pining, easy to neglect—it was a deep aching that called out from parts of her she didn't yet know. The girl she was now hardly felt a response when she looked at Lycidius, but it was clear that the ghost of her did. Hesitant to be left alone with him, she decided she'd go to the café down the street until Desya returned home.

Over at the stove, a three-armed robot grilled fish while pouring Desya a cup of green tea. Desya, who wore his navy bluecoat uniform—a beret stitched with eight silver stars, white gloves and a steel-plate vest—swiped up the tea and chugged it in three gulps.

"Avoid the south sky-tunnels," Lycidius advised, trading his skateboard for a laptop. "They were just bombed and the whole skyway is blocked off."

Desya cursed. "How bad?"

"57 dead. 28 critical."

Desya rubbed his eyes, cursing again, and then grabbed a trench coat off the table. "Check the north sky-route."

Snofrid's nerves wound up like a music box. With the rise of city bombings, she penciled out her plan to leave the mansion. Hopefully Lycidius was nicer than he looked.

She moved to hang up the suit jacket and something fell out of the right pocket: *a photo*. She picked it up and looked at it. Why she'd be anywhere near the steps of a grand log cabin, she could only guess. She was hugging a young man. His face was covered by a gasmask, but the sureness of his stance and spirited blue eyes spoke for his personality. His blond hair was slicked back so precisely he could've been a manikin. The jacket she'd found definitely belonged to him, for it matched the white silk suit he wore, which was tailored to the cuffs. Nervous that he might be her boyfriend, she decided to catch Desya on his way out and ask him.

Once clothed in a blue cotton dress, she climbed into the kitchen with the photograph in hand. Flames crackled in the fireplace and the air was rich with the aroma of miso soup, grilled fish, seaweed and green tea.

"Desya already left," Lycidius said as he stalked from the washitsu. Unlike Desya and Neko, his aura was detached and his presence seemed to fill up the whole room.

"How did you know I was looking for my brother?"

"Who else would you be looking for? You've forgotten me."

"Well, I—" He met her eyes directly and Snofrid's reply stuck in her throat. His gaze picked her apart, slicing her into smaller and smaller pieces before being examined. Even more alarming was that his left eye looked like it possessed a will of its own: it was cloud grey and bared frustration, while the right, which was sky blue, seemed to dismember her under its scrutiny.

She cleared her throat, trying to disguise her discomfort. Why hadn't his left eye been as frightening in her dream? And how could her past self possibly be drawn to it? It was like the eye of a monster.

"You're not the first person," he remarked.

"I'm not the first person to what?"

"Be afraid of my eye."

"I'm sorry. I didn't mean to stare," she said.

"Don't apologize."

As he heaped her a plate of grilled fish and steamed rice, she observed that his bearing was becoming more and more rigid, like screws being tightened. It made her wonder if his severity was really a natural trait, or if it was being generated by *her* presence.

"Go ahead and eat," Lycidius said, sliding the food on the table with a pair of chopsticks.

"I don't remember your name," she prompted. "But I'm assuming you're Lycidius—the *friend*."

"It's even simpler than that. We just live together."

"I'm sure you mean well, but since we're not friends, looking out for me seems inconvenient. It's also unnecessary. I don't need a babysitter."

"Having amnesia makes you vulnerable," he countered. "Saying the wrong thing in public, or forgetting the safety rules will get all of us shipped to a death camp. Without memories, you have the intelligence level of a child. Children need babysitters." He chewed something in his mouth. "Sit and let's get this over with."

She hid her annoyance for the sake of getting information and seated herself on one of the zabuton table cushions.

"I've put in an order with a contact for three new identities," he started. "We're moving in a week."

Snofrid felt a nip of guilt, for she immediately knew the reason behind the decision to move: *her*. All the attendees of the slave auction had seen her face, which risked their exposure as Inborns. "Clearly you're not happy about moving," she said, "so why don't you stay here? Desya and I will be fine on our own."

"You two couldn't last on your own," Lycidius answered. "Your savings wouldn't last six months; Desya's still paying off your adopted father's debts."

"I said we'll be fine," she assured.

"The decision's already been made." Lycidius crouched on the cushion across from her, and his eyes dipped to the photo in her hand; his face betrayed a struggle. "You're wondering about the man in the photo and want to have a talk," he guessed. "The one we're about to have will give you answers, not closure."

"I don't expect all the answers to be happy ones, but I still want to have them."

"Then you're setting yourself up for disappointment. It's naïve."

She frowned at his patronization. "In my position, anyone would want the same. I have a right to know the truth."

"You do," he conceded. "But the truth isn't always satisfying."

"Like I said, I still want it."

His eyes sparked at her persistence, but the spark perished with his words. "He's Atlas Bancroft. He's a munitions dealer, authorized by the New Global Union."

"Is munitions dealing his only profession?"

"Yes."

She referred to the photo, perplexed. Thanks to the Inhuman War, munitions dealing was widely popular. It was almost as common as being a soldier, so unless Atlas held a high position in a large corporation, she didn't see how he could own such an expensive-looking house. She lowered her chopsticks at a thought. *Unless he was a dirty munitions dealer.*

"You met him this past October," Lycidius continued, stroking his temple as if it pained him. "You were rock climbing in the Cascades."

"What class of Inborn is he?" she asked.

"He's British—raised in Sweden."

A tentacle of fear looped around her and she fought against letting it tighten. "But we were only friends," she blurted.

"No. You dated the human."

She resisted decisively, slack-jawed. "You're wrong. That's borderline *treason*. I wouldn't have broken our laws and I *definitely* wouldn't have betrayed our kind."

Lycidius rapped his knuckles on the tabletop; the skin was nicked with scars. He plainly hated that this briefing session had fallen to him, but he kept on. "Satisfying or not, what I said is the truth."

The tentacle of fear tightened, causing her hands to shake. "If it is, then why didn't Desya tell me?"

"Desya lets his fear of hurting people get in the way of confronting them. He's always had a misguided conscience."

Snofrid couldn't accept that she'd chosen to be with a human. If word of her crime somehow spread to the Inborn police, she'd be shamed with the title of vagrant and expelled from Inborn society. She'd been sorry for Desya last night, but now she feared for herself. "Where is he?" she asked. "Atlas."

"You don't want to know the answer to that question," Lycidius advised.

"*Tell me.*"

He met her eye, deliberating. "All right. Atlas is gone. You broke up."

Her hand trembled on the table. She felt naked, even in her clothes. *They broke up.* She'd committed a Level Three Offense to be with him and they'd broken up! Her anger flash-fired and her ravaged pride collapsed. She wanted to—*needed* to—believe there was a redeeming reason for this choice. "Why?" she said, her voice cracking.

"Desya will tell you in a few weeks. Clearly you can't handle what I'm telling you."

She rose up in protest. He had no justifiable reason to deny her. She wanted the choices she'd made to make sense, not to leave her with the belief that she'd had no morals or self-respect. "I need to know *why* I would do this."

"You don't need to know, you *want* to know," he corrected. "You're asking for facts without thinking of how they'll affect your life. Have a conversation with Desya in a few weeks." Lycidius parted his mouth, flashing a silver tongue barbell. "He says you were doing better before you lost your memories."

Her frustration sizzled, so much that her ears flushed red. She hadn't denied the possibility of discovering negative or shocking things about her life, but having dated a human was too much. Dealing with the situation wasn't a matter of moving on or accepting the past; it would stain her life permanently.

THE KING OF TERRORS

Lycidius noted her despair, and a flicker of regret tempered his face. At first, it seemed he might offer a consoling word; instead, he said, "Don't feel sorry for yourself. You've lost memories, but have some resilience."

"I'd only be weak if I *were* feeling sorry for myself." Her words broke off when a phone vibrated in her pocket. She angled away from him as she drew out her phone.

"Tell me who's calling," he said.

Ignoring him, she held the phone to her ear. "Neko? I know its Hatred Day, but I'd like to leave the house."

"You're in luck," Neko said. "Your assistance is required at the northwest barrier watchtower. Remus Leathertongue has been killed."

Snofrid had to verify she'd heard him clearly. "You want me to come to a *crime* scene?"

"Under normal circumstances, I'd never ask," he explained. "But since all thirteen of Hollowstone's beast specialists failed to identify the beast that killed Remus, I've acquired special permission for you to visit the scene."

"Why me?"

"Beast Biology is your major and you hold the top scores in your class. Also, you've successfully assisted us once before," he answered. "I'll brief you on further details when you arrive. That is, if you feel well enough to come?"

"Yes. I'll be fine," she said.

After he hung up, Snofrid lowered the phone in wonder. She hadn't expected the day to include being called to a crime scene, but then again, most of what she'd seen since leaving the slum had been far from what she'd expected.

"I'll fly you to the crime scene," Lycidius offered.

She disliked the idea of him tagging along, but there was no way of getting there on her own. "The body is at the northwest barrier watchtower."

"Tell me who was killed."

"Remus Leathertongue."

Lycidius's face fell dark.

"What's the matter?" she asked hesitantly.

"Remus Leathertongue is the Chancellor of Hollowstone's only son." Lycidius grabbed a black jackal-head gasmask off the rack and accessed the antechamber. "Get your supply satchel and come with me. Hatred Day just started."

The Halo Eater

W alk faster," Lycidius urged, as he strode into the garage.
"I'm right behind you," Snofrid called. Unlike him, she
wasn't keen on visiting the crime scene. Although beast attacks
were a common cause of death, the Chancellor's son falling victim to one—
especially on Hatred Day—was suspicious.

"Identify the beast quickly and then leave the crime scene," Lycidius
directed. "Don't stop for reporters and don't talk to the authorities. They're
going to try to get you to make a statement, but you need to get in and out
without problems." He jerked his chin at a red tarp. "We'll take my
Steelrunner."

The Steelrunner was a flying transport he'd designed and built himself.
Apparently, he'd sold the design a year ago for fifty-seven million silvers.
Upon first glance, she understood why someone had paid so much for the
gold-and-black titanium transport's design, but kept all flattery to herself.

With a black carbon fiber frame and swingarm, the Steelrunner stretched to an impressive twelve feet. It sported gold ape-hanger handlebars beneath which gleamed two deadly toroid pulse guns that could be operated by a foot pedal.

"Ride on the pillion," he said. "Hurry."

As she mounted the back of the Steelrunner, he swiped his Tag over a scanner display on the control panel; the vehicle awoke, belching blue fire from its exhaust. Its long seat arched upward and holographic radar, scope and course-plotting displays sprung from the windshield. She scooted back when he rocked himself into the seat. "There are no grip bars," he informed. "Hold onto me or you'll pancake on the platform. This hits three-sixty."

She wrapped both arms around his torso with calculated indifference. "It might be a good idea to put grip bars on a two-seater," she hinted.

"This isn't a two-seater." He skewed his body left and the Steelrunner rotated to face the exit of the garage. Her stomach did a flip as the transport lunged forward, speeding from the platform.

"You should *make* it a two-seater," she cried, tightening her grip on his waist.

The sky traffic was white-knuckle pandemonium, but luckily, Lycidius proved to be a highflier. He piloted with greedy domination, gunning the engine as he dusted off slowpokes. Snofrid found the experience both exhilarating and terrifying. The city had burst to life; she was shocked to see so many people out of their homes on Hatred Day.

Blinding sunlight coursed into a jungle of buildings which bowed around and beneath one another, forming arches, sky bridges and tunnels. The rain had made a frozen shell over the snow, which paved the streets like rivers of stardust. Along the sidewalks the people walked with purpose: crowds spilled down office blocks, some stopping to buy from vendors and hawkers, and others leaping from the paths of careless drivers; crowds streamed down the steps of churches, temples and mosques, praying for aid; crowds rushed toward transportation stations, hoping to catch the next bullet train or skyline vessel; crowds carpeted the trade docks, haggling for first pick of the produce, meat and liquor flown in by confederate merchant vessels; and crowds basked outside cafés, pubs and restaurants, relishing the perks of the morning as if this day were like any other. Students congregated on snowy university campuses, smoking in alcoves, chatting under trees, and typing last minute assignments before the first classes of the day. Bluecoat transports were parked on every street corner, radioing in the day's first disturbances. Tanks patrolled the streets downtown, flanked by heavily armed military units and fighter crafts. Attack helicopters and drones defended the airspace and deployed soldiers who fast roped onto rooftops, platforms and walkways. Everywhere, memorials were in service. The largest of these was held at the Bluecoat Headquarters in the Golden Circle where the Chancellor was addressing the city at a Hatred Day Memorial Parade for fallen troops.

Hither and thither, the roar of working machinery was echoed by honking horns, blaring Jumbotrons and wailing sirens. Electronic music pulsed above all other sound by the time they slowed in the sky traffic near the city square—a major commercial intersection located in Vancastle, just outside the threshold of the Golden Circle. A mingle of smoke, gasoline and grilled food scented the air. Coupled with an influx of tourists, the city square was a blend of delightful chaos and flourishing anarchy. On the highest platforms of the square, Inborn protests were in progress. The activists popped in their cardinal-red clothing as did their signs, which were plastered with demands for a city-wide Inborn extermination.

"The Inhuman War is a government conspiracy," people yelled. "It's not about freedom; it's about CONTROL!"

"Protect our youth," others pleaded. "Without peace, there's no future for any of us!"

"Bomb Inborn cities!" more demanded. "Send in an airstrike and end this war!"

"We don't negotiate with aliens!" a group of shirtless teens chanted. "We *kill* aliens. Kill the aliens! Kill the aliens!"

Snofrid blocked out the noise, though in one way she did find herself agreeing with their pleas: there wouldn't be a world to fight over if the war endured much longer.

Wailing sirens blasted from the south sky-tunnels where she saw police and news helicopters hovering over the area. From the extent of the damage, she guessed that multiple charges had been detonated. The support beams had been ripped out like weeds. Piles of rock, bubbled plastic, and broken glass were strewn about the collapsed tunnel, which had melted in the flash heat. The dozens of tarps spotting the rubble converted her exhilaration into dark curiosity. How many more people would die before this year's Hatred Day had run its course?

A transport with colorful wings abruptly cut them off. It was piloted by a burly man with purple dreadlocks, who made a crude gesture before releasing black smoke into their faces. Snofrid coughed and stiffened her hold on Lycidius. The Steelrunner pulled up, speeding to safety of its own accord, as if it had sensed that the other transport was too close. Grounding out a grunt, Lycidius accelerated and forced the man out of the stream of traffic, sending him swerving around a cell tower.

"Go back to your slum!" Lycidius yelled.

They left Vancastle and soon Snofrid saw the north barrier watchtowers of Westerbridge through the smog. Sky-high at two-hundred stories, the towers resembled a ribbon of lighthouses, their spotlights sweeping the forest like yellow eyes. It seemed that Remus's death was being considered a high profile crime. Forensic teams were already conducting a walkthrough around a black tarp near the base of one of the towers, collecting trace evidence into biohazard bags; sketch artists were drawing out the area and photographers were capturing photos; and around the main area of disturbance, beast specialists consulted heatedly with police detectives. People in yellow jackets closed off the scene with barricade tape, holding back waves of reporters.

"All unauthorized personnel must remain *outside* the perimeter," a yellow-jacket man shouted as he taped off the scene. "That includes reporters."

"Can you tell us the identity of the victim?" more than one reporter demanded. "Why are so many law-enforcement officers present?"

"*Outside* the perimeter!" the man roared.

Lycidius touched down on a parking platform crammed with news crafts and Wildlife Department vehicles. "Keep an eye out for Neko," he advised. "They'll arrest us if they think we're civilians."

"He's over there." Snofrid pointed at a beat-up Wrangler jeep that had swerved up the walkway behind them and parked beside the steel fence. A young man with a green clipper-cut hairdo and suspicious green eyes slid from the pilot's seat, slamming the door behind him. His gasmask, which rose just above his nose, overflowed with sharp teeth and his grey-plaid suit was worn and frayed over his slim frame.

"Neko," Lycidius called. "What did you find?"

"Not a thing," he muttered, handing Snofrid a navy coroner jacket. "That rat-bastard Fergus Dripper has denied me access to the body. It's fortunate he likes Snofrid so much."

"She'll get you in," Lycidius guaranteed. "Does the Chancellor know it was his son?"

"When he knows, we will know that he knows."

"Call me after you wrap up. We need to be ready if this thing goes from bad to worse." Lycidius cocked his jackal gasmask at Snofrid. "I'll come for you in one hour," he said. "May we meet again."

Snofrid uttered the phrase for the sake of courtesy. She dismounted the pillion. While the men exchanged a last word, she scanned the sky for signs of the Chancellor's aircraft, the *Black Dagger*. Only police crafts zipped through the haze. She felt a flash of empathy as she pictured his reaction to Remus's death.

Lycidius accelerated westward off the platform. Neko offered his arm to Snofrid. Glad to see a familiar face, she circled her arm through his— which stiffened slightly—and they headed toward the entryway.

"I didn't know forensic pathologists came to crime scenes," she said.

"They don't. I'm here on your behalf." He peered down at her, his voice gentling. "Yesterday, you mentioned that you remember the city. But what about people? Have you remembered anyone at all?"

"Just bits here and there," she said, "but nothing concrete. Which is why I'm so grateful you agreed to do an examination."

"I respected the girl you were. If I can restore her, I will." He snapped on a pair of latex gloves. "Additionally, I have a medical interest in your case. The conditions of your lost memories are peculiar, which reminds me, how much do you recall about beasts?"

"Well, if something is missing, I wouldn't know."

"What's a Snapping Reefer?" he tested.

Snofrid's tongue started off at full throttle, as if she were reciting extracts from a glossary: "Snapping Reefers are lengthy, legless, flesh-eating reptiles of the suborder *Serpentinus*. With multi-jointed mouths and overlapping scales, the Reefer has the ability to ingest prey larger than itself. The Reefer's venom is a form of—"

"That should do," Neko interrupted. "Fortunately for us both, your knowledge seems untouched." He handed her a visitor's badge, a pair of latex gloves, some boot covers and a smock. "Let's be brief and thorough. I don't care for the stench of this one."

"I'll do my best," she promised, trying not to let intimidation bully her confidence.

After rechecking the sky and finding no sight of the *Black Dagger*, she suited up and then followed Neko through a body scanner at the entry to the crime scene. They were forced to sign a waiver with their thumbprints, stating that they would refrain from discussing the identity of the victim until it was made public by the Chancellor's administration, under penalty of prosecution.

Then they were finally granted access.

On the way to the kill site, the crowd of personnel bustled and shoved aggressively while others loitered in groups, consulting in aggravated tones.

"Chancellor Leathertongue is going to demand a *logical* explanation," a man with a shiny detective's badge yelled. "Find me security footage even if you have to pull it out of your own ass!"

"The unprofessionalism of this crime scene is embarrassing," a female sketch artist nattered. "And…it just got worse. Take a look, Callahan. They're bringing in that teen off the street again."

Snofrid let go of Neko's arm when she caught sight of Remus's corpse.

It was girdled by a ring of yellow evidence marking tents and the tarp was drawn back to reveal the boy's upper half. His bejeweled gasmask was shredded, revealing a purple, bloated face, glossed with blood. Runny fluid leaked from his smashed nose, split mouth and ears. His abdomen had also bloated, and was wiggling, as if something were alive inside. Maggots had hatched and begun to feed on his tissue and the unnatural curve of the spine suggested that it had been snapped.

"The cadaver doesn't disturb you, I hope?" Neko inquired, prying open a blood collection kit. "The maggots can't be removed without removing evidence."

"The smell is worse," she said, cupping a hand over her mouthpiece. "But still not as bad as Gehenna."

"Dr. Aberthol," a team leader blurted, as she broke from a group of her colleagues. "What have you and your assistant determined?"

"We've been with the body all of three seconds, so only that it is dead," Neko muttered, as he fastened on a pair of goggles. Flipping a switch on the side, he examined the ground around the body.

Snofrid watched him swab clear sludge from the neck. "Saliva?"

"It is. But since all the security cameras in this section of the city were being replaced, we're on our own finding who's responsible. Go on. Make your analysis."

Dropping her hand, she braved the stench and reminded herself to begin with the physical characteristics. Fighting off a gag reflex, she wrestled up the lip of Remus's gasmask, where she discovered severe bruising along the jawbone. *He was dragged*, she realized immediately. *But why to here? It's not a secluded feeding site.* Leaning closer, she studied the gashes in his skull, which indicated that he'd struck rocks along the way. She couldn't help but pity the human, for she knew his death had been slow and excruciating. In her opinion, being torn apart by a beast would be among the worst deaths.

After coming up for a short breath, she examined the claw lacerations on his neck and figured this injury had been the one to kill him—the carotid artery had been cut like a rope. Working her way down, she prodded his abdomen and was horrified when the skin broke open and spills of fly larva ran onto the tarp. "I think Remus was feasted upon while still alive and then dragged here hours after his death," she said.

"You're correct," Neko granted. "But it's peculiar—it almost seems as if the beast wished us to find the boy."

"Beasts don't have reason, so I doubt that was the case." She lifted up the sheet that covered Remus's lower half and alarm struck her chest, reverberating like a tower bell. His right leg, from the ankle downward, was missing. "Neko, look at this." She pointed. "The leg."

Neko's eyes widened. "Damnation."

"Do you think—?"

He held a finger to his lips, quieting her. "Let me have a look," he said, and hovered over the body.

Snofrid peered over his shoulder, hoping her suspicions were wrong. The boy's right ankle was missing, and the right ankle was where the Halo of a *Spectral* was located.

To her knowledge, Spectrals were spirit-like Inborns with the ability to possess living hosts. Once they'd fully possessed a host, a Halo would mark its right ankle. For a Spectral to possess any host other than a beast was frowned upon in Inborn society. If one had indeed possessed the human, Remus Leathertongue, the Chancellor would surely take out his wrath on the Inborns of Hollowstone. The more Snofrid contemplated her suspicions, the more obvious they seemed. Spectrals had possessed powerful human public officials, oligarchs and military leaders before, but this had ceased since the humans had determined that Stonewall Spells could block Spectrals from possessing their bodies.

"Neko," she whispered, putting her head on level with his. "Do you think it's possible a Spectral possessed Remus?"

"It's not just possible, but likely. It's also curious. Why didn't the Chancellor protect the boy with a Stonewall Spell?" He glared at the corpse, his eyes condemning. "The Spectral deserved to die a far worse death than this. Minds are sacred, even *human* minds."

"It was an Inborn that done it," a man with scraggily orange braids and a massive, hooked nose announced as he stepped from the crowd. Snofrid took in the man's freckled complexion and thought his lanky build resembled a stretching cat. He wore a white hazmat suit, which sagged off his shoulders, and a hairnet that made his head look cone-shaped. His Government Issue gasmask bore the chimera emblem of Hollowstone and his badge revealed his name was Fergus Dripper, the man who supposedly liked her.

"Get off my crime scene, Dripper," Neko spat.

"Actually, it's *my* crime scene." Fergus puffed himself up importantly. "You're a forensic pathologist so you shouldn't even be here. I've already examined the body, *before* you even arrived I might add, and uncovered evidence of foul play."

Neko spun around, black brows knitted. "The security cameras here aren't working, so *how* do you have this evidence?"

"That's confidential information." Fergus widened his stance. "What've you found, Snowball?" he asked.

"I disagree that foul play was involved," she answered. "Based on my analysis, I think a beast was responsible—a grinoire to be specific. But I'd have to run some tests to verify."

"No need." He rubbed her back appreciatively. "Like I said, we've already got our evidence." Whirling around, he ordered his assistants to pack up the body.

Neko waved them back. "My inspection is incomplete."

Snickering, Fergus aimed a crooked finger at Neko. The finger was on the end of a hand so dirty, half the crime scene's evidence might've been crammed beneath its nails. "First come, first serve, Aberthol. But don't worry, you won't go home empty-handed. A bluecoat walked into one of them cannibal-worm nests while canvassing the forest. Poor bastard didn't have a chance. And he ain't got no family so...guess you'll be cremating some sludge tonight."

Neko watched him walk away, raising his blood kit as if to hurl it at him. "Go," he told Snofrid. "You don't want to be here when the Chancellor arrives."

Snofrid didn't argue. As she removed her boot covers and smock, she wondered why Fergus had been so evasive about the alleged evidence of foul play. Her heart caught in her throat at a thought. *Maybe Fergus came to the same conclusion Neko and I did. Maybe he knows Remus was possessed by a Spectral.* If her suspicions were correct, the beast no longer mattered. The crime would be blamed on the Inborns of Hollowstone. Suddenly thankful for Lycidius's and Desya's decision to move, she raced to the exit of the crime scene.

As she passed the news crafts, high-powered engines drowned out the tumult of conversation. Looking up, she spotted a windowless silver aircraft, much larger than any other present, signaling to land. Bluecoats scampered in every direction to get clear, forming orderly lines at a distance, and Stellar Ops units funneled toward the craft in a wedge formation.

Snofrid ducked behind a local news craft to watch. A logo of red roses entwining a black dagger was emblazoned above the cockpit, marking the aircraft as Chancellor Leathertongue's.

The aircraft landed on a platform some ways off, its engine expiring with shots of steam from all sides. Two ramps lowered at the tail and a twelve-man private security detail filed out, their assault rifles leveled with the crowd. They formed a corridor with their bodies as a door slid from the fuselage and a ramp extended into their ranks. The main door popped open with a hiss, revealing a fat man.

A personalized blue energy shield was erected around the Chancellor like a second skin—not even a hellfire missile would make him miss a step. Inside the shield, his white silk suit glowed aquamarine. From the distance, Snofrid made out a waxed head and a fleshy, round face, one that was twisted in pain like a corkscrew.

Two of the Chancellor's senior advisers, his press secretary and the President of Vancastle exited the aircraft after him, all wide-eyed and pale-faced. When the Chancellor galloped down the ramp, sobbing so hard that he stumbled several times, the crowds fell into shocked silence. In waves they backed away—slowly at first, but when the President of Vancastle gave the order for all unauthorized personnel to be arrested, they scattered like rolling marbles. Panicked cries gored the air. People plodded over one another, banging into parked cars and transports.

Snofrid fought through the uproar, trying to keep pace with the fleeing crowd. A steel-toed boot crushed her foot. She cried out, flexing her toes to ease the pain, and narrowed her gaze on the perpetrator: *a bluecoat*. She flashed him her visitor's badge and then darted further into the crowd, searching wildly for Neko.

Ahead, more than half the crowd was dispersing in the direction of the Speedrail Metro Station. Snofrid followed until she'd wriggled into the clear. Her lungs felt fit to burst. She crouched behind a parked transport, heaving for air, and again swept the crime scene for Neko. He was nowhere. Aware that she couldn't wait for Lycidius, she pulled out her phone and sent him a message:

> *Don't come to the crime scene or you'll be arrested. I'll ride the Speedrail Metro and meet you at the house.*

Fear fueled Snofrid's steps as she sprinted toward the Speedrail Metro Station. The beast couldn't have chosen a worse person to kill, or a worse day to kill him.

Machinegun Tag

Snofrid bolted toward the Speedrail Metro Station like a spider toward a fly. It stood on the corner of *Melpomene Parkway* in a gaudy spectacle of marble arches and dichroic glass windows. At six dizzying stories, the station's elevated tracks sent bullet trains north, south, east, and west, whisking civilians to every part of the city.

She kept on the right side of the lobby escalator so as not to be trampled by the mad dash of people. Aside from extra security guards, nothing gave cause for panic; but their alertness mirrored her own. She wished she could get out of the city today, before authorities started pointing fingers regarding Remus's death, but admitted that relocating so hastily wouldn't be smart. It would look suspicious to the authorities if civilians abandoned their jobs and left Hollowstone the day Remus died. She just hoped the week would progress without too much backlash.

Tugging nervously at her sleeves, she rode the wave of people to the sixth-level ticket counters. After a ticket vendor had downloaded a boarding pass into her Tag, she, along with thirty others, were cruelly selected to undergo additional security checks. She sighed as a security guard directed her out of line. What had she done to give cause for suspicion? Maybe it was because she looked so restless. Either way, Hatred Day security lengthened simple tasks into exhausting formalities, making even an elderly monk lose his patience.

Snofrid quietly awaited the additional safety procedures while fishing through her satchel. Inside, jammed up against her pistol, was a silver box. She hadn't noticed it earlier at the crime scene. Cracking the lid, she found a gold necklace with a drop-pendant, on which was inscribed a Swedish phrase. She frowned. Lycidius had mentioned Atlas was raised in Sweden. Thinking it likely the human had gifted her the necklace, she tossed it back into her satchel.

Her train screeched to a halt on platform thirty-three a few moments after her final body scan. A dozen people bum-rushed open seats and were fired dirty-looks by disembarking passengers. Snofrid intentionally boarded last and settled into a position near the doors, in case there was an emergency evacuation.

Tension clouded the train car in whiffs of sweat. The passengers looked jittery, aggravated, or dog-tired. She figured that, along with Hatred Day norms, news of a high-profile crime had added to the general excitement. Remus's identity hadn't been made public, though rumors that the Chancellor had personally visited the crime scene had recently been confirmed over a live broadcast.

"Shut your damn mouth, Enzo," an Italian man spat into his phone. He wore a tailored black business suit and his red face seemed to inflate with his words. "Just shut your damn mouth. Hematic guerrillas are killing civilians and you're talking about bloody carbines. You're just like the rest of the schmucks who can't tell crap from pudding."

"Dad, you're not listening to me," a wide-eyed girl in a plaid uniform sobbed into her phone. "He was *in* the sky-tunnels when the bombs went off. I don't care what your stupid girlfriend says. I'm not going! I'll run away before you make me!"

"Attention passengers, in the event of an emergency, an attendant will direct you to your nearest exit," a young train attendant announced over the car's loud speaker. He sported a traditional black uniform and his ginger blond hair was combed neatly in a side-part. "Remain calm and be advised that this train does not tolerate concealed carry firearms. Weapons must remain visible at all times. Thank you for your cooperation."

The train jerked forward and Snofrid, failing to snatch onto a straphanger, stumbled into a middle-school girl standing in front of her. "Sorry," she huffed.

"Not at all," the girl assured, then rolled her eyes. "If you were a sweaty, old man, I'd have a word."

Snofrid smiled. "And I'm sure he'd blush."

"No doubt about that. I love your dress by the way." The girl gave it a quick glance. "Carter and Roke?"

"Is it written on me somewhere?"

"Nope, I've got the eye. *And* I'm friends with most worthwhile designers," she bragged, flipping her braids to one shoulder. "My mom works for Imperial Black." Her phone rang and she propped up a finger. "Ooh, I have to take this one. Stay safe, fashion-sister. Crazy things happen on Hatred Day."

"So I've been told."

Snofrid spent the next few minutes scrolling through news articles on her phone and taking great pains to ignore the occasional gawker. Security cameras winked from every corner of the car, which allowed people to breathe easier; usually, criminals thought twice about breaking the law when the eye of the Bluecoat Headquarters was watching.

Except the Bluecoat HQ wasn't the only pair of eyes watching.

During her routine scan of the metro car, Snofrid noticed a young man—probably in his early-twenties—staring at her. He stuck out so vividly, she couldn't say how she'd missed him before; no one sat within five feet of him.

Her first thought was that he belonged to the Swangunners—the super-gang of ex-military who ruled Gehenna. He sat alone on a rear bench in the car, flicking ash from a cigarette. There was a foreign air to his appearance, largely due to his sandy complexion and refined, Grecian nose. With hard angled brows, light stubble and full chapped lips, he was an untidy sort of attractive; but his badger-grey eyes harbored a calculating flare. Hair as black as a thundercloud plunged to his shoulders, framing his face everywhere except above his left ear where a thick stripe was shaved. The quilted black jacket he wore was in novel condition—it looked pricy, in fact—and equally expensive biker pants stressed the ridged muscles of his legs. Clicking rang from the machine pistols, hand grenades and knives packed into his chest harness.

Unease turned its cold breath upon Snofrid as she stared back at him. The sleek metal tubes that contoured his breastbone, serving as air filters, were a trademark of the Swangunners; still more, the red band tied around his left bicep indicated that he was a gang Captain. Being war-veterans, Swangunners utterly despised her kind. Their hatred thrust them into all manner of violence when Inborns were found squatting in Gehenna; usually, after torturing and killing Inborns, the Swangunners decked their armor in their victims' bones.

It was now that the look in his eyes registered. Like a beast observing its prey, he planned to do her harm. She retrieved the pistol from her satchel and backpedaled until her spine touched the wall.

"Civilians," the Swangunner called in a coarse, Lithuanian accent. He drew a machine pistol and instructed, "Clear a path or I'll make one."

Faces looked up from their phones, eyes popping, and mouths took to startled gasps. No one spoke. No one took defensive action.

"Move! That guy's Lucian Lozoraitis!" someone screamed.

"Get out of my way!" snarled others.

A groundswell of terror rippled through the ranks. The cries started low before the train car tumbled into chaos. Citizens hurled themselves at the walls, shoving past one another to get clear of the line of fire. A column of people toppled to the floor. Yelling curses, their eyes wild and panicked, stragglers scrambled toward the walls and clung to them with desperate pleas.

"I have a baby," a woman cried, cupping her child to her breast. "Please. Don't shoot!"

"Your baby is not a shield," the Swangunner informed, shunting through the packed train car. "Use him as such and I'll shoot you for pleasure."

"Stop!" the ginger blond train attendant barked, jumping onto a car bench. "Holster your weapon or you'll face arrest."

The Swangunner made a 'tsk' sound. "You speak these rules with such authority. But, like the civilians on this train, you don't matter."

He lifted his pistol and fired. A bang echoed throughout the space, sucking away Snofrid's hearing, muffling fresh screams. The attendant's head whipped back, sending a streak of blood and gore at the faces behind; people scattered as his body collapsed.

Snofrid hammered her fists against the doors until a crack formed in the glass. She didn't understand why no one was choosing to defend themselves. Around her, people smacked into one another, pinning her to the door and trampling those on the floor.

"Let us out!" people sobbed. "Please! Open the damn doors!"

"I'll pay you whatever you want, Captain Lozoraitis," the Italian man in the business suit promised, using his own body as a buffer for a young boy. "Just don't shoot anyone else! Please!"

Snofrid checked her flank at the sound of amplified shrieks. The Swangunner was less than an arm's length away. His hand shot out like a viper and grabbed her jacket.

"Get off me!" She thrashed about as he dragged her toward him. "Let me—"

He drove her into the wall, whacking the air from her lungs, and then pinned her with his chest.

"Let me go or I'll shoot you," she coughed.

"No, mieloji. Drop the weapon or you'll be the one who loses fingers this time," he said, now speaking in a crisp Lithuanian dialect. Jarred by surprise, she found herself as familiar with the language as she was with English, Russian and Japanese.

She dropped the gun, searching for an escape even before it struck the floor. The train sped thousands of feet above the city, so unless she jumped, she was a rat in a corner. "Please," she started, also speaking in Lithuanian. "I won't run away. Just loosen my wrist."

"You performed this trick last time. I won't be polite again, mieloji." He tilted up her chin with the still-warm barrel of his gun. "My boys tell me Atlas Bancroft left Hollowstone, and, without his guns, you're sadly unprotected."

"You're wrong, I'm protected," she assured. "My brother is a—"

"I warned you," he broke in. "Struggle and the pain will be worse."

She flicked her eyes up at him, confused and angry that Desya and Lycidius hadn't thought to warn her about this man. "Why? What have I done?"

His face darkened. "If you're going to play this game, then Aušra will play too." He tossed his cigarette to the floor—she noted the missing thumb on his left hand—and unzipped his coat pocket. Snofrid lurched back as he fished out a wriggling yellow viper and held it palm-up, until it coiled around his forearm. "You remember her?"

"Y-yes." Somehow she did recognize the eyelash pit viper. It had a triangular-shaped head and a set of bristly scales over its eyes that could almost be eyelashes. She knew that the pit-viper's bite was as painful as getting your hand slammed in a car door over and over again. This recollection was so potent that she was certain she'd been bitten before.

"Then you remember how painful her kiss is." He held the viper's fangs to her neck and spoke into her ear. "I'll *keep* my dignity and you'll keep yours, mieloji. This means you won't insult me. We respect each other. It wouldn't please me to take your life unfairly."

"Then, don't."

"I don't cheat. You know this. I plan to let you off at the next stop," he said, tilting the viper away from her neck. "There, you'll run and I'll follow. This deal is fair."

She wasn't of a mind to argue, but knew she'd be outed as an Inborn if she was shot and then healed. She'd need to leg it fast. "We have a deal. I'll run."

"Good, girl." He loosened his grip, then slid the viper back into his pocket.

A hundred pairs of eyes watched her. All were fat with terror, wet with tears, and the faces freckled with blood. Most denounced her with their stares, as if she was responsible for the killing. She didn't know. She didn't know anything. Maybe she'd once done horrible things. Or maybe this Swangunner had targeted her because of Atlas Bancroft. *Atlas probably is dirty.* Losing focus, she held tight to her rock shard from Oubliette; outside of her fear, it was the only thing she felt.

Minutes later, the bullet train squealed to a halt at a pick-up station. Snofrid scanned the platform for the best route of escape. The least congested path was near the train information displays.

The Swangunner nodded at the doors. "Run, mieloji. I'll follow in ten seconds."

She dashed from the train car, smacking into people she couldn't dodge fast enough. She stumbled, but bounced off a pillar and gained speed. Zooming past the ticket counters, she sprinted up the stairs two at a time. A brief glance over her shoulder confirmed that her time had run out. The Swangunner broke into a run.

She exited the station and leapt from the walkway onto the flat roof of a building. The Swangunner cleared the building with a grunt, landing on a walkway further below.

"Run faster, mieloji," he advised, taking aim. "Otherwise, I'll kill you too quickly."

On instinct, she rolled across the roof and plunged down the opposite side. Her feet struck the ground amidst a troop of street performers. Wedging herself among them, she willed them to accept her and resume their acts. She waited, knees trembling, counting seconds that felt like hours. Finally, she stole a glance around her. The Swangunner was nowhere. She walked briskly, parting the audience until free of their bodies. Breaking again into a run, she kept pace alongside an electric hypercar.

"Watch it, sweet legs," the driver snorted. "This isn't a damn pedestrian crossing."

"You watch it," she shot back. "Pedestrians always have the right of way."

Skirting the car, she passed by a group of teen protestors in red shirts and then swung into a vacant alley, which ran its course and T-boned into a gypsy trade market. She checked her peripheries, dodging low-flying transports and rounding stacks of whiskey crates. The Swangunner was nowhere to be seen, but even so, she went on running.

All types of people browsed the stalls, which exhibited purebred horses, guns and liquor. They overlooked her as she struggled to squeeze by. Just when she'd secured an opening, the Swangunner emerged from a rifle booth and charged her. He fired shots into the crowd. Crying out, she scrambled behind a pile of metal crates, maneuvering on her haunches. *My hell. Run,* she told herself. *Don't think, just run.* Sprinting across an exposed patch of walkway, she ducked into a tavern.

It was a task to move through the knot of sweaty, dancing bodies inside. Beer glasses slid down counters and curvy prostitutes clad in lingerie catered to those who remained conscious; half a dozen bodies littered the floor, some vomiting onto the checkered tiles. There was no other exit.

She slipped into the bathroom where laughing girls with sweaty hair and smoky eyes jostled for the coveted space before the bathroom mirrors. She did a sweep of the floor, her memory recalling that such dives sometimes had secret hatchways to spirit away shady but well-paying customers if there was a raid.

She found it: a trapdoor just beneath the girl's shuffling feet. "I need the door, girls," she pointed. "A Swangunner is stalking me."

"Go for it, hon." A redhead lifted the trapdoor and Snofrid dropped inside. "Don't let him push you around!" the girl called before sealing the door shut.

Snofrid found herself in a dank passage girded with corroded steel. Water dripped from the ceiling, dampening her hair and clothes. She followed the tunnel, imagining that it moved under several buildings, platforms and walkways. *If he finds me in here, I'm a sitting duck.*

The passage ended abruptly with an elevator large enough for one person. She rode it down and got off on a support beam beneath the city: it was safest not to return to city level in an elevator.

She took hold of the nearest support strut and swung herself over to a wide beam. She worked her way along in this manner. Her heart pounded so quickly it seemed to catapult her over the struts. Now and then, her shoes brushed the treetops, heightening her fear of falling. Being under the city, she had no idea where she was going, only that more distance meant more safety.

Or at least she thought it did.

She glanced over her shoulder and suddenly glimpsed the Swangunner racing across the beams. The girls in the bathroom had probably given her up. Terrified, she dropped down a level and snagged a metal cable. She moved along the cable, hand over hand, dangling over the abyss, until she alighted safely on a beam. The Swangunner's footsteps grew louder; he was gaining on her. Heart thrashing, she again glanced over her shoulder and noticed something strange. His head was swinging back and forth, searching, as if he couldn't see her. Thinking she'd gone mad, she searched for an explanation. She nearly cried out, sandwiched between shock and relief, when she found she couldn't see her arms, torso, legs or feet. *Someone* had raised a Concealing Spell over her.

She turned in a full circle, scanning, until she spotted a person in a full-face gasmask, watching her from a nearby beam. The person remained still, like a block of granite, and flecks of purple magic gleamed on its gloves. Immediately, Snofrid mistrusted the person's motive for helping her, though she was still thankful. She waited until the Swangunner was a speck in the distance before saying, "Thank you."

"Protecting you wasn't a kindness. As you shall soon see."

Snofrid tensed, struggling to combat the hypnotic effect of the person's voice; it was the most spellbinding voice she'd ever heard, so sultry it could've charmed a bull.

The person sprang onto Snofrid's beam. Purple magic billowed from its hands, threading along Snofrid's body until it had eaten away the Concealing Spell.

"Who are you?" Snofrid managed to ask.

"Someone whose side you will want to be on." The person pulled off its gasmask and ran a gloved hand over its bald head, which was as smooth as an eggshell.

Fisting her hands, chin held upright, Snofrid's first thought was that this person was infinitely more dangerous than the Swangunner. It was a Seer, Necromancer Inborns who rejected standard magic, and instead, risked their physical beauty—and sometimes even their lives—trying to master a hazardous branch of the spirit element, known as the *Leaky Spells*. Fortunately, the ivory facial armor this Seer wore covered its grotesque features that, if shown, would likely terrify even the most stouthearted soldier. There were surgical scars below its neckline, probably where its breasts had once been. Her violet eyes were the lone feature Snofrid could make out through her mask; they appeared blank, as if emptiness lay beyond them. She wore a corseted tunic beneath her green wool cloak, which cascaded down one shoulder, exposing half of the House insignia that embossed her breastplate—a Komodo Dragon enclosed by a wreath of purple monkshood blossoms.

Before daring to utter a word, Snofrid warned herself that the majority of Seers could petrify creatures, communicate through the mind and manipulate people with their voices. However, this one had clearly been subdued. The iron three-ringed collar around her neck meant that she'd been tamed by a master.

The girl fitted on her glove and said aloud, "I'm Hessia Nabash. Address me as Hessia."

Snofrid recognized the name and raised her left hand in salute. Hessia Nabash was rumored to have been enslaved by a Skinwalker Commander and was famed for her victories in the Middle East. It made no sense for her to be here. "I'm Snofrid Yagami."

"I know who you are."

Snofrid furrowed her brow. "How?"

Hessia didn't reply. She buckled on her gasmask, then circled around her. "I've wasted time enough searching for you, so I'll make this brief. I've been sent by my master to propose a trade. If you agree to it, you'll be rewarded."

Snofrid ballooned with curiosity. "I'll listen, but I can't promise anything."

"I've requested nothing more than listening at the moment." Hessia lifted a piece of Snofrid's hair, which was still thinly crusted in blue slime. "Fifteen days ago, you were marked by a beast in the woods outside of the Gehenna slum. Its saliva still clings to you."

Snofrid touched her hair reflexively. She was aware that various species of beasts marked prey with their saliva and scolded herself for not making the connection. It made tracking the prey effortless when they needed to feed. "Why does a Seer care about a beast?"

"I've been tasked to ensure that the beast dies. That's why I've been sent: I want you to offer yourself as bait."

Snofrid suspected the girl was delusional. "Why would I just offer myself?"

"To please me."

"Your voice is hardly powerful enough to control me."

Hessia fingered her glove threateningly, as if she was going to strip it off and paralyze Snofrid with her touch. "My master and I were sent to destroy the beast by the Empyrean City. *You* have been given the honor of assisting us. Before you decide, keep in mind that, either way, the *welx* that marked you will come for you in thirteen days."

"Scaring me won't convince me to help you," Snofrid assured. She wondered why a Seer and her master had been sent to kill just one beast in particular. The Empyrean City was home to three of the five Inborn Lords, making it the most powerful Inborn city on Earth. "I've studied many beasts, but I haven't heard of the one you're searching—"

"Only a select few have," Hessia cut her off. "Join us and you'll be among them."

Snofrid froze up. Notwithstanding feeling indebted to Hessia for the Swangunner, she was leaving the city with Lycidius and Desya in a week. Still, she felt it would be smart to gather as much information about the welx as possible. If the beast would come for her in thirteen days, she needed to be prepared. "I need more information about the welx before I decide."

"You'll never know more than what my master wants you to know," Hessia notified. "The beast is a welx, a rare species in the order *Bashea*, but the one we are hunting is possessed by a Spectral."

With this new information, Snofrid's courage wobbled at the thought of the beast coming for her: Spectrals could raise magic, even if inhabiting beasts.

"The welx hibernates for seventeen years at a time. Upon waking, it feeds thrice," Hessia explained. "Its feeding cycle spans the course of six weeks; its diet is very specific: it feeds on Inborn Halos. As of now, it's already taken two victims—one in Salem and another discovered this morning: the Chancellor of Hollowstone's son."

"*Remus Leathertongue?*" Snofrid asked.

"Yes."

Snofrid doubted this day could get any worse. Remus *had* been possessed by a Spectral spy, which meant there would be catastrophic political and military repercussions when the human authorities also confirmed this. "Why do you need to kill the beast?" she asked. "Is the Spectral possessing it a traitor?"

Hessia's tone morphed into a croak, shedding its beauty. "Spectrals are lower than traitors. They're abominable. The rest is confidential."

"I'm sure you can give me a hint without breaching your confidentiality agreement. At least tell me why it's a threat."

"I will. But only because my master allows it. The Spectral possessing the welx has mastered the earth element."

"That's not possible," Snofrid protested. "Spectrals aren't strong enough to master Elements."

"This one is strong enough."

"Then tell me how."

"You're not privy to that information. Obeying my master is your only concern. The welx is not only being hunted by us. Others search for it as well, not to kill it, but to use it. Preventing them from doing so is also our mission. If you join us, you'll report to my master until the mission is finished. Make your choice."

Snofrid wasn't going to agree, regardless of her plan to leave Hollowstone. Few Spectrals or Necromancers ever mastered one of the six elements fully—earth, air, fire, water, spirit and metal—and it generally took decades to do so. Having mastery over the earth element gave the Spectral possessing the welx the ability to manipulate soil, rocks and plant-life at ungodly capacities. This made her want protection, especially considering the welx would track her when she left the city. But her decision was already made. "I can't help you."

"Why?" Hessia demanded, her tone intolerant. "You have a healing ability. There's no risk."

Snofrid's mind did a one-eighty. "*How* do you know I can heal?"

"My master, Commander Hadrian, briefed me before he sent me to recruit you."

Suddenly, the events of the past few days converged and made sense. Snofrid realized that the Commander had bid so high for her at the slave auction because she'd been marked. He'd wanted to use her in his hunt. It took all of Snofrid's willpower not to turn around and walk away. She never wanted to be within range of the Commander again. "Like I said, I can't help you."

"Consider what you're saying, civilian. Then understand that my master won't accept a refusal. It's *expected* of you to pay service to your kind, to do your duty. Otherwise, I'll see to it that you're shamed."

"That's blackmail!" Snofrid pointed out, her temper flaring.

"Duty isn't blackmail. It's merely an *honorable* choice."

Snofrid, feeling the weight of worry, took into account that Desya might also be condemned when news of her refusal reached the proper channels. Even if they were both vagrants already, it wasn't widely known. If Hessia made good on her threat, the result would blacken their names in every part of the world.

"We're stationed in a war bunker under the city," Hessia said, fishing a pair of gold-plated goggles from her pocket. "These are globus goggles. Should you decide to choose *duty* over fear, they'll direct you there. Meet me the day after tomorrow, at 2000 hours."

Snofrid snatched the goggles from the Hessia's hand, convinced that the Seer wouldn't allow her to leave unless she accepted them. She turned on her heel, eager for freedom, but was stopped by Hessia's hand on her shoulder.

"As I said, this information is classified. You'll be expected to swear into a Covenant Spell."

Snofrid was now doubly relieved that she'd rejected Hessia's trade. Like any contract, Covenant Spells bound two or more parties together, each pledging to do something for the other; but, if broken, the spell preyed upon the betrayer's greatest fears, often times making them a reality. The only known ways to break the spell were if both parties agreed to end the arrangement or if one party died. "Please let me go," she said.

"For now. May we meet again." Hessia released Snofrid's shoulder.

Snofrid stuffed the globus goggles into her satchel in bitter frustration. When Hessia was out of sight, she set off in search of a service elevator. Panic burrowed its way into her conviction, fracturing it. The past few days had been a whirlwind, and she hardly knew what problem to focus on. Learning why the Swangunner wanted her dead was her top priority. However, she didn't see a sure road to answers. It was like being tossed into an exam that she hadn't studied for. Nothing fully registered. The girl she'd been two days ago wasn't the girl she was now. This one was purposeless. The moment this thought entered her mind, she flushed it out. Such thinking wouldn't help her. Instead, she needed to gear all her focus towards her forgotten past.

The Divine Hound

Snofrid stared hard at the photograph of her and Atlas Bancroft, trying to imagine what he looked like. His gasmask covered most of his face, leaving only his blond hair and steel-blue eyes visible. She wondered if she'd chosen to date him impulsively or if she'd truly loved the human. She hoped it was the latter. Risking the title of vagrant for anything less than love was insanity. Questions raced in her mind, so many questions.

Sighing, she folded the photograph into her satchel and glanced at the wall clock. Only eight minutes had passed since she'd last checked the time. It felt infinitely longer. She'd awaited Desya's and Lycidius's return for hours last night before finally dozing off sometime after midnight. Lycidius hadn't come home or even called in for an update. She had no idea where he could've gone, but Desya had messaged her a while ago, letting her know that he was working a second patrol shift until 7:00 a.m.

Grabbing a knit sweater from her drawer, she climbed down from her bedroom into the kitchen. On the television, a news bulletin was giving a Hatred Day summary, listing damages to the city. She nibbled on a bowl of *Natto*—fermented soy beans on steamed rice—and watched. The horrors of Hatred Day still clung to her body, driving her restlessness. Yesterday hadn't been as violent as last year's Hatred Day, but the death toll still ranged in the hundreds; this had foreseeably delayed Neko's examination of her.

She'd spent half the day researching the welx. In learning that she attended the University of Hollowstone, she'd contacted one of her college professors, Dr. Darther Cricket, for information. Even with his aid, they'd turned up nothing. Since the welx only woke from hibernation for six weeks every seventeen years, she figured it had never been sighted. This or all knowledge of its existence had been wiped from the beast database. Accordingly, she decided to focus on answers that were closer at hand— like Atlas and the Swangunner. Peace of mind was something she desperately needed.

"In the words of John F. Kennedy, 'conformity is the jailer of freedom and the enemy of growth,'" an earnest voice spoke from the television.

Snofrid glanced up from her Natto to find the station airing a rerun of a speech by the New Global Union leader, President Sebaster Leathertongue. His spryness reminded her of a fox, but she didn't trust his 'flawless' image. Only 26 years old, he'd been nicknamed the *Divine Hound*, for he was a mixture of almost two dozen nationalities and was as handsome as a Greek sculpture.

The address had been filmed in an outdoor stadium with rows of policemen securing the stage platform and a roiling audience of wildly cheering and sobbing people. A black gasmask screened all but Sebaster's soft green eyes and his bespoke navy suit gave a nod to his well-heeled upbringing.

"This administration does not tolerate conformity," Sebaster went on, planting his blucher shoes apart in an alpha pose. "Terror is unacceptable. War is *not* absolute. People of the world, we are united in suffering, and what is suffering if not a means to overcome frailty? Loved ones have been lost, but in grief, we cannot lose sight of ourselves or of our purpose. In all desolation, we must take comfort in the certainty that storms *always* break. The sun *will* shine on humanity again. History has consistently proven our resilience. Humanity *will* endure as a civilization and as a species."

Her phone jingled. "Television off," Snofrid ordered. She found a message from Desya:

Be home in five.

Jumping to her feet, she buttoned on a red parka that was hanging on the coat rack. After carting her dishes to the kitchen, she jogged onto the plaza platform.

Storm clouds muted the sunshine, draping the buildings in wind-whipped rain and lackluster shades. With one hand on the pistol in her pocket, she perused the shops that bordered the main street: The Tradehouse of Exotic Teas, and beside it the Alaskan Fur Emporium, and a couple of platforms down was the Sun Wheel Cafe.

"Hi, Sno!" a girl in a violet scarf called from across the platform. "Hey, where's Lycidius? I haven't seen him in weeks. Is he finally single now?"

"I'm not sure," Snofrid called back.

She perked up at the sight of a Brute jeep making a turn for the house. Desya cut the engine outside the garage and grabbed his rifle off the console as he slid from his seat.

"Sorry, Sno," he puffed. "It's been chaos out there since Remus. I would've tried to get off if I'd known Lycidius would skip out."

"Don't apologize," she urged. "I was fine on my own. The robot showed me where things were stored."

"Yeah, that's the butler-maid, Threearms." He put a hand on her back and steered her toward their shop, the War Lobby. "I got listed for another shift tonight, so Lycidius will pop by around six to help you close things up. But I'll show you the ropes."

"I would imagine the shop is beside the point right now."

"I think you'd be surprised how fast Hatred Day blows over, Sno. Everything will be fine in two days tops. It's best to go on as normal."

She fixed a doubtful eye on him. "Even with the death of Remus?"

"Yeah, Neko filled me in on the leg. But they can't *prove* he was possessed by a Spectral and they'd need evidence before cracking down on anyone."

"Maybe, but from what I can remember, humans usually blame us when something goes wrong," she said, walking around a beheaded snowman. After taking a moment to reign in her anger, she added, "Desya, there's something we *need* to talk about. Yesterday, I ran into a Swangunner on the metro and he forced me to play machinegun-tag. He would've killed me if I hadn't hidden under the city."

Desya stalled in his tracks. "Was his thumb hacked off?"

"Yes."

"If you *ever* see him again, hide and call us."

"Why? You know why he wants to kill me, don't you?"

"Hang on." He did a quick sweep of the area, then changed directions and headed toward the house. "The guy who tried to shoot you is Lucian Lozoraitis. I don't know how much you remember about Gehenna's pecking order, but the kingpin goes by the code name, the Warden. Lucian is the Warden's youngest brother."

"Shoot me," Snofrid cursed. Immediately, she realized that if Lucian Lozoraitis was a warlord, she was little more than a blade of grass in his backyard. No wonder the passengers on the Speedrail Metro had been too afraid to put up a fight.

"We dug up everything we could on the Lozoraitis brothers a few years back," Desya went on. "Their organization has deep roots and it's all backed by silver. They quit Europe eighteen years back and it took them less than two years to get established here before they started expanding across the west coast. They're packing more than Swangunners now."

"Why does he want to kill me?" she demanded.

"It's a long story, Sno. I don't—"

"Desya." She grabbed his arm. "Tell me."

"Okay…uh…Lucian has this thing about respect. You earned a nod the first time you stole oranges from his bike. He thought you were cute, so he started calling you mieloji and hired you to do deliveries. You became friends and for a while it was great because he saved our skin more than once." He paused, then pulled off his beret and dusted it off. "Last year, he got engaged to some Brazilian dancer, but she didn't want kids, so he tossed her. That's when he made a move on you. Things got bad when you told him you weren't into him. Atlas finally stepped in and sent some guys to give him a scare." Desya wiggled his thumb. "They cut off his thumb as a warning to back off. Not even stiches could fix it."

Snofrid's mind staggered in heated confusion. Lucian had tried to kill her over a *thumb*?

"Lucian mentioned he came after me because I was unprotected," she said. "I'm guessing that means Atlas and I aren't on good terms?"

"I'm not sure, Sno. You're more secretive than a newt." Desya shrugged. "You know, at first I thought Lucian had something to do with you going missing, but when I checked in with a contact who works at his club, she said you weren't with him. I wasn't too surprised because Lucian hasn't bothered you for weeks. I thought maybe he'd decided to leave you alone for good, but we're gonna have to deal with him now."

"What does that mean, Desya?"

"I don't know yet."

She decided that any plan to strike back was idiotic. Lucian was a linchpin for the Swangunners. They were civilians. If he wanted to hurt her, she'd need an army of her own to stop him. "Lucian said Atlas had hired guns. Was he dirty?"

Desya shook his head. "I don't know that either. He was a boss in the Aracnid Munitions Company, but I think he got his stacks from other investments."

"Do we know anyone who can do a background check?"

"Lycidius checked him out a few weeks back, but he told me he came up clean. It could be drivel though. He could've paid to get his record wiped. The guy has the stacks."

Snofrid swept back her hair, unsatisfied. She still had nothing. Desya's account left her with the same questions on the same shadowy bluff of uncertainty.

"It's okay, Sno," he comforted, rubbing her back. "Don't stress about it. I'll talk to Lycidius later and we'll figure something out."

"No. I don't want you doing something that gets you hurt or killed. I think we should leave the city sooner than planned."

"We will if we have to," he promised. "But first, we're gonna sort through all our options on how to deal with Lucian."

"All right. But please, let's leave if none of our options pan out within a day or two."

"Two days tops. The Moonlentar Express docks tomorrow morning. We can grab supplies and be ready to leave in a tick." They strode into the garage and he slid open the genkan door with a nod. "Chin up, Sno. We've run up against worse and we're all still kicking."

She regarded his eyepieces, through which she could see the hazy outlines of his eyes. "Is that the truth, or just something you made up to make me feel better?"

"It's the truth, Sno. I swear." He rotated to enter the kitchen and then doubled back. "Oh, and I checked in with the Hematic Inborn Cell. None of them know why a Commander would be in the city. If you want, I can—
"

"Don't worry about the Commander," she said quickly. She no longer wanted to waste energy on the Commander, not after refusing Hessia's offer. Yes, there would be consequences, but at this point, she had to choose her battles. "We're leaving in less than a week anyway," she added. "I do have one question, though—about Lycidius. Did we have some kind of falling out before I lost my memories?"

"Uh…" Desya scratched his head, "not that I know of. Why? Has he been acting weird?"

"You could say that."

"Okay. I'll talk to him." Desya thought for a moment, then sighed. "I'm not trying to make up any excuses for Cid, Sno, but I should tell you he's a pretty extreme guy. It took you guys years to get on friendly terms. He's probably just frustrated over the whole memory thing. It's hard for me, too."

Snofrid didn't buy this excuse. If Lycidius truly wanted to be her friend, all he had to do was treat her nicely. "Okay, thanks Desya."

"No problem. Oh, and just a note; you always called me Dez. Not that I mind my name, it's just weird hearing you say it."

Snofrid wandered the snowy plaza after Desya returned to work. This time, she carried two pistols—one open carry, one strapped under her parka—in case Lucian Lozoraitis made a second appearance. All throughout the shopping center, people were frantically stocking up on survival gear in fear of more bombings. That or the fear that Hollowstone would become militarily reinforced. The humans called it Martial Law.

After eating *wagyu* steak at the *Cosmopolitan Lounge*, she took a stroll down the lamp-lit sidewalks, and, in a store window, noticed Lycidius tailing her at a distance. She couldn't mistake his tawdry red hair, or his ominous jackal-head gasmask. From the way he remained in vantage, talking on his phone, she knew he wanted her to see him. In a similar way, she wanted to see him, too. With subtle urgency, she tried to repress the uninvited response arising within her. She again felt a compulsion towards him, but this time, it surfaced stronger. And this time it stirred her senses until she found herself experiencing an acute attraction towards him.

Immediately, she convinced herself the attraction wasn't real. It was nothing more than a different person's yearnings hemorrhaging so heavily into hers that they only *seemed* to be her own.

Continuing down the sidewalk, she tried to put him out of her mind—he lingered there, in a corner she consciously ignored. She browsed a few gun stores with nearly empty shelves and then bought an apple cider to go. Just as she stepped onto the icy street, Lycidius cut her off. She dropped her cup and it burst open against the asphalt, the boiling liquid melting holes into the snow.

"My presence earns a loud reaction," he observed, and hunkered down to retrieve the cup.

"My reaction wasn't a compliment," she assured, recovering from her start. "You scared me." He'd appeared out of nowhere, like a hitman. "You were following me since I left the Cosmopolitan. Why?"

"I already explained why you need to be looked out for. That Lucian almost shot you yesterday proves it."

"Well, I might've been able to avoid it if you would've told me about him. Hundreds of people could've witnessed me getting injured and healing and then all of us would've been outed."

"Had I known he was still an active threat, you would've been told. But really, you were never supposed to go off on your own. Either way, we're leaving the day after tomorrow."

This hardly excused him, but she felt reassured. "Good. I think it's for the best. Not just because of Lucian, but Remus too."

"Without proof a Spectral possessed Remus, people will get over it. They always do." Lycidius chucked the cup into a trash incinerator. "Let's go. Neko is waiting at the mansion and has a dog's patience."

"Wait." She reached out and touched the arm of his jacket. His eyes shot to her hand, and instantly, she let go, as fast as if she'd touched a hot stove. "W-what? What did I do?"

"Nothing," he snapped. He swung back, his anger plainly directed towards himself.

She guessed that he disliked being touched. Still flustered, she had to recall what she was about to say. "Um...I thought Neko couldn't look at me until tomorrow."

"That was the original plan," he replied. "It changed when Lucian showed up."

Exhilaration strengthened her resolve: with the restoration of her memories, her muddled tragedy of a life would be ordered. Whole.

As they once more hit the pavement, a wistful feeling fell over her. It was as if she was walking with the wind, her steps light and natural. This had happened before, she was sure of it—she and Lycidius strolling this very sidewalk, exactly like this. All was the same, down to the pedestrians clearing a path, reluctant to breach Lycidius's personal space. Their behavior was similar to the way people had regarded Lucian on the metro—with tremulous caution. She couldn't understand the lengths they went to avoid crossing paths, but granted there were sinister traits about Lycidius—his monstrous eye for one.

"Have you decided where we're moving to?" she asked, as they passed a vendor selling holographic newspapers.

"The Satar Stronghold. We'll stay there until we find a permanent location."

"I've never heard of it."

"It's in Alaska."

"Alaska?" Bewildered, she halted, then hastened after him. "Desya can't stand the cold."

"There's less trouble in ice caves and glaciers," Lycidius clarified. The wind picked up and he raised his chin, as if he enjoyed the breeze on his face. "It's short-term and Desya has survived worse. You don't need to complain for the man."

"Complaining and concern are different things," she pointed out. At his sudden curtness, she said, "Even without memories, my instincts have been sharp. I get the feeling you dislike being around me, and I can only guess it's because I'm a vagrant."

Sunlight reflected in one of his eyepieces, giving the appearance that it winked. "If that bothered me, you wouldn't be living in my house. Who told you I don't like being around you?"

"No one. It's obvious through the way you act."

His hands flexed in his pockets. She expected him to respond, but he struck the pedestrian button too hard at the crosswalk, tapped his boot impatiently, and then treaded across the street.

She followed in his wake, guessing she should change the subject. "If you have family nearby, they could be an option," she suggested. "Staying with our kind might be safer than tramping into the wilderness."

"My family doesn't live close. And they wouldn't welcome two vagrants."

Snofrid was mindful that she'd earned no welcome. Still, she felt a sting at his bluntness.

"My adopted brother lives in Norway," Lycidius went on, fingering a silver ring on his left hand. The ring had a seal depicting an upside-down tree. "You called me heartless once," he reminded. "If you met my brother, you'd find new meaning in the word."

Snofrid took this as an admonition—moving in with his brother wouldn't be a smart idea, even if she wasn't a vagrant. "I think I'd prefer to brave Alaska," she said.

Lycidius was no longer paying attention. Not to her anyway.

She stared at him with a feeling that mounted the steps of unease and slowed her stride. He walked without watching, his fingers swaying, as if he were counting secret numbers. The way the cords in his neck protruded made her think he was arguing with someone. *Not me.* Not even someone in their general area. The idea seemed farfetched, but the person he was talking to would have to be *invisible.*

"No," he said to no one in particular. Then he glanced her way. "The Moonlentar Express docks tomorrow morning," he said. "My contact will fly in on the train. He has our new identities."

She ended the conversation with a short nod.

At the mansion, she traded her wet boots for house slippers and then went into the kitchen where Neko was loitering near the irori hearth.

"Hi, Neko." She greeted him with a smile and his mouth twitched. His features were tenderer than his aloof character. His doughty scowl endured, but he possessed a unique air that, on second glance, might be considered approachable. Due to his willowy build and wide, hooded eyes, he appeared far younger than his true age. The great size of his feet was difficult to overlook. Paired with a lean frame, they put him a bit out of proportion. His white trousers were spotless—pressed to perfection—and he wore a metal chest-harness overstuffed with roots, plants, serums and other medicines.

"At last," he huffed, turning on Lycidius. "The distance from the Cosmopolitan should have been a two-minute walk."

"You waited six minutes," Lycidius said, shrugging off his bomber jacket. "You've survived worse."

"Never by choice," Neko insisted. He pulled out a zabuton cushion at the table. "Go on and sit down, Snofrid."

"Thanks." She seated herself, her stiff joints thawing in the room's warmth. "How are you?"

"I'm a little closer to death than the last time I saw you. Other than that, little has changed." He fiddled with his harness. "So…I hear you plan to leave?"

"The day after tomorrow."

"I see." Neko's mouth tucked down. He handed her a vial of blue liquid from his harness, his hand juddering a little. "Drink this, but take heed not to spill. It'll stain your skin for thirty-four days."

Snofrid read the label, De-Fogger Draught, and knew it would make her mind more visible to him. Taking the vial, she drank it down and sucked in her breath. "Oh, that's sweet."

"The sweetness is to mask the taste of the wortpods." Neko crouched on the table. He removed a pair of red goggles fixed with a series of square lenses from his harness and strapped them over his eyes. "Alright, Snofrid. Magic can't enter a mind by force; for this to work, you must willingly let me enter."

"I know," she replied. "I'm clearing my thoughts right now."

"Then let's begin." He flipped a switch on the side of the goggles, illuminating them, and set his hands on either side of her head. They were *freezing*. Gooseflesh sprouted along her arms, which she smoothed away with a shudder. "Do my hands make you uncomfortable?" he asked.

"Not at all. They're just cold." Closing her eyes, she made an effort to concentrate. As she laid down the walls of her mind, a fountain of green light unfurled from her head, causing her ears, nose and mouth to itch. She lifted her chin, trying to watch him work, but it made her eyes throb to look straight up. He moved closer and closer, until the tips of his green hair poked her eyes, forcing her to close them. Lycidius's heady rainwater scent made her highly aware of how close he'd come. She loosed a rickety breath, wanting him to leave and stay at the same time.

Ten minutes dragged by. Twenty.

The strings of her patience snapped one by one, making it difficult to fake a calm bearing. The only hints she'd received about Neko's findings were scowls, grunts and glowers. But maybe the lengthy timespan was a good thing.

Another ten minutes passed before Lycidius spoke. "You're making a face, Neko. What have you found?"

"The problem isn't what I *have* found, it's what I *haven't*. Look at this."

"What do you mean, Neko?" Snofrid gripped the sides of her cushion.

"Give me a moment, Snofrid."

"I can't see her mind," Lycidius said, glancing at the light beaming from her head. "We tried before and I failed."

Snofrid was unconvinced. There was no way she could've been stupid enough to allow any person, other than a doctor, to see her thoughts. She had no idea what was inside her mind. As far as she knew, it held incriminating information. "Why did I let you see my mind?" she asked.

"To win a bet."

"It matters little, for I've seen all I can," Neko assured, sliding off the table. He held off, perhaps to spare giving Snofrid only bad news. "Before I give my analysis, I must know if any spells were raised over Snofrid before her memory loss."

"No," Lycidius said. "She took my bottled Slumber Spells to sleep, but that's it."

Neko's eyes tapered. "Slumber Spells wouldn't have caused the problem, or perhaps I should say *problems*." His tone grew apologetic. "I'm very sorry, Snofrid, but thirty-nine percent of your memories are gone."

Her jaw dropped. "Thirty…" Distress started as a warm flicker, before it exploded into bitterness, clawing at the heart of her hope. *Gone*. Thirty-nine percent of her life had vanished like dust blown off an empty street. She cupped her mouth as remnants of the De-Fogger Draught pitched up her throat and faced Neko. "They were destroyed?"

"No. As far as we know, magic can't destroy memories," he reassured.

"I believe someone stole your memories. But as I mentioned earlier, this person couldn't have taken your memories unless you'd given them access to your mind."

Snofrid couldn't blame anyone but herself. She clearly *had* been stupid enough to allow other people apart from Lycidius and Neko access to her mind.

Neko removed his goggles. "Strange as it sounds, your remaining memories are in a dormant state. Tampering with them may lead to additional damage. The wisest course of action is to wait for them to wake on their own."

Snofrid had no concept of how long that would take: weeks, months or even years. Everything she knew was faceless, everyone she met was nameless, and every object she saw was colorless. She needed her eighteen years to give her sight. Her lost experiences were a platform of confidence she needed in order to stand as a whole person. She feared hesitation would rust her from the inside out if she didn't find some means of clarity.

Then it came to her.

Like a small piece of paper slipped into her mind, a possible solution came: a *Mania Mirror*. For centuries, her kind had used the mirrors to reflect memories of the person who gazed into them. Raising her head, she let her eagerness hover on the edge of *maybe*. "What about a Mania Mirror?" she asked.

"A Mania Mirror will fail if the spell on your memories is too powerful," Lycidius told her. "But that doesn't mean it's impossible."

"Mania Mirrors are rare entities," Neko mused. "But I know of a hawker who may be able to get us one. However, he's a booty-pincher, so it will cost no less than fifty-thousand silvers."

"A booty-pincher?" she asked.

Neko arched a brow. "That means *cheapskate*."

Snofrid rose to her knees, too high on hope to feel disheartened by such a minor inconvenience. Even if the hawker demanded a steep price, she was willing to pay whatever she had in exchange for a glimpse of her past.

The Butcher of Hollowstone

S no, get a move on," Desya hollered from the kitchen.

"I'm almost ready," she called as she weaved her hair into a fishtail braid. Done, she zipped up her hooded toggle coat and shimmied down the loft ladder into the kitchen.

Desya was waiting for her by the antechamber, her satchel and gasmask on the tips of his fingers. He looked winter-proof in a wool overcoat and a black beanie and had a guilty itch in his step. "Sorry, Sno, I didn't mean to yell. It's—"

"It's all right, Dez. Are you and I driving together?"

"Yeah, but we need to scram or the traffic's gonna be nasty."

They traded the warmth of the kitchen for the chill of the garage. The open door invited in snow flurries; the glacial pre-winter cold burned her skin like sand paper.

"Where's Lycidius?" she asked, noticing that his Steelrunner was gone.

"In the sky waiting for us."

Shivering, Snofrid hopped into the jeep after Desya. Once heat was fanning on her face, she said, "Do you mind if I ask you something about Lycidius?"

"Not at all," Desya said, strapping on his seatbelt. "Ask as many questions as you need, Sno."

"We've obviously lived together for a while, so why aren't we friends?"

"You guys used to be really close actually."

"So something happened then? We fought?"

Desya fired up the engine with a shrug. "I have no idea, Sno. One day you just weren't friends anymore. If you want to know what happened, you're gonna have to ask him."

She wanted the explanation now. A part of her felt outraged that something had broken them apart; then she wondered at herself. She didn't even know him. Curiosity aside, it seemed best to figure things out after they'd safely left Hollowstone. "All right," she said. "Let's get to the city square before the train comes and goes."

The drive to the city square evolved into two hours of honking battles and bumper cars. Desya proved his skills as a bum-rusher in the parking garage. Way at the top of the 87th parking platform, the people in the city square looked as small as stars in the ether. Snofrid kept close to Desya in the mad dash of people and even closer to her satchel after a snide-eyed boy made a reach for it. They suffered a smelly, jam-packed elevator ride to the street before whizzing through the security gates. One of the benefits of Desya's job was line-cutting privileges. In a gunshot of time, he jogged toward the loading docks to buy provisions for their trip to Alaska. This left Snofrid, with Lycidius in tow, free to browse the thousands of stalls in the city square. In Lycidius's own words, he didn't want to leave her alone in case Lucian made an appearance. She didn't argue.

The city square was crazier than it had looked from the sky. Humans of all ethnic groups swarmed the streets and flooded in through the gates, decked out in face glitter, costumes, and festive hats. Clearly, Desya hadn't exaggerated when he'd said Hatred Day blew over quickly. Here and there, people donned turbans, corseted dirndl dresses, flower-patterned kimonos, cowboy hats, sequined sari dresses, or black Hijab veils. Loudest of all were the frat boys, with writing on their bare chests. One read: *Kiss me, I won't even remember.*

The coming of the Moonlentar Express equated to a holiday even though it came to Hollowstone once every month. The energy was frantic. Security guards kept the cheering crowds in check as famous musicians, illusionists and acrobats performed incredible acts on raised stages. Families camped out on the platforms under sun umbrellas, the children laughing or whining for attention; parents pushed their toddlers in strollers through the shops and fashionable-looking people walked dogs down the sidewalks. Fortune tellers predicted fates in closed tents, mimes in striped shirts slunk through the crowds like jailbirds, and lines of hypnotic belly dancers reeled in university boys.

Wooden stalls, shaded by white cotton canopies, enclosed the square. Paper lanterns floated in the lanes above the canopies, under which local and foreign traders exhibited their chattel. Snofrid had never seen such commodities and had a hard time resisting a shopping spree. She found exquisite batik cloth and ornate shadow puppets from China—the puppets gave her a nostalgic feeling, maybe because she'd played with them when she was younger. There were clay *moqueca* pots from Brazil and elephant *djembe* drums, bone-tooth necklaces, and wooden masks from Africa. She went on to see tree-pattered Persian carpets from Iran, dyed *tenugui* towels from Japan, sparkling *shamballa* bracelets and wool *Jamawar* shawls from India, silver fox ushanka hats from Russia, and beaded ornaments from Thailand.

Snofrid reveled in the festive aura as if it were the last day of her life. She tasted Belgian Craft beers; modeled kimonos; greeted people she didn't recall, but who apparently knew her; and drew swirling chalk designs on the streets. Lycidius followed her at a short distance, never speaking, though his eyes were fixed on her at all times—as if she might vanish should he look away. The skilled way in which he tailed her made her think that shadowing her was something he'd done often. It was mildly off-putting.

After ditching a clown who wouldn't stop dancing circles around her, she stopped to watch a troop of fire-eaters. She had seen no sign of Lucian Lozoraitis. Perhaps he'd given up trying to kill her for a while. That was probably wishful thinking, but it was enough to satisfy her for the time being. As a last hurrah, she sent one of her college professors into a dunk tank. As 11:00 a.m. drew near, she and Lycidius made their way toward the loading docks in search of Desya.

"Sno, we just got in a new travel promotion!" A young man in a blue suit waved at her from a Skyline Air stall. "Three minutes. Come on, I'm bored to tears back here."

"Not interested, Lochan," Lycidius said, and then guided Snofrid from the area.

Snofrid glanced over her shoulder at Lochan, knowing why Lycidius had refused the man's offer. Lycidius had already secured them passage to Alaska through the Doubloon Raiders. The shady sky-pirates practically charged body parts for a ride, but they were known to have no problem with providing passage when it came to Inborns.

Rotary blades buzzed suddenly in her ears and she gazed skyward. Through the glaring sunlight, she counted thirteen drones whizzing below the clouds. Four news helicopters lagged in their wake, filming the festivity from the air, and, occasionally, a fighter plane jetted past. This seemed peculiar. Scanning the rooftops in a full circle, she spotted sniper teams positioned on every building. *Such high security doesn't seem like standard protocol*, she thought. Perhaps the police department was simply taking precautions after Hatred Day.

"Attention traders," an automated female voice announced over the sound system. "Please form orderly lines before each drop station. Those who refuse to cooperate with trading policy will be denied service."

Rumbling engines again drew Snofrid's eyes to the sky, but this time, she saw something else entirely. A ship designed like a dais soared overhead, shading several hundred yards of the square. It took a position near the wall screens and young girls with baskets tossed fistfuls of flower petals over its railings. The petals fell like painted rain across the people's gawking heads. Snofrid, certain that this was Chancellor Leathertongue's entourage, faced the wall screens just as the cameras panned to Parisa Namdar. The crowd jumped with feverish cheers.

"Parisa, we love you!" girls claimed.

"Parisa, you look like a goddess!" more flattered.

Parisa gazed upon the multitude with glittering eyes. She *did* look like a goddess in her dazzling tulle gown of pale feathers and golden rhinestones. Her bronzed skin gleaned with shimmer powder that was as vibrant as her aura. Black hair ruffled at her waist, tousled by the breeze, and a pair of metallic wings inlaid with pearl sprouted from her back. She was closely guarded by soldiers in black graphene armor.

Parisa held her chin high as she addressed the people. "It's a great honor to be tasked with initiating this month's Moonlentar Trade," she declared, her voice sweet and sultry. "Hatred Day's losses have been great, but let today be without grieving. Gentlemen, drink hard, and ladies, put on those little black dresses I know you've all been saving and rock this year's new *Louve* Gasmask Collection!"

"Marry me, Parisa!" a mime demanded. The crowd broke into cheers.

"Open the crates, loaders," Parisa charged, with a twirl of her fingers. "This month's Moonlentar Trade has officially begun!"

Snofrid kept on toward the trade docks. She tried to imagine having been friends with Parisa and couldn't. She seemed worlds away from the one Snofrid existed in. By the way the humans adored Parisa, Snofrid figured she'd done important things. A feeling of insignificance too difficult for Snofrid to ignore bubbled up. She recalled Lucian's words to the train attendant: *Like the civilians on this train, you don't matter.*

She finally reached the private loading dock where Desya and swells of other shoppers purchased crates of goods from supply trucks; anti-gravity braces were strapped to the shopper's arms, increasing their strength by five times.

"Hey, Sno," Desya called, adding a crate of barley to their stock. "Did you grab me some Sake?"

"Ginjo." She handed him a glass bottle from her satchel with a smile.

"They had Junmai, but I figured it would chill too much on the way."

"This is awesome. Thanks."

"From nothing." She looked up the crate towers, which stored a medley of seeds and grains. "How much will you buy?"

"Enough rice to last a year. Maybe a crate or two of millet, but that's about it."

"Rice and millet in Alaska. At least we'll have plenty of fish." She made a mindful glance at the snipers on the roofs. "Did you know about the Stellar Ops units?"

"No, actually. There wasn't any chatter, so it must be off the record." He stuffed the bottle in his coat, then added, "It's probably just a precaution, but still, it might be best to stay in the area."

"I will," she promised, and stole a side-glance at Lycidius. He was talking with a scrawny girl, maybe ten years old, with her brown ringlets twisted up in Bantu knots. Snofrid guessed she was African American from her chocolate skin. The girl laughed shamelessly, tipping her head all the way back, as if she were about to howl, and clasped her hands, which caused a chorus of jingles to sing from her gold arm-bangles. Dressed in a jade parka and trousers, she had a spring to her step, which made Snofrid think she might shoot off into the sky at any moment.

"That's Jazara Popplegoom," Desya reminded, jerking his thumb at the girl. "She's like you and me...but a little more like you."

Snofrid took his insinuation to mean that Jazara was a Mystish Inborn. But, apart from rare instances, all pure-blood Inborns were white-skinned. "Does Jazara have black skin because of mutation?"

"No."

Snofrid tensed, suddenly aware that Jazara had black skin because she'd been born from one human and one Inborn parent: she was a *halfbreed*. She glanced the girl's way again, afraid for her, because being a halfbreed was far worse than being a vagrant. Not only were halfbreeds shamed and expelled from Inborn society, but most of them were hunted down and executed by Halfbreed Hunters—Inborns who considered halfbreeds to be abominations. Swallowing hard, Snofrid asked quietly, "Dez, do any of the

Inborns in Hollowstone know what she is?"

"No," he whispered. "She poses as a human." He put a hand on her shoulder, squeezing it. "Don't worry about her, Sno. Jazara doesn't look at herself as different from us. Oh, and by the way, she's claimed you as her big sister."

"Really?"

"Yeah. Watch out, though. She's kind of a nut." Desya picked up another box, then cleared his throat. "Did uh…Parisa talk to you?"

"No. But why would she? I thought she cut ties with us."

"She talks to you every once and a while. It's me and Lycidius she's dusted off."

"I'm sorry." Snofrid held off from saying what she truly thought. It seemed like he was still hurting. "How long were you together?"

"A long time, since we were kids, actually…but I didn't date the glitter-puff, I dated the other one."

Snofrid's brows sprang upward. "There are *two*?"

"No." He let out a short laugh, but then his manner grew regretful. "I meant she used to be different. The old Parisa smuggled abandoned babies off Gehenna's field of exile. It's like her heart got sucked out or something. She's got stacks, but she hasn't even lifted a copper to help our old friends in the slums."

Snofrid pursed her lips, feeling a sudden blister of shame. "It's okay if you want to say it, Dez. I know I was a booty-pincher, too."

"Maybe. But I have no idea what a booty-pincher is, Sno."

"It's a *money-grubber*."

"Ah." Desya tugged her braid like a church bell. "You're not, but you do got a skill for getting guys to buy you stuff without asking. Especially Lycidius."

Snofrid bit her lip. "It sounds like I was a—"

"Dez!" Jazara cried excitedly. She clamped her arms around Desya's torso from behind, squeezing hard, causing his eyes to pop.

"Jazara, my back!"

She released him with a sigh, "You're my best guy, Dez. But let's be real. You're kind of wormy." She spun Snofrid around and led her toward the landing tracks, bangles chiming. "So…how was your beast survey trip?" she gushed. "Tell me all."

"Beast survey trip?"

"Yep. Dez told me it's why you didn't come to my party." Jazara sighed. "You were gone a long time. You better have brought me back something good."

Whaaaaat?" Jazara's yellow-brown eyes grew as large as her bangles. "Why in the heck would you go to *Alaska*?"

"Because we need to get out of the city for a while," Snofrid explained, feeling like she just killed a kitten. "It's just temporary, Jazara."

"Then…" Jazara cast a crushed glance at the loading docks and her eyes glossed over. "I'll never see you all again. And Dez…" Her brows bumped together. "I've *got* to go with you."

"I don't think your parents would let you just leave."

"Parents?" Jazara narrowed her eyes. "Sno, I ain't got no parents."

Her heart skipped, and she quickly added, "I just had a major brain fart. I'm an idiot. Sorry Jazara—"

"*Pleeeeease* let me come. I'll ride in the trunk if there's no room. And I'll even work for my board."

Snofrid fell silent to think, before nodding slowly. "It's not up to me. I'll talk to Dez."

"Yaaay!" Jazara squeezed her arms and Snofrid gasped at her iron grip. Luckily, a sudden wave of anticipation rippled through the crowd, causing Jazara to release Snofrid. "It's starting!"

"Attention," the automated voice echoed over the sound system. "For safety reasons, all civilians must remain ten feet from the tracks. Failure to comply will result in removal from the city square."

Snofrid and Jazara pedaled from the tracks, not a moment before a large black object descended from the clouds: *a train car*. As the train neared the landing tracks, titanium skids engaged from its tricycle undercarriage. A second train car rocketed from the clouds behind it: Snofrid realized it was descending in pieces. Dozens followed the first two until black cars spotted the sky. The train assembled upon the tracks in a neat row. With a click, the cars connected, as if someone had flipped a magnet switch, and the train rose and hovered above the loading docks.

Snofrid tried peering into the observation deck, but, finding the arched windows plated with ebony glass, examined one of the car door insignias instead—a man sitting cross-legged on a horse with his hands cupped to form a circle. She crooked a brow, impressed. The train belonged to the *Romeo Gypsies*. Legend had it that these gypsies were more than quiet traveling folk; since the start of the war, many had allegedly become lethal assassins for hire.

"For the convenience of the merchants, all traders standby until the cargo is unloaded," the automated voice announced. "Thank you for your cooperation. Have a pleasant trade."

Desya and Lycidius joined up with Snofrid ten uneventful minutes later, carrying pints of lager, hamburgers and cotton candy. Jazara climbed onto Desya's shoulders and tried to pinch a paper lantern from the decorations while Lycidius let a stray dog lap from his beer mug.

Snofrid, growing impatient, searched the head car for movement. The train hovered silently like a ghost-machine; seemingly, it navigated the skies with no engineer.

Murmurs swelled through the crowd as people seemed to come to the same conclusion. Eventually, Desya cupped both hands around his mouthpiece, and shouted, "We're waiting!"

"Unless you want a bullet in your throat, that's not smart," Lycidius advised.

"I'd take a bullet for you," Jazara whispered to Desya, now cradling four stolen lanterns in her arms.

Suddenly a hatch in the head car popped open, startling Snofrid as well as some onlookers. A man as thin as a pole's shadow arose, his feet planted on a circular platform.

Silence fell over the crowd.

Snofrid thought him the scariest merchant of them all. His bearing was erratic, as if he were standing barefoot on a bed of hot coals. Thin reddish-black hair curtained his sunken face, which was hidden behind a pale horse-head gasmask. Spikes forked from the toes of his boots and matching claws extended from his fingertips.

The gypsy took a wide stance, swishing his red cape, and stretched his fingertips skyward. He snapped his fingers and the tops of the train cars shot open like rippling dominos. "Come out, come out," he invited.

Trapeze artists in red leotards emerged, performing flips across the cars.

"Greetings, beautiful citizens of Hollowstone," the gypsy sang. "We come with fresh invention for each and every buyer! We come with goods to render, we have what you require! We come to you in friendship, we come to slake your greed! Come close, eager peoples, you shall find everything you need!"

As he dropped back into the hatch, his cloak broke into a flock of metal birds that dispersed above the surging crowd. Whistles, cheers, and applause resounded. An elderly woman standing beside Snofrid called, "Come back, handsome!" Staircases cascaded from the train doors and anchored themselves on the docks. Some people formed lines, only to break formation when others stampeded past.

"Dez said he'd *think* about me going to Alaska," Jazara told Snofrid. She waved a hand toward the platform where Desya and Lycidius were caught up in a haggle. "So, obviously, I gotta go to the orphanage and pack. But I'm coming by tonight, just so you don't get ideas about leaving without me."

"Call me and I'll come get you," Snofrid said as Jazara dashed into the crowd, spilling paper lanterns in her haste. Strangely enough, Snofrid spotted Fergus Dripper perusing a kite stall nearby. He looked conspicuous in a lemon tracksuit and was chuckling with two freckled-faced orange-haired men—his brothers perhaps.

"Snowball!" He frisked toward her, sipping a container of beer from a specialized gasmask-straw. "I thought I was hallucinating there for a second. And boy, I'm glad I wasn't. Having a grand time?"

"As good a time as any," she replied. "Are those your brothers?"

"Cousins, actually. They popped in from Jamaica last night. How's your research paper coming along? Still need a source?"

"I do. Thanks for the offer," she answered. She squirmed as she recalled the giant heap of college work she still needed to catch up on. "Back at Remus's crime scene, you mentioned you have evidence that an Inborn killed him. Is that evidence still confidential?" she asked.

"Sorry Snowball, but it is." He slurped harder on his straw, his brows wiggling. "You single now?"

"Why are you asking?"

"Just making conversation."

She removed her gasmask cartridge, and, after taking a bite of the cotton candy Desya had brought her, answered, "Atlas and I broke things off."

Fergus's brows bounced up in delight. Reaching into his pocket, he slipped her a folded piece of paper. "My digits. Ring me and we'll pop by a tavern. My treat."

"Sure. But Fergus, I think of you as a friend."

"Ah, but victory comes to those who persevere." Winking, he stretched his arms out at his sides with a sigh. "Lovely day, isn't it?"

"It is." His determination impressed her.

One of the train cars behind her started to shake causing its chains to clang against its doors. It was like an earthquake had taken root beneath it.

"It's just a technical malfunction," Fergus assured, still sipping on his straw. "Happens to everything, even the best transportation."

Wobbling thumps bent out the side of the car, loosening screws.

"My word!" Fergus dropped his beer.

Panic snaked through the crowd. The car shuddered faster, frightening away those who still stood near.

"What the hell is going on?" traders demanded.

People stumbled, falling onto their faces and hands. Worried cries stabbed the air as people trampled over one another, knocking over crates and baskets of fruit. Snofrid tried to pass through the jungle of bopping bodies, yet the flow forced her toward the train. She searched wildly for an exit and nearly treaded on a fallen woman. Snofrid hoisted the woman to her feet. Then, whirling, she continued to search for an escape. An elbow jabbed her ribs; a knee dug into her thigh; then she was caught— sandwiched between stomachs and backs.

"Form orderly lines to all available exits," the automated voice rang out. "Use of firearms will result in arrest."

At first Snofrid thought she imagined it, but the train was *rising*. Struggling to stay on her feet, she watched the ladders retreat into the cars.

"Good God!" a woman screamed.

"Emergency evacuation personnel are en route," the automated voice broadcasted. "Form orderly lines and seek your nearest exit."

Snofrid, fighting to distance herself from the train, saw the train doors reopen. First came the ladders. Then the *combat robots*. Hundreds of them funneled onto the platforms, steel giants into a mob of panicking dwarves. When her eyes locked on the Ninth Underground City logo—N.U.C.— airbrushed on their chests—her stomach plunged in terror. This wasn't a trade train, it was a military transport. The hydrocop's were two-and-a-half-meter humanoids assembled from black titanium; each sported a full-face ballistic helmet with an infrared visor, from which emerged modulated voices, stark and authoritative.

"Close off all exits," one of them commanded the others. "Permission granted to open fire on any target who refuses instruction or attempts to exit the area."

Doubling her efforts, Snofrid rode the waves of the riot toward the gates. Her nerves flailed as she drove her body forward leading with her knees. Hands clutched at her, tearing her clothes, stomping her ankles, yanking on her braid. "Let me go!" She jerked away and staggered backward into a cushioning knot of bodies.

Ahead, the hydrocops formed up into rows. She sprinted through them toward the freight hold, keeping a desperate eye out for Desya. Her lungs burned by the time she'd made it through. Safe against the wall of the freight hold, she took a moment to catch her breath. What the hell was happening?

She watched two hydrocop units remove a vibrating titanium crate from the chained car. Something was *inside*. One of the hydrocops shoved a Taser rod through a hole and a horrible wail went up. The last hydrocop descended and, one by one, the cars separated and soared into the clouds. Snofrid watched with a sinking realization that the safest place to be was probably onboard.

Gunshots! She spun on her heel, tracking the shots to the wall platforms. The low ground blocked her line of sight. Hopping onto a crate, she stared at the floating dais at the north end of the city square. The Chancellor stood atop it, his silken white robes flapping around his squash-shaped figure. His head tilted heavenward, catching the sun's rays in a majestic pose. He donned a half-face gasmask in the mold of a chimera and his brilliant, aquamarine energy shield sizzled around him with hundreds of hydrocops, together with his security detail, just beyond.

As he raised his arms, his image appeared on the lofty screens behind him. Snofrid knew that whatever happened next would be broadcasted to the entire city.

"*True* children of Hollowstone," he thundered, his voice gravelly and operatic. "Remain calm."

"What's going on?" people cried out.

"Why are there soldiers here?" others shouted.

"Do not be afraid," he consoled, his tone now fatherly. "You will not be harmed. The message I carry is for the maggots who are burrowing into the flesh of my city. The enemies of peace and the bringers of suffering."

"Inborn scum!" several voices shouted.

"There is no insult appropriate for their obscenity." He paused to scan the crowds, his hands fisted in suppressed fury. "Most of you are aware of my son's death. Most of you knew him. He was only sixteen; he wanted to be a soldier, to fight and defend his homeland and his people. He wanted, more than riches and success, to dedicate his life to the service of others. But all of these noble dreams were snatched away by *them*. I tell you now that I've been delivered proof of Inborns' involvement in his death."

Some people gasped, while others covered their mouths. "No!"

"*Yes!*" he bellowed, his chest engorging. "Like you, I have lost much to this war, but like the true patriots of our time, I will not let it be in vain. In the words of President Sebaster: *We will not be bystanders to tyranny any longer.*" He spread his arms wide like a falcon taking flight. "Our loved ones deserve retribution! No, not only retribution, but *justice.* This *will* end now. We will honor them with a stand like no Inborn army has witnessed and put an end to these gruesome acts of terror. And we will begin that stand with the execution of every Inborn in Hollowstone City."

"Yes!" a choir of voices approved. "Yes!" The people were no longer frightened. Heads lifted and hands rose, saluting the fallen in reverence. Snofrid heard low, indistinct chanting ripple through the crowd. It rumbled into an earsplitting roar.

"Retribution! Retribution! Retribution!"

"Kill the Inborns!"

"End terror!"

"Children of Hollowstone, we have kept the fight from these walls, but is it just?" the Chancellor questioned. "Is it *just?* Why should our neighbors bleed while we doze? The truth is *simple.* We should not. So my cousin, President Sebaster, has sent us aid." He slammed his fist into his hand. "The purge begins NOW."

A deafening sound like a hundred screeching tires shuddered beneath Snofrid's feet, quaking the stalls, stages and platforms. Bracing herself on the wall, she glanced down in dread. The crate on which she stood was glowing. A flash of blue drew her eye to a dome rising over the city, which enclosed her heart, along with her hope and her bravery.

The dome was an *energy shield.*

The Chancellor's security detail shepherded him from the dais and thirty hydrocops marched onto center stage with their forearm-guns aimed at the crowd. They formed two ranks behind a hulk of a man clad in blister-red armor and iron gloves. A Roman numeral nine was stamped on his breastplate, branding him as the Hydrocop Chief; but he was human and he terrified Snofrid even more than the bull-head gasmask of the Inborn Commander. Grisly hooks flowered from his spaulders and a spike-studded gasmask alike to a porcupine masked his face.

He pointed a machine pistol and fired a dozen shots into the sky. "Get used to this sound," he advised. "You're all going to be hearing it for the next two months."

"Fire again!" voices insisted. People jumped onto the wall platforms and thrust their fists into the air. "Fire again!" The crowd's inhibitions blew to the wind, but their frenzied excitement fed Snofrid's frenzied horror. A heavy hand clamped down on her arm and she reeled around in a quivering start. Lycidius stared up at her, his cloudy eye as black as funeral smoke. "You're a target. Get on level with the rest of the crowd."

She dropped onto the platform. Desya had also come and she took his arm before looking to the holographic screens displayed from the wall.

"I'm Chief Reznik Stoker," the man informed, "your new god. I'm not a forgiving god and I'm not a merciful god. No Inborns will be spared under my command." He took a wide stance, while steadying his gun barrel on one shoulder. "My message for humanity's enemy is this: you're trapped. Three minutes ago, Hollowstone went under lockdown. The energy shield will ensure that no one enters or leaves. Barrier patrols have been tripled. All civilians, irrespective of species, caught trying escape will be shot without question. Effective immediately is a 10 p.m. curfew. Civilians who break curfew will be put in holding until the purge ends. If you're stopped for a Tag scan, obey without hesitation or you'll be shot." He aimed a metal-sheathed finger at the crowd. "Humans, your part is simple. If you're harboring Inborns and come forward within the next twenty-four hours and beg forgiveness for your treason, you'll be imprisoned, but spared. If not, when we find you, you'll be shipped to death camps with your Inborn lovers."

"Turn them in!" people urged across the crowd. "Don't protect those murderers!"

Snofrid's muscles pulled tight in fear and she held fast to Desya's arm; Trojan Mortals harbored her kind all around the city. If any of them were scared enough, hundreds of Inborns could be exposed and murdered. Her eyes dug into Reznik with hatred. They were at the mercy of humans: the shield would stay in place as long as necessary, and people would eventually give into fear. Trojan Mortals had children too; if given the choice, they'd sacrifice her kind to protect their own.

Desya wrapped his hand around hers and started invoking the protection of the Inborn Promethia Flower under his breath. Then he said, "Stay calm, Sno."

"Why are you warning me, Dez?"

"Just *stay* here. If you run, know I'm gonna come after you."

"Dez, of course I won't run." She tried with all of her strength to have courage, but it wasn't enough. Her insides roiled in terror as hundreds of the crowd yelled out names and addresses. Hundreds of her kind would die. The wall spotlights zeroed in on men, women, teenagers and children, all of whom were identified on the screen behind Reznik. She stared at their faces, knowing she could easily be among them. But she wasn't. Not today.

Today it was Neko.

Snofrid felt Desya's hand go limp in her own. She stared at Neko, oblivious to all that was around her, except for him. *Run Neko*, she thought frantically. *RUN!*

Hydrocops charged all those who'd been accused while bystanders tackled them so they couldn't flee. Neko took a combat stance and flicked his hands upward; green magic blasted from his palms, then rushed to his toes, encapsulating his body in a small energy shield. People were shoved backward like flicked peas while sniper bullets were vaporized by the shield. His arms quivered when a drone flew overhead and shot a hellfire missile; the energy shield vaporized the missile, shrouding the area in black billows of smoke. Neko's face remained composed. Snofrid felt as if all the fear that should be raging in him was tearing her apart. She wanted him to move, to run, or at least to attack the humans back. But he didn't.

Then she saw it.

A shadow of acceptance touched his face. He cast her a final glance—

his eyes glossy and haunting. She pled with him to run. But he didn't; instead, he looked to Reznik and spoke stridently "I've chosen to live peacefully among humans. Now I choose to die peacefully among them." He shut his fists, severing the flow of magic. A whizzing sound skipped through the air. His head flapped back and his gasmask split down the front, before he collapsed amid a gust of cheers.

Snofrid bit down on her tongue until it bled. Desya grabbed her wrist and guided her between two stalls. She couldn't see through her tears. Around the square, hydrocops began amputating Halos to hinder any attempt of an Inborn stand. Their electric forearm blades buzzed as they sawed off arms and legs amid shrieks and pleas for mercy.

Reznik, watching from his dais, tapped his gasmask. "They wear our human faces, but don't be cheated. They've stolen them, just like they've stolen our planet. And now we'll pass judgment."

Reznik gestured to three of his hydrocops. They saluted him and rolled the iron crate from the train onto the center stage. He used the iris scanner on the crate and with a beep it opened, revealing a giant, knotty tree with a single hole in its trunk. The hole contracted like a hideous mouth. A *bonecopse*—a carnivorous tree from Armador. It writhed and wriggled horribly, stabbing the air with its screeches as it tried to pry its roots from where they'd been strapped down.

"Their reckoning begins now." Reznik nodded at the hydrocops. "Destroy them."

The hydrocops muscled their way toward the bonecopse, hauling bludgeoned Inborns behind them. The tree seemed to know that it was going to be fed, for it ceased writhing.

"Kill them!" people demanded with flashing eyes. "Kill them!"

The hydrocops shoved the wailing people through the tree's opening. Then, they chucked in the amputated limbs. The bonecopse wiggled faster, bulging in and out, as if it were chewing. Blood seeped down its craggy bark. The screams escalated into high-pitched shrieks; paired with the echo of ripping limbs, it was the most hellish sound Snofrid had ever heard. Cupping her ears, she tried to run from the square, but the churning throng ensnared her like a fisherman's net. Immune to the brutality, half of the crowd went on cheering.

RETRIBUTION!

The Devil's Notebook

Snofrid, Desya and Lycidius abandoned the city square. Desya's bluecoat clearance got them exempted through the evacuation queues until they arrived at the plaza.

As they drove, Snofrid clenched the sides of her chair to still her shaking. Deep inside the nub of her terror, she embraced the same impulse she'd had in Oubliette: *survive*. But this scenario was different. She had a family that she needed to look after now. Protecting them was an automatic instinct, like it had been encoded into her brain; still, she sparred with the desire to run and hide. Neko's bravery had given her a shot of strength, though not one strong enough to smother her dread of watching Inborns be tortured and killed. Her courage shrank inside of her. She feared this purge would turn out like Memphis: an energy shield had been thrown up there a few months ago. No Inborns had survived. There was nothing to give her hope that this purge would end differently.

"Lycidius and I are gonna hit the Trojan bunkers," Desya told Snofrid as he braked outside the garage. "They might give us shelter if we get there first. But we need you to stay here and wait for Jazara."

"I'll stay. But Dez, I'm…"

"I know. Come here." He stretched across the console and she clutched him tightly. "We have to keep our heads up until we're clear of this," he encouraged. "We'll be back in forty-five minutes and I'll call you if anything goes down."

"Be careful, Dez. Please."

"We will. I promise."

Snofrid hopped from the jeep just as Lycidius skated past her. "Go inside the house," he said. "Put the system in lockdown and don't open the door for anyone but Jazara."

"I won't, Lycidius. May we meet again." She jogged through the garage into the dim kitchen. "Lights on," she called, pulling off her gasmask. "System lockdown."

The lamps flickered on and the door locks engaged. Night was descending fast, presenting a blushing, silver moon. Snofrid stood frozen in the silence, cupping her mouth to stifle a sob. Of the people she'd met, Neko had been one of the few who meant something to her. She didn't know how to, and didn't want to, come to terms with the idea that he was gone.

Choking on tears, she scaled the ladder to her loft, only to be reminded of her cage. Out her window she watched electrical currents spark at the apex of the energy shield and ripple down its edges with the vigorous flash of lightning.

Desya had described the shield as a sphere. Half stretched over them, blocking escape by sky, and the other half extended below them, blocking escape from under the earth. The shield was programed to allow in news signals, select aircrafts and atmosphere such as rain, wind and snow. Only the mightiest magic stood a chance against a human energy shield. They'd need at least thirty Lambent Necromancers, all masters of the fire element, to breakout. But, as far as she knew, they didn't even have one.

Her phone jingled and she swiped it up, counting on a message from Desya.

Hey, Snowball. Just making sure you're alive.

She tossed the phone onto her mattress. If Fergus knew she was an Inborn, he'd hand her over to Chief Reznik without a second thought. "Television on," she said, wiping her eyes. "N.U.C. Broadcasting Company."

The orange screen above her desk switched on, presenting an impressive young man seated in a wingchair on the bottom floor of a grand library. She made a move to change the channel, but stopped.

Behind the man, a gilded butterfly staircase rose into a warren of mahogany bookcases. He reclined with one ankle propped over his knee, dressed in a grey-silk, two-button suit, with his rich black hair slicked back. His lean physique and powerful radiance reminded her of a black stallion. She read the name on the screen: *Julian Forsberg.*

"Wars will always make certain individuals and organizations wealthier," he told the pretty interviewer, who was seated across from him. "As they destroy, they also create opportunity. This is a fact of life, Miss Dallan. Soldiers *need* guns. The black market will always exist, our military will always require contractors, and public officials will always accept bribes." His mouth stretched into a bored smirk. "You refer to me as a war profiteer, yet my family's companies ensure that our troops receive weapons, clothing and supplies. And we do not overcharge. So, Miss Dallan, in your practiced criticism of what you do not understand, tell me how I am hurting the New Global Union?"

I know this man. Snofrid stared at Julian's face, thinking she'd be unsurprised if he looked at her and said 'cheers'. His voice was the kind that made one want to listen all night, and his Swedish accent glided through her ears as naturally as her own Mystish language, *Prenax.*

While he talked on, she analyzed his voice, hoping it would spark a memory of him. To her regret, he proved to be a ghost of a memory like all the others.

She took to pacing her tatami mats, hatching escape plans until she lost track of the time. Her ears pricked up at imagined sounds, which propelled her to the window to check for Jazara. Whenever a hydrocop patrol marched by, she was barraged by a cyclone of ghoulish images from the city square—in particular, the haunting look Neko had given her before the bullets had split his gasmask. Yanking the rock shard from Oubliette out of her satchel, she scraped blisters into her palm until her panting slowed to cool, even breaths.

By the time 6:11 came, Snofrid was exhausted from worrying. Thinking a cup of tea might give her a boost, she went into the kitchen. Her hands shook as she suffused green tea leaves in a porcelain teapot, until, sudden as a fluttering wing, an idea popped to the front of her mind; she froze, hands on the teapot. *Hessia Nabash.* The Seer had promised payment in exchange for acting as bait for the welx hunt. The specifics of this offer were vague, so demanding an escape from the city might be too steep of a request. But there was still a chance.

Before making a decision, Snofrid took into account that assisting the Commander and Hessia would require confidentiality—more specifically, she'd have to lie to Desya and Lycidius. This made her question if she was being impulsive.

Or maybe she was just afraid.

She flipped the rock shard around in her palm, face heating up in shame; fear was the real reason she didn't want to act as bait. But what did she have to fear? *She* could heal; Desya and Lycidius couldn't. Rocking on her feet, fingers gripping the countertop, she urged herself to be brave. *Daringly dared, half of it won,* she told herself. She didn't know where she'd learned this phrase, only that it gave her courage.

Behind her the genkan sliding panel opened and she reeled around. Lycidius strode into the kitchen, his jackal gasmask in hand. Snow dappled his hair and bomber jacket, and his left eye was as dark and as glowering as a solar eclipse.

"We can't stay with the Trojans." He pitched his mask onto the table. "They're only harboring Inborn children and babies."

"We'll hide in here, then," she said, her voice smaller than she'd intended. "The humans won't find us if we go on as normal."

"It's all we can do for now," Desya agreed, as he came in on Lycidius's heels. "Chief Stoker's gonna wait for our kind to bite back. We need to act like the humans would, and that means doing our jobs and acting normal until we can get help."

"Help?" Snofrid stepped forward, hopeful. "From whom?"

"The Empyrean City. The shield can only block technological transmissions, not one's powered by magic, so we can use a transmission globe. Ours is busted right now, but Cid knows a few guys who've got globes of their own. We can check in with them. But trust me, Inborns all across the city are probably calling the Empyrean City as we speak."

"Dez, there are four-thousand Inborns living in Hollowstone at most. In Memphis, there were six-thousand. The Lords would never send a Sky-Legion to Hollowstone for so few."

"No one can say anything for sure at this point, Snofrid. We just need to try." He scanned the kitchen with a frown. "Where's Jazara?"

"She didn't come," Snofrid said. She caught a trace of worry in his face. "But it's still early, Dez."

"Not for her. She zooms here the minute she gets off of school almost every day. I'll call her." He cracked a trapdoor in the floor by the stove, then glanced up at Lycidius. "Grab the hard drive. I'll boot up the computer."

"Give me a minute," Lycidius said. He faced Snofrid. "Come with me when I drive out to borrow a transmission globe."

"I can't," she answered. If she was going to meet Hessia Nabash, she'd need to leave in less than two hours. "I want to be here when Jazara gets here."

His tone was disappointed. "That's fine."

"I'm sorry about before, I don't mean to panic." Snofrid pressed her palms over the painful knot in her chest. "Desya told me Neko was your friend before—"

"He was your friend, too," Lycidius reminded. A hint of compassion softened his features, then faded as he drew back a retractable wall in the cupboard. Behind the wall was a safe, and after using a security iris scanner, he took out a hard drive. "Let's go," he said.

She entered the trapdoor after him and descended a spiral staircase, which led into a basement *zen garden*, designed with heaps of mossy rocks, pruned trees and leafy ferns, and a bamboo fountain. Crisp gravel raked to mimic water ripples bordered the wooden pathway.

"Took you long enough," Desya remarked. He sat on a tangerine cushion in the center of the room before a low desk with a hologram computer screen.

"Sorry, I didn't realize we were talking so long," Snofrid said, taking a cushion beside him. "Did you—?"

She cut off upon feeling something, like a pair of fingers, tugging gently at the tip of her braid. Turning, she found Lycidius standing behind her, his arms folded over his chest. Her suspicions dispelled. Maybe she'd imagined the feeling.

"Did you reach Jazara?" she asked Desya.

"Yeah, her housemother is driving her over. She got a pass to crash here tonight, but don't let her talk you into planting roots. If she leaves the orphanage right now, it'll make her a target."

"I know. I'll make up a bed for her in my room."

Lycidius tossed the hard drive to Desya. "Pull it up."

Desya swiped the hard drive over the computer, connecting it, and then began interfacing with the holograms. Lycidius booted the third cushion into the gravel, puffing up dust, and crouched beside Snofrid.

"Why are we looking at this drive?" she asked Desya. "What's on it?"

"Dirt." He coughed croakily; it sounded like he was coming down with a cold. "It has the IP address and access codes to a deep-web system called the *Devil's Notebook*."

"Is the 'dirt' criminal activity?"

"More. The system's a fat pile of dirty laundry. We can use it to pull Chief Stoker's records."

She narrowed her eyes, getting a foggy feeling of distrust. "This really seems deep, Dez. How did you get the system?"

"Lycidius stole it from a guy in Gehenna."

"Who? Is he a Swangunner?"

"No. You didn't know him," Lycidius said. "He was one of the Lozoraitis intelligence contacts, but he's buried in a hillside now."

She wasn't comforted. "As long as no one knows we have it. This could be a huge security risk."

"Ryuki was a top-level white-hat hacker," Lycidius reminded. "Desya learned from him." He pointed out a red and black pictogram at the top of the screen: a horned beast leering from the heart of a five-point star. "Everyone who uses the Notebook stays anonymous. The human government couldn't name the real Devil if they tried."

"I think I got something," Desya said, and accessed a file called the *Helios Society*.

Lycidius's face hardened. He rocked forward on his toes. "Verify that Reznik has real ties to Helios."

"Yeah, give me a second, man. I don't have tentacle hands." Desya tapped on a link and loaded another page. Photos hugged the middle-text, showing white labs, pillared bank buildings, grand country estates, thought-controlled plane prototypes and plasma weapon systems. He scrolled farther down before halting on an insignia of an emerald serpent coiled around a fiery-orange sun disk. "Stone me," he cursed.

"This is bullshit," Lycidius muttered. He elbowed Desya aside and took the cushion before the computer, then entered a long string of code.

"Is the Helios Society a political party?" Snofrid whispered to Desya, as he crouched on the floor beside her.

"It's more like a secret club with strong political influence. They popped up in England about eighteen years ago. Some banker named Sir Northrup Castle started everything, but now, most human world leaders have been initiated."

"They mean nothing," Lycidius said, now flipping through criminal records. "Only three families threaten us: The Forsberg's, the Leathertongue's and the Castle's."

Snofrid thought back to the interview she'd watched and wondered if she'd been hallucinating. "Dez, I'm almost positive I know Julian Forsberg."

"What? Why would you think that?"

"I recognized him during an interview."

He exchanged a skeptical look with Lycidius. "If somehow you're able to bilocate and have a couple hundred billion golds stacked up somewhere, then you probably do."

"Dez, I'm serious."

"Okay…" He mulled over the idea, before shaking his head. "You never met him that I know of."

She believed he was telling the truth for he had no reason to lie. Claiming to know a Forsberg was probably the same as claiming to be close friends with an Inborn Lord, and yet, the sense that she knew Julian lingered like perfume in an elevator. "Do you think the Chancellor is a member of the Helios Society?"

"If he is—" Desya sneezed abruptly, then wiped spittle from his mouth. "If he is, then Chief Stoker sure as hell is, too."

"Why are they a threat to us, though?"

His expression turned sheepish. "They finance Regulative, Sno."

She stared at the beast pictogram with as much fear as if it might spring out at her, for Regulative was her kind's *worst* nightmare. A year after her kind had come to earth, the humans had formed the Regulative organization to study her kind. Rumors claimed that their first objective was to find a way to extend the human lifespan through Inborn DNA.

"Hey, pull up the lab photos," Desya asked Lycidius.

"Let me finish. Show her the pictures after."

"Don't worry about it, Dez," Snofrid interrupted. Lycidius didn't look like he'd budge even if a bulldozer tried to force him. "Just tell me what Regulative is, and I'll have a look later."

"Yeah, fine." He rose up on the balls of his boots, gesticulating. "Regulative scientists cross-engineered human clones with our DNA, but they always turned out more like beasts, so we call the things *Mongrels*.

The Helios Society created a couple Mongrel batches and tried storing existing consciousnesses in them. Basically, these guys wanted to be able to jump from body to body without losing their knowledge."

"So, it didn't work?" she asked.

"No, the project bombed." Desya turned abruptly and coughed hard into his sleeve.

"You should drink some tea," she advised, rising from her cushion. "I'll make you a cup upstairs."

"It's fine." He sniffed, his eyes blinking, and wiped his nose. "It's just a crappy cold."

She didn't believe him. It was clear he was trying to hide the fact that he was crying.

"Got it," Lycidius announced. "Reznik Dalek Stoker. Age thirty-four. Unmarried. Born in the Czech Republic. Used to be a Colonel until he was honorably discharged in forty-six...worked as an Inborn Terrain Analyst until forty-eight. And in forty-nine, he was initiated into the Helios Society and became a Spotter Agent."

"What the..." Desya reread the report, his jaw tight. "This isn't a purge, it's a bloody harvest."

Snofrid scooted closer to the computer and studied the picture of Reznik dressed neatly in a military uniform with a red beret. At first, she was too petrified to do anything but gawk at the flaky purplish scar on his neck; it looked like his throat had been slit. Gradually she came to fully grasp Desya's implication and numbness bloomed across her body, decelerating her heart rate. Hundreds of her kind would be captured and shipped to diagnostic zones to be classified. Most would be condemned to death camps, while those who had valuable abilities would be flown to Regulative facilities. If the Helios Society was searching for a way to extend the human lifespan, she knew her ability to heal would be of interest. Some part of her acknowledged that being studied in a cage could be worse than death, yet she felt she'd rather see Desya locked in a lab than executed because being captured still offered a chance at escape.

Inside the Spyderweb

W here are you going?" Jazara asked Snofrid, as she zipped up her parka.

The girl was nestled in a cocoon of blankets on Snofrid's bed, a stuffed giraffe tucked under one arm. Her eyes were puffy, though she hadn't cried since her housemother had dropped her off at the house, lugging two bursting suitcases and a polka-dot bicycle.

"I have to go meet someone," Snofrid answered, tying on a pair of hiking boots.

"Who? You don't remember anyone but us."

Snofrid's eyes widened in surprise. "How did you—?"

"Secrets are bad friends," Jazara said, rolling onto her stomach. "I asked Dez why you're acting weird. He told me someone swiped your memories." She shrugged, twirling a finger in her ringlets. "I thought you didn't like me anymore cause you didn't even hug me, but I'm glad it's not that."

"I didn't know how to tell you," Snofrid admitted. "I thought I'd get my memories back soon, so I didn't want to make a big deal about it." She paused upon noticing Jazara's kinked brows. The girl had the advantage of knowing her better than she knew herself. "All right, I have to do something important. I can't tell you what, but I need you to cover for me if Lycidius comes home before me."

Jazara dropped her giraffe and sprang to her knees. "We *got* to stay in the house, Sno. The metal soldiers took two boys off the sidewalk and put them in an armored van!"

"No one will see me," Snofrid promised, motioning for her to quiet down. "I'm going to take the secret elevator under the zen garden and stay on forest level."

Jazara's mouth pressed into a stubborn line. She continued this way a moment, before picking up her giraffe. "I can keep Lycidius's nose out. But only if you send me words every half hour. That way I'll know they didn't find you out."

"I promise." Snofrid stuffed a Taser flashlight into her pocket. "I'll be back in two hours tops. Use whatever you want."

"Uh uh. Wrong." Jazara pointed her giraffe at the horror novels in the bookcase. "You always told me the ones on the middle shelf are too scary for me."

Snofrid skimmed one of the titles: *Blood Fall.* "Everything but the horror novels, then."

She tiptoed to the kitchen. The shower in the boy's bathroom was running providing a perfect cover. She plucked a 1911 colt pistol with pearl grips from the gun rack before shuffling into the basement where she crouched over a patch of gravel below the bamboo fountain.

"Open hatch," she whispered. The gravel crawled back, exposing a spacious antechamber-elevator inside the hollow trunk of a tree. Dropping inside, she rode to forest level. Her body danced with nervous tingles. She blew out a long breath. *I won't be found,* she encouraged herself. *If I stay near the support pillars, no one will see me.*

At forest level, she strapped on the globus goggles; they colored her vision bottle-green and projected holographic labels onto the environs. Chiming rang in her ears and a somber voice stated:

Current Location: SUN PROMENADE PLAZA; SECOND RING
Destination: RECONNAISSANCE BUNKER; SECOND RING
Distance: 2.1 MILES
Estimated Time of Arrival: 23 MINUTES

Snofrid headed northeast at a brisk jog, using her flashlight to navigate the rough terrain. It seemed as if she'd descended into an other-worldly place, more mysterious and beguiling than the city, with its soaring trees and frosted moss veils. The trunks were intimate, sometimes growing into one another, branching into a dense canopy that stymied the rubicund sunset. Craggy boulders were slapped across beds of pine needles, and hither and thither shrubs with sticky antennas thrived amongst the native plant life. The air smelled fragrant, like fresh pine—a welcome change after the city's smoky streets.

She skidded down sloping ravines and clambered over begrimed logs for about a half-mile. In the distance, trees fringed the mountain peaks like fur. Cold wind chilled her neck as she broke into a clearing. She felt good, pumped enough to run another few miles at least.

Ducking, she moved farther beside the city's support pillars. The trees offered extra-cover and she kept stride this way for another mile. The globus goggles led her into a glade of fir trees and she heard voices.

"Unit 021 investigating sound disturbance. Over," an automated voice buzzed from somewhere not far off.

Her heart bucked at the sight of red lights advancing from the direction she'd come. Trying to outrun a hydrocop patrol, with their long-range guns, would be suicide. Scanning the glade, she settled upon a giant hollow log, not twenty feet away.

She loped across the glade and tried to scurry into the log. *Thump.* Her skull struck an iron-hard object, sending her cringing backward. When she glanced up, a pair of reptilian eyes watched her, their pupils dilating as they met her gaze.

"You look afraid," a husky voice observed. "Running from something?"

She drew back. Crouched in the entrance of the log, a man watched her; he was so still he could've been cut from rock. Monstrous spikes studded the pauldron of his red exoskeleton armor and iron skulls were perched in place of shoulder spaulders.

She knew from the sudden polychromatic ripples that the suit was made with particles of *Swoegar*—an impenetrable Inborn alloy that was rarer than Californium. Since only Commanders, Governors and Lords were privileged to wear it, she identified the man as Hessia's master, Commander Hadrian—one of the three Skinwalker Commanders.

"I need to hide in here," she breathed. "A hydrocop patrol is headed this way."

"I hear them." He flicked a raptor claw authoritatively. "Come, cower in the log."

She crawled over him swiftly, with the tense feeling that she was slipping past a spider. Mud and leaves clung to her knees, smearing along her dress.

Hadrian produced a bottle from his boot. Snofrid knew it held a Red-Heat Spell. She held out her hand, allowing him to empty the liquid into her palm, and quavered as it washed over her flesh, chilling her. The spell might just save her life, for it would make her invisible to the hydrocops' infrared vision.

Hadrian spun toward the log's opening on the toes of his boots, as if ready to pounce. He was unarmed. If the hydrocops discovered them, they'd be fish in a barrel. Her worry escalated as she looked at him: what lay *beneath* his red bull-head gasmask was like the face of a predacious beast. His pupils were vertical, like an alligator's, and almost dissolved against the camouflage paint that was smeared in an X-shape across his face.

"Attention civilian," a hydrocop commanded. "Reveal your position and you will be unharmed. If you do not comply, we will shoot to kill."

Hunching, she peered through a narrow slot in the log. Warm blood rushed in her ears as she watched four hydrocop file into the glade.

"Sweep the area," one of them ordered. "Shoot to destroy." The hydrocops fanned out; three uprooted the underbrush while the fourth radioed in their position. "Transmitting current coordinates. All available units standby. Over."

"Clear," one of the hydrocops stated. "Unit 021 proceeding to northeast checkpoint twelve. Over."

Snofrid stared from the slot again, seeing that one of the hydrocop units had left her line of sight. She kept motionless. The seconds lagged like minutes; she dared not even scratch her chin. Hadrian's gaze shot to footfalls crunching the frosted leaves beside the log. Snofrid lifted her pistol, but he flipped up a claw in warning.

Five minutes ticked by. Then ten.

Snofrid again peeked from her spy hole, this time with relief. The hydrocops' red visors still streaked the darkness, but were moving *away* from the glade. She steadied herself, not letting relief run away with her. It would be smart to wait a few minutes before abandoning the log.

The crackle of leaves drew her eyes to Hadrian. He was trading gazes with a fat, triple-horned reptile that was slithering toward the log. She wheeled back on her heels. A bite from a Snapping Reefer caused death in eighteen seconds.

Hadrian curled a claw at the Reefer, and it rose like a blooming flower, swaying, as if hypnotized. Then, quick as a whip, he speared the Reefer's skull with a claw, pinning it to the dirt. The action was almost soundless.

But the hydrocops still heard.

"Target Acquired. Terminate." Crashing footfalls were making for them.

Hadrian punched his way through the log. With a yelp, Snofrid shielded her eyes from the wood shards that flecked the air and rolled over. Metal striking metal crashed above her: Hadrian was battering the skull of a hydrocop into a dented crater with a rock. He wrenched back the robot's head and sent his claws through its jaw; sparks and smoke whiffed from its visor.

A fragmented, automated voice blared, "Terminate," before the robot buckled to its knees and fell face-down over the Reefer's carcass.

Snofrid staggered to her feet, heart thumping like a Ping-Pong match. She swore all four hydrocops had left at the same time. This one must've been patrolling in another unit, which meant more were waiting nearby.

"In eighteen seconds we'll be in range of two more units," Hadrian told her, tramping out of the glade. "Run."

She broke from the log after him, dodging tussocks of blood grass. Her single thought was to bargain with Hessia for an escape. It strengthened her against how frightening he was. Her adrenaline pumped and she ran harder. They didn't break pace, not even when a combat helicopter flew overhead, aiming spotlights at the trees.

Hadrian finally stopped at a sharp bend in a creek. He drew an assault rifle from a carpet of ferns and pulled back the bolt, engaging the first round. "There is a military base a mile southeast," he said, plodding through the water with powerful strides. "They have long-range snipers. Keep your head low."

"I want to know where we're going," she panted, wading in after him.

"We're going underground."

Hadrian maintained a sprint for another half-mile before slackening in the gnarled shadow of a Sapling Ward sentinel-tree. Its bulging trunk was plastered with fissured bark that twisted up into boughs that stretched heavenward, as if to touch the moon, while its roots thrashed below in the slush.

Snofrid stooped to ease her wind-burnt lungs. At a sideways glance, she identified the sapling as part of the *Spyderweb*—a secret reconnaissance network that spanned across every continent, excluding Antarctica. She couldn't explain how she knew this: civilians weren't privy to such covert military information. When she straightened, Hadrian was watching her disapprovingly.

"In situations where there is a live threat, each moment I stop to explain myself to you is an opportunity for the enemy to eliminate us," he told her. "So, the next time I order you to do something, don't open your mouth—except to obey."

She stole a small step back. "I'm sorry. I just wanted to know where you were leading me."

His eyes raked her with contempt. "Know that when you swear into this Covenant, one of its most basic provisions will be *obedience*. In the Inborn Army, when a soldier defies his superior once, he is shamed and tortured. Twice, his Halo is scalped. I shoot a soldier the first time he defies me." He slowly clicked his raptor claws together. "Choose your next words carefully."

Snofrid suddenly wanted to return home. He held the right to chastise her in whatever way he saw fit due to his rank. Whatever sentence it was, she didn't doubt that it would be vicious. There was a subversive edge to his manner, like a fine perfume mingled with a stench. Drawing a cautious breath, she said, "Yes, Commander."

"That was once. The second time, you'll be disciplined." He made a fist and the armor-plate above his wrist evaporated, unveiling a tattoo of a black skeleton key on his left forearm. "We'll seal the Covenant here."

Snofrid waited, choosing her words carefully. "Before we make the Covenant, I want to talk about a trade. Your Seer promised me recompense for being your bait."

Hadrian frowned; the black paint on his face creased, giving him a savage look. "What did Hessia promise you?"

"Nothing yet, but there's only one thing I'm willing to trade—a way out of the city for my family and myself. There are four of us, total."

"After we destroy the welx, I'll point out an exit and leave you and your family to go at it alone."

She cleared her throat. "I'd like my terms included in the Covenant as insurance."

"Anything else?"

"No."

"Then our negotiations are closed. From this point on, you'll report to me until the welx is dead and our contract ends."

She nodded stiffly. "Yes, Commander."

He peeled off the tattoo and the ink changed into an iron key. She'd seen this *trux illusion* work with more than keys; knives were most common. He used a claw to flip up a tuft of ivy, beneath which was a knot of bark wrought like a mouth. Shoving the key into the knot, he twisted until the roots slunk backward, revealing an iron hatch at the tree's base. "Follow after me."

Crouching, he propped the lid open and dropped inside. She stared into the dark hole and fear permeated her senses. It wasn't the hole or even the Covenant that gave her pause, but *who* she was about to seal herself to.

"Come now, or the roots will crush your legs," Hadrian advised.

She jumped and landed inside a dark stone passage. He activated the wall lamps, flooding the passage with garish red light. A huge iron mawbeast skull was mounted at the end of the passage, its seven-forked tongue drooping between its fangs.

"Follow," Hadrian ordered again.

He strode toward the mawbeast skull. She'd heard of gateways like these, but they were rare and typically used in the Empyrean City. Hadrian drove a raptor claw through the skull's cracked mouth, twisting, until the jaws cracked open.

"There is information you'll need to know about Spectrals," he said, stepping over the teeth. "The information is never documented on computers. You'll read a book."

"Yes, Commander."

They entered a drafty, damp atrium. It was designed as a two-story courtyard and reeked of wormwood and burnt cloves. A six-tier chandelier, whittled from branches, flowered from the vaulted arch-ceiling, casting rickety shadows on the walls. Purple thistles and woodland ivy choked the pillars and gnarled tree roots grew out of the stone walls. Hyalite opal lanterns, a spiral staircase, and a table cut from black coral accounted for some of the fixtures; she peered up the staircase, but the upper chamber was shrouded in darkness.

"The book is upstairs," Hadrian said, unpinning his breastplate. "Have a seat at the table."

She minced toward the nearest chair. After removing her gasmask, she glanced around the room: something was off. Picking out a specific detail was difficult, for the room *looked* normal, only she couldn't find anything of sentimental value. Not a photo, a warm interior touch, or even a pair of boots. Desya always left bits and bobs lying around. She'd found his shirts in the kitchen, his electronics in her loft and even his beret in her bathtub.

She tried to send Jazara a message and was irked to find she had no reception. She made a note to text the girl when she'd left the bunker. Not a second later, footsteps shuffled on the stairs. Every part of her grew alert as Hadrian descended. One glance confirmed that his alligator eyes had been contact lenses—probably used to terrorize his enemies—because his eyes were a clear green now.

He'd changed into a red cassock adorned with simple brass epaulettes. Standing tall and erect, he emanated an aura of indomitable authority, which made him appear to occupy more space in the room; she felt reduced to a tiny creature. He'd washed off his face paint, baring the arresting precision of his features; but he had one crudely chipped incisor tooth that offset his symmetry. One might say he'd deliberately cracked the tooth in defiance of all things perfect. Instead of the traditional military single-strip shaved above the ears, he had three on each side, so that it looked like a bear had slashed the hair off. In one raptor claw, he held a tablet, and in the other, a leather bound *Demented Book* decorated with oak leaves and bindweed.

"Read Section 23 of this book," he instructed. "That's all. This book appears small, but the further you read, the longer it becomes."

"I'm familiar with Demented Books," she assured.

"Then you'll be prepared if something goes wrong when you open it." Hadrian flung the book on the table and then fished a satellite phone from his cassock. "This is how we'll communicate."

She eyed the satellite cellphone, suspecting it was wired with a GPS, though he probably already knew where she lived. As she tucked the phone inside her satchel, a light clatter sounded on the floor.

Hadrian picked up the gold necklace Atlas had given her, which had fallen from her satchel.

"You speak Swedish," he observed.

"No."

"Why purchase something without knowing the meaning behind it?"

"It was gift," she said.

He dropped the necklace in her hand, saying, "The inscription translates to: *daringly dared, half of it won.*"

So that's where Snofrid had heard the phrase. She wondered if she'd learned it from Atlas.

Hadrian locked his claws behind his back and stood across from her. "Tell me why you were at a slave auction."

"It doesn't matter. It's over now."

"Wrong. Your face was seen by humans. That's a security risk."

"My brother is a hacker. He wiped my photo from Oubliette's database," she explained. "As for the humans who saw my face, we planned to leave the city. But now, with the quarantine, I wear a gasmask whenever I leave the house."

Hadrian tapped the tablet with his claw and referred to the information on screen. "It says here that you run a supply store. What would you rather do?"

She glanced at the file, disconcerted that he had so much information about her. Her palms grew clammy and she wiped them on her coat. His interest in her didn't register as small talk. She felt like she was being analyzed, not as a person but as a *thing.* "I'd rather be a PAWN for one of the Mystish Governors."

"A Personal Assistant Whenever Needed? Most Governors exploit their PAWNS. Apply to be Lord Drakkar's PAWN."

She immediately ignored this advice; in order to be the Mystish Lord's PAWN, she'd have to be a highborn.

"Sit and ask me a question," he told her.

She sat down slowly, keeping both eyes on him. "Did you choose to be a Commander?"

"No. My uncle is the Skinwalker Lord. He prefers war over politics."

Snofrid did a double-take. Being the nephew of a Lord meant he was a *Royaler*. If she'd know this earlier, she would've acted far more respectful. All at once, she felt crude sitting across from him, like she'd come face-to-face with a mighty soul.

Rising, she kissed his cheek in formal salute. "Saldut debokter."

His nose wrinkled. "I don't accept greetings from halfbreeds. Pick up your mask and cover your Asian eyes before my Seer arrives."

Heat blazed in her face. "W-what?"

"You have a *human* parent."

Snofrid turned on him in steadfast defense. "That's a severe assumption, but it's even worse to accuse it wrongly. I'm a *pure-blood* Mystish. My eyes are like this because of mutation."

"What a sad liar you are."

Snofrid contested the allegation. Yes, her eyes were slanted, but Desya would *definitely* have warned her that she was a halfbreed. Regardless, if any other high-ranking Inborns in Hadrian's company undertook the idea that a halfbreed was amongst them—even though she wasn't a halfbreed—the results would be far worse than reprimand.

"The girl is a *halfbreed?*" a furious voice cut in.

Snofrid put on her gasmask at the sound of Hessia's voice. When she turned, the Seer was stalking toward them, dropping a half-eaten lizard to the floor. Pine needles clung to her black robe, which bared her breastplate, and rainwater crept down her bald head and ivory facial armor. Her hands were gloveless, showing her filed black fingernails. At the sight of the longsword in her hand, Snofrid groped for the pistol in her satchel.

"The girl should be punished for coming into our presence as an abomination," Hessia growled. "I'm a Halfbreed Hunter, Commander. Let *me* be the one to slit her throat."

Hessia looked to Hadrian for permission and Snofrid drew her pistol. In a flash, Hessia's hands were around her neck, shooting boiling streams of paralysis through her body. Her knees buckled. She staggered, heaving wildly and clawing at her neck.

"Release her," Hadrian ordered. "Until my dealings with her are finalized, she'll remain unharmed."

Hessia snarled. "If anyone in the Empyrean City learned that we employed a halfbreed for this mission, it might jeopardize the dignity of our mission!"

"Dignity doesn't concern me, only success. Now release the halfbreed, or I'll tear out your tongue."

Hessia freed Snofrid with a hiss, her skin flushing like a ripening apple. Snofrid sank to her knees, gasping, and cupped the blistered ring around her throat. A tornado of rage swirled inside her, making her burn to strike back at the Seer. Lawfully, they needed *proof* to punish her. This was wrong. She hunched over at the compulsion to vomit.

Hadrian stared down at Snofrid. "Stand up," he said. "Then tell me how you knew Neko Aberthol."

"He was my friend," she choked. Water leaked from her eyes as she wobbled to her feet. "I've known him since I was little."

Hadrian, seeming satisfied, stood and paced toward an arch mounted with beast sculptures. "Follow after me."

Snofrid had healed, but her anger still festered. She hastened in Hadrian's wake, reluctant to be left alone with Hessia, who lurked on her flank; the curved shadows of her nails were like claws, making her appear much like a demon readying to devour her. Snofrid pressed herself to calm down. She couldn't think clearly. *A few days,* she urged herself. If she could somehow withstand Hessia for a few days, she'd be so far from Hollowstone the Seer would never be able to find her.

Tugging at her sleeves, Snofrid followed Hadrian through the arch. What she saw on the other side of the arch brought to mind an Inborn history book she'd once read and a spur of wonder eased her disquiet.

The chamber was lofty; Inborn architecture often was. Pillars adjoined a grey stone fireplace with an ornate mantle, and crossways, three arches led out of the chamber, into sprawling passages. A peaceful pool glistened at the heart of the refectory; rainwater trickled down the walls and in rivulets along the floor before draining into the pool. Antlers dotted the furniture like thistles, stone beast heads snarled from the walls and glass lamps flickered from the ceiling.

Ten *Dracuslayers*—the special forces of the Inborn Army—lolled about the chamber, chatting, working on computers, studying graphs, or spitting fruit seeds onto trays from a distance. Most were shirtless, exposing arms and chests of hard muscle and scars; the rest wore low-necked, sleeveless robes. All of them had single-strips shaved above their ears and unit-number tattoos inked on their left knuckles. When Hadrian entered, they leapt to their feet and formed two uniformed rows down the center of the chamber.

"At ease," Hadrian said. He rested his boot on a chair and unfastened the buckles. "A seal will form below your ankle after the Covenant is raised," he told Snofrid. "Take off your left boot."

She crouched and untied her boot laces. Thankfully the seal would disappear several moments after the Covenant took effect, so she wouldn't have to worry about hiding the mark from Desya and Lycidius. She tried to ignore the stares of the Dracuslayers as she jostled off her boot, but their looks cut into her with the power of a blade; rather than as a comrade, more than one regarded her in the same way as the slave-owners had.

At the table, Hessia cracked open a vial and distributed pink powder evenly among thirteen goblets. The liquid inside sizzled, then bloomed into a cloud of black smoke.

"The spell is already prepared," she called. "Choose your glass."

Snofrid picked up a goblet and sniffed the beverage; it carried the aromas of wine, honey, mugwort and pimpernel.

"The rules have been set down and agreed upon by both parties," Hadrian briefed, swiping up a goblet. "The only additional detail is that the girl and her family will have freedom from the city as her reward."

The soldiers busted into riotous laughter; Hessia threw her head back, hissing a hideous laugh. Snofrid frowned. She knew they were ridiculing her for something; she could only imagine they were getting a much *larger* reward.

Hadrian continued. "The covenant will follow the standard guidelines. Whoever breaks his end of the bargain will be tortured by his worst fear. Each partaker will do his duty until the welx is destroyed." Hadrian turned to Snofrid. "Agreed?"

Snofrid felt the gnawing fear of last minute hesitation. She wanted to save her family, yet she was terrified of every one of these people. To be bound into a Covenant with them seemed like more of a risk than taking up guns against the Swangunners.

He cocked his head. "Yes?"

"Yes."

"Duty over fear." He tipped his glass and drank. The soldiers raised their goblets, repeating the phrase "duty over fear", while Snofrid followed with a single sip. The spell gushed down her throat, poking her innards like a thousand needles. When it reached her foot, it burned and she curled her toes. Below her ankle the flesh bubbled and swelled until a circular scar formed. Her muscles unwound as the pain faded. She glanced at Hadrian's foot and then the other soldiers'. An identical circle branded each.

"We have a debriefing, master," Hessia told Hadrian, setting her goblet on the table. "Lord Alcander will contact us at 2220 hours."

"Assemble in the briefing hall."

Snofrid waited until the Draculayers had funneled from the room before catching up to Hadrian in the atrium. "You told me you'd show me a way out of the city. Where?"

"In the sky." His cassock swished as he faced her. "The Lords know Neko Aberthol was killed in the city square. They're sending a Sky-Legion to bring down the shield and execute Chancellor Leathertongue."

Her feet cemented to the floor as she abruptly realized why the soldiers had mocked her. Cobwebs of restraint blew from her body, making her words emerge crisply and harsh. "Then my family and I would have been free without your help."

"Yes," he admitted, his tone remorseless. "But your capacity to be manipulated is a fault of your failure to ask questions."

"You're a cheat!"

"No. I merely identified your naïveté as a weakness and used it against you. To do so isn't cheating. It's strategy."

She steeled her anger this time. Of course he'd tricked her, just like the trafficking ring had tricked her in Gehenna. She could have requested the restoration of her and Desya's honor as payment, but that window had closed and it was her fault. Having no memories *did* make her naïve. She wouldn't be so trusting any longer.

"Why is the Sky-Legion coming to avenge Neko Aberthol?" she asked quietly. "Was he someone important?"

"He was one of the *Crowning Five*."

Her mouth parted in disbelief, but he didn't appear to be lying. The *Crowning Five* were the Inborn heroes who'd made the crossing from Armador possible.

"You know little of our history," Hadrian observed, "and even less about your friends."

"When will the Sky-Legion arrive?"

"After the welx is destroyed."

"That's over *two weeks* away," she protested.

"You weren't planning to leave *before* then, were you?"

"No, of course not. But thousands of us could be dead in two weeks."

"Millions more will be destroyed before the war ends," he guaranteed. "The shield won't fall until the welx is destroyed. It works for us: it confines the beast."

She studied his face; it was dark, like a moonless night. Clearly this mission was far more urgent than she'd been led to believe, for its outcome wouldn't only determine the fate of Desya, Lycidius and Jazara, but of *all* the Inborns captive in Hollowstone.

The Demented Scholar

Y ou're alive," Jazara chirped when Snofrid emerged from the bathroom the next morning. The girl wriggled from her blankets, stuffed giraffe in hand, and bounced off the bed. "I would've stayed up, but after you sent me words, I got tired."

"Don't worry about it." Snofrid gave an encouraging smile, and traded her toilet slippers for a pair of leather house slippers. "Did Dez or Lycidius come in here?"

"Lycidius stuck his nose in twice and I told him you were on the potty."

"Both times?"

"Uh…" Jazara twirled her finger in a ringlet. "Yeah."

"Well, as long as he wasn't suspicious," she put in, though she was sure he'd been suspicious. "Thanks, Jazara."

"Easy peasy." The girl rummaged through her suitcases until she'd found a green corduroy jumper. "I packed five green outfits, but you got to help me pick the best one."

"Sure, let's have a look." Snofrid knelt beside the suitcase. "Why green?"

"For Neko's *Venethereal.* Green's the Necromancer color if you don't remember. Dez told me people are gonna come this morning and celebrate his life."

Snofrid looked at the door; she'd just noticed the echo of clinking glasses and droning voices in the kitchen. "It sounds like a lot of people came."

Jazara nodded slowly. "Neko was grumpy all the time, but he was never mean to people who didn't deserve it." She chose a jade-green dress with ruffles from the stack of clothes. "I'll wear this one," she sniffed, "cause it l-looks like his h-hair."

Snofrid wrapped her into a hug. "Neko didn't die for nothing. He's saving a lot of people."

Jazara's eyebrows quirked into a frown. "W-what do you mean?"

"I mean we're not going to die in this quarantine."

A shrill ringtone warbled from the corner, halting her train of thought. She cast a dreaded look at her satchel; the unfamiliar ringtone meant that Hadrian was calling.

"I'm sorry, Jazara, I have to get this," she scurried to answer the phone. After digging it from her satchel, she slipped into the bathroom. "Hello?"

"You're local, halfbreed, so you should know the Alley-Out-of-the-Way." It was Hessia. Her tone was cutting. "Where is it located?"

Snofrid wished she'd use her tactical resources to locate the hidden Inborn shopping village instead of bothering her. But maybe bothering her was the point. "It's in Toddy Common."

"*Where* in Toddy Common?"

"In a gastropub called the *Red Oxygen Bar.* Go to the attic. An attendant will show you the hidden entrance from there."

Hessia purred something to someone in the background. "My master has sent you files on the Dracuslayers you'll be working with," she continued. "Memorize their proper titles and ranks before your first briefing. It will be on Thursday at 1900 hours."

The call ended.

Snofrid wedged the phone into her pocket, jangling the keychain. The Seer would have to put in a little bit more effort if she wanted to rattle her.

"I'm gonna go eat food," Jazara said, peeking through the door. Her tears had dried, but her eyelids were veiny and enflamed. "I'll save you some *umeboshi*."

"Before you go, can I ask one more favor?"

"You don't remember people and want me to be your whisperer?" Jazara guessed.

"Wow." Snofrid wondered if her thoughts were written in her eyes.

"I'll be your whisperer if we sit by Dez."

"Deal."

"Awesome. I'll be waiting with the umeboshi."

Once Jazara had gone, Snofrid put on the only green-patterned dress she owned and then gazed out the window of her loft. All the rooms were bursting at the seams with guests, most of whom she didn't recognize. The sight was a bit overwhelming, and she had to walk off her nerves before joining the Venethereal.

Downstairs, the elderly reclined on couches before the fireplace, swirling their wineglasses and gabbing in melancholy tones. Tiny children darted about, flinging seaweed at Threearms and slapping one another with the cushions; the robot twirled from one end of the room to the other, offering cider, wine, Sake and whiskey to the guests; occasionally, it took a low bow if it was thanked.

Snofrid spotted Desya standing beside Jazara at the irori hearth, a bottle of Sake in hand. He was cooking cream stew over the fire, while chatting with a group of people, who, by their haircuts, appeared to also be bluecoats.

She made a beeline for him until an impatient voice called, "Snofrid!" Following the voice, she locked eyes with a rosy-cheeked girl as she broke from a group of somber-faced teenagers. She moved with intent, in a floral-patterned dress that bared her freckled arms. She wore her brunette hair in a fringe.

"That's Caviah," Jazara whispered, suddenly at Snofrid's side. "She's a vegan. She has a lot of friends and her dad's a vestment banker."

"Thanks," Snofrid said, assuming she'd meant 'investment banker'. "I thought I was going to have to do the slip."

"Easy peasy." Jazara planted her hands on her hips. "But I'll be real. Caviah likes you, but even more than that, she wants to kiss Lycidius."

"Where's Cid?" Caviah asked Snofrid, her nose flaring in frustration. "He's not in the garage or the washitsu. Did he leave, or something?"

"I don't know," Snofrid answered.

Caviah rolled her eyes at the ceiling. "Seriously, Snofrid, you're never a help." She grabbed a glass of wine from Threearms and rejoined her group.

Snofrid felt certain that Caviah had *never* been her friend. She did a detailed sweep of the room but couldn't find Lycidius amidst the commotion. She felt his absence potently, as if all the sunshine had been sapped from the room.

Snofrid mingled with the crowd. Jazara whispered the names of numerous other guests before she was confident enough to go her own way. There was Marcus Hobb, a friendly Hematic who day-lighted as a fireman while covertly working with Desya in the Hematic Cell; there was Elko Deventer, a Skinwalker conartist, who sold bogus jewels to humans—and loads more.

Snofrid finally reached Desya at the irori, Jazara skipping at her side. The girl hopped onto a chair and made different-shaped ears above his head with her fingers. Snofrid squeezed into an open space at his side.

"Did all these people know Neko?" she asked.

"Yeah. Most of them were treated by him at one time or another." Desya leaned in, cutting his voice to a murmur. "It must be weird not remembering anyone."

"Well, since I don't remember them, not really." She checked the wall television. "Has anyone else been found?"

"Not yet." He adjusted the hearth's pothook, raising the bubbling stew higher above the coals. "Chief Reznik's been holed up in the Golden Circle since the city square strategizing."

"He hasn't been searching?"

"No, but it's only gonna be a matter of days. Our orders right now are just to do extra Tag checks."

She brushed her thumb across the Tag in her wrist, then stared blankly at the plates of rice balls and pickled vegetables stacked around the hearth. "Dez, I have something to talk to you about. Do you have a minute?"

"Yeah, wait for me in the genkan, Sno. I need to put away the damn seaweed." He set down his Sake and rose. "Hey! Drop the beer, Nereus, or I'll make you lick the rice off the rugs."

As Desya scooped up a chubby boy with spiky blond hair and seaweed lodged up his nose, Snofrid retreated into the genkan. She prowled the tatami mats, each moment dragging by in ever-increasing expectation. As she sat on a bench built into the wall, Desya arrived.

"Okay, this is better," he said, shutting the genkan panel. "I can't hear myself burp in there."

"I'm sure Neko would've liked it."

"Yeah, right. If we had his body, it'd get up and walk out." Desya slid onto the bench beside her. "Okay...what's going on, Sno?"

"I have a question and I hope you'll answer it truthfully, Dez." She looked him in the eye, fidgeting with her sleeves. "You told me that Ryuki raised us because no one else would. Was the reason no one wanted me because I'm...because I'm half Japanese?"

Desya dipped his gaze to the floor. "What makes you say that?"

"I have *Asian* eyes, Dez."

He hunched, setting his elbows on his knees, looking smaller. "I would've told you. I only waited because I didn't want to dump too much on you at once."

His words echoed in Snofrid's mind like a ball bouncing off walls. She struggled to draw a redemptive thought from this truth. Nothing. Realizations crackled all around her, pumping her with skittish panic. That she was a vagrant no longer mattered. No amount of shame was worse than what Desya had confessed. She *was* a halfbreed.

"I'm...I'm related to Ryuki?" she choked.

"He was your uncle. His sister, Lorna, was your mother."

Her hopes toppled like a leveled building. The opinion of her past self that she'd been able to gather over the past few days felt violently wrenched inside out. "Desya, that means—"

"It means beastcrap," he cut in. "Your Inborn family abandoned you. Ryuki never did. That's the only thing that matters."

She pushed herself to believe him. It would make her situation far easier. But each time she managed to soothe her anxiety, Hessia's vicious tone wheeled back into her mind, along with her dooming words: *She should be punished for coming into our presence as an abomination.*

"Only a few people know what you are, Sno," Desya added quickly. "Just me, Lycidius, Jazara, and Neko knew, too. All the other Inborns in Hollowstone think you're a human, but none of them give us any flak for living with you because you pose as a Trojan Mortal. And even if they knew what you were, none of them are Halfbreed Hunters."

He was wrong. Hessia was a Halfbreed Hunter. And she'd probably try to kill Snofrid the instant the Covenant's hourglass ran dry.

"You don't have to take my word for it," Desya said, putting a gentle hand on her. "We have a Mania Mirror, Sno."

She forgot Hessia's face in a flash. "How? I thought…I mean, Neko was murdered."

"He got it before the quarantine. Lycidius is staking-out on his house right now. It's still being searched, but he's gonna bring it over in the morning." Desya rubbed her back soothingly. "It's gonna be all right, Snofrid. By tomorrow you'll know everything."

Snofrid wanted to know everything now. She needed to understand how she'd existed safely in a world that detested both sides of her. The humans would never accept her Inborn side and the Inborns had already condemned her human side. She felt like a patched up doll, stitched together with slapdash pieces that were either too large or too small, and mismatched in color or shape. But instead of pacing furrows into her bedroom floor, she accepted Desya's offer of a tour of the War Lobby.

As they marched down the icy sidewalk, she was too preoccupied to be bothered by the cold. The Venethereal had ended less than an hour ago, and since then, she'd assumed a dark outlook—partly from Desya's admission that she was a halfbreed, but mostly due to a sudden wave of sadness over Neko's murder. The total comprehension that he was dead had cut a ragged wound in her heart. It began after she'd viewed a broadcast stating that his remains had been stolen. The human authorities had identified him as one of the Crowning Five and made a gruesome display of his body. After axing him up and nailing his limbs above each bluecoat precinct, someone had somehow managed, unseen, to swipe them all.

Jazara's misery did little to cheer her up. As soon as Desya had begun his farewell speech to Neko, she'd burst into tears. Snofrid had done her best to console her, but her comforts felt hollow. She didn't want to lie to the girl, or fill her with false hope, especially because her sympathy for Jazara had amplified. Being a halfbreed allowed her to experience the humiliation and ostracism firsthand. She wouldn't wish the lifestyle upon anyone—not even her worst enemy.

The War Lobby turned out to be an ideal getaway. It was a survival supply shop, but housed a lovely Japanese teahouse and a charming rock garden. Desya had previously mentioned that she'd designed the place, which explained why she liked it so much.

Bamboo shoots and pink orchids grew in seas of pebbles packed in wooden cribs along the bay windows. Behind the register, a stone fireplace was set in the glass wall that strategically revealed the teeming street outside. Rows of handcrafted shelves framed the right and left sides of the shop, leaving a spacious aisle down the center. Tea tins, urns of roots, berries and plants, a wide variety of autonomous robots, and tactical and survival gear were arranged on the shelves.

"Who's this?" Snofrid asked. She pushed a finger into the cage of a white rat on the register counter.

"Right, that's Quibble," Desya reminded, his mouth twitching into a grin. "You found her in a dumpster. Her food's under the counter, but I fed her this morning, so don't worry about it."

"She looks pregnant."

"Nope, you just feed her a lot. Okay Sno, jump in if you have a question," he started, waving his beret at the shelves. "All the prices are labeled, so you shouldn't have a problem. If people ask about the products, use the register computer. All the info is there."

"Can you remind me of the password?"

"*Cid-23-Sno-16.*"

She entered the password, thinking she really had been close with Lycidius.

Desya pointed at the register. "Just a couple safety tips. There's a machine pistol behind the counter. It's loaded, so just make sure to switch off the safety."

"I see it." She spotted the gun propped up inside an alcove under the counter.

"Also…" He tapped his boot against a titanium door beside the teahouse. "This is a panic room. If crap hits the fan, hole up in here until we come get you. Cid and I will both get a phone alert if it's accessed."

"Have I ever had to use it before?"

"Not yet. And hopefully you never have to."

Nodding, she sat in the armchair behind the desk. "All right, I can take it from here. Thanks, Dez."

"Yep." He strode toward the door, then turned around and continued backwards. "Oh, by the way, if you have any questions, call Cid. I'm doing programming today and can't have my phone."

"I will."

After Desya had left, Snofrid opened up shop. If there was one thing she was good at, it was blocking out her surroundings—a trait she shared with Lycidius. The day zipped by while she distracted herself with schoolwork, watching the news, and doing anything that would take her mind off the Mania Mirror.

She was still brimming with energy by the time the clock struck six. After watering the plants, she closed the doors and jogged all the way home. The kitchen felt barren compared to how it had been that morning. Jazara stood between her suitcases, her head drooping as Desya lugged her polka-dot bicycle down the ladder.

"Hey, Sno," Desya called, setting the bicycle on the floor. "How was the shop?"

"Busy. We sold that ugly barrel." She left her coat on the rack. "Are you taking Jazara home?"

"The orphanage *isn't* my home," Jazara protested, clapping her hands on her hips. "This is my home."

Desya pinched the girl's nose and she bit her lip, fighting, before breaking into a giggle.

"That was cheap," she accused.

"Everything's cheap when you lose." He nodded at Snofrid. "Yeah, we're gonna head out now. Her housemother will have a conniption fit if she's back later than 7:00."

Snofrid gave Jazara a weak smile as they hauled the luggage into the genkan. She'd miss her; the girl was her only friend. "I'll see you Friday." She gave her a quick hug. "Stay safe and thanks again."

Jazara winked.

Once the door had closed, Snofrid climbed to her room. She had the thought to pass the time with a movie, but tossed out the idea when she recalled her promise to read the Demented Book. This was a derogatory title for a book that had gone mad as a result of the information it contained.

Her mouth formed an 'o' shape as she fished it from her satchel. The title read: *Spectrals Imported: A Short History of Mystery by Poppy Van Todder*. Oak leaves and bindweed adorned the book cover and intertwined around an orbicular lock.

After bolting the door, she sat on her bed, and said to the book, "I'm not scared of you. I'm also not stupid, so I won't look in the fake appendix." She pressed her Halo to the lock, until she heard a click.

"Let's test your courage, then," a sultry male voice suggested. "Choose your section."

She dropped the book and scooted back on the mattress. She'd never known Demented Books to speak calmly, only scream their demands, which meant this one might have an agenda.

"Section 23," she told the book's Scholar.

The pages turned, flipping faster and faster until cool wind fanned her face. Then the book flattened with a thump.

She peered into a moonlit chamber on the right-hand page. A broad-shouldered man reclined in an antique wingchair with one leg hooked idly over the armrest. He managed to look refined in his burnished steel mask even though cage bars lined the eyepieces and the mouth was molded to imitate grinning skull teeth. In one hand, he held a brass goblet; smoke rose from a silver hookah in his other hand, screening his black silk robes in violet clouds. Adorning his shoulders were epaulettes fashioned from onyx gemstones. Tribal chest tattoos spread in an exquisite array across his collarbones—probably trux illusions like Hadrian's key—and strips were shaved above his ears, leaving a wide swathe of black hair plunging to his chest.

"Welcome," he announced, clicking his skull teeth open and closed. "I'm feeling tolerant this evening, so I'll try not to confuse you."

"Are you Poppy Van Todder?"

"That's for you to decide." He inhaled from the hookah bit and blew a column of purple smoke her way. "You have four questions left. Choose them well."

"I know. You're not my first Demented…" Her words scattered with a cough. The purple smoke swam into her nose, stinging her eyes and leaving the air reeking of *skull blossom*, a hypnotizing herb that left victims oblivious to the nature of their actions, yet still fully conscious. Fortunately, neither the man nor the skull blossom were real. The man was simply a projection of the book's author, there to guide her through the book.

"If I'm not your first Demented Scholar, then I'll expect you to be clever," he finished for her. "That is, if you're not telling me lies."

"I might be, but you'd feel comfortable, then. Demented Scholar is just another name for liar."

"That's a fool's generalization. I enhance some truths with falsehood. Being able to discern between the two will depend upon your cleverness."

She gave him credit for one thing: he was the most astute scholar she'd ever met. "All right, let's play the game, then."

"Lovely." He balanced the hookah bit on his knee, delighted. "I have six historical facts to please you. But I need the little bookworm's permission to begin."

"You can start," she said.

"Fact One from Someone-Who-Wants-to-Please-You: Spectrals appeared on Armador in the year, 3092. Lord Theodolfus Luvon, currently deceased, confirmed these spirits had reason, as well as the ability to raise magic. In response, Spectrals were formally recognized as the fifth Inborn species, despite most Inborns viewing them as abominations."

"Where did Spectrals come from?" she asked.

"Their origin is unknown."

Snofrid's mind ballooned with distrust. "I'm not believing that, Scholar. I think someone *does* know their origin. A thing can't create itself."

"When you discover the answer to that question, come find me."

She made a 'psh' sound. "For all I know, you really *do* know their origin and would only want me to come and find you because it would give you a chance to bury me."

He laughed deeply. "That could be true. But I'm not in the mood to verify."

"Of course you're not. Go on, then."

"Fact Two from Someone-Who-Wants-to-Please-You: The *Law of Spectral Possession* states that Spectrals are prohibited from possessing all Inborn species except for Hematics." His skull teeth cracked open, showing a grinning mouth. "This Law doesn't apply to Hematics because it's impossible for a Spectral to possess a Hematic."

"Why is it impossible?"

"The answer is unknown. Two questions left."

She deliberated a moment, and then lifted her brows. "Oh, I see. You're leaving out details on purpose. Thanks, Scholar. I won't ask about the mysteries again."

He clucked his tongue. "What a pity. Perhaps you're not so daring after all." He swiped up his hookah bit and continued. "Side Note to Fact Two: On Armador, it was lawful for Spectrals to possess beasts. But beast bodies are inherently weak. For this reason, after the crossing, Spectrals eventually took to possessing humans."

"I know about this," she said. "You can keep going."

Disappointed, he rotated on the cushion and rested his boots against the chair's headboard. "Fact Three from Someone-Who-Wants-to-Please-You: The ability to raise magic is limited to Spectrals and Necromancers. A Spectral can't destroy anything with its magic." He tipped his head backward, eyeing her from an angle. "One exception: a Spectral *can* destroy things if it possesses a Necromancer body. To do this is a violation of the law of Spectral Possession."

She tapped the side of the book, curious why Spectrals had no power to destroy anything with their magic. *I'll save it until the end*, she decided. "Go on, please."

The Scholar chewed something in his mouth, clearly growing irritated. "Fact Four from Someone-Who-Wants-to-Please-You: If a Spectral conquers more than half of a host's mind, it will become permanently imprisoned inside that host." He propped up a red-gloved finger. "Nevertheless…in order to acquire the power to master an Element, most Spectrals choose to fully conquer the host's mind. To do so permanently prevents it from being able to abandon its host."

She scoffed. "That's an idiot's price."

"It is for some," he granted, and swirled his goblet. "Does the little bookworm want me to continue?"

"Yes."

"No questions?"

"No. I know you want me to waste them."

"Waste?" He broke into a wide grin, flashing a brass barbell in his tongue. "Curiosity is *never* a waste. It's a tender weakness…and the most rewarding to exploit."

She suddenly pitied him. He'd probably never sustained a full conversation with anyone. No wonder he was mad. He was entombed in a book, with only his knowledge for company. "I have no questions. Go on, please."

He sipped from his goblet, swishing the liquid around in his mouth. "Fact Five from Someone-Who-Wants-to-Please-You: Possessing a host is necessary for Spectrals to raise magic and use the five senses. There's a side note to this: Both inside and outside a host, Spectrals are weakened by heat and strengthened by cold."

"Just like Hematics are strengthened by heat," she mused. "That's interesting."

"It's a fact, nothing more." Setting down his goblet, he propped his arms behind his head and sighed. "The Final Fact from Someone-Who-Wants-to-Please-You: There are only two known ways Spectrals can die."

Snofrid waited with accumulating anticipation while seconds ticked by. Then, eyes narrowed, she caught onto his game. "Alright, Scholar. What are they?"

"Are you sure you want to ask this?" he tested.

"I just did."

"So certain…where does so much certainty come from, I wonder?"

"It comes from me wanting to know how Spectrals can die."

He crouched on the chair, as if this were his serious pose. "Then be certain of this…Spectrals will die if they remain outside a host for longer than forty-eight hours. And Spectrals will die if the host they're possessing dies while they are possessing it." He stuck up a white-gloved finger. "One question left. Choose your last question carefully."

"I need a minute." Concentrating, she mulled through asking him to explain why Spectrals couldn't destroy anything with their magic. Of the bunch it seemed the best question, only, she had a strong sense he'd tell her the cause was *unknown*.

"Tip One from Someone-Who-Wants-to-Please-You," he offered. "The last bookworm didn't choose her questions well and Poppy Van Todder found her *Door to Submission*."

"I still don't know if you're Poppy Van Todder or if he's someone else," she pointed out.

"That's your question?"

"No," she burst in. "My question is: what's a Door to Submission?"

"Exactly what it sounds like, little Japanese bookworm." He winked, and then stretched back in his chair, wallowing in his victory. "That was your last question."

"You manipulated me."

"Solution: Don't be easily manipulated."

She rose to her knees in frustration. "Whatever you think you've found out about me, you're wrong."

"I'm *never* wrong, bookworm." His skull teeth cracked in a grin. "Rule One from Someone-Who-Wants-to-Please-You: The next time a stranger offers you free information, you should take care to know who he is." He tipped the goblet. "It's been a pleasure pleasing you. May we meet again."

The book slammed shut, locks clicking in place.

Snofrid stared at the book's cover, blinking in confusion. *You should take care to know who he is.* She had no idea what this meant. Except maybe that he *wasn't* Poppy Van Todder. *Or was he manipulating me again?* Flipping the book over, hot with annoyance, she scanned the fine print at the bottom:

Inborn Imported: A Short History of Mystery
Narrated by:
Current Mystish Governor of Court One, Dhiacula Sykiss
Penned by:
Dhiacula Sykiss under the pseudonym, Poppy Van Todder

"Shoot me," she breathed. If she'd known he was a Mystish Governor, she would've asked far different questions.

Turning the book back over, she searched for the orbicular lock and sighed. After a moment of denial, she laid down the book in defeat. In meeting Governor Dhiacula, she couldn't say her surprise trumped her disappointment.

Where the lock had been was now the icon of a black poppy.

Through the Memory Glass

Tuesday, 10 Days until the Hunt

Snofrid found Desya's loaded Glock in the bathtub beside a bottle of tea tree oil. Picking up the gun, she rubbed the soap scum off the grip with a hand towel. He seemed sidetracked so often that it wasn't surprising to find his bluecoat gear in the most bizarre places around the house.

Hearing him call for her, she hastened down into the kitchen. He was leaning against the stove, clipping on his duty belt and blinking sleep from his eyes.

"Thanks, Sno," he sighed. "General Babbage would make me polish his boots with my hair if I showed up to work unarmed." Desya groped his belt and his mouth twitched guiltily. "Shoot. I'm missing my Taser flashlight."

She consulted the clock, certain he was going to be late. "Okay, think,

Dez. Do you have any idea where you left it?"

"No…but check the futons in the washitsu." He laced on a pair of combat boots, aiming a worried eye at the clock. "Just don't shock yourself, because it has a spastic handle. I'll look in the ima."

"No, I already looked in the ima for your gun. The Taser's not there. You should check in the basement."

She slipped on a pair of mittens and then tiptoed into the *washitsu*, a Japanese-styled room where they received their guests. As she reached to flip over the futon cushions, she noticed a shrine on the fireplace mantle. A bamboo incense stick was burning on the censer, as if someone had lit it only moments ago, and an assortment of silver picture frames glistened in the lamplight. She immediately understood that the photos were memories.

Needing a closer look, she picked up a weathered photo of Ryuki, Desya and herself posing beside the polar bear exhibit at the Hollowstone Zoo. She couldn't fail to see how happy she was with her toothy smile and frilled pink dress. The three of them appeared to be people from a different time, a better time.

As she set down the frame, a smaller picture caught her eye: it was of a Japanese girl sitting in an outdoor garden beside a bed of frosted beryl barb flowers—Inborn flowers that blossomed continuously throughout the year. Snofrid cupped her mouth as she realized the girl was Lorna, her biological human mother. But she was young, no older than Snofrid was now, and there was a haunting sadness in her face, like she had a secret. On her ring finger was a gold band jeweled with sapphire teardrops, all set like a beryl barb blossom; the picture had been taken after she'd married Snofrid's Inborn father.

"Sno, I found it," Desya hollered.

Snofrid stuffed the picture frame into her sweater and then returned to the kitchen. Desya was shutting the refrigerator. Her jaw dropped at the sight of his Taser flashlight in hand. "It wasn't in *there*, was it?"

"Yeah, by the wasabi mash. Sorry, Sno." He slung a duffle bag over his shoulder. "I have to run. Don't forget about the Sterling shipment. We have to get it out by today, or they'll get a full refund."

"I know, I finished the forms last night. And I have the numbers of the loaders."

"Awesome." As he paced toward the genkan, she sat cross-legged on a cushion at the table. "Wait, one more thing, Sno." Desya peeked around the door, his tone grave. "If you need to go out, don't go alone...or at least, don't go downtown. Chief Stoker has bluecoats doing Halo scans now, and sometimes the Halo camouflage draughts don't hold up."

"Okay. If I have to go somewhere, I'll ask Lycidius to come along when he gets back from Neko's house."

He nodded. "Stay safe, Sno. I love you. See you tonight."

She sat in silence until the garage door squealed shut. His absence left the kitchen feeling like a deserted bar, a cheery place that was now glum and full of absence. Loneliness blew in around her with only the squeak of Threearms's wheels to fill the emptiness.

Unbuttoning her sweater, she pulled out the photo of Lorna. In all likelihood the picture held hints about her past life, clues which she had only to decipher. But the longer she looked, the more her mother's tender dark eyes drew her in. Snofrid bit her lip, wondering what had happened to sadden her so terribly.

With little more than two hours until work, Snofrid finished up a research paper for Dr. Cricket. Her old self might've found the class fun, but she found it grueling; there were other things she'd rather be doing. She didn't dare brush off the work though, because failing to hand in assignments could be viewed as out of character; humans were supposed to be unaffected by the quarantine.

She was writing on the preservation of near-extinct beast species in their natural habitats and, oddly enough, Fergus Dripper had been her leading source. Apparently, he had top connections in the Union Houses of Science and Research. She found in her files at least a dozen messages from him, all opening with the salutation: *Hey, Snowball, get a whiff of this.*

Her mind slogged through beast facts until morning sunshine lit the kitchen. During this time, she noticed her phone had filled up with messages from contacts she couldn't match faces to. Most asked why she was ignoring them, or why she hadn't joined the Hatred Day protests, or why she'd skipped out on some music festival. She assumed the majority of them were human, which dulled the pride she felt at being so universally missed. She worked her way through the inbox, excusing herself with the explanation that she was recovering from an injury and then rose to get ready for her shift at the War Lobby.

As she packed up her laptop, Lycidius strode in from the genkan. She wanted to smile as he entered; the house again seemed full. A padded sniper case was slung over his shoulder and his right eye was vivid, like a patch of blue sky. He carried the scents of wet bark and rainwater with his steps—he'd most likely been staking-out Neko's house from the forest.

"You were gone the night before last," he said, laying the sniper case on the table. "Where?"

"I didn't go far," she assured, fiddling with the zipper on her computer bag. "I was down in the woods."

"Next time, tell someone when you leave." His tone was firm, but gentle. "If you get caught, there's not much I could do to help you."

"I know I should've told you, but I'm still curious—did you follow me around all the time before I lost my memories?"

"We've looked out for each other since we were young. With the quarantine there's a greater need." He grabbed a towel from the countertop and scrubbed the rainwater from his hair, eyeing her hands. "You used to do that before."

"Do what?"

"Pull on your sleeves when you were nervous."

She glanced at her sleeves, her skin warming. She hadn't thought about it earlier but was curious how many traits of her old self she'd retained. Was she a wholly different person now or just a few shades different? "I should get to the War Lobby."

Lycidius dropped the towel with a shake of his head. "You're not working today. I brought the Mania Mirror and you're going into it right now."

"Now? But Desya said it would take time to prepare."

"It will take time, that's why we're starting now." Hauling open the refrigerator, he began heaping food into his arms. "The mirror could keep you under for hours...sometimes they lay up people for days. You need to eat and drink as much as you can before going in. If you're still in there tomorrow, I'll put you on an IV drip."

She set down her computer bag, suddenly energized. "Okay. What should I do?"

"Eat this." He dumped a stack of bento boxes into her arms. "Go put on loose clothes, and make sure you use the bathroom."

"What if I'm under for weeks?"

"Don't worry about it," he said. "I'll think of something."

She pursed her lips. "Uh...actually, don't. I'll leave a note for Dez."

In her loft, she changed into the softest pajamas in her drawer. Then she used the restroom, scribbled a note for Desya about keeping Lycidius away from her bathroom needs, and plopped onto her bed. She ate through the bentos and followed it with cabbage rolls, pickled vegetables, cubed tofu and broccoli, and braised kale with bacon and potatoes. The hollow void in her mind might be filled—or, at least, the majority of her memories could return. Her entire body itched with longing at the idea. She'd no longer need to rely on others for explanations, like why she'd dated Atlas Bancroft; why people she couldn't remember were familiar; what had happened between her and Lycidius; and how she'd ever willingly lived in Gehenna. Most importantly, she'd know who she'd been before all of this had happened.

"Try to eat it all," Lycidius said. He slid a wooden trunk through the doorway. "And make sure you hydrate."

"Wow, the mirror is huge." She drank a glass of water and watched him finger a cork that was in place where the trunk's keyhole would have been. "No wonder it cost so much."

"Some Mania Mirrors are bigger than this house. This one was made with eighty-five kilos of *asrul dust*. Eighty-five kilos weigh one-hundred and eighty-seven pounds. The dybbuk scales, sivariel metal and memory crystals make it over two-hundred and forty-three." He laid a pillow on her legs. "Lie on your back. Even though you heal, we need to minimize the stress put on your body."

"You've really thought this through." She left her water glass on the nightstand. Resting her head on the pillow, she positioned herself comfortably; her belly was so full she felt like a stuffed animal. "I know there's a chance it might not work," she said, staring at the Japanese lanterns on her ceiling. "What then?"

"Then we'll try something else. Daringly dared, half of it won, Snofrid."

She tilted her head toward him, certain now that she hadn't learned the saying from Atlas. The way Lycidius spoke her name was caring, almost tender. "When I wake up, I might remember you."

He halted, as if something very specific had just occurred to him, and then dropped into a crouch at her bedside. "If it works, you'll remember all of it. The bad and the good. But…" he chewed his tongue barbell, his expression conflicted, "look, whatever you remember about us, know that everything we decided has a reason behind it. It was and still is for the best."

Snofrid couldn't explain it, but she suddenly felt a deep sadness. It was the kind of sadness one might experience from recalling a former suffering—still bitter, but eased by time. Clearly, her past self regretted the decision he was referring to. "I'll try to trust in all the decisions I made," she said.

He nodded, looking even more conflicted. He glanced at the trunk. "I should open it now."

"Okay," she said. "Do it."

"Make sure you're ready. There's no going back after I pull out the cork."

"I know." She looked in his bright eye, needing the comfort it offered. "But I'm sure."

He tugged out the cork.

Snofrid, fisting her blankets, watched glass tentacles wriggle out of the hole. They dove onto the mattress, clinking, and latched onto her arms. "Oh, they're cold," she breathed.

"They're memory crystals. They need to be chilled or the glass will warp." He got to his feet and crossed his arms. "But they won't work if they sense fear, so calm down. I've gone into a Mania Mirror before. It's not as bad as it seems."

"Did it work?"

"No."

She faced the ceiling, hoping she'd have better luck. The tentacles glided up her shoulders and suctioned to her temples. She blinked, seeing grey shapes in place of the ceiling lanterns. "Okay, something's happening."

"I know." He leaned over her face, so close his breath tickled her forehead. "Your pupils are dilating. Stay focused and look directly at whatever shows up in front of you."

The room burst into brightness.

She squinted, trembling, and shielded her face with her arms. The rays formed a dazzling, spinning hole that shone as if the sun had melted and flooded the room. Aureoles glowed around the objects in the room, until, one by one, they washed-out in the light. She stared into the hole, not wanting to enter, but feeling her body slowly tipping forward.

"Lycidius," she called, hearing her own voice from far away. "I don't think this is right."

"It's right," he called back. "Don't fight it, or the crystals won't touch your mind. Just relax and let go, Snofrid."

She shut her eyes, bracing her fear, and abandoned herself. The walls of her mind collapsed and she screamed as she was sucked into a hole, into a place that held neither light nor darkness, only silence. How much time passed she could only guess before she crashed into a toddler with braided black hair. Seated on the floor of a dark bedroom, the girl stared hopefully at the door.

PART II

A Girl and Her Ghost

I lived alone in a room without windows. It had one door that only opened on the last day of the month. There were giant chests of toys in the room. I kept my dolls in a wooden trunk with beryl barb carvings, and my thirty books, I stacked in neat rows along the walls. All of my dresses were stored in a wardrobe beside my bed; if I left one on the floor, it was hung by the morning. Each time I woke, a tray of meat, fruits and vegetables, and a pitcher of water was on the table. Someone took care of me; I didn't know who, but I think the person liked when I was neat. I named the person *Ghost*. I wanted to make Ghost happy, so I always made sure my toys, books and clothes were put away before I went to sleep. I used to stay awake, hiding my face with my covers, waiting to see Ghost when it came in, but nothing ever happened. Once I stayed awake for hours, and by the twenty-ninth hour, the food still hadn't come. I stopped trying to see Ghost after that.

But I talked to Ghost every day.

I told it about the things I read; I sang for it; I told it stories; I told it when I was sad, or afraid, or when I felt lonely; and I asked it questions, even though it never answered back. Almost every time I did these things, the floor creaked on the other side of the wall, so I knew Ghost was listening. This usually made me happy, but sometimes it made me sad. I wanted Ghost to let me see it and play with me in the room.

I didn't know where the room was. I'd stopped wondering a long time ago. I hadn't seen sunlight, or beasts, or plants, or the stars; I only knew about these things from pictures in my books. My favorite pictures were ones of the sky, and of giant towers with windows, and of beasts with bright feathers and furry tails.

I had no idea what I looked like. I'd never seen my own face, only a blurry reflection in my food tray. I knew my eyes were large and that I was very small. I hoped I was pretty like the highborn women I read about.

The two tall, masked men who walked me to the library each month to choose thirty new books were the only people I'd seen. One of them was skinny and so white he looked sick. He wore a black cassock and always tugged on the sleeves until strings fell on the floor. The other one was as big as a warrior. I'd learned by heart the House insignia on his breastplate—a cold blue wyvern head with seven silver horns above five golden keys. Around it were silver cypress leaves and golden anemone flowers; if I looked closely, I could see the soft outline of a solar eclipse behind the wyvern's head. I liked the swishes his blue cassock made as he moved; the clicking sounds his spurs made when he walked; the way the light made his silver pauldron shine; and even the slow way he breathed.

When the man in the black robe would lift me up to reach the books, he'd say in his raspy voice, "Don't only choose science books. Some of the history books might have sweets behind them." The man in the blue cassock never let me stand close to him. I didn't think he liked me. His silver eyes looked sad, sometimes mad, through his mask eyepieces. Every time I stared at him, he squeezed something in his pocket. It must've been sharp, because afterward his pocket would have blood on it.

Then one day I left the room forever.

I'd been drawing a picture of a snow-ferrier beast for Ghost when the door opened. I was so afraid, I dropped my pencil. The man with the silver eyes picked me up and carried me down a passage for a long time. He didn't talk to me or look at me, only held me in one arm, and kept the other one behind his back. I tried tickling his chin, but he didn't smile. He had a big black Mohawk on his head and I touched it to see if it was sharp. It was poky *and* soft. When he didn't talk to me, I told him about my friend Ghost. He stayed quiet. I fell asleep on his shoulder.

When I woke up, he was setting me down before a metal transport. I'd seen a picture of one in a book and knew the guns on the side were dangerous. The door in the transport opened and I moved back when a young man with short black hair came out, smiling at me. He was handsome like the highborns in the books I read, but his brown eyes were slanted funny, and he didn't wear armor. He crouched in front of me, and said, "I've waited to meet you a long time, Snofrid. My name is Ryuki Yagami and I'm going to take you to a new home."

I was afraid and hid behind the silver-eyed man's leg. No one had ever spoken to me before—except for the raspy-voiced man behind the wall, who taught me about Inborn etiquette, and how to read and speak English and my Mystish language, *Prenax*. I didn't want to go to a new home. I liked my room. I liked my books and my beryl barb chest, and I didn't want to leave Ghost. The silver-eyed man picked me up and put me inside the transport. Then, for the very first time, he talked to me, and said, "Daringly dared, half of it won, Snofrid."

I didn't know what these words meant. I wanted to ask him, but he'd already put his back to me was talking to Ryuki in a language I didn't understand.

There was a little boy with golden brown eyes sitting in the back seat eating dried leaves. It was the first time I'd seen a person as small as me before. I wanted him to like me, but I was too afraid to sit close to him, so after I greeted him saying, "Saldut debokter," I sat behind him. He stared over his seat with wide eyes, and said, "Stone me! You look just like my Aunt Lorna." His voice was loud, and I didn't know how to answer, so I just nodded. The boy talked a lot more after that and I listened. He told me his name was Desya, and that we were going to live in a place called Hollowstone City, and that Ryuki was a good dad, and that we'd never have to be afraid with him, even though we were shamed. I didn't know what he was talking about really, but after a while, I started saying things back.

We drove through the passage for a long, long time. When I first saw the sunlight, it happened so fast that I screamed. It was the brightest light I'd ever seen. It was brighter than all my candles and lamps, and it burned my eyes. Desya gave me a pair of black goggles. As soon as I put them on, I was able to see the mountains, the trees, and the flowers. I thought of Ghost right away and was sad I couldn't tell it how happy I was.

Age 4-6
Hollowstone City, Borough of Eastwick

Desya had told the truth about Ryuki. He *was* a good dad and I was happy he was the one who'd come for me that day.

We lived in a fancy, Japanese-style house on *Quintree Quay*. It was only a mile from the Hollowstone Zoo, so Ryuki took Desya and me there every time we asked to pet the animals and run through the poison maze. Our house was very different from my old room. Lots of plants grew inside and the doors slid open instead of swinging. After a few months, I got used to the things Ryuki and Desya did, like wearing house slippers on the tatami mats, sleeping on low beds, doing meditations, and eating with chopsticks. But it only took me a few days to become best friends with Desya. He was a Hematic, so he was fast. He knew how to swim all the way to the bottom of the pool; he wasn't afraid of the dark; he always shared his toys with me, and if I was scared at night, he'd let me sleep in his bed.

I'd lived in the house for almost a year before Ryuki said he wanted me to be smart and enrolled me in preschool. When I told him I already knew how to read, he said, "*Nou aru taka wa tsume wo kakusu.* The hawk with talent hides its talons." He didn't want me to be proud, but sometimes it was hard, because I knew more than the human children in my class. I wanted to make him happy so I pretended to need help from my teacher, even when I didn't.

I always kept my Halo hidden. I knew my classmates would tell on me if they found out I was an Inborn, so I didn't sleep over at girls' houses. Ryuki didn't have humans over to our house either. When I asked Desya why Ryuki didn't have human friends, he told me, "Dad had bad deals with the Hollowstone Trojan Mortals. Now they won't let him in their club." He didn't tell me what the bad deals were, but said it had something to do with Ryuki and his gambling. I didn't know what that meant.

I thought about Ghost every night before I went to sleep.

Sometimes when the floor would creak, I'd think it was watching me and tell it things. I told it how much I loved Ryuki and Desya; I told it that I missed it; I told it that I was learning to speak Japanese and that I'd be a Beast Specialist when I grew up. I even told it about Mandek Skala—a big Polish boy who lived in the house above us. He wasn't nice. He didn't like me because I laughed when I found out he was afraid of dogs. After that, he started calling me *maggot*, and the other children did too. I was smaller than all the children on my street, but no matter how much I ate, I stayed skinny and short. Everyone on the street liked Mandek because he was a leader. He told all the children not to talk to me, so I didn't have any friends except for Desya.

Mandek and his friends only called me names at first. But after a while they started to hurt me. It was small things at the beginning, like twisting my wrist, pushing my face in the snow and stealing my gasmask. Whenever they stole my gasmask, I got really scared because I thought I'd get rashes on my body from breathing the bad air, but I still didn't tell Ryuki. I didn't want to be a snitch.

But then it got worse.

Mandek broke one of my ribs with his fist. He made me eat dog poo, and once, he told his friend, Gunther, to throw a rock at me. Gunther threw it so hard, I went to sleep. When I woke up, I was in my bed and Ryuki was screaming at Mandek's father. Desya had carried me inside, so no one would see the cut heal. Even though Ryuki yelled at Mr. Skala, Mandek never got in trouble. Desya told me it was because his father was a Bluecoat Captain, but I didn't see how that was fair. I wanted Mandek to be punished.

Ryuki didn't get mad a lot, but when he did, it was scary. I'd never seen him so scary as the day he yelled at Mr. Skala. Desya started walking me home from school every day to keep me safe; Ryuki couldn't do it because he had to work. Mandek stayed away for a while, but I knew he'd come back.

A month after he'd cracked my skull, his friends cut us off at the end of Quintree Quay. It was the most dangerous street because it was close to the alleys. There were six boys with Mandek and they all had metal bats.

"You think you can tell on me and get away with it?" Mandek hissed at me, twirling his bat around his hand. "Well, you can't, little maggot."

I knew what would happen, but still, I held tight to Desya's hand and tried to run. Ryuki had always told us never to use our abilities in public. I wished Desya hadn't listened. When he yelled for me to run home, they hit his face and I saw blood come out of his mouth. His eyes got big, like he was surprised, before he fell on the ground. As I heard the bats cracking his bones, and his cries, I became madder than I'd ever been in my life. My body got so hot it felt like fire, and my eyes went blurry. I jumped on Mandek and bit his neck as hard as I could. He screamed and swung his bat, his face scarier than any monster I'd seen in my books. He ripped out my hair, squealing bad words, and then beat my ribs with the bat. Even though I cried, he didn't stop. I'd never felt so much pain as I did then. When everything turned red and black, I thought I was going to die.

But instead, I woke up. I was fine—I had healed.

Desya's face was puffy and bloody, his arm was bent, and his breath sounded raspy. I was so afraid I ran all the way to Ryuki's office downtown and told him. He drove Desya to a young Inborn doctor who lived in a tower named Neko Aberthol. The doctor told Ryuki, "Your son has a physeal arm fracture and fractures on his seventh and ninth ribs. Most Hematics earn these types of injuries through their wild lifestyle, so there's no need to worry, but I still recommend he stays here for a few days."

I felt better after that.

Three days later, Ryuki came home with important news. I'd been drawing a picture of a warrior troll for Desya in the washitsu when I smelled Ginjo Sake; Ryuki's brown leather jacket always smelled of Sake. After he picked me up and held me, he said, "I was able to get ahold of your uncle and we made some changes. Traditionally highborns get their *Shadow*, which is a protector, when they turn ten, but you're going to get yours now, Sno. His name is Lycidius Heidrun. He's a Lambent Necromancer and he's served as a Dracuslayer for five years."

I smiled because I was happy about this news. It meant Desya and I wouldn't ever be hurt again and that I'd have my own warrior friend, who was also a student of the fire element. Shamed highborns weren't supposed to get Shadows, or even be recognized by Inbornkind. That's why Ryuki told me my Inborn uncle was doing it in secret. Then he told me my Shadow was flying from Norway and would be here Friday. I wanted my Shadow to be here now, but decided I could wait five days, and started drawing pictures of what I thought my warrior would look like.

Soon after, the men who always yelled at Ryuki came through the antechamber with guns. I hid under the futons, as I did whenever they showed up. The men got mad at Ryuki about money and even though I hated it, I stayed in my hiding place; Ryuki would be upset if I came out. After they left, Ryuki took me out of the house to the zoo, where I told him that I wanted to move away. He shook his head, and said, "We can't leave Hollowstone, honey." Then he held my hand and told me, "But I swear, I'll always protect you, Sno."

I saw that he was sad, so I asked him, "Are we not allowed to leave because of the debt men?"

"No. Those men have nothing to do with it." He rubbed my back, the same way he'd done the first nights I was here when I'd cried, and said, "Suki dayo", which is in English, "I love you."

I didn't go to preschool for the rest of the week. I went with Ryuki to his government job and played in the office playpen with human babies and toddlers. We visited Desya at Neko's tower every day and each time, I brought him a new drawing and a box of *daifuku*—sweet rice cake. By the time Friday came, I'd already told Ghost all about my Shadow: that he was nine years old, that he was a powerful Lambent Necromancer, and that he'd fought in the Inhuman War under a famous Skinwalker Commander. I also told Ghost that I wanted him to be nice, handsome like a highborn, a fast runner, and a strong fighter.

He turned out to be three of these things.

The day I met Lycidius, I wore the blue floral kimono that Ryuki had given me for my fifth nameday, with a headdress I'd made from silk sakura flowers and a pink obi-belt. He'd flown to Hollowstone on a Doubloon Raider vessel, so we met him at an illegal port in the Hollowstone Underground. We waited for a long time before I finally saw a tall boy with red hair wearing the traditional button cassock of Inborn men. He had black beast-fur on his shoulders and carried a leather rucksack and a weapon case. He looked strong and his face was handsome, but he only knew how to frown and his eyes scared me. Especially the dark, cloudy one; I thought it wanted to hurt me.

To follow Shadow traditions, we greeted each other alone. I bowed to him, in the way Japanese humans did when they greeted each other and then gave him the Inborn salute.

Lycidius just grunted and chewed the barbell in his tongue; a lot of Inborn rulers and warriors had them because the barbells reminded them not to talk without thinking. He said to me, "Because you're a halfbreed, I'm your enemy. I'll protect you according to our Law, but I won't ever like or accept what you are."

I was hurt he was so mean. I glared at him and told him, "I'm still a highborn and you'll listen to whatever *I* say, Shadow."

That night we sealed a Covenant Spell where Lycidius promised to use his life to protect me.

At night, he slept on a futon in my room and I'd see his dark eye peeking at me after he fell asleep. I hated his dark eye and, after two weeks, I knew it hated me too.

Lycidius walked me to and from preschool every day, but the only things he'd talk about were his adopted Skinwalker brother and the Inhuman War. And he never held my hand like Desya had. When I asked him why, he just said, "Shadows don't touch the body they protect."

I still talked to Ghost every night. One night in autumn, Lycidius asked me who I was talking to and I told him, "I'm talking to my best friend. And it's not you." He kept asking me for weeks and I got tired of it, so I told him about the room I used to live in and about the person behind the wall. But I *only* told him this because I wanted him to tell me about the invisible person *he* was always talking to. It didn't work. Lycidius got mad and told me I was nosy. He slept in the washitsu for three weeks after that.

I was so happy the day Desya finally left Neko's tower. I made up a futon in his room so I could read him books at night and so we could play shadow puppets. Lycidius would peek through a crack in the door at times, and I always told him, "Go away, Shadow. This room is only for *friends*."

At first, Lycidius ignored Desya because his parents were traitors; but then, after a few months, he started talking to Desya without saying mean things. I knew Desya liked him because he thought Dracuslayers were awesome and because he'd always wanted to be a soldier. But the war didn't hurt us here. I'd hear students and teachers talk about the war at school sometimes, but no one ever got bothered over it. Only Lycidius did. He wanted to go back to his unit and be a Dracuslayer again, and I knew it was the biggest reason he didn't like me. Ryuki told me that the only way to make Lycidius stop being mean was to be nice to him. I tried doing it for a long time. I let him have the last of the rice balls at dinner; I gave him my fuzzy sakura-print blanket when it was cold; I shared my candy and my books with him; and I even tried not to get mad at him when he was mean.

But even after this, he wouldn't be nice. I didn't care after a while. He was a bully, just like Mandek Skala.

Mandek figured this out too and stayed away from me for almost three months. When I'd walk home from school, he'd stare at me from his window, or he'd hide in the alleys with his friends and watch me. I knew he'd try to hurt me again.

He shouldn't have tried.

Lycidius and I were in the poison maze at the zoo, arguing over the proper uses of phasgora thistles and creeping sprouts, when Mandek and four of his friends surrounded us. I tried to run, but Lycidius grabbed my hand and made me stay. I was more scared than I'd ever been because this time, Mandek had a knife.

"I've been watching you, maggot," he told me, holding the knife at Lycidius's throat. "And your new boyfriend needs to know who the law is in this neighborhood." He tapped the knife on Lycidius's neck. "Come on, Ginger. Squeal and maybe I'll let you run back to your daddy."

I'd never seen anyone move as fast as Lycidius did then.

He locked Mandek's wrist and punched him in the neck. He grabbed his shoulder, kneed him in the privates, kicked his face, and then yanked the knife out of his hand. Mandek was screaming so loud I cupped my ears. When the other four boys saw what Lycidius had done, they ran away. I thought Lycidius would leave with me right then, but he didn't. He grabbed Mandek's hand and forced it through the security fence, under a poky black plant. Then he said, "This is a Death Tassel. They digest the flesh of small rodents; its why cannibal worms build their nests in the leaves."

At first, I didn't think Lycidius would really let Mandek's hand get eaten. But when he pushed Mandek's hand closer to the cannibal worm nest, I knew he wasn't playing tricks. "Stop, Lycidius! Stop!" I screamed.

Lycidius yanked Mandek's hand out of the fence. His cloudy eye was so dark, I thought it wanted to kill me.

Mandek tripped three times as he ran away. His face had turned redder than Lycidius's hair and he was crying and squeezing his hand. I was crying, too. I thought I'd be happy if Mandek was hurt, but I wasn't happy then.

"You shouldn't have interfered. That bastard *deserved* to die," Lycidius growled. "I thought you wanted protection."

"That wasn't protection," I told him. "You were being *bad*."

Lycidius frowned the whole way home to Quintree Quay. I laid in my bed right away, with the blankets over my head, and told Ghost that I didn't want a Shadow. But that was only the first time Lycidius hurt someone to protect me.

Age 7-9
Hollowstone City, Eastwick

The children who lived on Quintree Quay stopped calling me *maggot*. They stopped throwing mud and snow at me, they stopped talking to me, and they even stopped looking at me. All of them were afraid of Lycidius. He was the new leader of Quintree Quay now.

Mandek never spoke to me again. For weeks, I found candy on our doorstep with my name written on the bag. I didn't know who'd left the candy until I decided to sit by the window and catch the person in the act (I hoped it was Tristian, a tall boy in my class, because he was smart, handsome, and funny). As soon as it got dark, I saw Mandek Skala drop a bag on the doorstep and then run away. I thought he was trying to thank me for saving his hand and I felt sad for him.

I stayed small while Lycidius got taller and stronger. Before sunrise each morning, he'd jog around the city for two hours. The only things he did were eat all the soba noodles in the cupboards, practice weapon techniques, do exercises until he was sweaty, read Demented Books, talk to himself, and work on his computer. Sometimes I'd find him doing video-chats with a young boy with long black hair and green eyes. The boy caught me spying once and growled at me; I didn't like him either. I thought he must be

Lycidius's only friend because Lycidius didn't make friends in Hollowstone and only talked to Desya sometimes.

But I made a lot of friends at my new school, the *Capstone Institute*. I was in second grade and at the top of my class, second to Sephora Wilder. She was nice, but I didn't like the way she bragged every time she outscored me. I still talked to Ghost, but not as much as I used to. Since I started making friends at the Capstone Institute, I felt less close to it. As I stopped talking to Ghost, Lycidius began talking to his invisible person more and more. He still wouldn't tell me who the person was. I thought it was because there really *wasn't* a person and he only made up the friend so he wouldn't feel so lonely. I was probably right because Lycidius would often watch children playing games in the streets from the window. Since all the other children were too afraid to play with him, he started talking to me more each week.

By summer, he wouldn't fall asleep until I did. He'd stay up for hours, staring at me while I read my favorite book, *I am a Cat*. I would get annoyed and tell him, "Staring is bad manners, you know." He didn't care and just stared longer. He talked a lot in his sleep and always sounded upset. Usually he talked about Norway, and about a war ship called *Vile*, and about an Unloved God, and about a woman with white hair. I used to think the woman was his mother. When I asked if he loved her, he snorted and said, "Love is why we're a weak species. People should hurt what they like and destroy what they love. I need nothing but the strength to never be defeated."

I just frowned and stopped asking him questions after that. I was afraid of saying something that would make him want to get revenge. If *anyone* did do anything bad to him, he'd make sure to get them back. Mostly, he'd use funny mind games and get them to believe things that weren't true. And he did it to me a lot of times. One of these times, I made him hold my flower basket while I gathered remedial plants in the woods. He didn't want to hold it because it was girly, so he got mad. I'd touched a lot of plants that day, and he said to me, "Your eyes are already starting to change. The seven-leafed plant you touched was Tearmoss and now you'll slowly go blind." I ran all the way home and checked my eyes in the mirror. They didn't look different, but for days I waited to go blind. I knew he'd been lying when Ryuki told me that Tearmoss was healthy and good with soba noodles. I got so mad at Lycidius I threw a rice ball at him. His dark eye smiled at me as he said, "Don't ever make me do something I don't want to again."

I didn't for a long time.

In autumn, I went into third grade and finally scored above Sephora Wilder. My favorite thing to do was to play in forest green-zones after school days with Desya and to swim at Paradise Pools; Lycidius always watched back from the water with a worried face. When I asked him why he was afraid of the pool, his dark eye turned black and he said, "I was left to die in water." But I knew he was just a scaredy-cat.

After a while, I started to get scared of things too.

In the winter, Ryuki started coming home later at night. I'd see him limping through the kitchen, holding ice packs on his knuckles, his mouth and his ribs, and become afraid. Sometimes, he'd have cuts and bruises on his face. Once, when I put Vaseline on them, and asked him why he was hurt, he smiled and said, "The other guy had a wicked jab-cross. But dad still won." Ryuki would have a pretty Spanish woman over sometimes, too. I was happy because I thought I might get a mother and asked him if this was his plan. He laughed, and told me, "Ask me in a month."

I didn't get a mother.

By spring, we'd stopped meditating. Ryuki wouldn't come home until early morning—always with a bruised face—so we stopped eating family dinners. And we even stopped playing family games. I didn't care so much about being smart after that. I only wanted the family to be a family again, even if we didn't have all the nice things Ryuki gave us. I got half of my wish. It was two weeks after my ninth birthday that Ryuki came home with red eyes and hugged me and Desya. After that, he told us bad news.

Age 9 - 12
Gehenna Slums

All of us were afraid to live in Gehenna, except for Lycidius.

Ryuki had to sell our house on Quintree Quay to pay a loan shark. Because he had no existing relatives, and since the bank and the Trojan Mortal club wouldn't help us, we had nowhere to go but the slums. I knew he was sad and angry about this; he'd cry at night when he thought we were asleep. He worked different jobs for food: doing fights at the bingo cages, sewing in sweat shops, and taking contracts from the Swangunners, or from one of the Swangunner's secondary gangs—*Kapa* and *Blackflag*—and even selling drugs to make more coppers. Even more than I was afraid of starving, I was afraid of Ryuki getting hurt during a job. But after each one, he'd come back to our hut and kiss me either good morning or good night.

We lived in a three-room hut at *Lamppost 23* on *Rue Street* with twenty-six other people. Most of them didn't trust us, but I knew that all newcomers needed time to become part of the community. Although the hut was cramped, we made our space as cozy as we could. It was built on the first level of the slums—there were nine in all—and had a tin roof, a gas lantern, and the dirt floor was covered with cardboard that Desya had scavenged. We each had our own wool blanket; Ryuki always made us fold them on the mat where we all slept. We had two pots that we hung on the wall, a portable gas stove, a flower pot of beryl barb, and a bucket where Ryuki made us wash before dinner. Even though we hung blankets on the walls, it was always hot in the summer and freezing in the winter. This wasn't as dangerous for us as it was for Desya. He got sick every winter. It was so bad one time that he almost died, but Neko brought him antibiotics.

Neko was sorry we had to live in Gehenna and even offered to let us live with him. Ryuki was thankful, but told Neko that the loan sharks wouldn't allow us back in the city until Ryuki had paid off at least half his debts.

I got used to slum life quickly because people would die if they didn't know the rules. At first, I missed my life on Quintree Quay. After two months, it felt like a different lifetime. The most important rules were to stay clean and dry, wear a rag over your mouth if you didn't have a gasmask, and never upset a Swangunner or trespass on gang turf.

Ryuki made us all learn who the bosses, captains and gang leaders were. It was easy to spot them. Gang members told everyone they were in a gang through tattoos, the colors they wore, the way they walked, and even the way they spoke. All the gangs marked their turf with their *sign* and would behead rival gang members and put their heads on sticks to mark their borders, so we knew where the red-zones were.

Recruiters tried to recruit Lycidius and Desya a lot. Desya didn't join, but Lycidius eventually was initiated into *Kapa*—a Russian gang managed by the Swangunners—as a Street Soldier, to protect us. I knew he had to do bad things, so I never asked him questions. Also, because I saw things. He would wash blood from his red and gold gang shirt in the lake before he came home. When he did come home, he'd have bruised knuckles and smelled like vodka and smoke. And people on the street started looking at him differently; it was the same look the children had given him on Quintree Quay when they were afraid.

I'd memorized all the rules so I'd be safe, but I still slipped up a few times.

Ryuki would give me and Desya more food than him—he'd grown so skinny that his clothes didn't fit—and I was afraid he'd die, so I knew I had to do something. One of the top rules was never to steal from gangs, so I knew stealing food was risky, but I had to do it.

A certain Swangunner always left his motorcycle unguarded by the base-head shacks, so one day, when the alley was empty, I searched it. There were poisonous snakes slithering inside his rucksack, guarding a bag of oranges. I picked up a stick and after pushing out all the snakes, safely stole the oranges. I got away with this three times.

The fourth time, the owner of the bike caught me.

I'd pinched five oranges when I heard a gunshot. I was so scared, I dropped the oranges. If I'd known it was Lucian Lozoraitis, the Warden's brother, that I was stealing from, I wouldn't have touched the bike. Lucian was only sixteen, but he was much bigger than me. He'd shot children before, so I knew he'd either kill me or send me to the Child Executioner.

"You're a greedy little girl," Lucian told me. "You should've stopped after the first three times."

"P-please…" I tried to leave, but he waved his gun at me. "I won't do it again. Please don't shoot me."

"You're too tiny to shoot. What's your name, mieloji?"

"S-Snofrid." My lips shook as I looked at the axe on his motorcycle. "P-please don't cut off my head."

"Which one would scare you more?" he asked. "Being shot or having your head cut off?"

"H-having my head cut off. If you let me go, I'll do anything."

He smiled and picked up the oranges. "Never offer deals, mieloji. Let the deal be spoken first and then manipulate it to your advantage. If you promise to be a Runner for me, I promise I won't cut off your head."

I told him, "If you don't hurt Ryuki, Dez and Lycidius, I'll be your Runner."

He shook my pinky, and said, "Good girl. This deal is fair."

After I told Lycidius about Lucian, he quit the Kapa gang and started to follow me everywhere. I lost count of how many times he hurt people to protect me—soldiers, pimps, luggers, drug pushers, watchdogs, and even child soldiers—but though I'd once hated him for hurting people to protect me, now I was thankful he was there.

I ran almost every day for Lucian's business, delivering packages. I wasn't a *real* Runner—those men delivered guns—so they all called me *Peewee*. Lucian lived in a fancy villa in the Golden Circle of Hollowstone with his brothers and the Warden, so I didn't see him often. But I heard a lot of rumors about him. Some said that he injected himself with snake venom to get high, that he was the only Lozoraitis brother on good terms with the Chancellor, and that he always kept his word.

My uniform was black trousers and a black shirt with a red wolf on it. Also, I wore a buzzer wristlet: each time it beeped, I'd run to *Gediminas Street* on the ninth level and wait outside the *Iliuzija Club* in the fancier part of Gehenna. A Swangunner named Vadimas would come out the back door and give me a cardboard box with instructions for delivery. I didn't know what was in the boxes I delivered, but after I saw blood leaking from one, I stopped wondering.

After about a year, Lycidius did start to act nice as Ryuki had promised. One day, he sat in the corner of the hut a long time, staring at me while I did homework (I'd enrolled in a tiny slum school on our street). He mostly watched my hands and his mouth tipped up, as if he liked the way I moved them. After a while, he said to me, "Do you hate your parent's for shaming you?"

I'd thought about this a lot myself and answered, "What makes us so different from humans? The only difference is our Halos. I'm glad my father married my mother."

He said, "You're wrong. You are different, Snofrid." Then he got up and left.

The next day, Lycidius was different. But instead of saying nice words, he'd make me gifts. I knew it was because he didn't want to tell anyone what he felt. If he did, he'd love and be *weak*. He was good at pretending, but I'd always known that he felt things deeply—more deeply than all of us. We were gathering sticks for a fire one day and he asked me, "Cedar or redwood?" I hid my smile, and said, "Redwood." The next day, he left a bracelet carved from redwood beads in the shape of beryl barb flowers on my mat. It was detailed, as if it had taken hours to finish. This was the kind of thing he did to tell me he wanted to be friends.

Summer and autumn passed in sad and happy moments.

Desya got a steady job making guns from bobby pistols in a sweat shop, which earned us an extra cup of rice; Ryuki worked every job available, down to dragging dead bodies to the waste pits, and I continued running for Lucian. When he was happy with my fast running, he gave me fruit, poppy seed cakes and chocolate, which I always brought home to share. When he gave me a pair of red sneakers, I ran even faster. He even gave me an expensive gasmask, and said, "Your skin is too pretty to be ruined by the air, mieloji. Find Vadimas every time you need a new cartridge."

I ran home smiling that day. Since I healed from air poisoning, I gave the mask to Ryuki, Lycidius and Desya to share.

During hot months, Lycidius and I climbed an abandoned tower overlooking the slum. I felt safe up there. I think Lycidius liked it because it was peaceful. Whenever there was wind, he'd lift his head up, like he loved the feel of it against his face. Sometimes we'd see fireworks going off above Hollowstone and we'd talk about how much we missed it. He promised me that he'd get me out of Gehenna one day. He told me he was working on a transport design that could make stacks of silvers. I told him, "If you get us all out of here, I'll love you forever."

As soon as I said this, his eyes grew large, like he was surprised. Then his dark eye grew blacker than I'd ever seen it. I didn't get scared, because his other eye stayed bright. After a while, it started to look suspicious, and he said, "You didn't love Ghost forever."

I didn't argue with him because I was suddenly very sad. I hadn't thought of Ghost in a long time. After we climbed down from the tower and lied on the mat in our hut, I told Ghost I missed it. Even though I'd promised myself I wouldn't cry again until I left Gehenna, I did that night.

My life changed when I met Parisa Namdar. And so did Desya's.

Three of the people we lived with were stoned for stealing food from other huts, so Parisa's family moved in. Her mother, Roshani, worked as a hostess at one of the Swangunner's clubs; her father used to be a Street Solider for a smaller gang, but he'd been killed in a turf war. We became friends right away. Parisa was Iranian and the most beautiful human girl I'd ever seen, but only her mother and I knew this because she wore a veil and baggy clothes like I did when in public.

Desya eventually found out, though.

His eyes would get big when she came into the hut. At first, he was too shy to talk to her, so he just stared at us while we talked, cooked rice or did laundry. Then he started to do things for her and Roshani—washing their clothes, gathering firewood, carving furniture. Parisa noticed what he did and smiled at him once. Afterwards, Desya stopped being quiet. He'd sit in the sand outside the hut and talk to her for hours; he'd share his food with her, walk her everywhere, help her haul water from the lake, and make her gifts.

About two months after this began, I saw Desya kiss her in an alley outside our hut. His red Hematic claws were sticking out, which only happened when he was mad or excited, and Parisa made him hold his hands behind his back so he wouldn't cut her.

Ryuki saw the kiss too. That night, he told Desya not to treat Parisa like men in the slums did, but that he should treat her better than he treated himself. Then Ryuki smiled and gave him the last of the vodka.

After this, Lycidius stopped him outside the hut, and told him, "Never let a girl tell you what to do while you're kissing her."

Desya smiled and said, "At least I've kissed a girl."

Lycidius chewed his tongue barbell and I knew he was embarrassed. But instead of losing his temper, he left the hut and didn't come back until morning.

Age 13-14
Gehenna Slums

As my body changed, so did my life in Gehenna.

I hated the way slaveholders stared at me and the crude things they yelled at me. I was afraid of being one of the girls or boys they kidnapped and sold off as pleasure slaves. Even though I was tall, skinny and dirty, pimps tried to recruit me. They told me I'd get food and nice clothes if I worked for them and that they'd protect me, but I knew they were all liars. I'd seen the way they treated their slaves and it was worse than slum dogs. Along with my mouth veil, I started wearing a mosquito net to cover my eyes. Parisa did too. These days, Desya never let her go anywhere by herself.

Lycidius was now tall and strong; no one even glanced at me badly when he was around. Desya also grew taller and came into his full Hematic speed. Parisa, who was one-and-a-half years older than me, helped me. She knew what happened when girls grew, so I wasn't so afraid when I did.

Ryuki was the only one that grew smaller.

He'd become so thin he was rarely hired for jobs anymore. I brought him all the food that Lucian gave me, but he usually vomited afterwards. This put more stress on his body and he stopped accepting the food.

One night, he set the bag of cherries I'd given him in my lap and said, "I'm happy you take care of me, Sno, but I love you too much to let you keep giving me so much food. I'd be a lot happier if you took care of yourself first."

I frowned, and said, "Are you not taking the food because you don't like cherries?"

Ryuki shook his head. "That's not why I'm returning the food."

"Then why?"

"Because I'd rather starve than let my daughter starve." He pinched my nose, and when I finally laughed, he whispered, "There's a lot I need to make up for, honey. Please help me try."

I did try. I tried my hardest to help Ryuki not feel guilty, but it didn't work. He'd cry more and more when he thought he was alone. But he was never sad in public. He always told jokes to children when he helped sick families. He even bought homeless slum squatters clothes and gave away spare coppers to the neighbors. I didn't understand the way he was acting, but because he seemed happier, I was too.

Lucian started to be kinder to me. As long as no one saw me, he'd let me sit behind the bar in the Iliuzija Club and drink soda or beer after hot days of running. He was always interested in how much I could drink and even said I had a gift. I did. My healing abilities made it impossible for me to get drunk.

One day, after a hot run, he showed me his second favorite snake—an eyelash pit-viper named Aušra. He even let me hold her, but she was cranky, so she bit me. Lucian picked me up and ran me to an emergency hospital room at the back of the club, where the doctor gave me antivenin, morphine and penicillin. Luckily, Lucian had to leave for a deal, so he didn't see me heal. I was left alone with the doctor. When she went to check on another patient, I snuck from the club and ran back home. Lucian found me the next day, demanding to know why I'd left the hospital. I told him that he had a good doctor and that I was all healed. He didn't believe that I felt as good as I let on, so he stayed by my side all day to make sure. Lycidius, who was always watching me from far off, didn't like this at all.

On June 24th, the Lithuanian *Dew Holiday,* Lucian let me go with the Swangunners' daughters, girlfriends and wives into the woods to find magic dew. He told me that the morning dew became magic on the shortest night of the year and that if I washed my face with it, I'd look younger and prettier and be cured of sickness. I wanted to be pretty so I washed my face longer than the other girls. Then I gathered a bouquet of magic herbs and made a head wreath. I was invited to go to a bonfire to greet the sun, but couldn't because I had to go to school the next day.

I was always happy about the presents Lucian gave me, but Lycidius hated it. Whenever I'd come home with a new gift from him, Lycidius would immediately try to make me a better gift (the best of these was a tower he'd built in the forest, out of logs, twigs and branches). Parisa and I would go to the tower where it was quiet when we wanted to talk. I'd grown used to the sounds of the slum, except for the crying that came from the *field of exile*—a field above the slum where all diseased people were abandoned, left to die and lie unburied.

Ryuki was the first to be brave enough to go on the field and bury the bodies. After a while, Parisa and I went too. We felt sad for the sick toddlers, so we carried them off the field and hid them in my tower in the woods. Even though we fed the toddlers fruit and bits of rice, they all died within a few days or weeks. It made me wonder if I'd die too: I always healed from sicknesses and injuries, so I couldn't know. If I never died, I knew I'd be unhappy because everyone I loved would leave me. One night in the spring, Desya and I both couldn't sleep, so we stayed awake talking. He told me that he had a secret. But before he could tell me what it was, he made me promise that I would keep quiet until he'd figured out the right words to tell Ryuki. I was curious to know the secret so I made the promise.

He smiled the brightest smile I'd ever seen and said, "Parisa and I got married last night. It was an Inborn ceremony, but Parisa still wanted to use rings. Lycidius stood in as the witness."

I was so shocked I didn't know what to say at first. When I realized he wasn't joking, I felt hurt and asked him why he hadn't let me go to the wedding. He looked embarrassed, and said, "If the Swangunners find out we're married, they'll tax us. I don't have the stacks to pay all the fees so I didn't want anyone to know." He held up a chain around his neck, showing me a metal ring. "Lycidius saw me making the rings, so I had to tell him."

I thought I understood better after this, even though I still felt hurt. But in all, I was happy about the news because Parisa was my best friend. Since she and Desya were married, we'd always be family, no matter what bad things happened. I told Ghost the news after Desya fell asleep beside Parisa.

I could only know when new seasons were coming by snow, rain and sunshine. It was in the summer of my fourteenth year that I first realized how much Lycidius liked me.

A terrible storm hit Hollowstone so we had to go into the underground part of the slum until it passed. After four days, it was safe to go above ground and the first thing I did was run to the river to swim. A foot of rain had fallen during the storm so the water was high and the current strong, but I went swimming in a shallow part of the river while Lycidius watched me from the bank. It happened so fast: I slipped and couldn't grab onto anything. The current pounded my head. I choked and swallowed so much water. The current threw me against rocks; I broke bones and got cut. I thought I was going to die, but then I saw Lycidius sprinting along the shoreline. I thought that he wouldn't help me because he hadn't touched more than two inches of water in a bucket since we'd met. I was so grateful to be wrong.

He got ahead of me on the shore and then jumped in. He was powerful—the current couldn't suck him under—but I'd never seen him afraid until that day. He reacted as if the water were fire. He was white-faced with wild eyes and his whole body shook. With one hand, he grabbed my arm and yanked me from the water. Then he dragged me to shore and fell down in the mud, panting so hard I thought he might faint. I held onto him, thanking him, and by the time my bones had healed, he was hugging me back. It was the first time he broke his rule about Shadows not touching the body they protect, and afterwards, he broke the rule almost every day.

He'd stand close to me while we walked. He'd touch my braid when he thought I didn't notice and sometimes, at night, he'd touch my fingers. I was nervous at first, because he looked at me differently, like he was thinking something he wouldn't say. But after a few months, I started to miss his hand while I was running. He'd held my hand so often that it felt strange when it was empty. We did things together: went to bonfires, street festivals, cage fights. He helped me gather herbs in the forest and didn't get angry when I asked him to hold my basket. He helped me do laundry, carve a chair for Ryuki, and kill an Elder-Ridge Back beast. I made him a necklace with one of the claws, which he put around his neck and didn't take off.

We still argued a lot, but I was grateful that he'd stopped doing mind games on me. Usually, he'd grunt and walk away before turning around and coming back. He'd never tell me he was sorry and I knew it was because he was too proud. Instead, he'd make me a gift to show that he wanted to be friends again. Sometimes I'd accept the gifts and other times I'd try to make him say sorry. One of these times he stared at me for a half-hour, chewing his tongue barbell, but he didn't say the words—it was against his soldier-code to apologize for anything. I tried ignoring him for a few days to help him change his mind. He *hated* being ignored. When he couldn't take it anymore, he followed me around, grunting to let me know he was there. I ignored him for a few more days before I spoke to him. He treated me nicely, so I knew he was really trying to be a good friend, and I never asked him to say sorry again.

But Desya always said sorry to Parisa. Often, I'd hear them fighting in the woods, or inside the hut, or by the lake, or in the back alley. It never lasted more than one day because Desya had a sensitive conscience. He'd find Parisa and make her forgive him by doing whatever she asked, then he'd invoke the Promethia Flower and ask forgiveness for what he'd done. One time, Parisa made him kill a beast, skin it, tan the hide, and then put the hide on her shoulders before she forgave him.

Lycidius heard about it, and told him, "I'd starve to death before letting a girl turn me into a wimp."

I felt bad for Desya, so I reminded Lycidius about what Ryuki told us about love: "Love is when the other person's happiness is more important than your own."

Lycidius didn't reply. He just sat there in silence, looking confused, like I'd just told him the opposite of what he thought. He was the most hard-nosed person I knew, but I still wanted to be near him.

Our lives changed in the winter of my fifteenth year when Ryuki didn't come home for two days. It was the longest he'd been away, so we knew something was wrong. We spent hours searching the huts; we even asked Neko to help us and rounded up a huge search party. Since all the neighbors liked Ryuki, over five-hundred people joined. We combed all nine levels of the slums, searched the forest, the river and even the waste pits. With each second, I became more afraid of finding him hurt.

We finally found him in a back alley near the loading docks.

He was lying in the sand, still wearing his work gloves. As soon as I saw the vultures eating him, I picked up a stick and hit the birds as hard as I could. I protected his body with Neko and Desya. Lycidius asked the loaders what had happened. Most ignored him, but one eventually told him that Ryuki had collapsed and didn't get up. I cried so hard that a man kicked me to make me be quiet. I barely noticed when Lycidius struck the man, sending him sprawling, and picked me up.

Desya brought Ryuki to the woods and we buried him in a glade of redwood trees under a rock that we carved with flowers and wings. I planted the beryl barb flowers from our hut pot over his grave, knowing they would always bloom. For the first time in years, I prayed my own prayer. I'd always believed in the one power of the *Promethia Flower*—a source of pure healing on Armador—and I prayed it would make sure Ryuki was never hurt or hungry again and that he'd find my mother, Lorna, in the afterlife. Parisa laid her beast hide on the grave. I had never seen Desya cry so hard.

Neko left two days later because he had to do a surgery. After four days, Parisa, and Desya went back to their jobs, but Lycidius and I stayed with Ryuki. Since I hadn't stopped crying long enough to eat, Lycidius got worried. He said, "The people you love never really die. They'll stay with you as long as you remember them. All you need to do is remember Ryuki and he'll be happy."

I knew he'd lost his family too, and it made me trust his words. A day later, I ate a piece of bread so he would stop worrying.

We stayed at the grave for a week, sleeping under a birch tree at night and planting flowers around Ryuki's grave during the day. Even though Lucian needed me for deliveries, I couldn't make myself leave because I knew I'd lost the only father I'd ever have.

Age 15
Gehenna Slums

I wasn't afraid of Gehenna anymore. I didn't cry when I was hungry and I tried not to complain when I had to eat insects or drink puddle water. Each night before I fell asleep, I asked the Promethia Flower, the pure healing, to free me from everything that hurt.

I talked to Ryuki instead of Ghost now.

Each day after running, I visited his grave and told him all of the things I thought and felt. I told him that Lucian hired me to be the nanny of his three nieces—*Drasa, Svajonė and Erelis*— and that each week, he paid me with new clothes, rice and ten coppers; I told him that Parisa was pregnant and that Desya had become a Street Soldier for Kapa to keep the three of them safe; I told him that I was 5'6" now; I told him that I missed him and that I thought of him every day; and I told him that I loved Lycidius and that even though I knew he loved me too, he said nothing.

One night, I knew for certain that he wanted to be more than my friend. It was a hot night, too hot to sleep. Lycidius was so big now, he didn't fit on our mat at night and had to bend down to walk outside the door. As he rolled over, I opened my eyes and saw him staring at me. He was not frowning. I didn't know what he was thinking at first. Then, when he looked at the veil over my lips, I knew. We didn't talk and I was afraid to. As he pulled the veil off my face, his dark eye turned violent-looking, so I only stared in his bright eye. He put his mouth on mine slowly and touched my face for the first time. When I started kissing him back, my heart beat faster and he held me even closer. That moment something changed between us. Lycidius changed. He became gentler than he'd ever been in his life.

For months, he followed me around in the same way that Desya followed Parisa—not because he had to, because he wanted to. He kept his eyes on me whenever I took off my veil, so he could see my face before I covered it again.

The first time I ever heard him laugh was when I let him read my favorite book, *I am a Cat*. He stayed up all night reading, smiling at almost every page. I didn't sleep that night, but I didn't want to. I just listened to him, covering my face with my blankets so he wouldn't catch me spying. I was glad that he could really have fun like other people.

My favorite times were when he smiled at me. It made me feel things I'd never felt before—things Parisa talked about, but that I'd never understood. Each day, Lycidius and I grew closer and even told each other our secret thoughts. During most of the nights since our kiss, he held me, so that it was hard to sleep on the nights he didn't. He told me he could only be happy if I was. If I had a bad day of running, he always tried to make it better. One of these times, he traded his extra shirt for a new pot of beryl barb flowers, because he knew they were my favorite. The gift reminded me of Ryuki, so I kept it in the safest place in our hut. I was still afraid of the dark parts of Lycidius, but I started to believe that the thing behind his dark eye wouldn't hurt me unless he told it to.

My fear left almost completely when he began to confide more deeply in me. We sat in the forest alone together from sunrise to sunset on days when I had no work or school, just talking. He always turned a little shy when he spoke of his past, like he was afraid I might get scared of him again and decide not to love him anymore. But by now, I loved him too much to let his dark eye scare me away. Some of the things he told me I already knew and other things surprised me. I learned that he'd respected Ryuki despite being human, and that he thought Parisa was greedy. He told me that the woman with the white hair, who he used to talk about in his sleep, was his adopted brother's mother. Lycidius told me she was the only woman he'd ever liked until he'd met me.

Sometimes, he closed up, though. I knew he felt uncomfortable at giving away all his secrets, so I started paying more attention to things he did. I discovered signs that showed what mood he was in. Over time, I asked him private questions and found out that he played the harmonica, that he had an eidetic memory, that he was taught to be ambidextrous, and that his favorite weather was cold wind. He even taught me a song on the harmonica called *Beyond the Sky* and I played it for Ryuki each time I visited his grave.

I never told anyone about our kiss. Mostly because Lycidius didn't kiss me again, even though I knew he wanted to. Each time I thought he might, he looked guilty and stopped suddenly. This was usually when we climbed the abandoned tower and sat together under the stars. One night, I was feeling confused about it and asked him to explain. He again looked guilty and said, "It's against the law for highborns and their Shadows to be lovers. My job is to protect you, Snofrid. We can be friends, but that's all."

My heart hurt badly at this. I knew the law but had always thought he didn't care about it. The law didn't apply to me because I was a halfbreed. I asked him, "But don't you love me?"

He said, "Snofrid, I love you more than everyone I ever loved."

I frowned, feeling more confused, and asked, "Then why can't we be together?"

"Because I made an oath to your uncle to keep Shadow Law. So if we want to be lovers, then you have to release me as your Shadow."

I hated this idea. He was property of the Inborn Army, so they could do whatever they wanted with him if I let him go. I said, "If I release you, you'll get deployed and we'll never see each other."

"I know, Snofrid. But we have to make a decision."

It was the hardest decision I ever had to make. I didn't want to give up Lycidius. I'd already given up Ryuki and Ghost. If I said goodbye to him, I thought I'd die. I hugged him tightly and said, "I don't want you to leave me, Lycidius."

At this choice, he seemed relieved, though not much happier. He thought about the problem for a long time, talking to his invisible friend, before he finally said, "I won't leave you, Snofrid. But it'll be easier for me if we spend less time together."

I nodded and tried not to cry in front of him.

After we climbed down from the tower, I went to Ryuki's grave and cried there. I wanted to be with Lycidius in the way Desya was with Parisa. I wanted it to be happy, but, from the way Lycidius acted after that night, I knew my dream would never happen. He grew distant, just like he'd been when we'd first met. I knew he was angry—not at me—at himself, at Shadow Law and at the Inborn Army. Even though he hardly ever spoke to me, I gave my love to him through looks, as if they could be touches. I think it made things harder for him, because sometimes after these looks, he'd grew even more distant. He never touched me again.

Once a week we would spend time together and talk about what we'd do when we finally left Gehenna. I wanted to go to university and Lycidius wanted to design machines. When I asked about the project he was working on, he told me, "It's something that will save you and Desya."

I wanted this so much that I told Lycidius again, "If you get us out of here, I'll love you forever." Instead of looking suspicious, he glanced at my mouth. He didn't kiss me as I hoped he would. He just rubbed his temples, as if they hurt, and turned away. When he stayed quiet, I asked him if the 'something' would save Parisa and Roshani, too.

He told me, "If you ask me, I'll save them, too."

It was one week after this that our darkest days in Gehenna came.

They began when Roshani was caught lifting coppers from one of her Swangunner clients. Parisa and I heard about it and ran to the platform where she was being held. A large crowd had gathered because the Swangunner wanted to make an example of her. He beat her with a crowbar. Parisa fought to reach her, but she was struck by a Swangunner with the butt of a rifle. Her head was bleeding and I was terrified she might die. Before I dragged her off the platform, I saw the Swangunner put a hose down Roshani's throat. I'd seen this kind of execution before so I knew he'd make her drink the water until her stomach burst. Just as I left the platform, I heard the Swangunner yell, "This is what will happen if a whore starts thinking she's worth more than the maggots that will eat her corpse!"

For days, I stayed with Parisa in my tower, holding her while she cried and telling her anything that would make her stop screaming. She cried so much, her face got grossly chapped. She swore to me that she'd kill the Swangunner even if she had to die doing it and that she'd humiliate him as he'd humiliated her mother. I didn't want her to get hurt or killed, so I tried to talk her out of it, but she wouldn't listen.

Two weeks passed before Desya and I finally convinced her to come home. He did whatever he could to help her: he stayed up nights with her while she cried and fed her because she wouldn't eat. Five more days passed before she told him that if he loved her, he'd kill the Swangunner. He said, "I do love you, Parisa, but I can't. If I do, the Swangunners will execute both of us."

Then she hit his face and yelled, "If I'd known you were a coward, I never would've married you!"

Parisa only got more depressed. She'd scream at Desya until her voice was hoarse and say even crueler things that I knew she didn't mean. One of these times, she threw a rock at his head and then laughed like she'd gone crazy. He just picked her up and took her up to the lake to bathe because she wouldn't even clean herself anymore. The day she miscarried their baby, Desya almost broke. But somehow, he didn't. After Parisa had fallen asleep, he sobbed in the corner of the hut for almost two hours before

Lycidius came to help him bury the baby.

Lycidius hated Parisa more each day. He even asked me if I wanted him to put her out of her misery. I got upset then. I knew how Parisa felt because I'd lost Ryuki and told him, "If you touch her, I'll never love you again."

He ground his teeth and said, "Parisa wouldn't do half of the things for you that you're doing for her. One day, you'll know that she only cares about herself and then you'll regret wasting your love on her."

Things got worse with the *Midwinter Insurgency.*

It was the bloodiest riot I'd seen since moving to Gehenna. The slum civilians had nothing but suffering. Their families were broken; their children and wives had been sold into prostitution; they were underfed and underpaid and treated with less compassion than the vultures on the field of exile.

So when they rose up against the Swangunners, it was a massacre.

Swangunner armies lined up thousands of rebels along the edges of the waste pits and shot them. They even killed the babies and toddlers. Most were left to starve or freeze to death on the field of exile; whoever tried to save them would be shot. People went crazy; they accused even their friends of being rebels, giving them up to the Swangunners to be tortured or raped and ultimately killed. Two families who lived near us accused each other. All of them were taken to the *Blood Shed,* the Swangunners' execution house, and I never saw them again.

A week passed. Gang wars broke out, as if to just get in on the killing. Blackflag and Kapa had always hated each other and this war almost destroyed both. I'd seen people die in horrible ways in Gehenna, but the way these gangs slaughtered each other was beyond anything I knew people could do to each other.

Lycidius refused to fight in the gang wars. Instead, he stayed by my side all day and all night without hardly even sleeping. Two days later, Desya got knifed in the stomach. Parisa came into the hut as Neko stitched up the wound and fainted. For three days she didn't wake up, and when she did, she was burning with a fever. We brought her to the woods and we took care of her in my tower. The fever nearly killed her, but Neko fed her tea from remedial plants and kept her face cool with a wet rag and the fever broke.

We went to the underground part of the slum. Bodies were everywhere. The mud was red and peppered with shells. People were crying and screaming and the smoke from the fires shrouded the streets in a stale fog.

The fighting got so bad that Lycidius was forced to save me with his magic. He arced a wall of flame from the fires and burned alive over a dozen Blackflag soldiers. No one even noticed in the chaos. Afterwards, Lycidius refused to even let me go to the river on my own. He stayed awake in the hut for days, holding a rifle and threatening to shoot anyone who tried to touch me or steal from us. His eyes got so bloodshot that he looked crazy.

One night, he tried to change our decision. I was sitting in the corner of the hut, trying to block out all the sounds of gunshots, when Lycidius dropped his gun and crouched beside me. He held my face and said, "I want to take it back. I don't care about the Law anymore, Snofrid." He pressed closer to me, holding me tight, and said, "I love you."

I knew he was just acting crazy because of all the death—we all were. He'd remember why we made our decision soon and I'd be hurt again. I started crying, and said, "Go away, Lycidius. Go away, or I'll order you to leave."

Lucian came to our hut three weeks after the wars began. He thought I'd been killed. I told him that I hadn't reported for work because of the fighting. He didn't forgive me, but he still gave me a blue shirt that was branded with the mark of a red viper, his symbol. No one tried to kill me as long as I wore it.

Finally, after five weeks, the Chancellor of Hollowstone addressed the insurgency. People in Vancastle had been complaining about the smoke and noise and had signed a petition, forcing him to meet with the Warden. In preparation for the meeting, the Swangunner district of the slums was blocked off by laser-wire. Stellar Ops units combed the area for days before his arrival; people who were caught in the red-zone were detained and questioned.

The day the Chancellor met with the Warden, Parisa went missing.

When Desya found out, something changed in his face. It was a shadow of the look Lycidius wore when he hurt people; I knew Desya would do anything to find her. Lycidius and Neko helped us search all day and when we found nothing, Desya offered to pay people the few coppers he had for information. This turned up nothing. So Desya went after the pimps. When they didn't answer his questions, he shot their fingers off or ripped out their teeth with pliers. Hurting them still didn't help—none of them knew where Parisa was. Desya became something horrible then. His mercy disappeared, and he surpassed even Lycidius in his violence. When the insurgency was put down, we expanded our search to every part of Gehenna. Desya believed she'd been kidnapped, but after three weeks, I believed she'd been killed.

We never found her body.

About a month after she went missing, Desya lost it. I found him in the hut, crying and telling me that it was his fault for failing to keep her safe. I tried to convince him that dying in Gehenna was no one's fault, but he wouldn't listen. After Desya passed out from exhaustion, I went to Ryuki's grave and cried too. I invoked the Promethia Flower, asking that it would allow Ryuki to help us from the afterlife.

The next day, Desya started breaking things. He awoke, raging in the night, and screamed so loud the neighbors threatened to shoot him. But I *couldn't* lose another person I loved. At this point, I knew I'd do anything to leave Gehenna forever.

Lycidius, who'd turned harder after I told him to leave, ignored the sadness. Instead of sitting with Desya, he made secret trips out of the slum and was sometimes gone for days, leaving Desya and Neko to protect me. When I asked him what he was doing, his face stayed as hard as a rock. He said, "I'll tell you when I do it."

It was three weeks before I turned sixteen when Lycidius burst through the door of our hut, breaking it off the hinge. He picked me up and hugged me so hard I couldn't breathe. Then, for the first time since I'd met him, he started crying. I was terrified that something had gone wrong and started crying too. But instead, he told me good news, and, as I listened, I knew that I was going to love him forever.

PART III

What You Fear Most

Fragments of memories floated around Snofrid like a sunlit ash cloud. Some memories were tangible; others were husks, darker than the patches between stars—Ryuki, tucking her into bed with storybooks; Lycidius, smiling at her from across the hut; Parisa, laughing as she raced Snofrid to their secret forest tower; Desya, rescuing her after she got stuck in a tree.

Snofrid tried to concentrate, to hone in on one single thought, but a sort of hot, pulsing stupor had settled over her, leaving her tongue flappy and her skull pounding. She wanted to vomit again. Her fingers dug into the mattress, twisting as she wept.

Desya, who'd been rooted at her bedside for almost an hour, caught her in his arms, saying calming words that only strengthened her urges to cry. She sobbed into his shirt until the skin beneath her eyes felt blistered. "Desya," she choked.

"It's okay, Sno. I'm here."

She clamped her arms around his neck, wanting to comfort him in return. The last image she recalled of her brother was his soot-dusted face streaked with tears as he screamed for his lost Parisa. All this had happened more than a year ago, but the memories were again fresh and she just wanted to hold him.

When she'd finally emerged from the Mania Mirror she'd lain paralyzed, vaguely conscious, with nothing but the feel of Desya's calloused hand to ground her in reality. As the paralysis lifted, she'd felt too nauseous to form words and vomited across the tatami mats. She'd managed to hug Desya, to embrace the overwhelming happiness that she felt at having him back. It seemed as if she'd just been snatched out of the jaws of a terrible fate—that if the Mania Mirror had somehow failed, countless moments, insights, and feelings would've remained unnamed and lost to her forever—she'd have lost herself.

"Where's Lycidius?" she said shakily.

"Asleep. He was awake for three days and just passed out."

Her eyes locked on the door. She ached to see him walk through it, to be here now and to tell her that he still loved her. That in spite of what they'd promised, or what was forbidden, they could love each other openly.

Desya pulled away, steadying her so she wouldn't fall over. "You weren't out that long, Sno. It's only Wednesday."

She managed a nod. Little mattered in the moment except finding answers to her remaining questions. Her attention caught on the chain around Desya's neck and, with a rickety hand, she pulled it from his collar. A welded band swayed from the end.

He eyed the ring guiltily, and she shook her head. "It's okay, Desya. I know why you lied."

He fisted the ring and dropped it back into his shirt. "No, it's not. I should've told you the truth days ago."

"If you had, I wouldn't have understood it. I might've judged you for marrying a human."

"But you won't now. That's all I care about."

The bedroom fixtures started to spin and she held onto his arm for balance. "Desya, I'll never judge you."

"I know, Sno." He propped her back against the wall. "But you need to rest or you're gonna fall over. How about we talk later?"

"No," she objected, a little hysterical. "I still don't understand everything. The mirror stopped showing me my life the day Lycidius got us out of Gehenna."

His forehead creased. "Damn. You're still missing about two years."

She closed her eyes, not wanting to think about the gaps right now, even though large and small holes speckled every tier of her mind. "I know it might be hard for you to talk about Parisa, but I didn't see what happened to her. She went missing…"

"She didn't go missing," he cut in. "She ran away."

Snofrid's eyes fluttered open. "What?"

"The day the Chancellor met the Warden, she broke through the security fence and was somehow able to get to him as he was deplaning. She made a scene in front of all the cameras, asking him for mercy and crying and stuff." He scratched a patch of stubble on his chin, his face betraying his regret. "She was never missing."

"What did the Chancellor do?"

"He let her squat in the Golden Circle as a publicity stunt. People called him the *Merciful Father* and other stupid things. After she turned eighteen, they had an affair. When it went public, his ratings took a nosedive. But guys that have the media up their sleeve never lose their sparkle. She started hosting charity events and funding political campaigns with the stacks she got from her clothing line. People eventually forgot that the Chancellor had a wife and now they all worship her like she's saved lives."

"But, Dez, you guys…you got married."

"Yeah, but everyone who knew about us is dead except you and Lycidius. We got married in secret; there was never any record that it even happened. What's my word against what people want to believe? Besides, it's not like I can tell anyone either way—the wedding was an Inborn ceremony."

She measured the resentment in his face and wondered if she was angrier than he was. "So, you're not mad anymore?"

His nostrils flared. "Of course I'm mad. I'm mad as hell." He leaned back, his jaw popping as he worked the muscles. "I'll never be obligated to take her back, but I can't be with anyone else."

Snofrid rocked onto her knees. "Yes, you can, Dez. You said it yourself: No one knows you're married. Which means Inborn Law can't punish you if you leave her."

Desya looked her in the eye with quiet intensity. "Sno, you don't mean that, do you?"

Her face flushed and she puffed up with shame. She'd only made the suggestion because Parisa was human and Snofrid hadn't considered their union to be a traditional Inborn marriage. In a traditional Inborn marriage, spouses remained together for life. Most of the time, a Covenant Spell was even raised to ensure fidelity. But, being too poor back then, Desya and Parisa hadn't been able to afford a Covenant Spell.

She faced Desya, who was still watching her expectantly. Despite Parisa's actions, he'd never talked badly about her, and he also continued to wear the ring she'd given him on a chain around his neck. Snofrid glanced at the ring, glittering in the lamplight, and wondered if her brother still loved his wife. "Did you ever talk to Parisa?"

"I tried, a couple times actually, but she wouldn't see me."

"You should've told the guards you were her husband. That would've got their attention." As she swayed onto her feet, Snofrid suddenly became aware of the wet diaper she was wearing. "Oh my gosh, Dez...tell me *you* put this on me."

"Yeah. But I swear I didn't look."

Heat flared in her cheeks. "I believe you." She shuffled to her dresser and gathered a clean pair of pajamas. "I'm feeling a little better, so I'm going to shower and change quickly. Don't leave."

"How about I get some food?"

Her stomach burned. "Please bring a lot."

In the bathroom, Snofrid cranked the hot water, steaming up the shower curtain and the mirror. For a long while, she stood under the scorching water, washing off the sweat and filth from her dark journey. Tears broke from her eyes and mingled with the water. Her pain was raw, unappeased by time. The things she'd seen in the mirror felt new. Yet she still felt as if she'd aged years, as if the girl who'd been sold into Master Mookjai's trafficking ring was a shadow in her periphery.

With each passing second, she missed Lycidius more, resented their situation more. What would he say if she spoke to him now? Would he reconsider if she appealed to him? Sadness filled her at the thought. Before she'd gone into the mirror, he'd been adamant about holding to their original choice to stay apart. Remembering changed nothing—only Inborn Law could change it. But the Law was inviolable. She covered her face with her hands, feeling helpless.

Drying her eyes, she dressed and then gazed into the mirror at the face she now recognized. Her skin was pale, puffy from tears. Forcing herself to accept the gaps the Mania Mirror had left behind was difficult. They were like tiny mouths, gobbling up bits of her existence. Fortunately, the mirror had returned her family to her, but without all the pieces of her past, she couldn't view the full picture. There was only one gap which required no explanation: Atlas Bancroft. Being heartbroken from Lycidius, she felt sure she'd dated him in an effort to move on.

"Ryuki mentioned that my uncle secretly assigned Lycidius to be my Shadow," she said as she left the bathroom. Desya was crouched on the tatami mats with a feast of bento boxes scattered around him. Easing herself into a sitting position, she picked up a glass of water. "Who is my uncle?"

"I'll tell you," Desya said, fiddling with his chopsticks. "But just know that you're not going to like everything I say."

"I didn't like everything I saw in the mirror, but I'm still thankful for every detail, Dez."

"This is a little different." He paused a moment, assuming a grave air. "Your birth parents weren't like mine. Your real father's name was Ludendorff Vondrak."

Her hand jerked, spilling water across her hand. "Dez...*Don't* mess around."

"I'm not. I wouldn't tease about something like this, Snofrid. Your uncle is Drakkar Vondrak, the Mystish Lord."

Her face paled and she battled this idea with all her will, completely slamming her mind shut to it; but the effort was like trying to plug up a bucket of holes. His words spilled out, rushing all around her, forcing her to act. "If...if my father married a human, then how wasn't Lord Drakkar shamed, too? The disgrace should've affected the whole family."

"They kept you hidden," Desya explained. "When Ludendorff died, Lord Drakkar couldn't look out for you, so he asked Ryuki to do it. After all that crap with Mandek Skala, Lord Drakkar pulled Lycidius from his Dracuslayer unit and quietly assigned him to be your Shadow."

Snofrid thought about the two men who'd walked her from her bedroom to the library at the end of each month. From his House Insignia, she guessed that the man with the silver eyes and the Mohawk had been Lord Drakkar. It made sense why he'd send her away; he would've been stripped of his lordship if his brother's shame had become known. She shivered in cold terror; her existence threatened the entire Vondrak family and would plunge the Mystish Lord Office into scandal. Unbelievable in itself was that her uncle had allowed her to live.

Snofrid's fingers juddered on her water glass as she turned to Desya. "Before I talk to Lycidius, I have one more question."

"Sure."

"Why did Atlas and I break up?"

Desya thought a while. He rubbed the bridge of his nose resignedly, as if he was struggling to give a straight answer. "I don't know, Sno. Sometimes things just don't work out. You guys still keep in touch, though. He gave you a couple numbers to reach him if you ever needed a favor."

She found no satisfaction in this reply. Broken bridges lingered, ones she needed facts to rebuild. She felt that truth alone could offer her closure, but only she could find it, somewhere in the shadows of her mind. Bracing herself on the bed, she wobbled to her feet. "When Lycidius wakes up, please tell him I'll be waiting for him in the basement."

Snofrid sat on the basement couch, staring absently into the gravel ripples of the zen garden. Each line flowed with faultless harmony, never interrupted. It provided to the garden a sense of openness, of possibility, and she found herself envying it. Ryuki had once told her that the way people observed the world, by the senses, was deceptive. He said that people should strive to arrive at a state of emptiness and only in that aspiration could undiluted peace be reached; it was the sole purpose of his meditations, and the result was supposed to leave the mind undisturbed by desires. According to his philosophy, desires were intrinsically negative and shook the mind off balance. But in her position, emptiness was unnecessary. Without Lycidius, she already felt empty.

At the sound of footsteps on the staircase, she clasped her hands in her lap, her heart beating like a drum. Lycidius rounded the bend, his boots disturbing the gravel ripples. She regarded him with a sidelong glance. He moved urgently, the chords in his neck tight.

Steeling herself, she raised her head and found his eyes awaiting hers. Slowly his widened; she understood why. She was *truly* seeing him for the first time since Desya and Neko had brought her home from Gehenna. She was seeing him as the boy who'd followed her around Gehenna, who'd carved her wooden bracelets, who'd confided to her his secrets. The boy who'd fallen in love with her and she with him. Unlike yesterday, his face was now naked of conviction. The certainty he'd possessed before she'd entered the Mania Mirror had completely drained away.

A pang racked her chest as he hastened toward her, his face lit with expectation. She tensed, fearing to greet him with joy. If she did, how then could she control what she felt?

When he rounded the couch, she was unable to restrain herself any longer. She stood and hugged him. His reaction was immediate and overpowering. She'd never felt so suffocated, yet so protected. He held her as if she might dissolve through his arms. She missed him. Violently. And it made the moment absurdly harder than she'd imagined. All at once, she locked horns with her desire to toss aside their promises. She threw herself into the fight to crush it. But she was already on the brink of crumbling smaller than the pebbles beneath her feet.

He said nothing, which she was grateful for. But as the moments passed, he gripped her tighter and tighter. She knew what he was thinking; she was thinking it too. Like during the Midwinter Insurgency, he wanted to find a way around Shadow Law. She'd thought it through already. Before he'd come, she'd strained to find a balance between what she wanted and what was right. *A lawful solution.* But there were no loopholes. The question of being lovers was devoid of middle ground. In this realization, regret and frustration ran through her as painfully as the day she and Lycidius had first agreed to stay friends. She knew what was right, and loving him while he was her Shadow was unmistakably wrong.

Furthermore, she'd discovered a separate, even greater issue they'd never considered before, something they'd both overlooked. She was a halfbreed, which meant that even if there was a way around Shadow Law, being together would shame him. It would strip him of his choice to rejoin the Inborn Army and would bar him from ever reentering society. He'd be an outcast and his pride would be ruined. Letting him lose face for the sake of love wasn't love. It was greed.

When she was finally able to step away from him, his hands became rigid, his face almost pleading. "Snofrid."

She made no response. If she said anything, she'd break down. One final time, she gave her love to him through her eyes, pouring all and everything she felt into a single gaze. Then she let go.

A Thumb for a Thumb

Thursday, 8 Days until the Hunt

Snofrid watched snowflakes flurry around the skyscrapers from behind the War Lobby register. Since dawn, holiday shoppers had flooded the sidewalks. Every tree in the plaza was festooned in twinkle lights and each lamppost donned a big red bow. The festive aura left her feeling homesick. The last human holiday she remembered celebrating had been spent in the Iliuzija Club, playing cat-and-mouse with Lucian's nieces, while feasting on tart cranberry pudding and honey kvass. She'd been fifteen. Men in Gehenna rarely took a girl's age into account; however, Lucian had been an exception. He had no inhibitions about a lot of things, but acted relatively just and chivalrous towards the people he respected. He'd never even permitted one of his Swangunners to tell her a lewd joke. That they were no longer friends left her feeling at a loss. She knew first-hand that he spared no mercy for people who let him down. That *she* now fell into this category wasn't only frightening, but downright unexpected.

"It's about to start again," Jazara hollered from the rug. She was cradling Snofrid's pet rat, Quibble, and blowing bubbles with her gum. "I bet two coppers that South Africa will win this time."

"I'm betting five on Japan," Snofrid countered. On the wall television, the 2052 *Sky-Tri Olympics* was airing. A screen behind two talk show hosts showed reruns of Russia's victory in the flying-transport race.

"Actually, if South Africa wins, can I stay over tonight?" Jazara asked.

"If your house mother says it's okay, then sure. We can play a game with Dez."

Jazara's face brightened. "I'll send her words."

Snofrid smiled and continued issuing a refund for *Sterling Suppliers*, a private company she'd failed to send a shipment of filters to on time. Not a moment later, a Louve Perfume advertisement hit the screen; her mood soured at the sight of Parisa, dressed like the Greek goddess of beauty, Aphrodite. She was lying on a mound of cushions in a crew of bare, oily chested men. Silky black hair spilled down her shoulders and onto a crystal bottle of perfume she held in her palm. With a slow, seductive smile, she glided off the cushions, parting the ranks of men.

"Wear *Séduire* with purpose," she said. "Spray *Séduire* with confidence." She pinched the perfume nozzle, releasing a puff against her neck. She sighed contentedly. "*Love Louve.*"

"Do you think I'm pretty?" Jazara asked.

"You're pretty and smart," Snofrid said, ignoring the television. "Why are you asking?"

"I want to be pretty like Parisa Namdar someday, so Dez will want to marry me when I'm older."

Snofrid knew this wasn't possible. "You shouldn't marry a guy just because he thinks you're pretty. You'll have wrinkles someday, Jazara."

"I know," Jazara sighed. She scratched the rat's belly and then made a beseeching face. "Don't tell Dez about my plan. I don't want him to laugh at me."

"He wouldn't laugh. But I promise anyway."

Jazara let Quibble scurry onto the rug and sprang to her feet. "I'm gonna go get another cocoa. Do you want one?"

"No thanks, I have tea," Snofrid said, tapping her mug of *Kocha* black tea.

"I'll get a cookie for Dez then."

As Jazara ran across the street to the Sun Wheel Café, Snofrid checked her phone inbox: no messages from Lycidius, just a few from various human friends. Since yesterday, he hadn't left his workshop—not that work mattered when they were leaving the city—but she understood it was a needed distraction. He had an astounding ability to hyper-focus. From the way he'd explained it when they were children, his brain could reach such a point of concentration that everything left his mind but his present task. It was as if his problems didn't exist as long as he was occupied. Or so he claimed.

A rush of air signaled the antechamber was in use. Snofrid glanced up, surprised Jazara had returned so soon, and saw a pair of badger-grey eyes staring at her from behind the glass.

"Hello, mieloji," Lucian said.

She kicked back her chair with a gasp. Grabbing the machine pistol from under the counter, she stumbled from behind the desk, just as the antechamber doors slid open. Her eyes zeroed in on the panic room. Letting out a frantic cry, she yanked open the door and skidded inside on her knees. The door slammed shut, locks clicking in place. Snofrid scrambled to steady her breathing, but her gut was so twisted she felt she might spit up her lunch.

"Your death would be prettier out here, mieloji," Lucian called. "If I decide to torch the shop, that room will heat up like a girl-sized oven."

"This has a cooling system, Lucian. Burn it and it'll feel like I'm in the tropics."

"I want to see you. Come up to the window."

"No, you're not in control this time."

A gunshot went off, so loud it sounded like a wrecking ball had shattered the wall. She peered out the spy grate. Lucian stood on the rug, his deadly A12 assault shotgun pointed at a furry stain of smoking blood. She winced. *Quibble.*

Lucian studied her, his face hungry. He appeared to be outfitted for a funeral in a crisp black dress-shirt and trousers.

"Come out, or next time the price will be greater," he warned.

"Why? Are you going to try to knock me with your words?"

He made a 'tsk' sound. "You speak like these sarcastic Americans. It doesn't suit you."

"You can't take advantage of me anymore. I'm not a naïve little girl."

"Too bad." He withdrew a silver cigarette case from his pocket. "In Gehenna, you were an innocent—the only one among thousands. I admired you for that. But without it, you're just another trick."

She groped the trigger of her pistol uneasily. "Only you would think like that, Lucian. I'm not like you. I'd never try to murder a friend."

"Our friendship deal is done, mieloji. You took care of that all by yourself. I held out my hand and you cut it off."

"You didn't leave me a choice."

"Wrong," he said firmly. "We always play with fair rules. I made the mistake of treating you with more respect than I should have." He lit his cigarette with a blowtorch lighter, his jaw clinched. "You spat in my face."

She glared at his scarred face, trembling against those grey eyes that had once been merciful. "I was never ungrateful," she said. "Rejecting your marriage proposal *wasn't* ungrateful—I just didn't love you."

He checked the clock. "Enough. We've been over this."

"Then what now?"

"We negotiate. We do a new deal." He moved forward but stopped short. Lifting his boot, he saw the chewing gum. Frowning, he scraped it off with his gun and wiped it on the counter. "The bubble-gum chewer looked happy when she left. Think about her before you refuse."

"Don't you *dare*, Lucian! This is between us!"

"When men disagree, innocent people die. Such is life."

A jingling sound drew her attention to the phone on the register; Desya or Lycidius was calling.

Lucian swiped up the phone and held it to his ear. "Alio," he said in Lithuanian. Shaking his head, he flicked the ash from his cigarette. "Ne. Viso gero."

He tossed the phone onto the counter and dragged a chair before the panic room, the screech of its legs like nails on metal. Sitting down, he scrunched his black leather gloves. "Your brother and the redhead are wondering if you're dead. They'll be here in twenty minutes, but that's time enough to be thorough."

Snofrid grappled for calm. The minute Desya and Lycidius entered the antechamber they'd be gunned down—unless she got him first. Laying down her machine pistol, she powered on the computer inside the panic room. The holographic target mesh materialized before her. "I don't want to shoot you, Lucian, but I swear I will if you don't get out."

Lucian looked up at a clicking sound. A slot had opened in the ceiling and the muzzle of a very large minigun glared down at him. He eyed the gun for a moment and then said, "Shoot me, mieloji, and you'll have eight-hundred Swangunners baying for blood."

She closed her eyes, trying to think. *Don't be stupid, Snofrid.* Killing him was the worst plan. *Eight days.* Last night, Lycidius had recontacted the Empyrean City with a Transmission Globe, confirming that the Sky-Legion would attack in eight days. If she killed Lucian, she, Lycidius and Desya would have a bounty on their heads that would attract every desperado in the city.

"You're quiet," Lucian observed. "What's on your mind?"

"My family."

"Good girl. This is how we closed a deal last time."

A Swangunner slid into the shop suddenly, swishing his crusty pink trench coat. He hissed, baring his bloody gums at Snofrid and then swung his hog-head gasmask over one shoulder. She recoiled. He rotated his crooked jaw, craning his neck as if to better display his pimpled skin which was strewn with purple blood vessels. Pink liberty spikes, matching the pink of his contact lenses, shot from his head. Snofrid knew him: *Cannibal Brongo,* the infamous Child Executioner of Gehenna.

Brongo opened his mouth, uncurling a pink tongue past his chin. "Yum. Yum," he croaked. "Baby bird's trapped in a cage." He wiggled his tongue. "Baby bird's gonna taste gooood in my mouth."

"Keep wishing, Brongo," she called. "The last door you tried to open nearly cost you your face."

He rubbed the shrapnel scars along his jaw. "Baby bird's got to come out sometime," he snarled. "And I'll be here when she does."

She took a breath, telling herself to calm down before she said something thoughtless. In her peripheral, she counted at least ten more Swangunners stationed behind the register window. The streets had cleared—the chainsaw, flame thrower, and gasoline hose guns held by the Swangunners were probably the cause of that.

"This street is lined with security cameras," she pointed out. "This isn't Gehenna; try anything in Vancastle, Lucian, and you'll regret it, no matter how many friends you think you have."

"You have too little faith in money, mieloji. The cameras went dark fifteen minutes ago. No police will arrest me if I decide to kill you. Not when I purchased your life."

"Maybe for a day," she granted. "But if you were going to hurt me, you would've done it already."

"Lengthening pain suits me better. You know this." He poured a cup of tea from the Japanese teahouse. "What suits you, Brongo?"

"Baby bird legs. Baby bird eyes. Baby bird liver."

"Thin-Man prefers Columbian neckties," Lucian went on. "Meeks likes to use a tongue tearer."

"What's your new deal?" Snofrid demanded.

"Good girl." He balanced the teacup on his knee. "The Warden wants something from Atlas Bancroft. You'll contact him about his safe deposit box in the *Forsberg Bank and Trust*. Then you'll deliver me the verbal and numeric access codes, a voice recording, and a palm print."

"How am I supposed to call him with the shield up all over the city?" she almost shouted.

"I won't help you this time. It's *your* deed to do. That means you use your resources." Lucian chucked his cigarette butt into a flower pot. "Start with your brother, the bluecoat."

"He's only an Eighth Star. He doesn't have the clearance to get through."

"Then this is your first test. Find another way."

She saw no other way. Atlas would probably not even take her call if she did find a way. There were the high-powered computers in the Spyderweb, but Hadrian would have his own price. For even the tiniest favor, she was certain he'd make her pay sevenfold.

"And if I can't?" she asked.

"Baby's bird's gonna loooose its legs," Brongo barked.

"Quiet," Lucian scolded. He turned to Snofrid. "If you can't, then Brongo, Thin-Man and Meeks will bring their toys to your house."

"How long do I have?"

"Seven days. This is fair." He snapped open his cigarette case, his tone severe. "Don't disappoint me, mieloji."

She stared at the metacarpal bone strung around his neck as he lit up another cigarette, and nausea swooped in around her. He wasn't like normal humans. Chivalrous or not, he'd never break his mold as a cold-blooded murderer. "I used to believe that you cared about me, but now I know better."

"You never knew me, mieloji. You only pretended that you did."

Maybe he was right. Maybe every favor he'd ever done had merely been down payments for her future affections. Either way, she hoped that she hadn't misjudged Atlas as she'd done with Lucian. Otherwise, she might as well buy herself a pine box. "All right. I agree to your terms, Lucian, so please leave now."

"No." He stood. "The deal is still too sweet. A thumb for a thumb, mieloji. You spilled my blood, now I spill hers."

Snofrid's head snapped to the antechamber as Jazara hurried inside, holding a cup of cocoa and a sugar cookie. "No. Jazara! *run!*" she yelled.

Jazara dropped her cup in a fright. Brongo swiped her up, pinning her arms to her sides, and carried her toward Lucian.

Kicking and thrashing, she screamed, "LET ME GO!"

"Lucian, *please*," Snofrid shouted. "I swear I'll do anything. I'm begging you, don't hurt her."

"I want nothing more from you, mieloji. This price the girl will pay." He pulled a pair of bolt-cutters from his chest-rig harness. "If you come out or if you look away, I'll kill her."

"Sno, who are these men?" Jazara cried, her voice quavering. She stared at the bolt-cutters and her face paled. "Snofrid, I'm scared!"

A jolt of fear ripped through Snofrid, thrusting her into a fit of panic. Once more, she accessed the ceiling gun. "Touch her and I'll shoot you!" she threatened.

"Pull the trigger and you'll be killing her along with your family," Lucian warned. He held the nose of his shotgun to Jazara's skull. "This fires five 12-gauge shots per second. Her head will look like a watermelon dropped from the Trinity Tower."

"Okay, don't." Snofrid held up her empty hands. "I won't shoot. I s-swear."

"I know you won't, mieloji." Lucian grabbed Jazara's wrist and slid the bolt-cutters around her thumb.

"Don't cut it off," Jazara sobbed. "Please, please, please!"

He tipped up her chin with his thumbless hand. "Learn to control your own pain and you'll fear nothing," he promised. "Now…look at my eyes."

"No!" she screamed, her cheeks streaming with tears. Kicking harder, she tried to wriggle free. "Snofrid, help me!"

Snofrid pushed her fists into the door in her helplessness. "Jazara, I'm sorry," she called out. "I'm so sorry!"

"Every time I do a deal, I understand there is chance I might die," Lucian told Jazara. "I accept there could be pain and I tell myself that I want it." He nodded. "Tell yourself you want it."

"I don't want it, I don't want it," Jazara moaned.

"I want it," Brongo screeched, wiggling his tongue. "I want it bad."

Lucian clamped together the bolt-cutters, slicing clean through the bone, and the thumb dropped to the floor. Jazara shrieked so loud her face flushed red. She buckled against Brongo's chest and her head flipped back over his arms. Lucian plunked the severed thumb into his teacup with a splash, then, holding the bolt-cutters between his teeth, fired up his blow torch.

"Keep her still," he mumbled to Brongo.

Jazara fainted as he cauterized the wound while Snofrid stared wide-eyed through the spy-grate. For a moment she felt like she was standing at the Gehenna loading docks, gazing down at Ryuki's half-eaten remains. Heaviness pulsed around her, curbing the airflow in her lungs. She stepped back, hands falling limp at her sides, and started to sob.

Brongo laid Jazara on the rug while Lucian switched off the blowtorch. "Seven days," he called, fitting on a black viper-head gasmask. "This is the last deal I'll do."

He strode into the antechamber, passing off the bolt-cutters to Brongo. The Swangunner licked the blood off the jaws before he strapped on his hog-head gasmask and they both vanished into the snowfall.

By nightfall, the temperature had plummeted. The streets were deserted except for a dozen sweeper machines plowing snow from the roads. Above, grey clouds veiled the stars, showing only the moon glistening in a spot of naked sky.

Snofrid stood before the kitchen stove, monitoring a pot of steeping witch hazel leaves. Green froth flowed across the leaves, bubbling into thick foam and wafting an earthy aroma. Her eyes blurred as she pulled on a pair of oven mittens. Throughout the day, she'd periodically flashbacked to what Lucian had done. At each recollection, she reflexively cupped her hands over her head. Her eyes had grown sore from crying.

Since leaving the War Lobby, Jazara had ignored Snofrid. She only spoke to Desya and refused to go anywhere alone. Snofrid accepted the full blame for what Lucian had done to Jazara and held off from defending herself.

When the witch hazel had boiled, Snofrid brought the concentrate to Desya as a disinfectant for Jazara's wound. He was at the kitchen table, changing the gauze dressing, and masterfully disguising his anger.

"Okay," he said to Jazara. "Don't look, I'm pulling the bandage off."

"I want to see this time," Jazara argued.

"All right. If you close your eyes, I'll give you ten coppers to buy that basket for your bike."

Jazara sucked in her breath. "Deal."

Snofrid left a syringe of morphine sulfate on the table and retrieved her gasmask before taking a walk alone around the engawa—a roofed corridor that bordered the mansion like a porch. The engawa outcropped a hill-and-pond garden; its evergreens, hedges and flowers had wasted under the biting breath of winter. A light snow was falling, piling up on the frozen water.

Her gaze gradually dipped to the floorboards and she stared until she could no longer see the cracks. Covering her face with her gloves, she cried into her gasmask in short, puffy breaths. *I know it's my fault,* she admitted. *But what else could I have done? Lucian would've killed her if I'd moved.*

"You shouldn't be so upset over what happened, Snofrid."

She lowered her hands. The sight of Lycidius walking through the dim engawa sent even profounder regret rolling through her. He was just a few feet away; she wouldn't dare touch him, though she longed to. She suddenly prayed that time would lessen the way she felt, because nothing else, not even her healing ability, could. He'd stay by her side, shadowing her like a part of her, constantly reminding her of what was beyond her reach.

He appeared taller in the low corridor—the ears of his jackal gasmask grazed the ceiling—and his jacket collar was flipped down, showing his neck tree tattoo. He acted far more collected than he'd been that afternoon. He'd broken through the skylight in the War Lobby like an assassin, armed with an automatic rifle, only to find her and Jazara alone, both in tears.

"I can't help being upset," Snofrid said. "Not after what I watched Lucian do to her."

Lycidius held up a tablet he'd brought with him. "I watched the store footage and you did what you could. Lucian gave you no choice but to stay in the panic room. Don't let Jazara's pain guilt-trip you into thinking the thumb was your fault."

"Her pain isn't guilt-tripping me. I wish it was only that, but it's not. It *is* my fault."

"No," he contested. "Jazara is a child. Avoiding responsibility is what children do."

Snofrid looked to the louvered windows, concerned that Jazara might be eavesdropping. The last thing she needed was to feel like losing her thumb was her fault. "We grew up with different perspectives of life. I know that, Lycidius. But would you have said the same thing to me if my thumb was snipped off with bolt-cutters?"

"I always told you what I truly thought, Snofrid." He stayed at a distance, resting his hand on the railing. She couldn't see his face through his mask; she wanted it to be conflicted. He'd always warred with himself over how to react in times like these. Usually, he wreaked bloody revenge on the perpetrator; right now, she just wanted him to be compassionate to Jazara.

"I was four when I became a Dracuslayer," he went on, as if to prove a point. "Part of our training was basic aptitude skills. My unit's captain would stab us and leave us to stitch up the wound or we'd die. The children who needed sympathy lasted until they bled out." Caution strengthened his tone. "If you and Desya keep coddling her, she'll never be able to take care of herself. Sooner or later, people need to grow up, Snofrid. Jazara needs to right now."

"Yes, she does need to grow up," Snofrid agreed. The wind blustered, jingling the garden wind chimes. "But not all people are built to be soldiers. Jazara isn't—I'm not, either. Some people need understanding to grow, not knives in their stomachs."

"You're right. There's nothing wrong with giving children a little bit of understanding," he granted, "but too much causes damage. If you indulge people's weaknesses too often, they'll start to expect it. And then they'll give into self-pity and become a victim." He shook his head. "If Ryuki had done that to you, you never would've survived Gehenna."

A tear spilled from her eye. "If you have children, will you raise them that way?"

He hesitated. Then, recovering, he replied decisively. "If I ever have children, they won't be dependent, Snofrid. From a young age, they'll be fully capable of caring for themselves. In this world, teaching children survival skills early on would be the greatest kindness."

She suddenly thought of Ryuki. Every ounce of affection he'd given her, she cherished. But she was also appreciative for the times when he left her to do things on her own. Despite agreeing with Lycidius to an extent, she wanted to change the subject. "We need to figure out a plan," she reminded, "for Lucian."

Lycidius let go of the railing with a nod. "We're going to disappear. He'll most likely put a tail on you, so we'll split up and set a meet point under the city. The humans will suspect us and the people we know of being Inborns if we go missing today, so we'll leave the night before the Sky-Legion flies in."

"What about finding a way to call Atlas?" she suggested.

"No. If there was a way to get a technological transmission out, I would've done it."

She didn't feel much confidence in hiding. "I don't think we should run."

"It's our only choice."

"Even if it is, I'm worried about someone getting hurt again." She leaned against the railing, staring into the frosted flower beds. "Next time, it could be worse than a thumb."

As was typical, Lycidius acknowledged the danger of their position objectively. "Don't waste your energy, Snofrid. Bad things will happen whether you worry about them or not."

"I know they will, but we can at least try to prevent it."

His eyepieces tilted toward her hands as she tugged at her gloves. "I know what I said wasn't what you wanted to hear. I'm sorry. I was only trying to be straight about it."

She turned away from the railing, frowning. "What did you say?"

"I said I was trying to be straight about what happened." He paused. "So if I said something to make you feel worse, I'm sorry."

She felt thrown. For years, she'd never seen him convey even the slightest hint of regret. So when had he started apologizing? Had he outgrown his unwillingness to comprise, too? Still reeling, she wondered what other traits of his had changed over the past two years—the years she hadn't remembered. Pondering the possibilities was tormenting. She wanted back every moment they'd had.

"It's fine, I'm not upset," she assured. "But when did you—"

"I first apologized about a year ago," he answered. He lingered, as if thinking back on the moment. "You were surprised then, too."

She wished she could remember it.

Lycidius glanced skyward, and she followed his gaze to the energy shield. It glowed like an ocean over the city, bathing their clothes in blue. For a short while, she stood alongside him, silent and growing evermore hopeful. Even without asking, she knew they were both in expectation of the same thing: seeing the shield fall.

An hour later, in her bedroom, Snofrid laced on a pair of hiking boots. Due to the weather, the hike to the Spyderweb for her briefing with Hadrian would be treacherous. All the blackness of the day had brightened with Lycidius's apology, until a few minutes ago, when she'd recalled her duty. Now she just had to find a way to slip out of the mansion unseen.

When she was bundled up in a winter coat, she eyed the photo of her and Lycidius on her computer desktop; it had been taken at the Hollowstone shooting range. In spite of his plan to hide, she knew that her only realistic option in dealing with Lucian was to fulfill their bargain: she would make a trade with Hadrian to use his phone in the Spyderweb. Lucian had been generous in giving her seven days, but the Sky-Legion was arriving in eight. She couldn't afford to go into hiding; if she hadn't delivered by that time, she, Desya, Lycidius, and Jazara would be hunted down by a Swangunner army in the next twenty-four hours—the same twenty-four hours that she'd sworn to spend hunting the welx.

The Stygian War

The clock chimes echoed six through the house.

Snofrid scanned the kitchen from her loft window. Desya and Jazara had traded their Mancala game at the table for video games in the washitsu, and Lycidius was cleaning guns in the garage. This was her chance. She stole into the basement and rode the elevator to ground level.

Hooting ricocheted through the forest. Cocking her pistol, she peered up through the crowded saplings at the clouds. The dew had frozen, caking bark in ice and encrusting ferns, nettles and poisonous foliage. No wind blew; not even a squirrel scurried across a twig. The forest looked dead except for the whites of a Dracuslayer's eyes. His rugged brown skin blended with the trees.

"Don't be afraid," he called coolly. "I'm here as an escort. I'll be your guardian until the end of the hunt. My House name is Bourkan but address me as Dracuslayer Coyote."

"I know who you are," she said. "I read your file."

"You were given my name and a list of facts. You don't know who I am."

He advanced, moving with the dexterity of a hunter, and propped his bo staff on one shoulder. A blue robe swished around his calves when he moved, identical to the color of his fitted trousers and tall leather boots. His breastplate was imprinted with his House insignia—six forks of black lightning—and, on his shoulders, a dusky fur mantle kept the frost off his pauldron. Strands of his blond hair were entangled in the bronze facial armor that plated his forehead and cheeks. She noted his eyes, twitching as if their lids were full of sand, and wondered if he had some kind of disorder.

He tilted his staff at her satchel and added, "I smell acid. Open the bag."

"I brought an acid grenade in case I ran into a bonecopse."

"That's why I'm here," he informed, holding out a scarred hand. "You don't need to be armed in the Spyderweb." She surrendered the grenade. "Let's move. Walk on my left side."

Snofrid stepped into formation. She kept an eye on his arm as they hiked, wondering at the blackish-white substance glittering on his wrist. It looked organic. Occasionally, a ripple of what looked like electrical static glided down his hands to his fingertips.

"You're expected to be on standby at all times," Coyote told her after they'd crossed the creek. "My commanding officer tried to contact you yesterday and was unable to reach you."

Snofrid had anticipated this would be brought up. "I couldn't answer my phone. I was inside a Mania Mirror."

Coyote raised a brow but didn't comment. "This mission is your top priority; everything else is irrelevant. You'll find a way to be on call until the shield falls. Understood?"

She nodded, suppressing her frustration. "Yes, Dracuslayer Coyote. Understood."

"If it happens again, you'll be disciplined," he warned. "You don't want to go there, take my word for it."

A half-mile later, the branches of the black tree emerged from the fog. They descended into the bunker in silence. Once in the atrium, Coyote pointed out a passage overhung with roots. "Commander Hadrian will brief you in the Canvass Chamber. Go into the tunnel. Hessia will guide you from there."

Snofrid headed toward passage. No sooner had she crossed the threshold, then Hessia's hypnotic voice, which, according to her file, had the telepathic range of a mile, strummed through her mind.

"I'm assisting you because my master commands it," Hessia informed. *"But it lowers me to even address you, halfbreed."*

"I already know what you think," Snofrid said, shuddering as she flashed back to the erupting pain of the Seer's paralysis. She scanned the vast passage, then the mildew-matted ceiling, making sure the Seer wasn't hiding anywhere inside. "But your opinions don't bother me."

"If you had any self-respect, my opinions would compel you to act. Honorable Inborns commit suicide rather than live as abominations."

Snofrid cringed at her words. It was true: many halfbreeds committed suicide rather than endure a life of shame. However, she refused to do it, not because she was afraid, but because she didn't despise either of her natures.

She switched on her Taser flashlight at a fork in the tunnel. "Tell me which way," she said to Hessia. "But if you lead me into a dead-end, know that I'll blame you for being late."

"Oh, but it's easy to get lost down here—even for the practiced navigator. Some get lost in these tunnels for weeks...without food, without water."

Snofrid scrunched her fingers around her flashlight. "You won't do anything to me. You need me to be your bait."

"Before the hunt we do, but not afterwards." Hessia hissed, like a deflating tire. *"After the hunt, I'm going to kill you, halfbreed. I'm going to scalp off your Halo with my teeth and bring it to the Empyrean City as tribute."*

Snofrid's last fuse blew out. "I'm helping you kill the welx. Isn't that ENOUGH?"

"Even if you laid down your life for me, it wouldn't be enough. You'd still be filth."

Snofrid's animosity toward the Seer busted its restraints, like an incensed dog. According to the Covenant, Hessia couldn't touch her until the welx was destroyed. But Snofrid was determined not to stick around that long.

Hurrying, she turned down a corkscrew staircase hewn from rock. At the bottom, she tottered into a cave with a buffed marble floor.

"Cross the bridge at the end of the hall."

Snofrid looked down at a rock pool as she crossed. Hessia continued to lead her through a number of drafty tunnels that descended for what felt like ten minutes. By the time Snofrid had descended her third staircase, she suspected that the Seer was leading her astray.

"How much farther?" she demanded.

"When you reach the end of this next tunnel, turn right. The Canvass Chamber is through the Mock Wall."

"There are two kinds of Mock Walls," Snofrid pointed out. "Which kind is it?"

"The kind that desolidifies in intervals. You'll have five seconds to run through the rock, no longer, or you'll be crushed inside."

"You're a liar," Snofrid accused. "The longest setting on a Mock Wall is three seconds."

"I won't confirm or deny."

Snofrid defied the impulse to falter. This fact about Mock Walls she knew for certain. It was stored away in her memories, unspoiled by magic.

Foraging onward, she channeled her focus on her impending task. If she could win Hadrian's compassion, she just might earn her phone call to Atlas. The tricky detail was that Hadrian didn't seem to respond to anything. He simply demanded obedience and forced submission. She tried not to let this kill her nerve. Even after being exposed to his manipulations, she wanted to believe that in every living being, no matter how perverse, there existed a trigger for empathy. Otherwise, she couldn't fully believe that all the people she cared about would survive the quarantine.

At the end of the tunnel she positioned herself before a craggy wall, her left foot out in front.

"Use your defiled Halo to access the passage," Hessia instructed. *"There is a seal on the upper left-hand side."*

Snofrid located the seal—a roaring wyvern subtly embossed into the stone. She hiked up her coat sleeve. The reedy strands of her Halo glinted blue on the flesh of her bicep. Pressing her Halo to the seal, she held still until she heard a click. Then, she lunged through the rock as if it were air.

She emerged in a dome. The cold air hit her like a freezer draft. She slipped, skidding on the icy floor, and snagged a dangling root.

"You're on your own now," Hessia told her. *"Don't touch the water."*

Snofrid glanced down. She was standing on a black coral path that roved through a maze of iridescent silver pools. Further down, was a table built from living trees with all their trunks bowed and knotted together. Arranged on top were two black wineglasses—one full and one empty—a tiny marble orb and a tall bottle of alcohol with a dead cobra floating inside.

Hadrian was enthroned at the table's head, his claws interlaced as he stared absently into one of the silver pools. He didn't seem to notice her presence, or if he did, chose to ignore it. A black velvet cloak with a silver fur collar arrayed his shoulders. His hair was neat, slicked back, and wet, as if recently washed. Looking at him now, her original impression of him being an indomitable, mighty soul metamorphosed. Since journeying through the Mania Mirror, she'd viewed the world through new eyes, ones with richer vision. What she saw presently was a man embittered by life's failings—a rock shaped by a merciless, crushing tide.

As she advanced, she felt like she was sharing a room with a statue. He hadn't moved, even as she reached the chair. Then he tipped his chin slowly.

"You're late," he said.

"I know, Commander. But fault your Seer."

His eyes flicked skyward, as if he knew Hessia was lurking in the chamber above them. "This briefing will end in twenty-six minutes. Have a seat at the table."

Snofrid slid into one of the open chairs, counseling herself not to show her intimidation. Once seated, two frost beetles scuttled into her lap. Her hands dove and swatted them off; they'd sting her worse than a common nettle.

"While you're in the Web, your guardian won't leave your side," Hadrian said. He looked at her with marked interest, as if he detected something different about her. "Coming down here was the one exception."

"You need a man to spy on me?" she guessed.

"Not spy. The Coyote will make sure that you do nothing you shouldn't."

"I'm sure he will." She drew *Spectrals Imported* from her satchel and pushed it toward him. "I finished Section 23. Governor Dhiacula was insightful."

"I doubt it," Hadrian declared, reaching for the marble orb. "You spoke to Poppy Van Todder."

"They're the same person."

"That's an obvious assumption," he granted. "But incorrect. The mask he wears is possessed by a Spectral. Dhiacula Sykiss and Poppy Van Todder are not the same man." Hadrian flipped back his left claw and activated his Halo. The silver strands flickered like a fluorescent bulb as they awoke. She watched him brush the Halo across the surface; the orb animated, sparks popping inside. "I'm going to tell you a story."

"About the welx?"

"About a range of issues."

She eyed the orb curiously. "Why do you need a spell for that?"

"A Meno Orb contains memories, not magic." Standing, he picked up the bottle. "In order to keep this brief, the next time you ask a question, you'll drink dragon-ale."

"I haven't heard of it," she admitted. "But I'm guessing its alcohol."

"That's a boring guess. It's also only half-correct. But I've already established your flaws." He proceeded to fill the wineglass with some kind of glowing, green liquid. Steam swiveled from the glass's rim as he raised it and sloshed the liquid around inside. Rounding the table, he set it before her; fumes sputtered from the glass and singed her nose.

"What's in this?" she coughed. "Aside from deadly venom?"

"A variety of ingredients. In this distillation, the venom isn't lethal; it's curative." His mouth twitched wolfishly. "Aim high."

Snofrid decided she'd pull through the brief question-free and shoved the glass away. The inkling that he wanted to punish her lingered. But punish her for what? Being a halfbreed? "Before we start, I want to talk about negotiating another trade," she said.

"I don't do favors," he informed, retaking his seat. "I have no desire to please people."

"A trade means we each get something," she pointed out. "It's not a favor."

"Tell me what you want."

"A phone call. I have to talk to someone outside the shield and you have tech that can penetrate it. I just need five minutes."

Ice was beginning to crust his hair. "Making the favor seem simple won't convince me any better. Who do you need to reach outside the shield?"

"His name is Atlas Bancroft. He's a friend of mine."

"That's not likely. In my experience men use women for pleasure or to complete tasks."

"In *my* experience men and women serve each other."

Hadrian braced his elbows on the table, his face taut with condescension. "Men permit women to think they have power purely as a means to control them. It's an effective delusion, but men have defined history since the beginning, and they'll define it at the end."

"You're a stiff," she accused.

"That term means nothing to me."

"It means you think you're superior and, therefore, have a right to oppress people."

Hadrian let silence fill up the chamber, his features so sanguine that the hair on her nape stood erect. He was *proud* of the accusation.

"Relationships are a matter of psychological dominance and submission," he explained, as if he were imparting an obvious principle.

"There's never a balance. The varying degrees depend upon the man's or woman's need to dominate. I have a need to dominate. In pursuing it, I grow to the fullness of my nature."

"And turn people into slaves like Hessia?"

"I turned her into nothing," he insisted. "She was always meant to serve. I merely helped her to become what she innately is."

Snofrid's whole being rose up in opposition. He'd mistakenly assumed that these so-called *innate slaves* would never challenge subjugation, that they'd accept oppression. Her own experience proved him wrong. She would fight slavery again and again until she was free. "Is this the way Inborns think in the Empyrean City?"

"It's the way every animal with reason thinks, though some are more inclined to power than others." Hadrian drummed a claw against the orb. "The story I'm going to tell you will prove that our need to dominate is a natural instinct."

"It's probably some people's instinct, yes, but not everyone's."

"The people you're referring to are the ones who submit to dominance. Enough. We proceed."

Hadrian rocked sideways and pitched the orb at one of the pools. White fog spun from the pool as the orb struck the water; the fog formed a vortex over the pool, generating a roaring wind that slammed Snofrid back against the headboard of her chair. She covered her face.

"Before we came to this world, Inborns stood unified in Armador," Hadrian called above the turmoil. "All were submissive to the Five Lords until a Spectral named Invidia opposed their authority."

Snofrid whimpered as the wind grew hotter, burning her face like dragon's breath.

"Invidia needed a Necromancer host to master the six elements and become all-powerful. Invidia broke the *Law of Spectral Possession* and possessed the body of a young, Lambent Necromancer woman."

WHOOSH. The tornado blasted into a hundred tongues of smoke.

Panting, Snofrid lowered her arms, her eyes darting about the chamber. The smoke was coalescing into colored shapes. Stretching, the shapes morphed into three-dimensional images that swayed, as if alive, above the pools. She saw a castle built on the slope of a volcano in the clouds; fiery birds flew over the castle ramparts, streaking past the war chamber walls and then dove into the water with a hiss. Above another pool, herds of purple forests were migrating into a desert, and fleets of ships, built as half-machine-half-creature, were warring on a red sea. Further down, multitudes of beasts were retreating into caves, and an ice fortress was melting in the heat of a giant orange sphere. The sphere's light was flushing dark, spreading into black vapors, and destroying all that it touched.

Screams erupted in the room so abruptly that Snofrid yelped. She shrank against her chair's headboard. The scene was so lifelike that, for a moment, she questioned if she'd been physically transported into it. Bodies writhed all around her, melting into puddles under the giant sphere's vapors. On the sea, horned beasts broke from rising black waves, splintering ships; and on land, Inborn army stood against Inborn army, spawning endless fields of carnage.

"What is this?" she cried.

"This is the blood of the *Stygian War*," Hadrian told her. "The Stygian War is why Inborns left Armador."

CRACK. The images vanished in a puff of smoke.

Snofrid looked at Hadrian, unblinking; fear crippled her tongue. She felt small, shrunken in the shadow of a sudden disturbing truth, one which she was in no way prepared to face. Cold enveloped her, cold like she'd never known, and it leeched her hope. For any species to forsake their planet was horrible, but this revelation was more terrible than what she'd ever imagined: Armador didn't die by some natural plague; it was ruined by her own kind.

"There is an abyss in Armador called Babadon," Hadrian went on. "Invidia disappeared inside Babadon for nearly a year. When she climbed out, she was almighty, able to raise blackchant."

"What?" Snofrid panted. "No one has ever survived Babadon."

"No one, except Invidia."

Old terrors that had sent her cowering under her covers resurfaced. As a child, whenever she'd ordered Lycidius to tell her a bedtime story, he'd terrified her with tales of Babadon. He'd described Babadon as the open mouth of evil, the threshold that, once crossed, stripped a person of his ability to know right from wrong. Supposedly, even the vegetation that grew on its slopes was poisonous. But she wasn't a child anymore and blackchant was no longer a story. It was real.

"What is blackchant?" she asked.

"Blackchant is almighty destruction. It feeds off chaos and grows more powerful as it devours." He honed in on her wineglass disapprovingly. "You'll take a drink of dragon-ale for asking this question."

Unregretful, she took up the glass and flinched when the vapors seared her nostrils. *It can't be worse than Lucian's homemade vodka*, she encouraged herself. She braved a small sip. The ale cooked her lips. Her tongue quivered as the ale fizzled like soda and then gushed down her throat. "Ah!" Standing, she wheezed hysterically for air. The boiling sensation sank low in her gut before it flash-fired up her chest. "Ah! M-my..." She thrust her head back, straining, choking a cry; she clenched her fists and burped flames.

Hadrian watched the fire waft from her mouth with a smirk. "That was the worst spit I've ever seen. Roar next time."

"Beastcrap." Snofrid scrubbed spicy saliva from her lips. "Dragon-ale isn't hot like vodka; it's hot like acid. Make me drink it again and I'm walking out of here."

"Choosing to remain ignorant rather than feeling a little pain tells me a lot about you."

"A *little* pain? My throat almost melted!"

"It blisters the first few times, but not seriously. Drink some milk." Hadrian sipped from his glass, savoring the taste, and, as he spoke, exhaled smoke through his nostrils. "I'm not finished. Sit down."

Bristling, she lowered herself into her chair, wondering what exactly *his* glass was filled with. It couldn't be dragon-ale; he wasn't even batting an eyelash.

Hadrian set down his glass, and continued. "Throughout Armador's history, all Inborns were submissive to the Lord Office, sometimes to the extent of slavery. Invidia promised Inbornkind an existence where Inborns would rule themselves without government and without natural laws. Despite being acknowledged as the fifth Inborn species, Spectrals were cast off and left to live on the outskirts of civilization. Most of them joined Invidia as revenge and started calling themselves the *All-Steam Hunters*. Thus, the Stygian War began."

"We should've seen it coming," Snofrid said. "When an animal is abused, it always bites back."

He considered her keenly. "I sense a double-meaning. Are you suggesting that if I continue to use you for my own end, you'll bite back?"

"Yes."

He plunked down his glass, unaffected. "For me to act defensively, you would need to have teeth. Now sit quietly until I finish."

Snofrid squeezed the sides of her chair, knuckles burning white. "Yes, Commander."

"When the Spectral Lord joined Invidia, it caused the final turn in the Stygian War," he went on.

Snofrid followed his attention to the pools where gray swirls were rippling through the water. The swirls formed into a pair of towering, arched gates erected on a blue mountain peak.

"Four years into the Stygian War, the Five Lords admitted defeat. But in knowing Invidia would never spare the millions who'd fought against her, they didn't surrender—instead, they chose to run. Lycander Learyum, the Necromancer Lord at that time, raised a portal, allowing Inborns to cross into this world. But when Invidia's army found the portal, Lycander sealed the door from this side."

Snofrid dropped the leaf to the floor, slack-mouthed. "That explains why some of our kind never made it across."

"It wasn't just *some*," Hadrian informed. "More than half of our species is still in Armador."

The sinking feeling that streaked her stomach gave her the sensation of falling. Nothing she could utter or think would fully encompass the horror of this fact. But she felt it—felt herself tumbling fast into sickening awareness: those left behind who hadn't bowed to Invidia had likely been butchered, or worse—enslaved.

Hadrian dispersed the images in the pool with a wave of his claw. "Four of the Lords agreed that allowing the portal to exist posed too much of a risk. Lycander alone disagreed. He believed it was wrong to destroy the portal, for it would condemn to death the millions of Inborns who'd been left behind. So he secretly hid the portal and shrouded it with a Concealing Spell. For nearly four years, Lycander didn't reveal the portal's location to anyone. Only his immediate family was aware of what he'd done. Eventually, however, his brother betrayed him. Lycander and his entire family—except for the betrayer—were executed. Before his death, Lycander infused his memory of the portal's coordinates into a Spectral comrade."

Snofrid's voice quavered. "The welx...or...the Spectral possessing the welx is Lycander's comrade."

"His name is Nox Wolba," Hadrian confirmed. "He consumed more than half of the welx's mind and can't abandon the beast. When we destroy the welx, Nox and the coordinates will be destroyed."

"You make it sound easy."

"Not easy. Simple."

She sat back, her ears stiff with shock, feeling overcome. She'd already sworn to act as bait, so she told herself it shouldn't matter why the welx was being hunted. But it did. When the risk was this high, it did.

Before speaking, she mentally tailored her next question. "You haven't mentioned the All-Steam Hunters."

"That counts as a question."

"It was an *observation*."

"It counts."

She cursed.

"Thousands of All-Steam Hunters are trapped on Earth," he answered. "They'll slaughter Nox Wolba after he digests a third Halo and the portal coordinates will become visible in the welx's blood. Then the All-Steam Hunters will invite Invidia into this world."

"Nox Wolba must care that Invidia might be freed," she reasoned. "It will affect every living creature on this planet."

"Nox cares for nothing," Hadrian countered. "He went rogue after the Learyum Massacre and has no loyalties now. If he could, he'd starve himself, but having inhabited a beast host, it's nearly impossible for him not to feed. He won't commit suicide either because he's a coward."

At the foul taste of this insight, Snofrid wanted to vomit. "I see why you're readying for a war," she realized. "You're going to go up against the All-Steam Hunters for the welx."

"Don't concern yourself with the All-Steam Hunters. My Dracuslayers will deal with them."

"I don't doubt your Dracuslayers' competence, but if the All-Steam Hunters were to attack during the hunt, who will kill the welx?"

Hadrian contemplated her as if she were excrement. "That's not your concern, halfbreed."

Snofrid sat motionless, and, for a long while, they stared at one another, communicating dislike and intimidation.

Suddenly Hadrian rose, sweeping aside his cloak. "The Coyote will come for you tomorrow morning at 0800 hours. We'll negotiate a trade for the phone call." He rammed a cork into the dragon-ale bottle. "But ignore my call one more time and I'll have the Coyote beat you with his staff. That you're a woman is irrelevant when you're under my command."

Snofrid got to her feet. Without a word, she grabbed her satchel and headed for the Mock Wall.

"Stop right there," he called. "Turn and walk back to the table."

She halted. Thorns of resentment made her teeter on the edge of an outburst. "Why?"

"You asked *two* questions," he reminded, nodding to her wineglass. "Take another drink."

The Unloved God

"Y ou walk like a duck," Coyote observed, when they reached the forest elevator.

"It's called out-toe walking," Snofrid informed, swiping her Tag over the tree keypad to summon the elevator. He'd been making offhand comments since they'd left the Spyderweb and it was beginning to grate at her. "It's no more awkward than your eye twitch."

"My muscles contract when electrical currents travel through my body," he explained. "I don't have an eye twitch."

"That's beside the point. The spasms still look weird."

He crackled his thumb; a foreboding black current flashed over his knuckles. "Have you ever touched a hot stove? It heats up to 500, maybe 550 degrees Celsius."

"Yes. Most children do at some point."

"At 28,000 degrees Celsius, my lightning whips are hotter than the surface of Earth's sun." Coyote waved his pinky finger. "One stroke would send 15 coulombs of electrical charge and 500 mega joules of power through your body. A scanner wouldn't even be able to identify your remains."

Snofrid remained impervious. "Touch me and, yes, I'd burn, but you know I'd also heal. If I fired a bullet in your head, you couldn't say the same."

"If you fired a bullet at my head, it would melt before it left the chamber." The haughtiness in his face faded and was replaced with a stark, unforgiving glower. "I'll be here tomorrow at 0800 hours. If you're late, I won't wait for you. May we meet again."

"May we meet again," Snofrid replied. She watched as he blended back into the trees, until only the crunch of his boots betrayed his path back to the Spyderweb. It was as if every Dracuslayer under Hadrian's command was soulless—or they all secretly knew she was a halfbreed, courtesy of Hessia. This could explain why they treated her like a stain on the carpet.

After hiding herself with a bottled Concealing Spell, she headed into the house. No one was waiting. She passed Lycidius in the kitchen. He was on the phone and seemed too absorbed to hear the creak of the ladder as she climbed to her bedroom.

The room was empty. All was orderly, apart from a heap of laundry on the floor. Jazara had settled down to sleep in the washitsu, giving Snofrid the perfect opportunity to do some research. She intended to dig up information on Invidia, blackchant and the crossing. Hadrian had shared the barest details of the Stygian War, and she knew there was a flipside to every story.

The night before, Desya had reminded her that she kept her Inborn history books hidden under her bathtub. The bathtub was encased, leaving a spacious storage area around the bowl.

She sat on the bathroom tiles, huddled beside the towel cupboard, and growing evermore unsatisfied as the clock drew near midnight. Her books related how her kind had abandoned Armador twenty-two years ago, but there were few to none first-hand accounts from survivors. It was as if

Inborns had wanted to forget what they'd left behind. Or maybe they didn't want humanity to learn about what existed on the other side of the portal.

Snofrid lowered her book, suddenly conflicted, for she'd recalled Hadrian telling her that millions of Inborns were trapped in Armador with Invidia. It was clear these Inborns would be left to Invidia if the welx was killed; on the other hand, the alternative was just as terrible: if the welx was allowed to live, the All-Steam Hunters would open the portal, bringing Invidia to conquer Earth as she had conquered Armador. The decision seemed impossible, and Snofrid found herself pitying the Lords, for they'd been the ones tasked with making the decision in the first place. Snofrid would *never* want such a responsibility.

When it was clear that she'd get no answers from her books, she crawled into bed. Her eyelids flagged, yet her mind worked, stressing on information Hadrian had entrusted to her and playing out possible scenarios of the hunt. Considering everything she'd learned about the welx, she now knew that the hunt was infinitely more momentous than she'd been led to believe. The Lords were undoubtedly monitoring it, which meant her uncle, Lord Drakkar, was in contact. Securing an audience with him as a halfbreed was obviously a fantasy, but she still imagined it.

A creak sounded behind the door and she turned toward the noise. For a moment, she stared through the curtain of darkness while old habits revisited her. She thought of Ghost, the first friend she'd had in the world, and wondered if it ever thought of her. As it had long ago, the idea of Ghost's presence soothed her. But then, naturally, she thought of Ryuki and all her good feelings grew heavier. She missed him now as much as she'd missed him the day he died.

The door swung open. Jazara clambered up the ladder, suspending Snofrid's imaginings. She was dressed in a frilled yellow nightgown and hugging her stuffed giraffe.

"Is something wrong?" Snofrid asked. Guilt soaked her tone at the sight of the girl's bandaged hand. She involuntarily curled up a little, nerves twisting, suspecting that Jazara hated her.

"Nothing's wrong," Jazara said, her voice tiny. She stared at her bare feet a moment before whispering, "I'm…not mad at you."

Snofrid sat upright, unblinking, praying she hadn't misheard the girl. She scrambled out of bed and swept Jazara into a vigorous hug. "What happened was my fault, Jazara. I'm so sorry." She drew Jazara closer, warming with consolation when Jazara hugged her back. Her eyes fell to Jazara's bandage. "Does it still hurt?"

"Not anymore. Dez gave me more medicine." Jazara's shoulders bounced into a shrug. "He also said bionic-replacement appendages are in style now, so I don't got to feel bad." Her eyes wandered to the mattress. "Can I sleep in here? It's really dark in the washitsu."

"Sure, but it's late, so you should probably just sleep with me. I'll make up a spare bed tomorrow."

"Okay." Jazara pattered to the bed. "Dez, snores loud, too. I put a pillow on his face, but it didn't help."

"I snore sometimes, too," Snofrid warned, taking down a stack of spare blankets from the bathroom cupboard.

"Yeah, but not like Dez. And he whistles, too." Jazara waited until Snofrid was in bed, before whispering, "Goodnight, Sno."

Jazara drifted off to sleep, leaving Snofrid alone in the dark. She fussed to find a comfortable position; she wiggled her toes restlessly and her focus bobbed back and forth, like a ship on a stormy sea. Unbidden, she kept reimagining Hadrian's face as he'd briefed her on the Stygian War. He wasn't shy about showing the satisfaction he found in upsetting her, and it was all too familiar: Lycidius used to draw a similar type of pleasure from torturing her as a child.

By 2:37 a.m., she'd given up on sleeping. The thought that she needed to rise in a few hours made her groan. She rolled towards the window to look at the moon; a knock at the door sent her rolling the other way.

"Yes?"

"Hey, Sno," Desya murmured. "You busy?"

"It's almost 3:00 a.m., Dez, what would I be doing?"

"I don't know. You're awake, so I thought you might be doing schoolwork."

"I've never been that dedicated." She squinted at Jazara, and added, "Jazara's asleep though."

"I'll keep it down," he promised. "I just need you to make Lycidius's Demented Book shut up."

Snofrid propped herself up on her elbows. "Lycidius isn't here?"

"No."

Hopping out of bed, she twisted open the door and cringed in the piercing kitchen light. Desya stood on the ladder, his eyelids drooping and claws protracted. "Where is he?" she asked.

"He went to grab supplies, but he got held up in traffic, so he's staying in a hotel until curfew ends." Desya eyed Jazara, asleep with her mouth open, and retracted his claws. "Sorry if I woke you. The book's been having a conniption for ten minutes straight."

"It's fine," she said. "Is it in the washitsu?"

He dropped down the ladder. "It's in the toilet."

"Why did you put it in there?"

"Because it hates water. And it's a menace. Cid tried to chain it up, but it busted the last three sets."

"It sounds like every other Demented Book I've seen."

"No, this one is different, trust me."

Climbing down the ladder, she waited, shivering, while Desya slid open the washitsu door with his foot.

He added, "It bit Cid's hand once. Almost took off his pinky."

Her lashes flew up. "And you want *me* to touch it?"

"Yeah, Sno. It likes you. Come on, I'll show you."

She trailed him towards the washitsu bathroom where a powerfully deep voice was chanting like a funeral choir. "I am war. I am death. I am the Unloved God. I am war. I am death. I am the Unloved God."

"Hey," Desya barked, elbowing open the bathroom door. "Shut up or I'll toss you in the paper shredder."

Snofrid recognized the book's chant as the phrase Lycidius used to utter in his sleep when they were children and dashed to the toilet. A ratty book was sloshing about inside the bowl. On the cover was a familiar insignia—

a black upside-down tree, plated on leather chrysanthemum petals; behind the tree was the faintest outline of a solar eclipse.

"I am war. I am death. I am the Unloved God!" the book roared. A black barbed wing shot from the pages, startling her and making Desya groan irritably.

"If you don't be quiet, we're going to sell you," she threatened, crouching low over the bowl. "You have four seconds."

The wing sagged and slithered back into the book. The pages wrinkled. "Snofrid?"

"Yes."

The pages crinkled again. "You've ignored me. Why?"

She glanced up at Desya, hoping for a hint.

"It's been obsessed with you since Cid first showed it to you last year." Swiping up the book, he used an embroidered hand towel to dry the binding. "It's a bloody seedy needy and I'm gonna bury it if it makes me lose one more hour of sleep."

"Read me," the book hissed. "You've ignored me and I'm furious!"

"I'll take it," she said. As her fingers touched the book, warmth flooded the binding. The cover blushed red and the pages exhaled a long, low sigh.

"Don't put me in the drawer again," it warned.

"That'll depend on you. Are you going to let us sleep?"

"I'll be good. I'll be good."

"Do you know what's in this book?" Snofrid asked when they'd returned to the washitsu.

"Yeah, Cid let me read it a while back." He skirted past a valet-stand draped with jeans and snatched his phone off the breakfront. "It has some history about famous battles and Commanders, but most of it's about the Unloved God."

Slumping onto an open futon, she pulled a crocheted blanket over her knees and inspected the book. "I've studied most of our Commanders, but I've never heard of him."

"Yeah, that's because dad wouldn't let you. You know how he rated books on how scary they were?"

"Yes. He wouldn't let me read *Talks with Twoface*."

"That book was nothing compared to this one."

Snofrid traced her fingertips across the black tree, her interest enkindled. "Well, you read it, so tell me the best parts."

"There are no best parts; it's just a bunch of sadistic ways to kill people." Sitting beside her, he shoved his phone in-between the cushions. "You know those stories Cid used to tell us, about how people went into Babadon? And how it sucked out all their goodness?"

"Yes."

"The Unloved God was like that—except he never went into Babadon. His birth name was Grieva Gravebane. He used to be a Skinwalker Commander around the time we made the crossing. Cid served under him until his death."

Snofrid cleared the prickly lump in her throat. "Lycidius mentioned he served under a Skinwalker, never who though."

"I don't think he wanted us to know…at least, not for a while."

"Why? I don't believe it was because he was ashamed."

"Cid wouldn't be embarrassed if he woke up with webbed feet." Desya folded his arms over his chest, now wide awake. "Some Native Americans used to believe that each time a photo was taken of them, a part of their soul went with it. That's kind of how Cid thinks about his personal info. Like each time he tells someone something, he's handed over a part of himself."

"That's nonsense," she assured. "He never told me that."

Desya shrugged. "He only told me to warn me. He thought I was telling Parisa too much."

Indifferent, Snofrid lifted her feet on the footrest. "He's always been proud, Dez. It has nothing to do with souls disappearing."

"Yeah. But, I said his belief was *kind of* like the Native Americans. He didn't say anything about souls. He said it weakened his influence when people knew too much."

"That sounds like something he'd say."

Desya rose, and said, "I'm gonna grab a beer." He strode into the kitchen and a wedge of light signaled he'd opened the fridge. He returned swiftly, carrying two Greenmarket Wheat beers by the necks. "If we don't drink these tonight, Cid will sponge them both." He popped the caps with one of his fangs and offered her one.

"Thanks," she said, her palm numb against the cold glass. As he flipped through TV channels, she urged him to finish the story of Grieva Gravebane. "Lycidius talked about the Unloved God before," she said. "But I'm guessing it's more of a derogatory title."

"Yeah, it is. For starters, he really thought he was a god. He was totally convinced that by transcending weakness, he could rise to a godlike status. Since no one liked him much, the name kind of stuck. Even the Skinwalker Lord kept him at an arm's length." As Desya wiped his mouth, his face puckered into a disgusted expression. "It's no wonder though. He was the second biggest mass murderer in our history."

Snofrid felt the air in the room thicken into a stifling haze. "Dez, it never bothered you that Lycidius served under a *mass murderer?*"

"No, it did. I was like twelve when I found out and it scared the crap out of me." He narrowed his eyes, then took on a thoughtful look. "When I first met Cid, he said a lot of weird things, so eventually I gave the book a read. Things made sense after I read the chapter on Grieva Gravebane's code."

"It's all about weakness and power, isn't it?"

"Sort of. It basically boils down to dominance and submission. At its highest practice, you torture what you like and kill what you love. We used to think certain human religions were kooky—wait till you read about this one."

"I already know about this one," she assured. *Love is a flaw.* With Lycidius's words, Snofrid's need for an explanation went out the window. Hurtful memories put on new faces as she thought back over all of the times he'd been cruel to her—calling her names, playing mind games on her, telling her she was a castoff. It seemed to her that all of this really hadn't stemmed from hatred, but rather, a twisted version of affection.

Using her Halo, she opened the book and skimmed the index, eager to study the code. "How did the Unloved God die?"

"Chapter twenty-three," Desya said. "But I wouldn't recommend reading it."

"Why?"

"Because Grieva eventually went insane and murdered his wife."

"What?" She scoured the book's cover, as if it would suddenly spit out answers. "Why?"

"He snapped, I guess. When his son found out about his mom, he flipped and tore off Grieva's head, arms and legs and then stuck them on poles around their warship."

"It sounds like his son lost it."

"No, his son is just brutal."

Snofrid thought this an understatement. The vague reasons for Lycidius's childhood cruelty began to take shape: to be raised in such an environment would've been similar to being raised in the Midwinter Insurgency. No good could grow from that.

Still leafing through the book, she paused on a picture of two boys. Both could be no older than four. They looked as groomed by war as the Swangunners—the kind that had garnered a thrill for fighting. Both were adorned in reptilian armor and full-face helmets with bloodied ram horns. They stood poised to fight on the blood-soaked foredeck of a hideous warship. Great, barbed, leathery sails shrouded their bodies like a living cloak of ferocity; the setting sun glinted off the gutted bodies about their feet.

She recognized the toddler on the left, armed with an iron Longxu hook, as Lycidius; he stared at her with mismatched eyes even more menacing than the first day she'd looked into them. His tongue hung between his teeth, displaying his silver barbell, and his eyes blazed with exhilaration. The toddler on the right, with his alligator eyes and venomous sneer, she also found familiar, though it took a moment longer to identify him. She checked the caption beneath the photo:

On Left: Dracuslayer Lycidius Heidrun. Also known as "Cid the Insidious"
On Right: Dracuslayer, Hadrian Gravebane. Also known as "The Red Prince"

"This *isn't* Lycidius's adopted brother, is it?" Her voice cracked.

Desya consulted the photo. "Yeah."

She sat up slowly and the crocheted blanket fell off her shoulders. Distress raked her body; she found it difficult to form a coherent thought. *You called me heartless once. If you met my adopted brother, you'd find new meaning in the word.* Had she known Lycidius had been referring to Commander Hadrian when he'd spoken these words, she would've told Hadrian to go stone himself. Or at least, she thought she would've. As her frustration raged, reality snuffed it. No. She *couldn't* have changed anything. She'd never had the option to choose.

Desya's phone rang. Curious, Snofrid set the photo aside. She figured not many people would call at 3 a.m. unless it was to share bad news. "Who's calling, Dez?"

"Ronan…a buddy from work." Desya answered the phone.

Snofrid threw off her blanket and rose onto her knees. Whatever Ronan was saying, it caused Desya's face to pale until it matched the whites of his eyes. When he finally hung up, she pitched toward him, asking, "Dez, what is it? Did someone we know get found?"

"No." He cursed and dialed Lycidius's number. "It's worse. For the past couple days, there have been rumors circulating around the precinct about possible blood tests. Ronan just told me they're not rumors. Tomorrow morning, all the city hospitals are gonna start doing verification blood testing. That means the humans will be able to weed out Inborns with one sample. Reznik's scheduled to announce it on the morning news."

Something hot zigzagged through her. She tried to lean back, to brace herself on the armrest, but her hand slipped and her beer bottle shattered on the floorboards. A dark shape flickered nearby. Snofrid snapped her attention to the door and spotted Jazara standing on the washitsu threshold with her stuffed giraffe. The girl's eyes were glossy with horror. Snofrid felt her fear like an updraft, yet her legs were too rickety to stand—to get up and reassure her.

Now, they had no choice but to run.

The Verification Days

Awintry darkness settled over the city—the kind that might entice someone to sleep in—but, since 7:00 a.m., the citizens of Hollowstone had been very much awake.

Snofrid was glad to be indoors, off the riotous streets, and away from the mobs of human rights protestors. On her way to get spare gasmask filters from the War Lobby earlier that morning, she'd nearly been struck by a flying rock that had been intended for a S.W.A.T. officer. Now, she sat on a bench in the indoor courtyard, clutching a mug of cold coffee and waiting for a phone call from Lycidius—one that would reveal whether or not they'd be spared from the blood tests.

The Trojan Bunkers and the Alley-out-of-the-Way could only shelter about twenty percent of Hollowstone's Inborn residents. This had set off a desperate bidding war that would only benefit those Inborns who could pay hundreds of thousands of silvers. Lycidius was presently in the midst of it.

The 7:00 a.m. broadcast, which had first introduced the Verification Days, had created mass hysteria and outrage. Snofrid didn't know which would be worse: if the Verification Days weren't cancelled, or if military reinforcement was called in to manage the situation. Every news station was in the midst of a full-throated debate. Some reporters had taken to pelting one another with their water glasses or swearing on live television and insulting the New Global Union. A few thought the blood tests were an excellent idea, effective and direct, while others claimed that it was an idiotic plan thought up by someone 'dumber than an ostrich'. *It's against our basic human rights to get this blood test*, was the general consensus.

"I think it's an exceptional strategy," had been one talk-show host's opinion, a robust man with a strong, jutting chin. "Inborns have been living in our society for decades virtually unchecked. It's about time new protocols were put into place. We're not only protecting ourselves here; it's future generations we need to be concerned about."

"The *Human Rights Code* gives citizens the license to deny participation in these blood tests!" a female lawyer had yelled into a weather reporter's camera. Then a bystander had cut her off, and shouted, "Go to hell, dump truck! The *Aegis Act* allows anyone who the law deems suspicious to be detained and questioned!"

The interviews left Snofrid feeling paranoid, especially the last one. It had been given by a talk-show host, who had completely lost his composure and had screamed at the camera. "If we let this blood test happen, we'll have New Global Union citizens all around the world subjected to more tests, all under the guise of exterminating Inborns! What's really going on here is a crowd control experiment! That's right, I said a *crowd control experiment!* Hollowstone citizens are being conditioned by an elitist puppet and his band of goons. First were the Tags, next it's going to be condensed housing. The guys we put into power are trying to create an environment where we can all be fenced in, spied on, and controlled!"

Despite the pushback, Reznik's broadcast had continued to replay, ripe with threats and intent. He'd given his address inside the *Blue Square*—a spacious blue marble stone courtyard in the Bluecoat Headquarters— probably because he'd be assaulted if he left its walls.

"All civilians, regardless of their station, will report to one of the fifty-eight Hollowstone Hospitals within the next five days," he'd stated. "Blood will be drawn directly from the vein, meaning all prepared samples will be denied. Failure to comply with this order will result in incarceration. Any civilian caught trying to bribe hospital employees and any employees caught accepting bribes will be sent to the Terminus Max Penitentiary to await justice."

Snofrid rose and dumped her coffee into a patch of azalea flowers. She was unable to stomach the predicament Inborns were in. Maybe she was too used to getting her way, because she felt like there was a way out of the situation for *everyone*. She just hadn't thought of it yet. Since the first broadcast, over a hundred Inborns had been caught, their abilities failing against the technology of humans. Despite Reznik's warnings, both drifters and medical staff had been rounded up for peddling blood and accepting bribes. These would either die by firing squad or be locked up in Terminus Max—the largest submarine prison on the west coast. The Inborns were slated for *Minos*—a death camp in western Oregon—by the week's end.

Snofrid felt crushed at the realization that Minos was no longer just a vague threat but a real fate for most of her kind. Those who squatted in the woods would fall victim to the hydrocop units. Those who took their chances in the city would be found.

The safest place seemed to be Gehenna. The Warden had forbade entrance to the hydrocop units and, as far as she knew, the Chancellor hadn't attempted to force his hand. The reason for this was quite simple: Gehenna's informal economy was a modern wonder. Although untaxed, rife with illegal trade, and administered by a shadow government, Gehenna's sweatshops grossed more than four-hundred million silvers annually. Clearly, someone was making stacks for letting Gehenna be. But the irony of her kind fleeing to Gehenna for refuge turned her stomach.

Most of them probably wouldn't survive, beginning with those who didn't understand that nothing came free, not even a patch of dirt by the basehead shacks.

"I'm heading to the precinct now," Desya said, poking his head into the courtyard. His bluecoat uniform was ironed to the cuffs and his combat boots shone like latex. "Did you get all the emergency codes?"

Snofrid wiggled her phone. "Yes, Lycidius filled me in."

"Okay...uh...Babbage assigned me to check Tags in Westerbridge, so I probably won't be back until late. Also, Jazara's housemother called and wants her back at the orphanage. But if Lycidius gets us spots at the Alley, I'll pick her up and bring her over."

Snofrid wrapped her sweater tighter, hating the idea of Jazara leaving their sight. She was ten. Not to mention, one slipup and she'd be shot without question. "What if the orphanage children go in for blood testing today?"

"They won't, Sno. The orphanage is in Warburton. It's the last borough on the verification schedule—sometimes it's better to be poor." He adjusted his duty belt, growing tentative. "Are you gonna be fine staying home by yourself?"

"Yes," she assured. "If anything happens, I know how to get out."

"Okay...uh...just keep your phone on. If anything does go wrong, I'll send you the emergency codes and we'll meet up at my old tree fort."

She remembered the fort. It was built in the forest under Quintree Quay. "If I do need to leave, what do you need me to bring?"

He pointed at the genkan. "I stocked my jeep with supplies; there are two bags of canned food in there. Load them on Cid's Steelrunner and meet us."

"All right." She hugged him, pressing her face to his shirt, like a child. "Be careful, Dez."

He rubbed her shoulder. "You too, Sno."

Teeth chattering, Snofrid scanned the shady forest looking closely for Coyote among the shadow and dark. Branches laden with ice dipped to the ground; beyond them, fog washed out the distant pines.

"Hello?" she called.

A man peeled from a fir tree. Instead of being startled, she felt calm; she was thirteen minutes late and had expected Coyote to have left. With his bo staff and unforgiving glower, he looked like his usual self, except his blond hair was pulled into a topknot.

"I couldn't help being late," she explained, hastening toward him. "The city is rioting; I was barely able to make it here."

"This meeting is a courtesy to *you*," he reminded. "If you're late again, the courtesy will end."

"I'll be on time from now on."

"I'll trust your word when you start keeping it." He slid his staff under one arm. "Let's go. We need to make up for lost time."

Snofrid hurried in his wake, keeping watch for hydrocops. As they crested a steep ravine, her phone rang. She made a quick reach for it and reduced the volume. The caller ID read: *Lycidius Heidrun*.

"Who is calling?" Coyote demanded.

"Someone I live with. I need to take it."

"Make it brief."

"I will." She held the phone to her ear. "What's happening?"

"I got us in," Lycidius said. His voice sounded distant among the clamor of working machinery. "But there's a problem. Before all this, everyone thought you were a Trojan, Snofrid. To get you in, I had to tell them you're a halfbreed."

She shrank down instinctively.

"Snofrid?"

She pawed at her scarf, loosening it, telling herself that this had always been inevitable. When people were backed into a corner, their inmost secrets usually came tumbling out. "What about Jazara?"

"They know she is a halfbreed, too. Her skin color makes it impossible to hide."

Snofrid cut her voice to a whisper. "So, they're just giving two halfbreeds spots that pure-blooded Inborns could've had?"

"No, I had to pay a little more."

"How much more?"

Coyote seized Snofrid's arm suddenly and she almost dropped her phone. "Stay still," he ordered.

"Why?"

Ignoring her, he hunkered down and drew a gilded case from his pocket.

"Lycidius," she murmured. "Thank you. Let's talk when you get back."

"All right, I'll be home around noon. Make sure you pack, we're leaving tonight."

"I will." After pocketing her phone, Coyote lit up a cigarette and she balked in disbelief. "You needed a *smoke break?*"

"I don't smoke tobacco; it's unhealthy." He took a drag and then waved the cherry over a stretch of mud. A fiery orange cord ignited near her boots. "Laser wire. It lights up with just the right amount of heat."

She counted herself impressed. "How did you spot it?"

"It buzzes."

"Really? I can't hear anything." Snapping twigs drew her attention to a narrow glade ahead. Coyote motioned for her to follow. Hopping over the wire, she followed him into a cluster of pine trees.

"It's probably just a beast," she whispered.

"It is," he said, crouching behind the trunk. "But it doesn't know we're here and it needs to stay that way."

Snofrid once more swept their surroundings; her eyes stopped on a craggy boulder, roughly four meters high, beside a mutated birch tree. A long-horned tail flicked from the boulder and she caught her breath. The massive rock heaved, limbs breaking from its silhouette; it was the largest beast she'd ever seen. She ducked behind the tree.

The beast shifted and she watched as it stripped the flesh from a mule deer carcass. Standing on four rippling legs, it had a prominent muscular hump to support its giant head, which was heavy with a pair of thick horns on its brow. A leathery, black tongue slipped between its jaws as it lapped blood from the deer's splayed ribcage. Greyish-black scales overlapped all the way to its clawed feet, and a crest of shiny spikes ran from its skull to its tail. She recognized the spikes as a characteristic of a *dunespike*, an apex predator.

The beast flung its head skyward, startling Snofrid. Coyote clamped down hard on her wrist, prompting her to be silent. Trapped, she watched the creature's bones snap like carrots and fold into new shapes. The creature snarled as it changed, furiously swishing its tail. Suddenly, it reared up on its hind legs. Snofrid recognized her error: this creature *wasn't* a beast. Its scales receded, exposing the pale flesh of a scarred ribcage. Its teeth pulled back and a man's head pushed through the jowls, heaving for air. His face glistened with blood and fluid, like he was being birthed. She recognized him by his burnt black hair and clear green eyes.

Hadrian stepped free of his beast form. His towering, naked body was still slick with blood, flesh and saliva. She looked away, her cheeks warm. The mighty soul she'd seen in him was still there, animating his every gesture. He wasn't an embittered soldier, sanded down by war; he was the sole existing offspring of the Unloved God—a warrior whose blade had severed nations.

Coyote kept a steady watch, his fingers latched onto his bo staff. His caution was wise: Skinwalkers were hardly conscious in their second forms; instead of reason, they relied more on the instinct of their beast.

In the glade, Hadrian scrubbed the blood from his face and released his Swoegar from his spine: a shell of thick black armor swam across his body, clicking into place around his wrists, toes and neck. He held his left palm over the beast carcass. The flesh, bones and blood were sucked into his Halo until nothing remained.

"Let's go," Coyote got to his feet. "He won't attack us in his original form."

A ruckus of laughter was echoing from the refectory as they entered the Spyderweb. Snofrid peeked through the archway. Five Dracuslayers were hunched over a holographic tablet computer on the table, belting out laughter and conversing in the harsh, guttural Hematic language, *Gostronoth*.

Coyote stopped at her shoulder, unclasping the fur mantle from his pauldron. "They're betting on whether they think you'll get hit or not," he said.

"Hit?"

"Killed by the the welx."

She lost interest in the racket. "I'm guessing you put your hand in that."

"Both hands. But I didn't bet that you'd get hit. I bet you'd wet your dress."

"How witty," she said. "I'll make sure I don't drink liquids on the day of the hunt, then."

A trace of irritation skipped across his expression. "Stay here," he ordered, "and wait for the Commander." Coyote climbed the spiral staircase, wrapping the mantle around his fist, and disappeared into the dark upper levels.

Hadrian descended the staircase after him, his iron boots clacking on the stone steps. Her toes flexed inside her sneakers. From his childhood photo in the Demented Book, she'd recognized him as the boy Lycidius had spoken to over video chats when they were younger. Lycidius had entrusted plenty of information about her to Hadrian, meaning that Hadrian had known Lycidius was her Shadow since he'd learned her name.

A metallic aroma permeated the air as he advanced, radiated by the dunespike innards that still coated his skin and Swoegar. "Because of the Verification Days, you'll be boarding in the Spyderweb until the hunt," he called. "The matter is non-negotiable."

She protested, "I'm staying in the Alley-out-of-the-Way. Keep me here and my family will go looking for me in the riots. Their deaths *weren't* part of our deal."

Hadrian lingered on the landing, considering her with his alligator eyes. "One problem and you'll be bunking downstairs with Hessia," he warned.

"There will be no problems," Snofrid assured.

He scraped back the sticky hair from his face. "I have an offer. In exchange for a phone call, I want you to forfeit your credit for the hunt. Your name will be wiped from this mission; in effect, no one in the Empyrean City, or anywhere else, will know that you participated."

Snofrid's cheeks blanched. "You mean you're going to take away any chance I have of being recognized by Lord Drakkar?"

"That would be one consequence of the trade."

She quaked, even before agreeing, because Hadrian's eyes brandished their usual dogged menace, as if he wanted to punish her. And he'd damn-well succeeded. Hadrian was the reason she hadn't been able to secure a pardon from Lord Drakkar for being a halfbreed when she'd agreed to be bait, yet there had always been a chance of being recognized if the hunt proved victorious. By agreeing to Hadrian's exchange, she'd be foregoing this chance. She'd fade back into obscurity. Into non-existence.

"Why this trade?" she insisted, jabbing her fingernails into her palms. "You don't want me to get recognition because I'm a halfbreed?"

"I'm doing a comrade a favor," he replied vaguely.

"I thought you didn't please people."

"This person I do please."

Snofrid did not care. All she cared about was freedom, and receiving honor for the hunt *was* freedom. But then so was getting Atlas to deal with Lucian. She fought to admit that even if her pride suffered, the injury to her family could be worse without Atlas's help. "I'll do the exchange," she decided.

Satisfied, Hadrian strode to the center of the courtyard and stomped on a stone. The floor shifted and broke apart, the stones spiraling downward into a winding staircase. "Follow after me," he ordered.

Snofrid obeyed. At the foot of the steps, she found herself in a crescent-shaped room with ethereal walls; she couldn't guess how far she stood from them. It was dim and drafty, like someone had left a window open in the dead of a winter night. Light beamed from a row of rectangular holographic screens that hugged the crescent wall. They cast blue blushes on the marble floor around glass computer desks whose electric innards glowed frosty blue. Three Dracuslayers were at work in the far corner, interfacing with the holograms and talking into headsets.

Hadrian sat before a desk. "Tell me which number you need to call," he said

"It's not one number. I may need to call two."

"The agreement was for one phone call," he stated flatly. "I have a meeting to get to. Call the other one on Tuesday before our tactical briefing."

Snofrid faltered, then pushed him. "I'll be five minutes."

"Choose *one* number, or you'll be walking around the city with your cellphone on a pole searching for a signal."

Bristling, she slapped her phone onto the desk. "Call the first one."

Hadrian entered strings of code into the computer. Snofrid took the occasion to snoop. The screens displayed satellite images of command posts in Egypt and Yemen; one played a broadcast of President Sebaster Leathertongue's Veteran's Day Speech; and a few others showed maps of European countries inked with multicolored dots. That Hadrian was still commanding one third of the Skinwalker Army had slipped her mind.

Peripherally, a flickering silver light caught her eye. She checked the hair falling down his neck and espied a silver web on his nape. Her jaw fell.

"You have a Halo on your neck," she said, her tone accusatory. "You're a *Selfsame*."

"Yes," he admitted absently. "And by your lofty tone, I'm thinking you're adding it to my sins."

"Why? Did you do it to yourself?"

Hadrian thumped a fist on the desk with impatience; the Dracuslayers in the corner continued working. "If you're interested in me, read a history book."

"I'm not interested."

He returned to typing. She studied his Halo. Having multiple Skinwalker Halos made him what her kind had come to call a *Selfsame*, which wasn't viewed as abominable so much as greedy. If Hadrian had Halos of *other* Inborn species, he'd be dubbed a *Mingling*, which *was* abominable; those who made themselves Minglings were condemned, along with their entire House without hope of redemption. Often times, they were hunted down to be brutally dismembered and then executed.

"Give me the phone," Hadrian said.

"It's right under you."

He picked up the phone. The interface exhibited a photo of her, Desya and Lycidius at a street parade. "Your family?" he guessed.

"And yours."

Hadrian's pupils dilated. "He finally told you we're adopted brothers."

"I figured it out myself." She paused. "You're doing the 'favor' for Lycidius, aren't you? If I were recognized for the hunt, I'd be famous, and then he'd never have a chance of being relieved as my Shadow."

Hadrian didn't reply and he didn't have to; it was plain that Lycidius meant more to him than his invulnerable demeanor would seem to allow. This affection for his brother could ruin her. Protocol stated that if she ever married someone other than Lycidius, Lycidius would be reassigned and she'd be protected by her husband's House; but if she was bestowed a title for aiding in the welx hunt, he'd be stuck with her until she died—regardless if she married him or someone else.

"When are you going to tell him you're here?" she asked.

"When the welx is destroyed and this city is a scorch mark on the earth. Then I'll see my brother and tell him that I've been working with the piglet."

She crossed her arms, blushing a little. "Of course. That's what you two used to call me over your video chats."

"When you turned ten, we switched to 'the hog'." His lips curved in amusement. "Or do you prefer maggot?"

"*How* much did he tell you about me?"

"Not much. We had more interesting things to discuss."

"Like about how many people want you dead in the Empyrean City?" she offered. His lips parted in surprise. "I heard what you two talked about."

"Exactly eighty-seven people wanted me dead this year," he elucidated. "The majority of them are now ashes." He spun in his chair to face her.

"Before I make this phone call, tell me why you need to make it."

"I need an important favor."

Unconvinced, he said, "The person you've chosen to call is currently under surveillance by our government. I want to know your real reason for contacting him."

Suspicion wormed its way into her mind. She set it aside momentarily. "I need him to give me a code."

"What kind of code?"

"A bank code."

Hadrian turned on her with condescension. "You're calling this man for *money?*"

"There are other things in banks besides money," she pointed out. "What I need is private." She eyeballed the keypad. "Why is Atlas of interest to our government?"

"That I won't tell you. What I will tell you is that you know even less about your friends than you know about Covenant Spells." Hadrian accessed a private server and pulled up a professional photograph of a remarkably large family gathered inside a grand hall. "Look at this photo," he told her. "Then ask me again why you think Atlas is of interest to our government."

Snofrid examined the photo closely. She marveled at the ornate pillars, Renaissance ceiling murals, and crystal icicle chandeliers; she'd never seen a more luxurious room. Under a dome-vaulted ceiling, the hall extended to a silver and gold butterfly staircase, which rose into a portrait hall, where roughly two-hundred more people stood; crossways, tall windows sieved light across the regal assembly. All the men wore bespoke tuxedoes with cufflinks, pocket squares and silk ties while the women paraded lavish evening gowns and costly jewelry. They looked like people who lived in the Golden Circle.

"Do you know yet?" Hadrian prodded.

"I'm still looking."

She eventually paused on a young man outfitted in a black tuxedo and a white bowtie. The precise way he'd slicked his hair back was identical to the photo she'd found in her room, and she recognized his spirited blue eyes. Her first reaction was confusion. She didn't understand why a munitions dealer would be caught in such a picture. He was obviously well-off, but most in the picture were beyond well-off. Among them was Julian Forsberg, Julian's infamous father, Bjarke Forsberg, President Sebaster Leathertongue, Chancellor Albanus Leathertongue, and Sir Northrup Castle. Also in attendance was the current Regional Monarch of Sweden, at least a dozen other Regional Monarchs, fifteen U.S. Senators, and a host of other foreign officials, entrepreneurs and businessmen.

"He's well connected," she finally said. "That's why he's of interest."

"That is your worst perception so far," Hadrian assured. "After his parents were assassinated, Atlas Bancroft was adopted by Bjarke Forsberg almost twenty years ago. Atlas is not only going to be a candidate for the next presidential election, he's a renowned anti-Inborn activist whose adopted family is responsible for the assassinations of five Inborn Governors."

The meaning of his words derailed her train of thought. She checked and then rechecked the photo, so shaken that her mind numbed for a few moments. If Atlas was a Forsberg then he was also a member of the *Helios Society*—the people who'd initiated Regulative, financed the Inhuman War, and created Mongrels—which meant that he wasn't just her enemy, he was her worst fear. She'd not only been romantic with him, she invited him into the lives of *everyone* she loved.

"It seems I was right about you," Hadrian remarked. "You *are* naïve."

The Earth Square Fortress

Snofrid left the Spyderweb without calling Atlas. She sprinted the shortest route home, breaking only twice while Coyote swept for laser wire. He seemed pleased by her new urgency; his sudden upbeat mood plainly communicated that he was thrilled to end the day's babysitting responsibilities.

At the house, she dug her wallet from her desk drawer, and then jogged down Sun Promenade Plaza. Since all hypernet activity was being monitored, she hit every corner store and newsstand within a three-mile radius, buying up all the magazines that featured Atlas Bancroft. The collection ranged from *Harvard Business Review*, to *Time* and *Forbes*, to the *New Yorker*, the *National Enquirer*, and *Vogue*. His brother, Julian Forsberg, was featured on the cover of *Fortune*, so she grabbed it just in case.

With her bag of magazines, she set out for home, blending with the blue streak pace of the city. Bluecoats had set up roadblocks on backed-up streets and were directing columns of bumper-to-bumper traffic down back alleys towards hospitals and clinics. Snofrid spotted three blood test protestors getting nabbed outside of the Cosmopolitan Lounge and pulled on her hood; they were lying face down in the snow, red-faced and cussing at the S.W.A.T. officers who handcuffed their wrists. All along the sidewalks, people funneled towards the hospitals like sardines—most on foot or speeding down the curb on bicycles. Many had stopped to view the arrests while others brushed past them in haste.

Near the War Lobby, Snofrid saw a thickset man in a grey business suit. He loitered outside the shop antechamber, smoking through a slide in his gasmask. "You work here," he called, upon her approach.

"Yes."

"You closed all day?"

"We are," she told him. "We open on Monday. 8:00 a.m."

He muttered an oath. "Open up for ten minutes, hon. I just need ammo."

"I can't do that," she said, put off by his pushiness. "Try Gun Supply down the street."

He eyeballed the *Vogue* magazine peeking from her bag and sniggered. "Turn on the news. There are more important things going on in the world than fashion." Flicking his cigarette to the pavement, he jogged toward a silver electric Cadillac parked on the curb.

"Jerk," she breathed.

Once inside the mansion, she dumped the magazines across the tatami mats and then flung back her closet doors. Atlas's white silk suit jacket still hung beside her coats. Taking it down, she flipped back the collar and examined the label. The initials were sewn into the inner collar, A.B.F., *Atlas Bancroft-Forsberg*.

"No," she said aloud. She refused to believe she'd been as naïve as Hadrian had stated. Perhaps she'd known nothing of Atlas's relation to the Forsberg family; this thought offered a dose of much-needed consolation. She wanted to believe her past choices would minimize her problems, not add to the pile. To her credit, she never would've told Atlas that she was Inborn. No Regulative agents had hunted her down, so she was reassured. It was likely that Lycidius had known all along about Atlas's adoption. Being her Shadow, he would've done background checks on all her friends—especially her boyfriend.

Once the house was in lockdown, she began sorting through the magazines. Shouts and screeching brakes resounded from the street as she leafed through the glossy pages; they covered topics from slum life to celebrity fashion and politics. In the *National Enquirer*, she skimmed through an interview Atlas had given three weeks ago concerning his views on equality rights for Inborns. He'd been on a talk show, and halfway through, he'd shown a video of a crowd of diverse people on a grassy field—one person representing each human nationality. Around them was dug the words: *Earth is our planet. On its soil, humanity will always be superior to Inborns.*

Snofrid flipped the page, finished. Yes, some of Earth belonged to the humans, but all the land humans had failed to defend now belonged to Inborns. Such was the rule of war. Moreover, neither humans nor Inborns had yet proved their superiority—hence, why the war was still ongoing. "No wonder we broke up," she murmured, tossing the magazine aside.

Time contained nothing insightful, just an article about a space shuttle his family had privately built called Areion. In *Fortune*, she read that the Aracnid Arms Company was one of 129 corporations either owned or financed by the Forsberg Conglomerate. Most prominent of these companies were *Oracle Enterprises*, which manufactured autonomous combat robots; *Landmark*, the number one transport defense company in the world; and *Explority*, which designed A.I. weapon systems.

Drumming her knuckles restlessly on the mats, she flipped open *Vogue*. The fashion magazine proved to be the most interesting of the bunch: it featured a two-page photo spread from a war refugee charity gala in the Twin Comets Spacecity. What caught her interest was a photo of Atlas, Julian, Lars Castle, and President Sebaster Leathertongue. They were grouped together on a glass balcony in tuxedos and masquerade masks with a surreal view of the starry cosmos at their backs. The caption below read:

Our favorite brothers, Julian Forsberg and Atlas Bancroft, get an intimate view of outer space with friend, Lars Castle, and cousin, President Sebaster Leathertongue.

Snofrid stared at Atlas's gold Greek mask, becoming steadily more apprehensive. He seemed powerfully connected at every turn. If his cousin was running the New Global Union, then his family surely had a hand in affairs of state—or two. And taking into account the three families combined assets—Castle, Forsberg, and Leathertongue—they controlled thirty-nine percent of the world's wealth, which meant they had the world on their dinner table.

Her phone chimed with a message from Lycidius.

I'm in my office. Come down when you have a minute.

Snofrid got to her feet, wondering when he'd arrived home. She hadn't even heard him come in. Tucking back her hair, she headed downstairs and through the kitchen. His office was adjacent to his bedroom, separated only by a sliding door. It had all the starkness of a barracks, with the exception of a pot of beryl barb flowers beside the gun rack.

She found him packing at his desk. His duffle bag was tidily filled with bottled spells, pistols and a toothbrush. He added a pair of desert boots as she walked in.

"Are you packed?" he asked. His confident stance implied that he was untroubled by their situation.

"No, I was reading," she answered. "I'll do it when I go back upstairs." Crossing the room, she leaned against his desk, her shoulders aligning with his. "I found out Atlas is a Forsberg," she said. Lycidius's hands halted in midair. "It wasn't hard. More than a few magazines confirmed it. I'm guessing Desya didn't know, but you did all along, didn't you?"

"Yes," he admitted. "I kept it from you because—"

"I get why you kept it from me," she assured. "You didn't want me to worry. Which is why I need to know: did I ever tell him I'm Inborn?"

"No, Snofrid. We set down rules as soon as we left Gehenna."

She felt like she'd been released from a noose. Atlas didn't seem to be a threat, at least, not directly. This was all she'd hoped for because it meant that calling him on Tuesday was safe. "Why did you ask me to come down here?"

"I need to show you something." Lycidius zipped up the duffle and then powered on his main computer. "We're leaving the city after the shield goes down. I found our new destination and I want you to approve it."

"It's not Alaska?"

"No. There's a stronghold in Crater Lake we can hold up in. At least until we find a permanent location." She sat in an open armchair before the computer as he loaded photos of a deep blue lake shaped like a bowl. "It's called the Earth Square Fortress."

Upon inspecting the photos, she took a liking to the freeness of the Earth Square Fortress more than anything else, though it resembled a human military base. The tremendous, snowcapped cliffs that picketed the lakeshore were a natural wall; a half-mile from the water, a titanium barrier fitted with anti-aircraft guns staked out the borders.

The central fortress stood on Wizard Island—a cinder cone jutting out of the west end of the lake—and housed an airfield and six helipads. Submarine facilities glinted through the water, linked to the fortress by underwater channels; the water had a translucent clarity, reflecting even the clouds in the sky.

"It looks more like a small city than a fortress," she remarked, using her hands to zoom in on the fortress. "How is the Union not all over this?"

"It has been," Lycidius assured, "but Earth Square is part of the *Sixty Sovereignties*. The New Global Union doesn't own the land or the airspace anymore. After World War III, it had to sell off land to the central banks to pay back war bonds. The New Global Union intended to repurchase the land eventually, but Crater Lake and the Satar Province in Alaska were two of sixty territories that declared themselves independent before it could get ahold of them again. The *Sixty Sovereignties* operate as separate countries and survive by trading with each other through secret, underground trade routes."

"That sounds like a war waiting to happen, Lycidius."

"It will likely come to that, but the Union is already in a war." He zoomed in on a symbol of a blue sand spider; it marked the fortress gate. "Earth Square is one of ten forts funded by a famous Trojan Mortal called Blue Spider. The Union listed him as a terrorist, but he's a die-hard advocate for peace. He started giving asylum to Inborns last year on the condition that they pay well."

"What is his real name?" she asked.

"No one knows his identity. Not even the Devil from the Devil's Notebook."

She studied the symbol again, fascinated. "It's really no wonder. A lot of people would try to kill him if he came out."

"Probably half the New Global Union." He rubbed his temple, as if he had a headache.

"Are you feeling all right?" she asked.

"I'm fine. Don't worry about it."

She hesitated, then rose from her chair. "You don't always have to be strong, Lycidius. We have some feverfew extract in the cupboard. I'll go grab it."

She turned to leave, but he snagged her hand. "Snofrid, really. I said I'm all right."

She noted his hand on hers and he drew back, flexing his fingers. "It's okay," she said softly. "You can still hold my hand." No sooner had the words left her mouth then his cloudy eye darkened. The pupil dilated, pooling outward like a puddle of blood. "Lycidius," she breathed.

"What?"

"Your eye...it's—"

He frowned. "What?"

Snofrid minced back at the impulse to defend herself. His eye turned blacker, fiercer, like it might sprout jaws and chomp out her throat. She didn't doubt that it wanted to. Since the first day she'd seen it, she'd thought his eye had seemed like a living, breathing creature with a mind of its own. Whatever lay behind it, the entity intensely despised her.

"Snofrid." Lycidius was more demanding. "What's wrong?"

"I need to ask you something and…and please be honest with me." She tugged on her shirt sleeve. "When we were younger, you used to tell me that you had a friend—one only *you* could see. Is that true?"

The inquiry clearly took him off guard. She was stunned when he reacted defensively. Angrily. "Go pack," he said, rising to his feet. "We're leaving in two hours."

"Lycidius—"

"No," he snapped. "I don't want to talk about it. Leave."

A retort crawled up her throat, but she forced it down. Turning quickly, she left the office and shut the door behind her.

Upstairs in her loft, she sat on her bed. Her knees quivered and she pressed her palms into her eyelids until she saw sparks. He'd never pushed her away like that, not since he'd kissed her. She couldn't understand it. And it hurt worse than all the things Lucian, Hessia and Hadrian had done to her combined. In every way possible, he'd opened up to her, except about his invisible friend. It was almost as if he was protecting it.

A while later, a fist rapped on the door. Snofrid, in the midst of packing a suitcase, didn't get up. "Come in," she said.

Lycidius stepped inside. Without looking, she could feel the regret fanning off him like steam. "Snofrid, I'm sorry," he said firmly. "Please don't be upset. There are some things I've never told anyone; things that would be too hard to understand."

She set down the knit sweater she was folding, now realizing why he'd closed off. He believed if he told her the truth, she'd feel differently about him, perhaps even change her mind about being around him. "Nothing you say will make me love you any less," she said. "I thought you knew that by now."

"I'm not used to trusting people on their word, Snofrid."

"Have I ever lied to you?"

"No."

"Then why do you think I would now?"

He scratched his neck tattoo. "I don't expect you would. But sometimes staying ignorant is better."

"You're wrong. The truth is always better."

He considered her expression, then nodded stiffly. "I'll tell you what I can." Sitting on a futon, he thought for several moments, tapping his combat boot anxiously. Then he crossed his arms. "I hear sounds, Snofrid—or more like a voice. It's been with me since I can remember. I think it was with me when I was born." His knuckles burnt white, as if he was practically shoving the words out. "My left eye looks different because it's not mine. It never was."

Snofrid stared at him in bewilderment. Her mouth opened as she took in his pale, vulnerable expression, trying and failing to make sense of what he'd told her. "A voice? You mean like a person?"

"Yes. His name is...I call him *Rima*."

Her fingers clenched around the folded sweater. His eye was changing again. And she'd seen it equally enraged only once before: the night Lycidius had kissed her. "He's a real person?"

"I'm *not* crazy, Snofrid."

"I know, Lycidius. I only meant—" She bit her lip, at a loss for what to say. "So...you talk to him, then?"

"Sometimes."

"About what?"

He flicked his barbell around in his mouth, clicking it on his teeth. "Everything."

"About *me*, too?"

"Yes."

Snofrid grappled. She didn't know how to feel—how to react. A positive side of her insisted that there was a scientific or magical justification for the voice. Another side wondered if he'd simply been traumatized by war. She frowned and discarded the idea. All the years they'd spent together spoke differently. He'd grown more than she could've ever hoped, and he'd always been rational, even if he was extreme.

Then the thought that perhaps a Spectral Inborn had possessed his mind occurred to her. But Spectrals either possessed and conquered a mind swiftly, or they were defeated and cast out. For a voice to have inhabited Lycidius's mind for twenty-two years without fully conquering it was unheard of. On the other hand, she reminded herself that the science of Spectrals was ever-expanding. Inborns didn't have all the answers, and, for all she knew, there might be a legitimate reason for the voice. If it wasn't a Spectral, then it was magic.

Clearing her throat, she said, "From what I can understand, Rima has no control over you. Is that right?"

"Yes. I've always controlled him. Everything I've ever done and said has been my choice."

"Well then…Rima doesn't matter—as long as you're still *you*."

Lycidius frowned, skeptical. "It doesn't bother you?"

"Of course it bothers me. *Someone* is in your mind, and you have no idea who he is or where he came from." Her elbows started to tremble. "It's scary, Lycidius. But," she paused, "it doesn't change how I feel."

He leaned forward, looking as if she'd just lifted the world off his shoulders. "For years I wanted to tell you, Snofrid, but I was sure you'd think I was crazy."

"I wouldn't have wanted to tell either." She gave him a look of reassurance. Setting down the folded sweater, she stood and wrapped her arms around him. It was as if this was all he needed, because his decisiveness returned. He buried his face into her shoulder, and from the way he held her, she wondered if he'd ever let go.

When she finally broke away, his cloudy eye was smoldering in a soundless rage. She braced herself and a chill danced all the way to her toes. The look Rima gave her seemed to imply that he'd lost some kind of battle. Somehow, she sensed that he had. But she also sensed the battle would only be the first of many.

The Alley-out-of-the-Way

Tuesday, 3 Days until the Hunt

D oes that stuff even work?"

"Yes," Snofrid told Lycidius, raising her voice above the commotion in the Alley-out-of-the-Way. "It's an astringent. It will stop the cut's swelling and slow the bleeding."

She was kneeling beside him in their designated corner of the Alley—the corner he'd paid out two-million silvers to buy—pressing a cloth soaked in witch hazel on his split cheek; the shattered blood vessels were already swelling into a reddish bruise, one that, indirectly, she was responsible for. Since gaining asylum in the Alley two days ago, she and Jazara had been repeatedly harassed, so much that Snofrid felt reluctant to even leave their corner. All the Inborns had unanimously agreed that pure-blood Inborns were more deserving of life; this was the second hit Lycidius had taken in their defense.

"How long do I need to wear a face bandage?" he asked.

"At least a few days," she said, "or it won't really even help."

"Fine." His eyelid twitched as she pressed the cloth into his wound. "When you're done, I'm going to sleep for thirty minutes. Make sure you stay with Desya."

"I know the rules." She fished a roll of gauze from the first aid kit, and, as she applied it to his face, went extra lengths to be gentle. He blinked slowly, becoming drowsy at her touch. He lowered his gaze and watched her hands while she worked.

Actually, one eye watched, the other eye fumed.

Snofrid attempted to ignore it. She hadn't yet had time to fully process the existence of Rima. But then, what was there to process? In the back of her mind, knowing that someone would always be intruding on their every conversation, their every look, and their every moment not only upset her, but made her extremely self-aware. Rima had stolen a piece of what she valued most. As was natural, she wanted justice—or revenge.

"Thank you," Lycidius said when she'd finished. He laid on his back with his jacket hood drawn over his face.

"From nothing. If something happens, I'll wake you." She brushed the tip of his glove, so softly he didn't notice. As soon as they escaped Hollowstone, she was determined to find a way to evict Rima. Then, when Lycidius had regained full possession of his mind, they'd raise a Stonewall Spell on it, so that it could never again be breached by outside entities.

Gathering up the first aid kit, she veered down a shaded stone path toward their supply pile. Just as she tucked the kit into a duffle bag, her phone alarm triggered. It was time for her final mission briefing. She'd dreaded this moment. She had yet to figure out how she'd manage the meet without arousing suspicion. Since the Covenant forbade telling anyone, or even leaving a note for Desya and Lycidius, she saw no option except to sneak out of the Alley. However, the briefing would take two or three hours, which meant someone would definitely miss her. She'd have to think of a sound excuse for her absence.

A short way off, Jazara was curled up on a bench in a stone alcove. Her eyes, red and bloated with tears, were staring into space. Desya sat beside her, his Hematic fangs bared in warning to all the halfbreed-hating Inborns loitering nearby.

Snofrid slowly wound her satchel around one arm, certain that Jazara would be safe with Desya. Her best chance would probably be to slip away while they were occupied—even if this would be cruel.

Retreating behind a pillar, she wheeled down a narrow colonnade, away from their designated corner. Immediately, she felt a sting of guilt. Lycidius and Desya would go wild with worry when they realized she was gone. The dark glowers from onlookers only added to her unrest. She felt trampled by their stares, like she was dirt under their fingernails or something to be thrown out with the trash. She remembered telling Lycidius that she was happy one of her parents was human, but at times, it was difficult to hold to this statement.

At the end of the colonnade, she gazed out across the small interior of the Alley. It was a rustic highland village bordered by rocky bluffs. All that she beheld fit inside a single stone in the wall of the Red Oxygen Bar. The magic worked like a *Non-Stop Pocket Spell*, shrinking people and objects that they might fit inside whatever object had been enchanted. Purple trees roamed the village plateau, forming a river of forest through the cabins; the doors were built facing east towards the rising sun.

In the main courtyard, she noticed that a heated debate was ongoing. The way people had gathered in a wide circle resembled a council. She shifted nervously, praying they weren't talking about evicting her and Jazara. Drawing up her hood, she rambled through the crowd until she arrived at a row of cage elevators anchored to the cliff face. After boarding a vacant cage, she spoke to the bronze leaf curled around the elevator's lock, "The Main Exit. Top speed, please."

The gates slammed shut. With a clattering echo, the cage shifted sideways, rising up the cliff wall. Cold mist sprayed her face as wind threaded her clothes. She watched the colors of the plants and trees blend together like a motley streak of paint until, all at once, the elevator accelerated, ascending so fast she imagined her insides had scrunched together.

The cage braked at the summit of the cliff. Buckling on her gasmask, she left the elevator and went to where the rocks were scabby like barnacles. She brushed her fingers across their surface until she'd located a rectangular-shaped stone with a round hole cut into its base. After a last glance over her shoulder, she stuck her finger into the hole. Little by little her body drew forward, as if the hole was slurping her up. The walls blurred around her, expanding wider and wider until she felt as small as a particle of dust. Her feet lifted off ground and the roar of wind came thundering to her ears.

Light suddenly burnt up the darkness.

She found herself standing in the basement of the Red Oxygen Bar, facing a squad of able-bodied security guards. They were lounging at a table, drinking pints of dark beer and playing *Quell*, a traditional Inborn board game.

"Saldut debokter," she greeted them.

The sound of cocking hammers pricked her ears. All the men drew machine pistols from under the table and took aim at her.

"Password," a bald man holding a lighted cigarette stated calmly.

"The Oleander Club."

He lowered his pistol. "Why are you leaving?"

"I need to meet someone. It's really important."

"It may be. But once you leave, there's no coming back in. Security purposes."

"Please," she insisted. "My family is in the Alley. And I *can't* miss this meeting."

He nonchalantly took a drag of his cigarette. "If your family is in there, then you don't want to get separated. Go back in and wait with them until the Sky-Legion flies in."

Snofrid held her ground. Reaching into her sweater, she held up the gold pendant necklace Atlas had gifted to her. "I can pay," she said. "As soon as I come back."

"The necklace is a start, but you're asking me to break Alley Rules. What else can you offer?"

"One-hundred coppers."

"A hundred coppers is slum change."

She groped her pockets and mentally ran through the items in her satchel. She carried nothing else of value. "It's all I have. Please."

He tipped his head back and forth, considering. "If I say yes, the deal is closed. On your way back in, if we catch you trying to smuggle in someone else, you'll both be thrown out. And the money is still mine."

"Okay. We have a deal."

He motioned for her to pass. "Go on, then."

Ducking past the table, she left the guards behind. The unforeseen deal had wasted precious time she didn't have. Quickening her stride, she entered a shadowy hall where Inborn tombs were slotted into the walls. She was startled to find that one of the triumphal arches was dedicated to Neko and wondered how she'd missed it on her way into the Alley. Beneath the arch lay a coffin with his remains. She closed her eyes in relief; it seemed that his body hadn't been stolen, but recovered. His friends were more loyal than she'd realized.

Glitter drizzled onto her hood as she melded with the crowds outside the bar. People were pouring through Toddy Common in droves, eager to join the parties of *Humanity Week*—the seven-day annual festival in which humans celebrated their own existence. The tradition had first begun three years after the Inborn crossing, and with each new year, the parties grew wilder.

Stepping clear of the flow of traffic, Snofrid checked her phone hopefully. Before moving into the Alley, she'd asked Fergus Dripper for a ride at this specific time. Last minute, Hadrian had expressed that he wouldn't risk sending soldiers to the Alley to collect her, so getting to their meet point on *Cassiopeia Avenue* was her responsibility.

Fergus's message read:

Hey, Snowball. Got caught in traffic. Be there in five.

Satisfied, Snofrid pocketed the phone. Then, standing up against the wall of the bar, she waited.

A Call Around the World

W atch out, Fergus. I don't think that bicyclist sees us," Snofrid warned, as he guided his BlueCar, skidding and screeching, amidst a ruckus of honking transports on 43rd Avenue. She was cradling a cardboard box of primroses in her lap, which he'd explained were intended for his sister-in-law.

"She sees us now," Fergus chuckled, flashing his headlights. With each jolt of the car, his orange braids leapt off his shoulders.

Snofrid peered anxiously over the flower box at the clock. She was scheduled to meet Hadrian on Cassiopeia Avenue in eight minutes. But if the hellish traffic endured, and if Fergus was forced to continue driving thirty miles under the speed limit, she'd arrive late. She didn't want to imagine the consequences of that scenario.

"You know, there are some great bike trails in Albanus Park," Fergus remarked jovially. "Ever been?"

"I don't have a bike," she said. "I usually take the metro."

"Ah, that's a shame. There's nothing like packing up a cooler and blowing through nature for an afternoon."

"You must not be too excited about moving then."

Fergus raised a finger. "Actually, the Ninth Underground City has some sensational parks. They're man-made, but a few of the trees are real."

She nodded as if she understood, but really, she wondered how people could enjoy a park with fake trees. "I'm sure you won't miss Hollowstone in that case."

"No, I'll miss her," he granted. "She has her gems, but when all's said and done, my new job has a *salary*. I used to—" Fergus slammed the brakes with gritted teeth, "I used to work a similar job about three years back, but ended up leaving for personal reasons. This time, it'll be better, though: I'm gonna work right alongside some of the guys I knew back in the Union Houses of Science and Research."

She started to feel curious how he made his connections. "You'll be right at home then."

"Just about." He grinned wryly, a low chuckle in his throat. "It'll have its perks."

His insinuation was hardly subtle. Working in the largest research center in the world was more than a perk. She eyeballed the clock again: six minutes.

"Oh, look at this fool," Fergus laughed, wiggling a finger at a high-end department store. Snofrid's brows sprang upward. A hot air balloon had crash-landed on the roof and a DJ dressed in a silver jumpsuit hung limply over the side, vomiting into the street.

Fergus winced. "That's gonna suck come sunup."

"It looks like it already does," she said.

"You know, Humanity Week gets weirder every year," Fergus mused, stroking his chin. "I think I saw a gal fall down a manhole a few blocks back."

"She didn't fall: there are parties in the sewer tunnels," Snofrid explained. "I went to one a while back with my stepdad. It was in a club called Battery X, I think."

"It sounds foul."

"The tunnel smells but inside the clubs it's fine. It has pretty great karaoke."

"I'd rather party where my food doesn't end up...if you know what I mean." He switched on a disco station and tapped his shoe with the beat.

She sat back, still cradling the flower box, and stared out her window. Soon, her attention was caught by fireworks, looking much like the glittering tops of palm trees as they burst, streaking the skies over Westerbridge. The spectacle struck a chord of bitterness inside her: ever since Humanity Week launched, the city had worn a new face, one that harbored no visible trace of anger. The Verification Days were still in effect, but somehow, the outrage had vanished in a bout of confetti and popping champagne corks.

Just like after the Midwinter Insurgency, city officials had completely ignored the turmoil. On camera, most discussed foreign issues, not even pausing to put in a word about the growing unrest in Hollowstone. Apart from the increased security, Snofrid was grateful for one aspect of Humanity Week: the curfew extension. It had been pushed to 2:00 a.m., allowing people to party until they dropped.

"What's this monkey doing?" Fergus snorted.

Snofrid broke from her thoughts and combed the sidewalks. "Who?"

"Six o'clock."

She glanced over her headrest at the horde of cars nipping their tail. Less than fifty feet behind, a black hypercar weaved skillfully through the traffic. She couldn't make out the driver through the tinted glass.

"Slow down buddy," Fergus huffed, tightening his grip on the wheel. "I volunteer at the Bluecoat HQ on weekends, so if need be, I can make arrests."

"Maybe we should just let him pass," she suggested. "It looks like he's going to try cutting us off anyway."

"Not a chance," Fergus chortled and hunched over the wheel. "This monkey's gonna see I ain't a pushover."

Snofrid watched the hypercar steer smoothly until it pulled in front of them.

"Well, I'll be darned," Fergus exclaimed. He upshifted into third gear, braids bouncing. "Do you think he wants a street race?"

"I hope not. I'm sorry, Fergus, but we'd get dusted."

He squinted at the car and his eyes rounded. "My word! Is that a Peregrine?"

"What?" She eagerly swept the car for logos; a golden peregrine falcon was etched into the bumper. "Stone me, it *is*."

"Peregrines aren't legal roadsters," Fergus said, downshifting to second gear. "I might just make that arrest after all."

"Actually, they are now," Snofrid corrected. "Since last year." If she remembered rightly, this model was worth more than the Chancellor's personal energy shield. It maneuvered like a predator, a lion stalking the veldt, with its aerodynamic body glistening in the street lights. Lycidius had regaled her with the details of this particular roadster in the infant days of his Steelrunner so she knew what was at work beyond the sleek paint job.

Deep at its core, a powerful system of servomechanisms actuated the car's endoskeleton, giving it unparalleled durability. Even more impressive, the vehicle was *landmarked*, meaning even a grenade launcher couldn't scratch it—not with its auto-regenerating energy shield. All high-end Landmark transports were installed with crypto—a computer code that would encrypt outgoing cellular signals—and most enjoyed the advantage of a laser weapon system.

The car's window lowered and a red bull-head stuck out. "Snofrid Yagami," a husky voice called. "Are you in the box car?"

Snofrid did a double take. "Hadrian?"

"Box car," Fergus muttered, his tone insulted. "You *know* this clown?"

"Not well," she answered, recovering from her surprise. "We work together sometimes. And it looks like he needs my help again." She unbuckled her seatbelt, guessing Hadrian had tracked her through the satellite phone he'd given her. "I'm going to jump out here, Fergus."

"You sure, Snowball?" Fergus eyed Hadrian dubiously. "He looks like the kind of guy you'd find in a Halloween corn maze."

"He's Lycidius's adopted brother."

"Ah. Well, then I'll lay down my guns with my pride intact." Fergus set the car in park, and flipped his braids over his shoulder. "Just be careful when you exit. I almost took a tumble getting in."

"I will," she assured, setting the flower box on the floor mat. "Thanks for the lift, Fergus. Best of luck at your new job."

Wind speared her pea coat as she stepped onto the icy street. She rounded the hood of the hypercar with her satchel in hand, bowing her head against the stinging sleet.

"Backseat," Coyote ordered, as the door popped open. "Hurry."

Clambering behind his chair, she settled down beside a boy in a white nylon catsuit that blazed red in the car's ghost light system; drop-leg holsters were strapped around his thighs, and a crocodile-skin sniper case rested in his lap.

"So…did you track me?" she called to Hadrian.

Coyote replied. "Yes." He tapped a radar display on one of the five onboard computers. "The dragonale you drank was laced with a carbon-based compound called Q.T. It's undetectable in blood."

"What?" She reflexively touched her throat. "Tracking my phone isn't *enough*?"

"You don't always have the phone with you."

Snofrid glared at Hadrian in the rearview mirror. He really did have a crippled conscience. He ignored her, as if he'd done no wrong, and swung the car around a trolley bus. "How long will it be in me?" she demanded.

"Your system will flush it out in five days," Coyote said.

"What does the *flushing* involve?"

"You'll feel like you have the flu…a few hours of vomiting and you'll be fine."

She hardly minded the vomiting. What she did mind was that Hadrian would know her location even after the hunt ended. "Stay off Highway 22 if we're in a hurry," she advised. "It's backed up all the way to Albanus Bridge."

"We're not going to the Spyderweb tonight," Hadrian said, eyeing the police scanner. "We're going to the hunt site."

"For what?"

"A walkthrough. You need to memorize the site."

Based on his affinity for precision, she expected this could take days. "My phone has a camera."

Hadrian left her comment unanswered. He proceeded to swiftly cut off transports, as if he were racing in the Dakar Rally, while Coyote typed away on one of the onboard computers, his eyes tapered in concentration. Dull silence drenched the very atmosphere; outside noises were muffled by the soundproof doors, but she could hear a slight popping sound. The sound persisted, increasing at such a rate that she hurled a peeved glance at the boy in the glowing catsuit. He was cracking his bare toes against Hadrian's headrest—which probably wasn't smart—and playing a violent video game on his phone with an amused grin. His platinum side-braided mohawk left an impression, as did the silver cuff-earrings that studded his cartilage. *Rhode Vortigern.*

Only thirteen, he was a Mystish Dracuslayer with the ability to contort into impossible shapes, allowing him to fit into the smallest niches and gaps. He was a bit gangly in physique, and the way he kept folding his arm down his back made it look like he was stretching. She would've thought him cute, with his rounded facial structure and rosy cheeks, if not for his pig-like nose. Strangely enough, he looked nothing at all like Coyote; the boy's file had stated that he and Coyote were half-brothers.

"Someone farted," Rhode complained suddenly. "Crank up the filters."

Coyote reached for the control panel until Hadrian ordered, "Leave it."

Coyote sat back. "Deal with it, Vortigern."

Rhode sighed loudly. He shoved his hand into a paper bag on the seat and dug out a fistful of gummy worms; he stuffed them into his mouth. "Must be the girl. Every time one of us blows wind, the entire car goes into overdrive."

Snofrid scoffed. "No one farted. It's your *feet*. They smell like old milk."

Rhode eyed his dirty toes and then went back to his game.

"All right…the sensors just picked up two hydrocop units two klicks northwest of the site," Coyote announced, looking at Rhode. "Where is Hessia's team now?"

"She didn't tell you?" Rhode rubbed his nose, still munching on the worms. "It must've been none of your business then."

Coyote's voice shed its tolerance. "Confirm her location or that paper bag is going down your windpipe."

Rhode rolled his eyes. He jerked his phone from the seat cushion and perused the inbox. "Just a minute, this message is old." He swiped the screen with his thumb. "Uh…that one's old too." He swiped the screen again, biting his nails. "This looks new. They just arrived at the warehouse."

Coyote slid a glass box across the console. "Have her send someone to draw the units away."

"Distance?"

"Five klicks."

Rhode took two objects, resembling electrodes, from the box and stuck them on his temples. Snofrid was fairly certain they were *bug dials*—magical artifacts that allowed the wearer to communicate telepathically over long distances. Dark blue veins surfaced on the boy's temples, and she lost interest, knowing she was right.

Sighing, she shifted lethargically in her seat and wiped sweat from her neck. Soon, the heater grew too hot to endure and she shrugged off her coat. A brief glance at the heater made her balk. It was set at eight-five degrees.

By the time they reached their destination, Hadrian had cranked up the heater to eighty-nine. Perspiring, dehydrated, and short-tempered, everyone sprang toward the doors the moment he finally cut the engine in the parking lot of a supply warehouse on the south side of Warburton. Only a sprinkle of cars occupied the lot. A murder of crows bobbed across the snow, pecking at trash under the street lamps.

"You're a bunch of weaklings," Hadrian affirmed. "Open doors."

The doors lifted open at his command, letting in a gust of fresh air. Snofrid exited the car after Coyote and aired out her coat, wishing she'd brought a water bottle. He handed her a duffle bag to carry, before lugging two over his shoulders; hers must've contained lead bricks because it weighed no less than one-hundred pounds.

"Pack up everything," Hadrian ordered. "The car stays here." He hauled three duffle bags from the trunk and then glanced around. "Vortigern?"

Rhode poked his head from the car, now wearing a half-face gasmask. "Sir?"

Hadrian slammed the trunk shut with his knee. "Sprint the length of the parking lot until you vomit *every last worm*. Bring me a bag with proof. Then report back at the Spyderweb."

"What?" The boy's eyes flashed. "Dragonshit. You *need* me."

"You're highly overestimating your worth." He aimed his bull horns at the boy in warning. "If you want to wait for a fair punishment, then Hessia will stun you until your brain drips out your nose. It's your choice."

Rhode stomped from the car and thumped his foot on the bumper, stretching out his thighs, and snarling at Coyote's quiet laughter. "You'll regret that, Bourkan."

Coyote rolled his shoulders in a shrug. "Not as much as you're going to regret hacking up gelatin. Duty over fear, Vortigern."

"Let's move," Hadrian called. "Follow after me."

Snofrid, tailing them towards the warehouse, strained to keep up. The duffle bag clanked as she carted it along, as if it was bursting with glass bottles.

Inside the warehouse, birds nested on rafters above lanes of tall metal shelves packed with rubber tires and plastic yellow crates. Hadrian led the way to a titanium door at the back, swinging his duffle bags in stride. After scanning his iris, the door popped open with a hiss.

"Touch nothing in here," he told Snofrid.

"I won't," she assured and plopped the duffle at her feet. "What is this place?"

"A Dracuslayer playground."

Snofrid nodded, though she was lost in the ambiguity of his reply. "Before we go in, I was hoping I could talk to you alone."

"Why?"

She side-eyed Coyote, who was subtly listening in. "It's private."

Hadrian waved at the door. Once Coyote had gone through, he said, "What do you need?"

Snofrid tried her best to make the favor she needed not sound like a favor. "I had to sneak out of the Alley to get here," she started. "Lycidius has probably noticed by now and I'm worried he'll go searching for me in the city. We both know that's dangerous."

"You're being purposefully vague. What are you asking me to do about it?"

"I'm asking you to help me," she confessed. "You're the administrator of the Covenant, which means you can tell Lycidius that I'm with you and that I'm safe without breaking it. He doesn't have to know where I am or what we're doing. Because you're his brother, he'll trust you on your word."

Hadrian produce a cellphone from his cassock pocket. "Go wait inside."

She blinked. "You're going to do it?"

"Yes. Now go wait inside."

She broke into a smile. She'd been convinced she'd have to cut off her own arm before he helped her. "Thank you," she said.

Heaving up the duffle bag, she strolled into a bustling room, still high on relief. Never, in all the time she'd known Hadrian had he been accommodating. But then, since the favor involved Lycidius, it wasn't a stretch for Hadrian to act. He was probably concerned about his safety. She felt sure that in any other scenario, Hadrian would've refused her.

Snofrid unloaded her bag in the room, which was either a seized weapon's storeroom, or somebody's arsenal; there were at least thirty racks stocked with rows upon rows of loaded guns. On the far left wall, a panel of screens displayed blueprints of the city and below the cage-styled floor grates roughly eighty people in black jumpsuits were assembling guns at work stations.

She consciously avoided Hessia's gaze. The Seer and seven other Dracuslayers were huddled around a desk computer under waning fluorescent lights; all were geared up in either white or brown ballistic camouflage armor. Each time Snofrid saw Hessia, her aura grew fiercer and her eyes grew more condemning.

"The site is clear," Hessia called out to Hadrian, who'd just walked in.

"Keep an eye on the sensors," he said, sliding his bags toward them. "Everyone suit up. We move out in fifteen minutes."

Snofrid looked at Hadrian expectantly.

"It's done," he said, answering her silent inquiry. He addressed Coyote. "Help the girl make her phone call outside the shield. She has ten minutes."

"Yes, sir." Coyote led Snofrid to a table in the corner, where he produced a laptop from his bag. "You have two numbers?" he verified.

"Yes."

"Enter the first one."

Snofrid eagerly punched in Atlas's private number. Her optimism wilted a little when the call went to voice mail:

"You have reached the tenth private line of Atlas Bancroft. Unfortunately, he will not be able to return your call personally. State your purpose in a brief message. If you receive no response within six weeks, your request has been denied."

"Six weeks?" Her jaw dropped. Lucian *wouldn't* be that patient.

"Go on and put in the second one," Coyote prompted. "We have things to do."

Uttering a silent prayer, she entered Atlas's home number into the keypad. She stepped back, clutching the lip of the table, and waited. The line rang three times before an automated voice droned:

"This call will transfer until it is accepted. If you wish to reach Mr. Bancroft at a particular residence then enter the district code of that area now. If not, wait until your call is received." A shrill beep blared from the computer. *"Dialing Stockholm residence, Sweden."*

"What did she mean, 'it's going to transfer'?" Snofrid asked Coyote.

"It's dialing more than one house," he explained. "The call will transfer to each residence until someone picks up."

She wondered if this was as fortuitous as it sounded. If the number routed through multiple houses, her chances of reaching someone might've just skyrocketed. Getting in touch with a maid, a butler, or a secretary wouldn't be bad, as long as she had a way to send a message to Atlas.

"No response," the voice buzzed. *"Redirecting call to Hong Kong residence, China."*

She noticed Hessia glaring at her with disapproval. Hunched over the table, her fingernails gouging into the wood. "When a contact makes it difficult to get in touch, its code for: blow off," she called.

"Maybe," Snofrid granted. "But I have eight minutes left, so maybe you could do just that."

"Watch your mouth if you want to keep your tongue," Hessia hissed.

"No response," the automated voice declared. *"Redirecting call to Peleș Castle residence, Romania."*

Snofrid found herself bouncing on her toes.

"No response. Redirecting call to Moorea Island residence, French Polynesia."

"We were in Moorea this past summer," Coyote commented, the tiniest trace of amusement in his voice. "The Commander fell asleep under a coconut tree. By morning, he had a skull fracture."

She eyed Hadrian, supposing that explained a few things.

"No response. Redirecting call to Zurich residence, Switzerland."

With each failed call, the tension became more smothering. When her stomach started to twist in knots, she exhaled a slow, easy breath. "How many houses can I reach in six minutes?" she asked.

"Thirteen."

"No response," the voice announced. *"Redirecting call to Moscow residence, Russia."*

There was a click. Snofrid's eyes flew open in astonishment.

"You reach Mr. Bancroft's private house," a woman said very slowly in a Russian accent. "This is Irina, Mr. Bancroft's maid speaking. How I help you?"

"My name is Snofrid Yagami," she burst out. "I'm a friend of Mr. Bancroft's. Can you please transfer me to him?"

"I express regret," Irina replied, her tone dreary. "Mr. Bancroft not here since March. I not talk to him since then."

"Do you have a number I can reach him on?"

"I express more regret. Mr. Bancroft only call me. I not call him."

Snofrid racked her mind. "I've been quarantined in Hollowstone City and I need his help. If there's any way you can get a message to him for me, it would be incredibly helpful."

"Ah, I see this on news." The sound of clicking heels signaled that she was walking. "But surely this is not why you call?"

"No," Snofrid assured, not wanting to give the wrong impression. The human she was pretending to be had no reason to fear the quarantine. "It's a personal matter."

"I still express regret," Irina told her. "I not able to contact Mr. Bancroft."

"Do you know anyone who can?"

"I only one of the staff in this house," Irina explained. "We just clean and leave. But I have second call coming. I take my leave now. Udachi, Miss Yagami."

Snofrid shot from her chair, batting away the desolation that swooped in around her. Before she could ask to be transferred to the next residence the line went dead. Her heart sank.

"There is camouflage armor in the back," Coyote said, gesturing to a row of lockers through the shelves. "Go put one on."

"I still have *three* minutes," she pointed out. "Please let me make one more call."

Coyote snapped the laptop shut. "Commander Gravebane specified that you only make two. You made the two, now go suit up."

Snofrid measured the severity in his tone. He wasn't going to budge. But securing Atlas's help was essential, even though Lycidius, Desya and Jazara were hidden in the Alley. When the Sky-Legion flew in, they still had to travel to the Hollowstone Underground in order to board a gunship; by air would be the soundest way to flee the city unharmed. Except, knowing Lucian, he'd have Swangunners posted around the city, searching for them. This was too much of a risk. Lucian's vendetta against her needed to be put to rest.

A beeping sound reeled her gaze to the door. It swung open and Rhode skidded inside, his face bright red; rainbow-colored vomit stained the collar of his catsuit.

Hadrian slammed his fist on the table. "There better be a good reason you're here, Vortigern. If not, think about what happened to Pollux when he disobeyed me and then beg for mercy before I do the same to you."

"I didn't disobey," Rhode panted, skittering back. "I have *intel.*"

"Intel you should've delivered through the bug dials. Spit it out."

"Yes, sir." The boy stood up pencil-straight and scanned the interested faces of the other soldiers with smug satisfaction. "There's going to be a major hit against the humans," he announced. "Inborn militia from the Alley-out-of-the-Way are planning to detonate RP's under the city square."

Hadrian traded an irritated look with Coyote. "What is the blast radius?"

"One mile."

"Kuzmic. Narwood." Hadrian beckoned two Dracuslayers. "Deal with it. Do whatever is necessary to make sure those RP's don't go off."

"Yes, sir."

Snofrid couldn't fathom why Hadrian was acting so composed. RP's were radial plasma bombs—explosives so hot, they melted the buildings that they leveled. She now understood why there had been a council at the Alley. Yet, with the Sky-Legion arriving in just a few days, this retaliation could cause more harm than good. Digging her hand into her pocket, she hastily typed a coded message to Desya. The Alley was outside the blast radius, but just barely. The debris would decorate the Red Oxygen Bar.

Doubling back, she hastened towards Hadrian. Her entire body pulsed with urgency, but encouragement came at the thought that Lycidius and Desya couldn't be in on this plan. They knew as well as she did that Reznik would call in even more reinforcements in the event of a strike back. "Commander…"

"You won't go with them," he decided, before she could finish. "The Alley is outside the blast radius. Send your family a message if you need reassurance, but you're coming to the hunt site. That's nonnegotiable."

Hadrian moved through a lane of gun racks and stomped on the floor. The grates slid open, revealing a hidden elevator. "Everyone except Vortigern follow me," he ordered.

Rhode kicked a shell casing at the wall. "What am I supposed to do here?"

Hadrian gestured to a box of rags under the table. "Your punishment. Polish the guns on these racks until I can see my teeth in the carbon fiber. Then sleep on the floor. I don't want to deal with you again until morning."

The Alchemy Sphere

nofrid could barely match the pace of the Dracuslayer unit. Purpose fueled their steps through the forest and reluctance weakened hers. Outfitted in a Concealing Spell, she was guided by the occasional push and pull of Coyote's hand. The journey from the warehouse to the hunt site required a perilous trek through high snowdrifts, thickets, and yawning ravines; only a short stretch was paved by a path.

All her combined efforts couldn't soothe her apprehension. Talk of detonating RP's cluttered the bounds of her focus, steadily creeping inward, until the bombs were all she could think about. Twice, she told herself she was stressing for no reason. Hadrian had sent Dracuslayers to deal with the plotters, and they pulled rank on Inborn militia. Within the hour, the plotters would be subdued and the idea would be forgotten.

Bone-cold, she trudged up a ravine slope with sluggish steps. At the top, a feathery sensation cut across her skull, as if someone was lightly squeezing her temples. She winced and rubbed her head until a chuckling voice rippled through it with the force of a current and pooled at the root of her mind.

"You know, the Coyote bet ten gems that you'll wet your dress during the hunt," it taunted.

She halted midstride. *"Rhode?"*

"Address me as Draculayer Vortigern."

Feeling violated, she spared no regard for his rank. *"How did you get in my mind?"*

"Cause I'm the god of bug dials. There's no way you can kick me out, girl. The wall around your mind is as thin as tissue paper. It was child's play."

She suddenly saw the boy. Or rather, she saw his dirty feet. He was sitting on the vault floor, dissembled guns piled about his legs, with his phone in hand, playing the same violent video game. Somehow, she was able to see through his eyes even as he could see through hers. The vision wafted before her, almost a ghost image, more annoying than impairing to her sight.

"The Coyote might act tough here, but back in the Empyrean City, he's whipped," Rhode went on. *"His courtesan pedals him like a bike. Everyone knows it except him. It's hilarious."*

Snofrid felt Coyote's hand yank her back on track. Roots caught her feet, making her stagger, but she braced herself on the branch of a pine tree. *"So, what? You're just going to dish out dirt on your friends to annoy me?"*

"I'm going to give you some particulars to let you know who you're dealing with."

"Why?"

He reached to one side, and when he brought his hand back; it was fit to burst with gummy worms. *"So you'll hate them all."*

Snofrid gritted her teeth. *"Get out of my head."*

"I think I'll stay."

"Get out or I'll rat you out," she warned.

"Empty threat. I'll just pull out and you'll have no proof."

She continued up the ravine, undaunted. *"I have a strong feeling that my word will be worth more than yours."*

"Go on, then," Rhode urged. *"Go tell Commander Gravebane that I'm bothering you. I'm sure he'll force me out, give you his fur, and then and ask how else he can accommodate you."*

Snofrid hesitated. *"I'm sure he'd love to know how you're shirking."*

"Not likely. As long as I get these guns clean, he doesn't care what I do." Rhode cracked his toes, one by one, and continued, *"The Coyote said some interesting things about you...want to know what they were?"*

"You're going to tell me either way, so why not?"

"The Coyote said: she probably keeps her face hidden because she's an ugly moose."

Snofrid grabbed onto a boulder to steady her climb. *"Maybe I am."*

"Could be. But I think there's more to the mask than the Commander wants us to know." Rhode shoved a gummy worm down the chamber of a gun. *"I think you're hiding something. And I think I'll find out what it is and ruin you with it."*

"You know, after three days, we'll never see each other again. Why waste the effort?"

"It wouldn't be a wasted effort," he assured, a low chuckle in his throat. *"It would be fun to watch you cry."*

Snofrid fumed. She tried to expel Rhode's presence. Muscles straining, she imagined that his voice was leaking away, spiraling down a drain, but it just hovered there. Trying to get him out felt like trying to move a wall.

"That was feeble," His tone was full of pity. *"Your mind is too weak to defeat mine. I told you. I'm the god of bug dials."*

"I'm a fast learner," she assured.

"Mastering bug dials is a five-year study, so good luck with that."

Ahead, the Draculayers shed their concealing spells in the tree line before a spacious glade; the area, once filled with forest, now filled with the trunks of men sporting white ballistic camouflage armor and armed with cables, wood axes, shovels, Grenade Spells and anti-materiel rifles—rifles so powerful they could demolish a tank.

Hadrian broke formation as the Draculayers filed into the clearing.

"Where is the bait?" he demanded.

"I'm here," Snofrid called, holding up her hand.

"You're still concealed," he informed. "Shed the spell."

Snofrid stared at him blankly. Usually, she waited until her Concealing Spells wore off; if she'd known they could be shed, it might have saved her a lot of trouble in the past. "I don't know how," she admitted.

A few of the Draculayers broke into tittering laughter.

"I'll show her how," one of them offered.

"No." Hadrian strode toward her. He grabbed a fistful of her jacket and hoisted her upward; the spell slipped off, like a skin. "Next time, *will* it off," he said.

She landed on her feet with a gasp. "Next time, just *tell* me and I'll do it myself."

"Hessia." He flicked a claw, summoning the Seer. "Show the bait the Alchemy Sphere, then bring her back here."

"It will be done, master." Hessia glided toward Snofrid, her fur hood slipping off her scalp. The only color to offset her pale getup was cast by her violet eyes, which glowed through the eye-slits in her smiling mask. "This is the last time we'll meet before the hunt," she told Snofrid, her tone strangely polite. "So listen carefully. Any errors you make will be your responsibility alone. Understood?"

Snofrid clutched her pistol grip. "I understand."

They trekked down an icy trail, back the way they'd come. "The pitiful help from the Russian maid wasn't surprising," Hessia remarked. "Russians are the disease of humanity."

Snofrid disagreed. The gang Lycidius and Desya had worked for, Kapa, had been the most honorable in Gehenna. "I'm guessing the Inborn Army keeps Russian contacts."

"Unfortunately," Hessia confirmed, skidding on a pile of rocks. Her eyes paused a moment on Snofrid's Halo, as if trying to unlock its secrets. "The St. Petersburg Trojan Mortal base is among the largest in the world. Their agents do business with us, on the grounds that we meet certain provisions; but, despite contrary claims, size doesn't necessarily improve the efficiency of a thing." She fingered the iron collar around her neck; it probably chafed at her skin. "Constancy is what makes all things bear fruit. And sacrifice."

Snofrid noticed flowers of flaky, purple skin peeking from the lip of her mask. "You're referring to how you sacrificed your body?" she assumed.

"I sacrificed my body for the strength to raise Leaky Spells. So considering what I gained, it wasn't much of a sacrifice."

Rhode barked a laugh in Snofrid's mind, a high-pitched tittering sound. *That's dragonshit, if I've ever smelled it. Hessia never wanted power—she wanted approval. The whole reason she started messing with the Leaky Spells in the first place was because she thought that mastering them would make her stand on equal ground with us warriors.* He sniggered, shooting through an army of fluffy white rabbits on his video game. *No one will marry her now, especially because of her gross, mutilated face.*

Snofrid hardly heard him, for she'd had a sudden thought. If Hessia's capabilities were truly so prodigious, it was incredible that she'd been overcome by Hadrian. "How did the Commander break you if you're so powerful?" she tested.

"By a cleverly laid trap," Hessia replied simply, her eyes again darting greedily over Snofrid's Halo. "Many others tried to subdue me before he did, but I always destroyed them before their collars touched my neck. Instead of using force like all the others, Commander Gravebane used seduction. He promised me a position, a title, and respect." She sneered. "Obviously, he was a lying crust of filth. But at the time, I believed otherwise."

Snofrid felt no pity for her. But she did admit that they shared a common trait: resentment towards chains. "Is there a way to get the collar off?"

"Of course. I can't remove the collar, but another person could. She would just have to be merciful."

A sudden alarming sensation pulsed around Snofrid. She felt like she was looking at Lucian's eyelash pit viper, with its gleaming eyes and shiny scales. Before it had bit her, it had slithered all over her body, garnering her trust. Then the moment she'd reached out to stroke it, it had sprung at her. "I'm sure you'll find someone who believes your story someday," Snofrid told Hessia. "But I don't."

The Seer's voice deteriorated into a guttural rasp. "Only good liars can recognize other good liars."

"Maybe. But some people lie because they're forced to, not just for sport."

Snofrid held Hessia's black stare calmly. She knew Hessia hated her because she was a halfbreed. But perhaps Hessia also hated her out of envy over her healing ability? The idea seemed sound. Hessia craved power above all things, even beauty. The ability to regenerate would give her superior power without having to watch her body fall into ruin. This idea would also explain why the Seer harbored a personal, almost bitter vendetta against her.

Hessia broke eye-contact. "This way."

Snofrid, leaving her suspicions for the moment, slipped between two redwood trees after the Seer. Flipping back a drape of moss, Hessia stooped over roots matted with fungi and ferns. She dug through the snow and exposed a neat line of orange rock crystals packed into the soggy dirt.

"This is an *Alchemy Sphere*," she began, her voice now like a tiny, fluttering moth. All the anger she'd shown before was gone, as if it had evaporated from her. "Do you know what the spell does?"

"No," Snofrid inspected the line closely, still touching her pistol. "I haven't studied magic."

"Then I'll give you a short lesson." Hessia stroked her black nail over the crystals. "An Alchemy Sphere is a vastly intricate spell only capable of being raised by Phasma Necromancers. This one runs along the perimeter of the site in a circle. It will imprison any living creature that crosses into it, apart from the spell-raiser and whomever she chooses to exclude from it—which is all of us. We'll use the sphere to confine the welx." She scraped the snow back across the orange streak. "This is the first line of attack."

"How long is the sphere's diameter?" Snofrid asked.

"Two-thousand feet." Hessia stood, sweeping her cape off her boots.

"Let's go. There's still much to see."

Snofrid got to her feet just as Rhode's voice flitted across her mind again. *"Ever seen a Seer's face?"* he asked.

Disregarding him, she followed Hessia back to the glade.

"I'll take that as a no," Rhode deduced. *"Just imagine a head that got shoved into a bowl of acid. Then smash in the nose, rip out the teeth, and add gross, puss-filled blisters on the skin."*

"How long are you going to drag this out?" Snofrid demanded.

"As long as it takes to break you."

Once she returned to the Alley, she'd ask Lycidius to help her boot Rhode out. For now, she decided to take advantage of his desire to spill information. *"Keep at it, then,"* she invited. *"I can be patient when I want to be."*

Chuckling, he stretched out a gummy worm until it snapped. *"All patience has a breaking point."*

At the tree line, Snofrid crossed a beam bridge onto a triangular island, which stood in the center of a triangular trench. The trench was roughly six meters deep and had been dug along the edge of the glade. Hessia left her to canvass the layout. Before taking her leave, she said, "Report to my master when you've memorized what you see."

Snofrid released her pistol as the Seer drifted away. She glanced at Hadrian, who was issuing orders at the trench, and wondered if perhaps Hessia wasn't as great a danger as she'd thought. Snofrid still didn't trust Hadrian, but, over the past few hours, she'd felt more inclined to put faith in his protection. This was mainly due to Hadrian's affection for Lycidius. Since Lycidius was her Shadow, he'd take the blame if she was seriously injured or killed by Hessia. Snofrid doubted Hadrian would permit this. From the lengths she'd seen him go for Lycidius thus far, it wouldn't make sense if he let his brother lose face over the vendetta of his Seer.

Snofrid pulled her phone from her satchel, determined to photograph the finer details of the site. The first angle she captured was of the forest canopy; it made a dense sort of ceiling over the glade—a domed roof of branches that provided cover. Verdant trees, as tall as masts, picketed the site like a fence. Openings had been cleared through the dense branches, probably pruned for the benefit of the snipers. Several Dracuslayers were fine-tuning their sniper nests, built under cover of redwood roots and inside hollowed logs; others were being lowered by cables into the trench while the rest were laying out rows of steel spikes across the snow.

"One hydrocop unit is two klicks northeast, heading this way," Coyote announced. He was seated on a tree stump, a laptop on his knees. "Nethers, draw them out."

A stalky man emerged from the trench and unclipped his harness. He moved like smoke, here and then there, as quick as wind. His faced was shaded by a large hood, draped back to show his elaborate, tribal throat tattoo; it dipped down his chest, and appeared to flare out across his clavicle. Above it, a scarf was tightened around his mouthpiece.

Snofrid watched Nethers jog from the glade.

"Like what you see?" Rhode sneered. *"I think I just heard your mouth water."*

She took a photo of the trench. *"I'm not interested."*

"Judicious decision," Rhode praised. *"Fingal Nethers is crazy. Crazy can be funny, but most of the time it's tedious."* The boy sighed, pounding faster on his game controller. *"He thinks his newborn daughter is still alive, even though she's been worm food for the past two years."*

Snofrid felt a pang of shock. It sank into pity, and then rose up in annoyance. *"No one told him his daughter died?"*

"His courtesan used to tell him every day." Rhode rocked forward, sliding into a front split. *"Everyone who served under the Unloved God went crazy to some degree."* It sounded like he was smiling. *"Nethers has an obsessive need to do everything twice. Turning out the light, closing doors... placing large bets."* The boy reached a new level in his game and cheered, *"Woo hoo. I'm so good!"*

"Yagami!" Hadrian called. "Stop wasting my time."

Snofrid switched off her phone and jogged toward the trench, joining Hadrian and Hessia near its edge. Inside, two Dracuslayers were lining the floor with steel spikes. "This is the second line of attack?" she assumed.

"Yes. If the snipers fail, the spikes will destroy the welx. It's called a Fail

Floor." Hadrian unearthed a sheet of overlapping plates that resembled lavender quartz. She touched one; the surface was so warm, it radiated heat through her glove.

"These plates will eventually be laid across the full trench," he explained. "When the welx steps on them, they will collapse and the beast will be impaled by the spikes."

Snofrid noticed a Dracuslayer in a hazmat suit was lacing the spikes with a jelled substance. "What is he lacing the spikes with?"

"Hematic venom."

"How is it—"

"The venom has been stabilized with Abalus Root," he interrupted. "It won't go airborne. These plates will only trigger if touched by the welx— we've primed them to its DNA with magic. So if you need to run across them, you'll avoid becoming a pin cushion."

She felt reassured. There was sure to be commotion during the hunt and anyone could touch the plate by accident. This thought made her grimace: death by Hematic venom was rumored to be agonizing.

"The last part is an added defense for your sake," he said. Standing, he reburied the plates with his boot before gesturing to the center of the glade. "There is a steel dome buried under the snow that will activate once the welx crosses the Alchemy Sphere. You'll be safe enough inside when all hell breaks loose."

"How do I get out of it?" she asked.

"There is a lever on the ceiling. Pull it down and the dome will flatten."

She frowned. "On me?"

"*Around* you." He flipped up a claw in warning. "But don't open the dome until the welx is dead."

"I won't. But tell me when it happens. I'd rather not be sitting in there after you all leave."

Hadrian smirked, as if considering the idea. "The Coyote will be your handler during the hunt," he went on. "He'll tell you when to activate the dome and when to exit it." Hadrian moved to walk away, before he stopped and faced her, rotating his fist in a circular motion. "Do another walkthrough of the site."

"I've memorized it already."

"Your assurances don't concern me. Do another walkthrough."

Snofrid sighed. "Fine." Whipping out her phone, she stalked toward the nearest bridge.

"*I'm sensing tension in the air,*" Rhode remarked. "*Where might it be coming from?*"

"*It's coming from how much I dislike you.*"

"*Lie.*" Rhode sprawled out on his back, holding the game screen right up to his face. "*It's coming from a strong resentment towards something else…maybe you want me to spice up your dislike of the Commander with some depraved details?*"

She took a moment to mull it over. "*No, thank you,*" she decided. "*I already know enough about him that's depraved.*"

"*You can never get too much filth on a person,*" Rhode assured. "*Commander Gravebane whacked his father. Messily.*"

"*I already know.*"

Rhode fell silent a moment. "*In battle, he eats people in his second form.*"

Snofrid thought of Cannibal Brongo and her insides churned. Ducking under a tree bough, she started doing laps around the site. "*That's disgusting.*"

"*It is, but you know nothing.*" Rhode snorted a laugh, suddenly amused. "*Because the Commander's a Skinwalker, he can hear high pitched sounds. He's also very sensitive to them. So if someone were to play the pitch, 67 Hz+, he'll turn dopey.*"

She fell short on what this meant. "*You mean he gets stupid?*"

"*Wait, while I blow up this rabbit den.*" Rhode's thumbs pounded the screen of his phone as he pelted a family of bunnies until they exploded. "*Nailed it…where was I?*"

"*Commander Gravebane.*"

"*Oh, yeah. If you play that pitch, then he'll…well, he'll be more easily 'persuaded'.*"

She wavered, feeling skeptical. "*If that's true, then why don't you use it and get out of gun cleaning duty?*"

He scoffed, firing down another row of rabbits. *"Because the pitch is on my other phone, and I left it at the Web."*

"I appreciate the lowdown," she said, climbing over a fallen log. *"But I don't need to persuade Commander Gravebane into doing anything."*

Rhode snorted. *"I'm not doing you any favors, girl. Don't start fantasizing about us being friends now."*

"Don't worry," she muttered aloud. "The fantasy wouldn't even enter my mind."

Snofrid completed two laps of the site, taking photos and marking where the sniper nests were. Snow was showering from the sky by the time she returned to the middle of the glade. The Dracuslayers were tiling the trench with lavender plates.

"Yagami," Hadrian hollered from the farthest bridge. "You're done. Follow the Coyote."

"Finally." She made a beeline for the stump where Coyote was packing up his laptop when her phone beeped. She switched the phone on and was stunned to find a message from Atlas Bancroft.

What girl calls a bloke and then doesn't answer his return call?
Give me a bell when you get this, Snofrid.

Snofrid read and then reread the message. How could he have sent it? In order for him to contact her through the shield, he'd have to be in Hollowstone.

"Let's go," Coyote said, nudging her arm. "I'll escort you home." He swung the duffle over his shoulder and circled back toward the bridge. "I'll come for you Thursday evening at 1800 hours," he went on. "The welx will feed from anytime between midnight on Thursday to midnight on Friday, so we need to be in position early. We'll do a run through before we put you in place. From that point on, you'll be on your own."

She nodded, still distracted by Atlas's message. "Uh…what do I need to bring?"

Coyote ignored her. He dropped his duffle bag and glanced around, his eyes tapered. "What is that?"

Snofrid followed his sight to tree line, thinking he might've heard hydrocops. She ditched the idea swiftly; the sensors would've picked up on anything in the area.

"Commander, do you feel that?" Coyote called. "There's something under us."

Hadrian hunkered down and felt the earth with his palm.

"The Coyote's senses are never wrong," Rhode said, flinging his game aside. *"Turn. I need a panoramic view."*

Snofrid turned. *"I don't see anything."*

Hadrian shot to his feet. Seizing Hessia's arm, he raced to the center of the clearing, and roared, "Take cover!"

In one swift motion, the Dracuslayers dropped and shielded their heads with their arms.

Snofrid felt a tremor start low in the earth, rattling her body like a leaf in a storm. She slid onto her chest and crawled toward the bridge. *"What's happening?"*

"If it's an earthquake, you're going to want to be away from the trees," Rhode pointed out. *"And you're...wait a minute."* The boy stood up, shaking off the guns with a clatter. His tone grew excited. *"This isn't an earthquake, it's an uprising!"*

BOOM.

The cloud from an explosion erupted somewhere in the city above. Body shuddering, Snofrid dug her fingers into the snow. Creaking metal and shattering glass echoed the upsurge, screeching even louder than the fireworks. She craned her neck skyward, and thought desperately, *"What the hell is happening?"*

Intense heat fanned across the area, evaporating the snow from the sky. For an instant, she saw fire ballooning over the tops of the trees. Fear tore through her like a rotary blade. A blue wave of wafting heat melted a section of buildings somewhere near the city square. Deep down, she knew what was happening, but felt too terrified to register it fully. The high-rises bowed like wet paper before splashing down over surrounding buildings.

"Oh my hell." She staggered to her feet as the wave expanded and then headed for the hunt site. Her gaze fixed on two paragliders sailing over the treetops, their wings catching the flare of the blast. Before the wave took them, their wings smoked, screams sliced the air, and they enkindled in the heat.

"*Ooh, bullseye,*" Rhode cheered, throwing an air punch. "*Don't worry, girl. The site is outside the blast radius. It can only be one mile and you're 1.6 miles out.*"

"*The Alley is 1.2 miles out.*" Snofrid bolted for the bridge. Just as she reached it, Coyote seized her arm and hauled her backward. She shoved him off, bucking and thrashing in his grip. "Don't you dare try to stop me! I need to see my family!"

"Your family is on their own," Coyote panted, struggling to restrain her. "You need to be *free* to assist in the hunt, which means you're coming with us. This city is about to go to hell."

Around the site, the Dracuslayers scrambled to their feet and packed up their gear. Snofrid twisted in Coyote's hold, freeing one hand, and switched on her phone. Coyote snatched it from her and stuffed it into his armor. Lunging, she pounded on him with her fists. "That's my brother's life, you bastard!"

"*Enough.* Don't make me silence you myself." In one hoist, Coyote flung her over his shoulder. She grabbed a fistful of his hair and yanked hard.

"Continue, and I'll allow the Coyote to knock you unconscious," Hadrian threatened. "You're coming to the Spyderweb and you won't set one foot outside of it until this is over."

The Third Door on the Left

Wednesday, 2 Days until the Hunt

Since moving in, Snofrid had learned two essential details about the Spyderweb tunnels. Firstly, they were a confounding labyrinth of dead-ends and violent traps. And secondly, they were vaster than one could chart in only a few days.

Standing before a rock wall coated with turquoise glowworms, she resisted admitting she was lost. She'd been tricked by Rhode. *Again.* Turning on her heel, she gazed back the way she'd come. Glowworms dazzled in the pitch blackness, extending a half-mile down, so that the tunnel looked like a boulevard through outer space. The passages magically changed to mislead intruders, which added further difficulty. This was the third dead-end and she was beyond aggravated at Rhode's taste for causing trouble.

She rubbed her aching temples with her thumbs. *It could be a lot worse,* she told herself, trying to generate her own encouragement. Hadrian had confirmed that Lycidius, Desya and Jazara hadn't been harmed in the RP bombing, which was almost all she'd hoped for. However, one important thing remained to be done: responding to Atlas's message. This was why she was down in the tunnels, tramping through the darkness and trying to outrun shifting walls. Without a phone, she figured her best alternative was to make a trade with Rhode before her time ran out—if she ever found his room that is. Tomorrow, Lucian would come to collect on their deal, making tonight her final chance to request Atlas's help.

Pulling off her glove, she pressed her palm to the rock and waited sixty seconds. She breathed a curse. It wasn't a Mock Wall.

"Lost?" Rhode's voice asked. He sounded entertained.

"I'm lost because you keep leading me in circles," she accused. *"It should've taken me fifteen minutes to find your room, not an hour."*

The boy chuckled. He was sprawled out on a high, four-posted bed in a chamber of blue coral, leafing through a horror comic book called *Bloody Claw*. Plush white beast furs were heaped across his stomach, and, at his feet, she saw piles of candy spilling from paper bags.

"You took a wrong turn back at the Orina Junction," he told her.

She whirled. *"That was WAY back there, Rhode. Why didn't you tell me sooner?"*

"To humble you." He licked his finger, then turned the page of his comic book. *"You need to understand how helpless you are without my contributions."*

"Your contributions are wasting my time." She stalked back down the tunnel, aiming her lunar stone light at the receding walls; the glowing lunar stone was encapsulated by a lantern, which could only be dimmed by shutting the metal lantern screen.

"Patience, girl. Remember that this meeting is a favor to you." A sucking sound slurred the end of his speech. A blue lollipop suddenly appeared and waved in front of his face. *"If I get caught shirking with you, I'll be on wash-duty. You should appreciate the risk I'm taking."*

"I'd say you're already taking a pretty big risk by being in your room. You're supposed to be doing endurance training right now."

"Nope. That's at 0900 hours."

"Then I was right. You're late. It's 0947 hours."

Rhode added a third viewpoint to the bug dials, zooming in on a circular arena paved with gravel. Grunts, shouts, and clanking wood tore the air. The other Dracuslayers were dragging each other across the gravel by ropes, beating one another in the chests with rocks and leaping onto each other's shoulders, forming Inborn ladders up the walls.

"It doesn't look like they know I'm missing." Rhode tugged a cord, letting loose a fabric canopy around his bed; the training images vanished as the curtain was drawn. *"I think I'll stay right here."*

"What happens when they do realize you're gone?"

"Someone will come get me. When they do, I'll squeeze through the filter system and be in the training arena before he reaches my lodgings."

She ducked under a bridge made of trees. This was something about Rhode she envied: he didn't ever seem to be intimidated by anything, including Hadrian's mighty discipline. *"Good luck squeezing through the strainers,"* she said.

"The strainers?" He snorted. *"Those are child's play."* He threw his lollipop stick onto the floor. *"Why are we having this meeting anyway, girl?"*

"I'll tell you why when I get to your room." Snofrid sped up, hopping over puddles of glowworm goo. At a bend in the tunnel, she shone her lantern on a grated iron door. *"What on earth?"* she murmured. *"Is that a dungeon?"*

"Indeed. If we take P.O.W.'s, they need a place to stay."

She resumed her urgent pace. *"Do you know every room in the Spyderweb?"*

"Every room, every tunnel, and every staircase."

"Where does the spiral staircase in the courtyard lead?"

"The Commander Lodgings. No one is allowed inside except the Coyote."

"Why just him?" she questioned.

"Because he's the Commander's pet." Rhode chuckled at his comic and muttered, *"I knew she'd die."* Licking his thumb, he turned the page again. *"So...how is sketch number seven?"*

She frowned, the lantern rattling with her steps. *"The Commander made me restart again."*

Rhode laughed. *"That's because the proportions looked like Hessia's face."*

"The proportions were fine."

"If the hunt site really looked like what you drew, we'd all die."

"Everyone except me," she corrected.

Snofrid exited the glowworm tunnels and scuttled across a marble platform. Commander Hadrian's perfectionism was a tack in her shoe. He'd ordered her to sketch the hunt site from memory, but the task had evolved into eight different sketches. Whenever she'd complete a new diagram, he'd skim it over and then chuck it into the fire and say, "The blind Hematic Lord draws with better proportions. Do another one."

It was a pain. She was poor at sketching, so she'd most likely be redoing the picture until the actual hunt. Refusal wasn't within her power on account of the Covenant, but her conformity to Hadrian's will in other areas was beginning to waver. It had begun when he'd hijacked her phone. Keeping the phone wasn't even necessary. She wasn't a threat to security; he simply needed to have control. Just like he had to control the RP bombs. Since they'd gone off, he'd placed the full responsibility upon Narwood and Kuzmic—for arriving late at the Alley and failing to track down the Inborns in possession of the RP's. In Hadrian's mind, failure was *defiance.* She turned squeamish at the thought of what Narwood and Kuzmic's punishment had been.

The sole information she'd heard on the bombing aftermath was from several news broadcasts the Dracuslayers had gathered to watch last night and this afternoon. Now, instead of the fireworks of humanity week, the flashing strobes of emergency transports lit the city. Hundreds of Red Cross personnel, firefighters, emergency medical technicians, and aviation units had been called in to provide medical assistance. On top of this, President Sebaster had issued two-thousand marines to Hollowstone and had allegedly begun negotiations to rally worldwide support for military action. Already, over two billion silvers in donations had been amassed, for the bombing would reportedly amount to seventy billion silvers in property and infrastructure damage. Citizens had swarmed the hospitals in their willingness to give blood donations, and memorial services were being held globally for the 109,000 reported deaths.

As Snofrid had feared, the attack had generated serious backlash. Presently, her kind were being hunted down by Hollowstone veterans and civilians. Before being executed, they were forced to admit their crimes against humanity on video and then made to beg forgiveness. Outside the shield, humans from neighboring cities had congregated with firearms, demanding access to the city, so they could do their part in the extermination of Inborns. Order was gone. Riots rose up in every borough; fear pushed people to accuse their neighbors, and grief made people forget who they were. Snofrid understood why they forgot. She'd lost a part of herself the day Ryuki had died, and then another, the day Parisa had abandoned them.

Eventually, she arrived at a junction in the tunnel that split into five passages. Heart-shaped green aroid plants and moldy fungi budded from the rocks.

"Okay," she announced. "I'm at the Orina Junction."

"Jupioper Fork," Rhode directed, swiping up a bag of jelly beans with his toes. "Second right."

Snofrid followed the fork into an armory. Everything from sniper rifles, pistols, acid grenades, to honed longswords, spiked morning stars, various bo staffs, brass Chakrams, and grisly Longxu hooks stocked the racks. She wondered why the armory wasn't better protected, until the walls started to shift and close in on her. She bolted from the room before it entombed her.

"Astros Fork," Rhode said. "Middle left."

"Did you really memorize all these tunnels?" she panted. "Or do you have a map hidden under your pillow?"

"I never rely on maps," he sneered. "They're a crutch. I have an eidetic memory. It's a Draculayer requirement." He flipped onto his stomach and reached for a new book. "But these tunnels are child's play. There are secret passages all throughout the Empyrean City called Wheezing Ways. Everyone— except us mnemonists—need a Meridian Map to navigate."

She bet that a mnemonist was some great thing he'd expound upon.

"Since you probably don't know," he went on, *"a mnemonist is someone with a superior capacity to remember what they see. Like numbers, minefield locations, bank information."*

"I figured. The context was self-explanatory." Snofrid, knowing that Lycidius had once been a Dracuslayer, was curious and asked, *"What do Dracuslayers need aside from a good memory?"*

Rhode chortled and flipped open a book called, *Legends of Flesh-Eating Monsters.* *"You couldn't handle it."*

"I'm not interested in joining. It was just plain curiosity."

He deliberated, rolling a pink jelly bean around in his palm. *"Dracuslayers are required to know all the Inborn dialects, plus a few dozen human languages. Most have to be ambidextrous, and limber like rubber bands."* He sprinkled two more jelly beans into his hand, his voice haughty. *"Tack on bug dials training. Lie detection training. Pain tolerance training. Body language training. Weapon's training."* He added five more beans to the pile. *"Geometry. Physics. Swim 6.2 meters per second. An IQ of 140 or higher. 20/5 vision…"*

"Wait," she interrupted, her tone skeptical. *"Dracuslayers need an IQ over 140?"*

"Indeed." He tossed the jelly beans in the air, catching them all in his mouth. *"Mine is 146."*

Somehow, she mistrusted this.

"What's your intelligence level?" Rhode goaded. *"Or maybe you're too embarrassed to tell?"*

She raised her head slightly, unapologetic. *"129."*

He blasted a laugh. *"Yeah. You definitely couldn't be a Dracuslayer."*

"Good thing I'd rather go into politics, then."

Rhode snorted, then twirled his toe in a circle. *"My lodgings are in the Ursia Vortex. Turn right at the end of this tunnel and keep walking in circles until I tell you to stop."*

"This better not be another trick," she forewarned.

"You're no longer fun to trick, girl. It's boring to keep winning so easily."

"We were never competing," she pointed out. This was another common

trait she'd found in Draculslayers. They turned everything into a game.

Following his instructions, she strolled down a spiral-like tunnel, around and around and around, until she felt dizzy; a major downside of the Spyderweb was that the designer had a fascination with swirling walkways. Arched doors padded the walls and colorful mosaics adorned the marble flooring.

"*Up ahead,*" Rhode said. "*The door with the winged-octopus knocker leads into my lodgings.*"

Just as she found the door, it flew open. Rhode stood framed in the doorway, wearing a cobalt silk robe that bared his skinny white chest. His platinum side-braided mohawk was rumpled from his pillow, and blue dye stained his lips.

"Still wearing a gasmask," he observed. "The guys and I are starting to wonder why that is."

"Never mind why." She cupped her gasmask filter, gagging at the awful stench that crowded the room. "Are you going to let me in?"

He propped up two fingers. "Two rules: don't touch my armor and don't look through my comics."

"Fine."

He stepped aside, granting her entrance. The chamber stunk and was messier than if it had been hit by a bomb, but the elaborate interior made her marvel; Draculslayer soldiers customarily had barren lodgings. Candy wrappers littered the floor, some stuffed into the velvet cushions, or kicked under the bed; a fabric canopy and gilded headboard decked out the king-sized bed. Candelabras and sunburst mirrors festooned the blue coral walls, matching the hues of the pillared fireplace in the corner.

"Is everyone's room this nice?" she asked, eyeing a living wall of evergreen plants.

He cracked a toothy grin. "Not even close. This room is a Governor Lodging."

She posed a guess. "You ran the fastest and claimed it first?"

"Nope. Nethers is the fastest sprinter. When he snagged it, I let a skunk loose inside." Rhode stretched his arms and paced toward the bed. "After it sprayed, he backed out and no one else wanted it."

She wouldn't have wanted it either. As she closed the door, she noticed the rows of boxes and tubes across the floor.

"That's my training gear," Rhode said.

"Wait." She gave him a look. "Don't tell me you squeeze into—"

"Believe it." He leaned against the bedpost. "All right. Let's get this over with. What do you want?"

"I need to use your phone."

"No can do. The Commander doesn't want you making calls."

"Not for a call. I'm going to use your phone to play the super high pitch to persuade him to return *my* phone—I need an important number from it."

Rhode stroked his chin thoughtfully. "What's in it for me?"

"Tell me what you want."

"Well, let me see." His eyes prowled the room. "Two things: I want you to clean my room before the hunt, and I want you to show me your moose face."

She lobbed up a hand in protest. "I'll clean your smelly room, but I won't take off my mask."

"No face, no deal."

Snofrid knew if she showed him her face, he'd peg her as a halfbreed flat-out. And considering his poor ability to keep anything a secret, the whole Spyderweb would know by lunchtime. She swung her head toward him in warning. "If I do show you, then I want your word as a highborn that what you see will stay between us."

"Silence will cost extra."

"I thought it would. How much extra?"

Shoving off the bedpost, he strolled to a trunk beside the evergreen wall. He hiked open the lid and gestured to a skunk sleeping in the corner. "Let him loose in the refectory during dinner."

She grimaced. "If I do that, everyone will get sprayed."

"As planned."

"Tell me why you can't do it."

"Simple, girl. I don't want to be on wash-duty again." Shutting the lid, he lifted up his leg and stripped off a trux illusion key from the sole of his foot. "This will get you into the baths. You'll need it after you do the deed. But go after 1900 hours.

"Hold on. I didn't agree yet." She eyed the dirty key, glad she was wearing gloves. "Why after 1900 hours?"

"Because I do laps at 1800 hours. My streamline is wicked; it needs the whole bathtub." He sat on a lounge before the fireplace, getting comfortable. "Okay. Show me what's behind the mask."

The devious twinkle in his eye made the hair on her nape prick up. There was a solid chance that Rhode could spill her secret, so she had to ask herself which scenario would be worse. Risking the lives of her loved ones, or being penalized if the other Dracuslayers learned she was a halfbreed?

Turning to Rhode, she said, "What assurance do I have that you won't break your word?"

"Blind trust."

"I'd sooner trust that the skunk won't spray me." She plunked the lunar lantern on the table in frustration as she faced the reality that everything had a price. Getting her phone was crucial, despite how the cost affected her. She reached for her gasmask straps, her tone severe. "If you do tell anyone, I'll make sure you regret it, Dracuslayer Vortigern."

Snofrid pinched her nose to block the foul skunk odor that clogged the bathhouse air. She was soaking in a private pool at the back with the lace curtain drawn. The foamy water had grown tepid, for she'd been required to wait two hours to bathe. Every Dracuslayer in the Spyderweb had flooded the bathhouse after the skunk sprayed at dinner and had lingered there, steeping for hours. She hadn't been allowed to enter until 8:30, but since Hadrian would be in a meeting with Lord Alcander until 9:30, she didn't feel rushed.

Lifting her chin, she gazed up at the marble sculptures that ornamented the bathhouse pillars. One sculpture of a female soldier with flaming hair stooped over the water. Snofrid found herself thinking about the hunt as she looked at the warrior's stouthearted face. She'd listened to heroic tales of war her entire life, existed on the brink of it, yet she'd never truly understood how people could give their lives to war. The most natural outcome was death; a risk she'd never felt with her healing ability. She wondered if soldiers felt fear. Maybe it took a certain kind of soul to fight— a great soul. She'd never been inherently daring. In the past, she'd forced herself to do things that frightened her for the sake of those she loved, but those things were merely trifles. They weren't the kind of bravery that would be deemed heroic. She'd need heroic bravery during the hunt, though she feared that when it counted, she'd prove to be a coward.

As she reached for her towel, Hessia glided into the chamber with a bag of clothes tucked under one arm. The Seer chose the nearest open bath and proceeded to unfasten the clasps on her cotton tunic. Snofrid clutched the pistol that was hidden under her towel.

"I'm in here, just so you know," she said, drawing back the curtain.

"I do know," Hessia called. "I caught the stench of halfbreed from the hallway."

In her peripheral, Snofrid watched the tunic slide off her shoulders, baring her blistered back and bony ribs; scars, bursting abscesses and hanging flesh plagued her skin, making Snofrid wonder how she wasn't moaning in constant pain.

When she lifted off her facial armor, Snofrid couldn't suppress a flinch. The Seer's eyes were crooked, like the eyes of a melting snowman. The flayed purple skin that stretched over her skull made her resemble a leprous monster. Her mouth was toothless and trimmed with decaying gums, but the sight wasn't nearly as horrific as her crushed nasal bone and skewed jaw.

"Your reaction is no different from others," Hessia said, wading into the pool. "Go on and stare if you wish. By now it's become more thrilling than demeaning."

Snofrid frowned as Hessia side-eyed her right bicep. "You always look at my Halo," she noted, "which makes me wonder: are you interested in my ability to regenerate? Or are you jealous of it?"

Hessia arched a brow. "I could never be jealous of a halfbreed."

"I think you are. I see it in your *face*."

Hessia went quiet, her nails curling around the lip of the bath. "As a soldier, I must destroy my vulnerabilities. But also as a soldier, I must face the realization that life is transient. Only a creature who can control whether she lives or dies is truly powerful. *Most creatures* want what you have."

Snofrid's hand had grown sweaty on her pistol. It seemed a lot of people wanted what she had. Invincibility wasn't only Hessia's goal, but the Helios Society's goal and it had been the goal of the Unloved God.

"I know they do," she said. "Which is why I'm thankful every day that there isn't a way for me to give it to them."

Hessia's eyes again flitted to her Halo and glittered darkly. "What makes you so certain?"

"Just *try* verifying it."

Hessia's lips peeled back into a wicked smile. "When the hunt is over, I *will*."

Snofrid let the threat blow past her. "When someone is truly strong, breaking the body does nothing," she said. "It's breaking the mind that destroys a person. So, in your case, getting a healing ability would be a small achievement. Your mind isn't unconquerable."

She yanked the curtain closed. Using it for cover, she dressed herself in the long blue skirt and knit sweater she'd been wearing since the Alley. She then packed up her belongings and hastened to her room, leaving Hessia stewing alone in the pools. Her room was a standard soldier's quarter, which was probably why it was neighbor to Hessia's.

Dumping her things onto the desk, she swiped up her latest sketch of the hunt site. It could fail, but the sketch would be half of her excuse to see Commander Hadrian. He hadn't left his lodgings since the skunk ordeal—which luckily no one had discovered she was responsible for—so she hoped he wasn't still in a meeting. By now, Atlas probably thought she was blowing him off. Imagining this made her want to sprint all the way to the Commander Lodgings, batter down the door and then shake Hadrian until he gave up her phone. Unfortunately, she'd need a more artful plan.

She jogged to the refectory. The jaunty commotion of the soldiers' recreation echoed down the halls long before she entered the chamber. Inside, they all donned exquisite floor-length tunics detailed with silver brocade. As they gambled with dice, guzzled down dragon-ale, and shucked clams, none regarded her with hostility, just the usual suspicion.

She ducked under Rhode, who was swinging like an ape on the ceiling beams, and ended at the table beside Coyote. He was playing a game of *Thaul* with Nethers and a Dracuslayer named Darling. It was an Inborn number game of strategy that used a latticed board and wooden spheres. Coyote didn't seem to be faring well. Sitting hunched with his forearms on the table, he spun a lustrous gem around in his palm, occasionally lighting it up with a burst of blue electricity.

"What do you need?" he asked her.

"To talk to the Commander."

"The Commander is in his study," he informed. "No one bothers him after the door closes."

Snofrid had anticipated some red tape but was far from quitting. "Please. It's important."

Coyote eyeballed her sketch. "I think the drawing can wait."

"That's not why I want to see him. Tell him I want to apologize."

Coyote arched a brow, incredulous. "For what exactly? How about you apologize for tearing my hair out?"

She stiffened in defiance. After how he'd handled her at the hunt site, he deserved it. "Fine. I'm sorry I ripped your hair out."

Laughter erupted in the room "Did she tear out your manhood with it?" someone jeered. "Or maybe she left some behind so you wouldn't be a complete wet bag."

"That's exactly what you're going to be, Narwood, when you're kissing my ass." Coyote skidded back his chair, tossing his gems on the table with a clatter. "I'll run it by him," he said to Snofrid, "but expect nothing."

She nodded. "Thank you."

As he left the refectory, she slipped a hand into her pocket and switched on Rhode's phone. The boy had downloaded a recording of the pitch 67 Hz+ from the hypernet, setting it to play on a loop. No one seemed to detect a change as it began to play, though she was certain Hadrian was within earshot; his hypersensitive Skinwalker hearing allowed him to isolate sounds within a ten-mile radius.

"What do you need to apologize for, girl?" Rhode hollered from the ceiling beams.

"Something you'll never hear about."

"Don't need to. I can guess." He swung back and forth on the beam, gaining momentum, before he heaved into a triple front flip, and fell into a side-break on the table. "You want clemency for denying us warriors our rightful respect?"

"No."

"Then you want forgiveness for entering into our midst as a deceiver in lady's clothing?"

Snofrid shot him a cautionary glance. Since he'd seen her face, he'd been trying to trip her up in some way or another. Thankfully, it seemed that he intended to keep the secret of her halfbreed nature, but this didn't ensure that he wouldn't try to make her spill it on her own. *"Remember our deal,"* she thought.

"I might." He shoved a dragon fruit into his mouth, grinning widely. *"I might not."* Rhode angled his head lazily at Nethers. "What do you say, Nethers? Do you think you're feeling a little dry in admiration from the girl?"

Nethers said nothing.

"Silence is consent." Rhode set his hands on his hips with an air of authority. "It looks to be unanimous. We want you to take off the mask and entertain us."

"What did I tell you about standing on the table, Vortigern?" Coyote called, striding back into the room. "Nethers. Give him a charley horse."

Nethers wrenched his scarf down and spewed rays of burning blue magic from his mouth; they speared through Rhode's calf. Knees buckling, he burst into shrieks and landed on his backside with a thump. Snarling, he clutched his leg to relieve the cramp. "Take it off!"

Nethers shut his mouth, cutting off the flow of magic.

"You'll regret this, Bourkan," Rhode wheezed.

Coyote was unmoved. "Not as much as you're going to regret whining. The Commander chose you as the fall guy for the skunk."

"Dragonshit!" Rhode aimed a foot at Snofrid. "It was the *girl* who did it!"

"No witness, no proof." Coyote jerked his thumb at the wash room. "Now go put on your apron and start scrubbing."

Gritting his teeth, Rhode slammed a foot on the table. "I've been working ALL DAY."

"What did the Commander say?" Snofrid interrupted. At Coyote's sudden mistrustful stare, she tensed up, wondering if Rhode had tricked her with the pitch.

"He said yes," Coyote finally answered.

Snofrid looked at the spiral staircase with hope. Murmurs of suspicion fluttered around her, but she ignored them. "I can go up right now?"

"Yes." Coyote sat down and scooped up his gems. "The Commander's study is the third door on the left."

Bull's-Eyes

The long corridor above the spiral staircase was lightless. Snofrid moved carefully, groping the walls to guide her steps. In the darkness, her senses were more acute and picked up scents of purple heather and blue anemone. The blend reminded her of a wild forest; she wondered if Hadrian kept an herb stash.

Rhode's phone was stored safely in her pocket; it still emitted the pitch in what was silence to her ears. A hunch that the boy might be deceiving her hung in her mind. All his spiteful games seemed rooted in the childish pleasure he got from causing trouble. One glance at Hadrian would likely confirm the boy's true motives.

The third door on the left led to a spiral staircase. She made the ascent and found another door on the top landing, crafted from mahogany wood and silver filigree. She mentally went through her plan. There was no room for mistakes. This time, if it was possible, she had to be slyer than Hadrian.

Before entering, she removed her gasmask and pulled back her wet hair.

"Stop grooming yourself," Hadrian called. "Come in and shut the door after you."

She dropped her hands, briefly embarrassed. After closing the door, she padded into a room that idolized two things: order and plant life. Certain details reminded her of Lycidius's style, predominantly the bed. All the pillows and furs had been stripped off, leaving a barren mattress; but the medley of ferns, fringed pink flowers and sneezewort was as vibrant as a greenhouse. All the plants were native to Norway. Around her, the wall stonework was seized by the lichen-caked roots of the black tree growing above them, so that the room looked overrun and abandoned.

Hadrian was nowhere.

"Where are you?" she said.

"On the other side of the arch."

Snofrid followed the sound of crackling flames. Soon, she found herself in an alcove where two armchairs basked in the light of a stone fireplace.

Hadrian sat before a high wooden desk, flipping through a Demented Book called *Ridley's Secret*. Though his face was in shadow, she swore it held traces of enjoyment. The red single-shoulder pauldron he wore bared his right arm, which was flexing proudly over a finely patterned breastplate with the insignia of a black upside-down tree. On the desk was a ceramic oil burner, from which the forest scents wafted. In all, he looked the same, except that he tapped his boot against the floor, as if he heard music somewhere off and was keeping time with the beat.

"How did Vortigern get you to release the skunk?" he asked. A silver barbell flickered inside his mouth.

"I figured you'd accuse me." He'd given her critical glances all throughout dinner. "I needed something from him. The skunk was the only thing he'd trade."

"That's unlikely." Hadrian snapped the book shut. "Vortigern used you, just as I did. When you know the desires of the person you're trading with, you control the exchange. Compliment Vortigern's intelligence and he'll lick your toes."

Remarkably, Snofrid suspected this advice would work.

Hadrian slid the Demented Book into a bookcase. When he'd returned to his chair, he looked her over and said, "You'd tell my Dracuslayers that you're a halfbreed before apologizing to me for anything. What is it you're really here for?"

"Actually, that part was true." She laid the sketch on his desk. "Sorry, I couldn't draw a perfect one. This is the best I can do."

He regarded the skewwhiff sketch with discontent. "That's worse than the last one. I still don't buy it. You have the look women make when they want something. Tell me what you're trying to con out of me."

He made women sound like leeches. "I'm not here to con you out of anything," she assured. "I'm here to make a *trade*. It seems to be the only way one can do anything around here."

"This is about the phone," he realized. "What is your strategy to get it, aside from asking for it?"

She reminded herself of Lucian's words about deals: *Let the deal be spoken first and then manipulate it to your advantage.* "What are you willing to trade?"

"On a normal day, I'd tell you to leave the way you came. You were informed that your family is alive. No further contact is necessary." He yanked a knife from his boot and hurled the tip into a dartboard above the fireplace, hitting the double bull's-eye. "But since I'm in a good mood, we'll play a game of Shanghai. The victor wins a favor."

She eyed the dartboard—its frame was wreathed in beast teeth—and confidence blew away all of her worry. This was a trade she could win. "All right," she agreed, her voice now jaunty. "But we'll play without the Shanghai rule. We have to go all the way around, hitting the sectors in numerical order—one throw each turn. Then we'll end with a double bulls-eye."

"You're worried I'll win in my first throw?" he guessed.

"Not at all. I want it to be challenging. That means no shortcuts."

His mouth twitched in amusement. Scooting back his chair, he retrieved the game pieces from a breakfront across the room.

Snofrid traced her finger across the phone in her pocket, now convinced that the pitch method was real. Hadrian had never been this accommodating where Lycidius wasn't concerned. In fact, for the first time, she detected a genuine attentiveness in his expression.

Upon returning, he handed her three darts whittled from bone. The tips were honed to points and the flights were crafted from bat wings. "Find something to record your score," he said.

"I won't bother. I'm sure your eidetic memory can handle it."

"You either have an interest in Dracuslayer life, or you've been talking to Vortigern."

"Both, actually."

Hadrian backed away from the dartboard, pinching the creases from his flights. "You should think before you believe everything he says. He's trained to manipulate and deceive."

She was deftly aware. "From living with Lycidius, I learned what to expect from a Dracuslayer. I never thought I'd meet someone more manipulative than him, but your training is truly terrifying."

"I was never trained," Hadrian corrected. "I've been manipulating the outcome of scenarios since I could speak. It's a natural skill."

She believed this as soon as the words bounced off his tongue. And his superiority about it was foreseeable, though his bragging air was new. "You strong-armed your mother into which brand of diapers you wanted?"

Hadrian smirked. "My mother never cared for me a day in her life. Soldiers are raised by their fathers." He snuffed the flame in the oil burner and then went on. "Essentially, I destroyed the belief systems of other child soldiers."

She noted the way he said this with a disturbed feeling, as if he'd murdered something. "Why would anyone want to do that?"

"To control them. To *own* them. By cutting down a person's confidence and condescending their moral codes, they question their own principles. This made the child soldiers feel foolish for thinking freely—for trusting in their ability to make logical decisions. Eventually, they didn't have enough self-confidence to think anything unless it was approved by me."

He leaned against the desk, aligning his shoulders with hers. "Within two months, the children had formed a completely new consensus of beliefs, which, in effect, changed their identities."

She found this far more horrifying than he made it sound. He wasn't just manipulative; he was borderline sadistic. "How?" she asked.

"Stress. Discord. Peer pressure. The children were conditioned and didn't even realize it."

"You're a tyrant," she accused.

"Yes. To survive in my position, it is what one needs to become."

Snofrid was faced with a new, uglier conception of his destructive mania. His strategy could give a person outright oppressive power without much effort at all. The manipulator simply had to rely on the natural self-doubt everyone possessed; on how people, especially children, want to belong—like she used to—and might sacrifice themselves to do so.

"Is that how you tricked Hessia into wearing her collar?" she wondered.

He launched a dart at the dartboard, striking the 1 double-ring. "Hessia is a skilled liar—better than Vortigern. It wasn't necessary to dominate her mind because she offered her services. In her head, if she served the Gravebane House, it would make her honored."

"From how she's treated now, it seems like it did the opposite. You treat her worse than humans treat their dogs."

"Hessia is treated no different than she always was. All Seers are viewed as filth and it will never change." He picked up a glass of dragon-ale from the table; instead of a cobra, a scorpion was steeping inside. "They're like gluttonous eaters, except what they crave is powerful magic. The deterioration of their bodies illustrates that fully."

Snofrid held off throwing, amazed at his nerve. "That's painfully hypocritical. Your need to dominate and doctor people's beliefs for power is *just* as greedy."

"Some greed is good; some isn't." He paused and reflected on his response while fingering the silver Commander ring on his hand. "Power is like poison. I'm out for long term authority, so I don't drink the full bottle, but take small doses incrementally. My father chose to drink himself to death; Hessia is doing the same right now. It's why my father lost his control and it's why Hessia is steadily losing hers."

Snofrid threw a dart, hitting the 1 triple-ring clean. "Power should be given to decent people who can't be bought, not paid for by ones who want to use it to control their people."

Hadrian flicked his eyes at the ceiling in deprecation. "A decent person in power is rarer than a woman without an agenda. It's why the Hematic Lord is the only honest ruler in the entire Inborn governing office. But Lord Wolfgang will repair nothing long-term, only slow the rot. Or more likely, he'll be assassinated. He has twice as many enemies as I do, and infinitely more death threats."

"Do you want him dead?"

"Lord Wolfgang and I stay out of each other's way. If he crossed my path, my opinion of the situation could change. But for now, I care little for what he does."

As Hadrian took his turn, hitting the 2 triple-ring, Snofrid studied his posture. His shoulders were loose and open; his chin was held high and his stance was lofty, poised as usual; and his eyes were as bright as sunshine on the ocean. The pitch seemed to have the same effect as alcohol had on humans. If so, he might have a loose tongue—if she played along, that is.

"What did you do to make so many people want to assassinate you?" she asked.

He seemed pleased at the choice of topic. "I have a few enemies, but my popularity is greater than my unpopularity. Everyone who is worthwhile has a mob of torch-wavers at their back door."

"You still didn't answer my question," she pointed out.

"I don't play Governor Games. They want puppets at their fingertips, not sharp teeth." He gulped the dragon-ale, then shot green flames out his nostrils. "But mostly, because of Governor Ariaxa's inability to handle rejection."

Snofrid recognized the name. Ariaxa was the Necromancer Governor of Court III in the Empyrean City. "You messed up her agenda?" Snofrid gathered.

"No. I crushed her brother's agenda. When she eventually offered to ally our Houses through a marriage, I explained to her that I'd sooner marry her decrepit, bloodsucking mother."

"It seems you would've had more power if you just married her."

Hadrian frowned, as if she'd just said something insulting. "I won't marry. I have too much self-respect to be a slave."

"You talk exactly like Lycidius used to," she said, getting a potent sense of déjà vu. For years, he'd also asserted that he'd never be pinned down by a woman. "I wonder if that has anything to do with brainwashing."

"It's called good judgment."

Snofrid faced the dartboard, turned off by his smug countenance. "You won't be a slave to children too, then."

A prideful undertone animated his features. He scooped the detoxified scorpion from his glass and fitted it whole into his mouth. Snofrid got a reminiscent feeling as he chewed the crunchy arachnid. Lycidius had often drunk his vodka in the same way, claiming that the scorpion curbed the acrid taste.

"To children, I wouldn't be a slave," Hadrian said after he'd swallowed. "Before I'm thirty, I'll have five sons, but all from different mothers."

"Because you couldn't possibly be monogamous."

"Men weren't made to be monogamous, but there is always the risk of attachment. Having five lovers will remove the risk of attachment to one." He glanced at the board, pursing his lips with displeasure. "You play this game often?"

Snofrid was too nettled to admire her triple scores. Hadrian had a penchant for sucking the joy out of everything. "I used to. When I lived in Gehenna, the Swangunners would let me play at their club."

His features animated. Stepping back, he hurled a dart with so much force, it rattled the board; he struck the double bull's-eye. "Make that shot," he ordered. "If you do, you win. If not, I do."

Snofrid suddenly felt put on the spot. She back pedaled into position and told herself to breathe. She'd made similar shots hundreds of times before. This was simple. She threw, missed by a hair, and struck the bull's-eye. Defeat washed over her, draining the feeling in her face. "Stone me."

"You lose," he announced. "Now hear my deal."

It was foolish not to have expected this. He'd probably had an ulterior motive prepared before she'd walked in. "What is it?"

"I'll give you the phone if you release Lycidius from being your Shadow."

She gaped. "That's the *worst* deal I've ever heard."

"I wasn't finished," he snapped, suddenly losing his poise. He pointed his glass at her. "I'll also give you credit for the hunt, to absolve you of your halfbreed shame. Instead of being scorned by Inborns, you'll be worshipped by them."

Snofrid trembled. Yes, he knew what she wanted most and wasn't above using it against her. "No. I won't do it."

"That's a selfish choice," he growled. His nostrils flared as he grew fiercely impassioned. "Lycidius is a *soldier*. He was made to fight for his Lord, not to protect a civilian. You'd be doing him a service by releasing him."

Snofrid strongly suspected that this was what Hadrian had wanted all along. He'd stripped her of all recognition from the hunt only to dangle it in front of her for a greater price. "You've hated me since we met," she said. "It's because of Lycidius, isn't it? You think I took him away from you."

Hadrian faced her squarely, his posture threatening. Snofrid went stiff with shock as she met his gaze. *Pain.* The emotion was fleeting, but she'd seen it. Pain meant that Hadrian *could* feel. It meant that, despite claiming to uphold Grieva's code, he'd allowed himself to love.

"My brother was destined for better," Hadrian asserted. "Serving as a Shadow to a halfbreed is an insult to his potential."

"That's for him to decide, *not* you."

"Being that my brother is bound to you by a Covenant, it *is* for me to decide."

The moment Snofrid started to consider his words, she felt like a tidal wave was descending upon her, crushing her into a hard bed of sand. Driving a hand into her pocket, she rolled the rock shard she'd taken from

Oubliette around in her palm. She could hardly remember a time when Lycidius wasn't in her life. If she freed him, he'd be deployed. He'd fight and perhaps die in the war like millions of others. But for a moment, she tried to study the positive side; there were some factors she couldn't ignore. Since they were young, Lycidius had longed to rejoin his Dracuslayer unit. Being a soldier was what had made him feel valuable. He hadn't spoken of his old life in years, though deep down, past her own desires, she knew that reenlisting was what he wanted. Additionally, since Lycidius would no longer be her Shadow, there would be no Law to forbid them from dating. Even more, she'd be absolved of her halfbreed title, which meant she could be with him without shaming him.

"Do we have a deal?" Hadrian prodded.

She squeezed the rock shard. "If I do this, I want my brother to be given his honor back, too."

"That's not part of the offer."

"*Make* it part of it. Otherwise, no."

Hadrian stalked to his desk and removed her phone from the drawer. "Release Lycidius after the Sky-Legion attack and you and your brother will be pardoned. But if you break your word—"

"My word is good, Commander. I don't need Covenant Spells to keep me honest."

His temper diffused, as if the world had just been lifted off his shoulders. "Then we have an agreement." He cleared his throat and offered her the phone. "Use it sparingly. The battery is low."

"*How* low?"

"8% lower than when I took it."

She panicked, a knee-jerk reaction, and checked the screen. The battery quivered at 4%, which was even lower than low. On top of this, the inbox displayed seven missed calls from Desya, twenty-seven missed calls from Jazara and six missed calls from Fergus.

"The Coyote will wake you at 0400 hours," Hadrian said, moving around his desk. "May we meet again."

Snofrid returned a hasty farewell and then left. On the way to her room, she skimmed through messages from Desya and Jazara—which had been sent before Hadrian had told Lycidius that she was safe. It was easy to hear the worry in their words. Initially, they thought she'd been kidnapped or arrested. Their fear chafed at her conscience, but only until two missed calls from Atlas caught her eye.

She powered off the phone, needing to think. The battery would probably only support one phone call, but it could allow a few messages. In her room, she sent a quick reply to Atlas. To her delight, he responded almost right away, so she began a dialogue.

Snofrid: *"Hi Atlas. Sorry I didn't answer sooner. Don't have battery for phone call. Tried to get in touch earlier because I need a favor."*

Atlas: *"The kind of favor that requires a phone call, or the kind that requires a personal effort on my part?"*

Snofrid: *"Both. Lucian threatened to knock me if I don't deliver your safe-deposit in Forsberg Bank and Trust. Deadline is tomorrow. Please talk to him."*

Atlas: *"Lozoraitis won't give you trouble. But now, it's my turn for a favor. I need to see you."*

Snofrid: *"Why?"*

Atlas: *"My reasons are of the sensitive sort. You'll know when I see you."*

Snofrid took a moment to ponder his request. She was curious, and even a little mistrustful at what he could want to talk about. She replied: *"Can't see you, a little tied up at the moment. But maybe Saturday morning?"*

Atlas: *"I'll make it work. 8:00 a.m. I'll send a bird."*

Snofrid halted at a sudden insight. She couldn't make this meeting. The Sky-Legion would be taking down the energy shield by that time and she'd be preparing to flee the city. But maybe she could call him quickly beforehand. She sent a reply: *"Okay. Need to go. Talk to you Saturday."*

Atlas: *"Just one more thing, Snofrid. Your location?"*

Snofrid: *"Pick me up at home."*

Exiting the conversation, she switched to the messages from Desya. Just as she opened the first message, her phone screen went black. "Shoot." Snofrid slapped the phone onto her mattress. Her tantrum petered out the second she realized that Lucian was no longer a danger. Even though

Lycidius and Desya didn't know this, it hardly mattered. They were safe.

The door swung open, and she sat up in a start. Rhode stood in the doorway, wearing a wet apron. "I'm here for my phone," he announced. "But first, how did it go?"

She tossed him the phone. "Good and bad. But really, I don't think the pitch works."

He caught the phone with a low chuckle. "Well, it would've been amazing if it had worked. I meant to tell you: I made up everything about the pitch's powers. Must've slipped my mind before." He slammed the door and strolled down the hallway, laughing.

The Hangman's Noose

Thursday, 3 Hours before Midnight

What *time is it?"* Rhode demanded. *"I can't feel my butt it's so cold."*

"You don't need your butt to tell time," Coyote informed. *"Suck it up."*

"Just tell me the time."

"2112 hours."

The boy grumbled. *"It was 2104 hours an hour ago."*

Snofrid stared over her shoulder where Rhode was perched in a tree. She sat alone in the center of the hunt site, wishing she could disconnect from the bug dial pool, at least until the welx showed up. In all imaginable ways, being plugged into Rhode's every sporadic thought was a special kind of torture, particularly because he thought in images.

Jacked into all the Dracuslayer's minds, she had twelve different viewpoints that supplied a vantage of the site from every angle. The soldiers' noisy, crude conversations cluttered her head, and she could almost feel the sweat of their eagerness trickling down their necks.

Presently, Hessia was sustaining an Isolation Spell that acted as a protective mantle over Hadrian, the Dracuslayers and Hessia herself; the spell masked three of the five senses, ensuring that they couldn't be seen, heard or scented by anyone outside the bubble, except for Snofrid.

Oddly enough, she had a view of herself through the scopes of the Dracuslayer's rifles; she sat on her calves beside a snowdrift, too numb to shiver anymore, a ghost in a white parka picking apart pine needles. A black-tail deer carcass was scrunched against her knees; for theatrical effect, she was supposed to gut the carcass upon the welx's advance.

Having ten sniper barrels trained on her gave Snofrid a burning sensation, as if smoldering matches were being ground into her skin. This wasn't exactly the way she'd pictured the hunt would go down—her sitting in the snow, so cold she could scarcely move—waiting to be attacked or shot. Maybe it was the weeks of anticipation, or maybe it was just the cold, but she barely felt any dread at the welx's coming.

Brushing pine needles from her gloves, she zipped up her parka over her bulletproof armor. She felt more and more weightless with each passing hour, like a snowflake lost in the sky. Each moment carried her farther from the Covenant and closer to freedom. Since she'd awoken, she'd checked the clock almost as many times as she'd breathed. She was ready to see Lycidius, Desya and Jazara; to leave Hollowstone; and to begin again. She hadn't given much thought to what beginning again entailed; she only knew that she wanted to finish college, start a career, and live a more peaceful life.

"*Who wants to hit a Short Stop and grab some coffees?*" Rhode asked, chewing his nails under his gasmask mouthpiece. "*What do you say, Nethers?*"

"*Nah. I don't want to miss anything.*"

"*Darling?*" Rhode questioned.

"*Don't want to miss anything either,*" a gruff voice responded.

"Narwood?"

"You go," Coyote broke in. He was rolling cigarettes in his perch, using baked herb leaves from a tin box. Snofrid glared when she noticed the acid grenade he'd swiped from her dangling from his belt. She'd probably need it in the battle to come, especially if the All-Steam Hunters made an appearance. *"If the welx shows up, and you aren't here, you'll be labeled as the guy who missed out on saving Inbornkind,"* he added.

"Never going to happen," Rhode snorted. He was positioned almost a mile out, with the post of his anti-material rifle nestled at his shoulder; it had a 4-chamber muzzle brake with an attached suppressor, which Snofrid assumed would make his location more difficult for the welx to determine. His side-mohawk was plaited into a fishtail braid, and the silvery fur mantle he wore glowed orange in the moonlight. *"Okay,"* he announced. *"I have another joke."*

"If this is another pun about Seers, I'll paralyze you," Hessia warned.

"It's not," Rhode promised, sounding like he was smiling. *"Okay. Want to know why I broke things off with my courtesan?"*

"Which one?" Nethers asked.

"The one with the lazy eye."

Nethers spit a stream of pepper tobacco over the side of his perch. *"Why, Vortigern?"*

He busted into laughter. *"Because she was seeing someone on the side."*

Rhode's laughter reverberated through Snofrid's mind, shaking her head until she thought it might split open. She drew up her hood with a sigh.

"Okay. Okay. I have another one," he said. *"Why did the cross-eyed teacher get fired?"*

Coyote blew out a column of smoke. *"What is it with you and crossed-eyes?"*

"Come on! Guess."

"She didn't get fired. She quit because you were in the class."

"Nope." Rhode's voice quivered, before he broke into another fit of laughter. *"Because she couldn't control her pupils."*

"What's rocky and bad for your teeth?" Coyote swiped up a stone and bounced it in his fist.

"You're 400 feet out. Make that throw and you'll be…"

Whizzing stroked the air. Rhode's head snapped up, just as the rock smacked his gasmask. *"Ow!"* he shouted, clutching his skull. *"Bourkan, you bastard!"*

Snofrid saw violent images leaking into the bug dial pool from Rhode's mind—Coyote being punched, being dragged behind a car by his neck, being grilled over a red hot grate. Unhooking from Rhode's perspective, she focused on Nether's viewpoint—which was always peaceful—and rifled a pouch of dried venison from her satchel. As she unbuttoned the pouch, Hessia's melodic voice poured into her mind.

"It's a shame you missed the formal salute," she said.

Snofrid narrowed her eyes as she thought back on the day. She recalled nothing about a salute, unless Hessia was referring to the curt speech Hadrian had given about how mistakes were unacceptable, before they'd left the Spyderweb. *"What formal salute?"*

"Oh, you didn't know?" Hessia plucked a beetle from the dirt, humming cheerily. *"The Lords contacted us and gave us their approval, as well as their profound admiration for acting as saviors of Inbornkind. They're calling us the Noble Twelve. All the Governors were present, too. It was quite something."*

Snofrid chucked the venison pouch back into her satchel as disappointment coursed through her body. *"When did this happen?"*

"An hour before we left the Spyderweb."

Snofrid used Coyote's gaze to hone in on the Seer's position. She fought to ignore Hessia's baiting, but she felt hurt nonetheless: she had no plans to travel to the Empyrean City, so the salute would've been her best chance at seeing her uncle in person.

Using the bug dials, Snofrid zeroed in on Hessia where she squatted inside a rotted log a half-mile north of the site, where Hadrian would be when he'd returned from his reconnaissance. The Seer looked hungrier for a fight than the Dracuslayers. A halter-neck breastplate of tarnished silver encased her lean ribcage, and brown leather gloves ran all the way to her knobby elbows; her faded green mullet-skirt left the front of her twill trousers bare.

"What did the Lords say?" Snofrid asked. Before continuing, she focused her thoughts, so as not to betray any information about her past. *"Or, what did Lord Drakkar say?"*

"Oh." Hessia stroked the beetle's shell. *"I don't remember, exactly. But I think it was something like: failure won't be tolerated."*

Snofrid frowned. *"That's all he said?"*

"Lord Drakkar speaks through non-verbal commands as powerful leaders generally do," Hessia explained. *"His administration has learned to translate his body language, particularly his PAWN. He doesn't open his mouth unless he has something specific to relay."*

Snofrid turned away, hiding her disenchantment. She checked out of Coyote's viewpoint and performed her routine sweep of the site. Wind purred through the branches; on her left, a bony badger trotted through the undergrowth. Not a single snowflake filled the sky, giving place to the rusty copper moon.

Above, the city buzzed with machinery; hundreds of construction workers were trying to repair the damage from the RP bombs. In the morning, the humans would wake to war, but for now, the night seemed to tick on without violence. Knowing what sunrise would bring made the moment eerily similar to the calm before riots broke out in Gehenna. Countless humans would be slain. Being aware that so many would die and having to stay silent made her feel like she had a role in their deaths.

Two hours lagged by, peppered with jokes from Rhode, discussions about offensive strategies for the war on Hollowstone, a massive trade route bombing in Paraguay, and a legendary Empyrean City event called the *Midnight Game*. Nethers, Rhode, Coyote and Narwood began a trivia match while the rest of the Draculayers took turns sleeping or traded shifts luring hydrocop patrols away from the site.

Snofrid didn't think she'd be able to sleep, even if she had a feather mattress. Tension had taken a swan dive behind her calm exterior. *Waiting.* It was something she'd never been good at. At each rustling leaf and snapping twig, she scanned the forest, expecting to see the welx. Coyote had explained that it stood over four meters high—it was the largest land beast in existence, even bigger than the African Elephant. Moreover, the welx had an armored shell, and a tail that could shish kabob a man.

She looked to the tree line at the sound of cracking branches. Hadrian broke from a netting of trees. Fog puffed from his white bull-head gasmask as he approached; his enchanted boots left no footprints in the snow. He'd been absent for hours, off on one reconnaissance, and then another. This was the first she'd seen of him since leaving the Spyderweb, though he appeared no different than he had then. He had the confident swagger of someone who saw his destination shining on the horizon; he'd been lively all day, as if battle was a thing that put him in a good mood.

His sweeping cassock, flapping in the wind, was pale as a shroud, and was cinched at the waist by a series of brown leather belts. The grey mantle that warmed his pauldron bristled like raised fur and hobnailed tailbone-armor crusted his spine; on both hands, his raptor-claws beamed with fresh polish.

"*Do you even know how to gut a deer?*" he asked through the bug dials.

"*Yes.*"

He slid a folder knife from his sleeve. "*Gut it on the Coyote's signal. The welx needs to think you're a hunter, not bait.*"

"*Maybe it will figure it out anyway.*" She slipped the knife into her pocket, and then said, "*Why didn't you tell me the Lords contacted you? We had a deal that I'd be given recognition for the hunt.*"

He closed his arms across his chest. With the force of a bulldozer, he shoved everyone out of the bug dial pool, leaving only their two minds connected. "*When you deliver your end of our deal, I'll deliver mine,*" he told her. "*Free Lycidius and you'll be given recognition. Not before.*"

"*You don't trust I can keep my word?*"

"*I trust no one at their word, especially halfbreeds.*" He flicked a claw. "*Stand up. I need to check your vest.*"

Snofrid rose and stumbled, gripping onto Hadrian's arm for balance. "*Shoot,*" she muttered. Glancing at her boot, she found the sole was glued to some sort of yellow mucus. She crouched and wiggled the boot, then stopped abruptly when a twinge pained her ankle. *"It's caught in something. I can't get it out."*

"I'll do it. Step back."

"I will, but don't rip it out."

He prodded the earth around her foot with his palm. Then he tilted his head and listened. *"Take the shoe off,"* he ordered. *"You've stepped in a mud-tusque nest."*

Her heart knocked against her ribcage in alarm; at any moment, her leg could be sucked into a carnivorous pit. Hastily, she moved to unlace her boot. Upon seeing the goo crawling up the laces, she froze and sucked in her breath. *"It's trying to take my whole shoe."*

Hadrian grabbed her ankle. *"Shift your weight back."*

Snofrid shifted her weight backward and checked their perimeters. More nests flared across the glade like widening mouths. *"Oh my hell,"* she breathed, jerking her leg faster. *"This area is infested with nests"*

He did a quick scan of the dirt. *"How didn't we see this during the environmental sweep, Bourkan?"*

Snofrid cut in. *"Mud-tusques are impossible to track. They burrow through the ground until they settle on a nesting place. Then they shoot up through the ground like moles."*

Hadrian grunted. Unable to budge her shoe, he rocked forward on his toes and yanked hard.

"Ow!" She smacked his gasmask. *"That* hurt*! You're going to break my ankle."*

"The bone will heal."

"Don't you dare," she warned. Snatching up a twig, she poked at the laces and unwound them slowly.

"Nine seconds until you lose the foot."

"I only need five." Snofrid continued with profound focus. When she'd unlaced three ties, she jiggled her foot; it was looser. She wrenched her foot free.

"You're lucky it was just a fledgling," he told her, getting to his feet. *"Step*

in a mature nest and no one can help you."

She was well aware. In one of her studies, she'd read that a mature nest had swallowed a man and his entire transport. Before taking a new position, she combed the ground and found several un-infested areas. *"I'm moving.*"

Hadrian kicked the deer carcass. It slid across the ice and stopped on a clear spot. Then he aimed his horns down at her. *"Move there,*" he said. *"And remember—stay in the dome.*"

She hunkered down beside the deer. When he started to walk away, she called after him in confusion. *"What about the rest of the nests?*"

"The nests stay. They could be useful."

Once he'd vanished into the trees, her mind reconnected to the pool, like a plug clicking into an outlet. The Draculayer's rough voices and wandering thoughts mingled with her own. Bored, Rhode was chucking pine cones at squirrels; Coyote smoked his herb leaves; Hessia focused on sustaining the Isolation Spell; Nethers rubbed his eyes tiredly; and the other Draculayers shifted restlessly in their perches.

Midnight struck. The moments melted into long hours of pitch blackness that brightened with the rays of dawn. Snofrid watched the horizon enkindle; its light half-drowned behind a veil of lazy snow. Spokes of sunlight pierced the clouds, reaching down through the treetops to ignite the sparkling snow. The morning was glorious. It reminded her of the times she'd hunted with Ryuki and Desya in the green zone—camping out in the early morning hours—and how she'd cried each time Ryuki had killed a deer.

Over the course of the morning, soldiers dipped into their supplies, digging out pouches of dried venison and olive bread with hard goat cheese. Laughs replaced dull moods, and jokes substituted complaints for the most part. It seemed that the soldiers sensed the end was close at hand.

"The welx needs to show up already," Rhode complained, unwrapping a Twinkie. *"This is the most boring mission I've ever done.*"

Coyote waved a hand and said, *"You know humans put cellulose gum in those.*"

"So what?"

"They also put cellulose gum in rocket fuel."

Rhode shoved the full Twinkie into his mouth. *"Powerful engines need similar fuel."*

Snofrid withdrew her attention from Rhode and Coyote to argue with Nethers about the correct way to burp a baby—Rhode had told a half-truth. Nethers had twin girls. One of them had died, though he'd only recently accepted it. She found it strange that Rhode had belittled the baby's death, because Nethers had made Rhode her Birth Patron. However, under his indifference, she sensed that Rhode really had cared about the baby, but put on airs of detachment. Most Dracuslayers did.

The debate broke at a sudden flash of red in her peripheral. Turning, she spotted a flock of fat red birds crowding the trees around her, hissing as they hopped from twig to twig.

Nethers and Coyote followed her gaze. Coyote frowned, and said, *"Gaper fowl are warm-climate beasts."*

"They sense something will die," Snofrid realized. From her memories, she knew the species had minor magical abilities. *"They can predict death and are here for breakfast."*

"They're right on point," Rhode chuckled, adjusting his scope height. *"When birds of prey come to see a fight, you know it's going to be wicked."*

Snofrid kept an eye on the gaper fowl, feeling put off. Worse than vultures, they didn't even wait for the victim to die but swarmed its wounds and stripped the flesh as it bled out.

"You know, I've been thinking," Rhode said, fluffing the branches of his perch. *"I can't wait to get back to the Empyrean City and be famous. I'm going to have my own fan club, like Lord Wolfgang. Except, my fan club will be Gorgons, not peasants and crusty old people."* He slurped punch from a juice box. *"What do you want, Nethers?"*

"Gorgons sound good." Nethers handed a piece of meat to a squirrel. *"But I'm going to see Fern first."*

"Why would you go see your daughter when you could have anything?"

"I don't know. I just want to see her."

"Lame." Rhode gurgled his juice. *"What do you want, Coyote?"*

"A chamber in the sixth level of the Sky-Dome Citadel…Gorgons…maybe a few hundred- thousand gems."

"Classic." Rhode spit some juice into the snow. *"Narwood?"*

"Governor Ariaxa."

Rhode blasted a snort. *"Not going to happen. If you and an orangutan were the last two creatures on earth, she'd choose the orangutan."* He made a quiet chuckle. *"Commander? What do you want? Aside from a Lordship?"*

Hadrian drew his eyes from his black-tree ring. *"Keep spitting, Vortigern, and I'll make you lick up every juice spot."*

Rhode heaved a sigh and screwed on his mouthpiece. *"We all know what Hessia wants."*

"What's that?" Hessia challenged.

"You want to become a Governor."

The Draculayers burst into laughter. *"Right,"* Narwood agreed. He glanced up from his scope reticle, his rattail slipping down one shoulder. *"I'd sooner become the President of the New Global Union before Hessia became a Governor."*

Hessia dipped her chin, glaring under squatted brows. Just as she looked like she might retort, Hadrian held up a claw in warning.

Throughout the conversation, Snofrid experienced the polar opposite of Hessia's anger. Each soldier was going to receive eternal veneration. They'd be regarded as gods and fawned over by all who crossed their path. Though she didn't desire such an extreme degree of praise, she did want to scrub clean her father's name, Desya's name and her own and enter Inborn society without eliciting death threats and insults.

Flipping open her folder knife, she tried to spin it around her hand. After a few failed attempts, she locked into Nether's perspective. Through his eyes, she spied a figure walking past his tree; it stood tall, and the clank of grenades punctuated its steps. She pricked up in alertness. Before she could determine if the figure was a patrolman or a hunter, it faded into the trees.

"Darling," Hadrian called. *"Take care of him."*

A beast of a man slid from a birch tree, right in Snofrid's line of sight. Brawny shouldered and scar-faced, his chest was twice as broad as Hadrian's and he sported a coarse brown flat-top. While he plodded deeper into the forest, she searched the tree line. *"Who is it?"* she asked.

"Darling will confirm and report," Coyote said, sucking his teeth. *"If it's a hostile, he'll eliminate the target."*

"You mean an All-Steam Hunter?"

"Could be." Coyote snuffed his cigarette in the snow. *"No one knows if they're even going to show."*

Rhode returned from using the restroom, wiping his hands on his trousers, and climbed back into his perch. When he was settled, he said to Snofrid, *"Getting girlish trembles, yet?"*

"Not even close."

"Just you wait. A little while longer and you'll be squealing. Right, Nethers?"

No reply.

"Silence is consent." Rhode placed his mil dots on the back of her head. *"Just don't think too many erratic thoughts while us soldiers are fighting. It can get distracting when someone is screaming through the bug dials."*

Snofrid turned around, looking for him in the trees. *"Take that off me."*

"Getting scared?"

"No. I don't trust you not to slip and pull the trigger."

He puffed out a snort. *"I've never missed a hit in my life."*

"Dragoncrap," Coyote called out. *"Nepal."*

"That was ONCE."

Snofrid caught a glimpse of a grey shape at her rear and did a double-take. She almost turned around for a better view, but stopped herself at the last moment. *"Wait, Rhode. I need to see behind me. Put your scope back on me."*

"Girls." He scoffed. *"They can never make up their minds."*

"Put it on me!"

"Excellence takes time, girl. Patience." Rhode readjusted his scope height, settling it on her head. *"Done."*

"What is that?" she demanded. *"Is that a rock?"*

He glanced up with a snort. *"You wasted my energy on a rock?"*

"Just look behind me."

Rhode scanned the glade and his eyes bugged out. *"Commander, are you getting this?"*

Hadrian had already left his spot in the log and was running through the forest, his Halo-hand ready. *"All units prepare to fire on target."*

Heart pounding, Snofrid stared at the grey shape through Rhode's rifle scope. It wasn't a rock, it was a *boulder*, roughly the size of a small car. And it was barreling toward her position, splintering the trees in its path. Wherever the welx was, it had a plan she hadn't foreseen—to use its magic from afar. To pin her under a rock so she couldn't flee.

"Start gutting the deer," Coyote ordered.

"Is that going to crush me?" she asked, shoving the deer onto its back.

Rhode chuckled. *"If it does, at least we won't have to carve a tombstone."*

"Shut your mouth, Vortigern," Coyote barked. *"Focus."*

Using her folder knife, Snofrid sliced the deer's belly open from its sternum to its crotch. She hauled the intestines out and then began clipping the membranes that fixed the innards to the spine. *"Is it still moving toward me?"* she asked.

"Yes," Coyote verified. *"You'll be fine. Keep gutting."*

As she cut the diaphragm, a ring of blood pooled across the snow. She yanked the guts free and set them in a pile to her right before smashing through the pelvic bone using the butt of her knife. With each movement, her bloody hands trembled and her pulse raced faster. All her mind could produce were spasmodic thoughts, cascading over themselves, repeating: *Don't look over your shoulder.* She froze when the cracking of the trees grew louder. *"My hell, that boulder is right on me, isn't it?"*

"Just stay where you are," Coyote said calmly. *"Nethers will tell you when to move."*

"I'm counting on you, Nethers," she called, and pulled the colon from the deer's body cavity. *"Has anyone spotted the welx?"*

"Not yet. It's probably raising the spell from a safe dist—".

"Now, Snofrid!" Nethers cut in. *"Roll left!"*

She rolled left just as the boulder breached the tree line. Fragments of wood peppered the air. Snofrid waited, nerves thrashing, until the boulder had crossed the clearing—flattening the deer carcass along the way—and then scrambled back into position.

A screech tore through the forest. Spinning around, she scoured the trees. *"Is that the welx?"*

"Target in range," Rhode announced.

"Take it down," Nethers shouted.

Rhode's mind cooled as he took aim. *"Height of target, 4.2 meters. Calculating distance."*

Snofrid saw nothing but wood, rocks and snow. The ground shook with thunderous footsteps, and the trees bowed. Something was moving through them. Fast. Math equations trickled into her mind even as the soldiers calculated their shots, *"4.2 times 1000; divided by 5 mils is an 840 meter distance."*

Rhode scrunched one eye shut. *"Wind adjustment, head on. No value, guys. Drop shells."*

Shots fired.

A beast tore through the tree line, roaring as bullets bounced off its hide. Snofrid skidded back in terror, ducking a flurry of sharp branches. For a brief moment, she saw her shuddering reflection in its scaly hide. Before she could fling her knife at the beast, a wall of metal sprang up around her, crashing shut and caging her in a titanium sphere.

Through the snipers' eyes, she saw the welx turn and gallop toward the tree line. One good look at the beast and she feared for everyone's lives. Its tail tapered to a bony, spiked mace. As it ran, it swung its tail-club at the trees, splintering the trunks. Its forelimbs were shorter than its hind-limbs, giving it extra thrust, and every inch of its body was coated in armored scutes—external plates overlapped with horns. Air sacs flared above its six eyes, and its snapping jaws spilled over with rod-like teeth.

The welx skidded to a halt at the edge of the Alchemy Sphere. Pacing back and forth, it shrieked in frustration. It was trapped.

"Why didn't the Fail Floor activate?" Nethers demanded. He took shot

after shot at the beast, but the bullets ricocheted off its shell like pebbles.

"I don't know, but Wolba is a sitting duck now," Rhode chuckled. *"Headshot takes it home."* He yanked back his trigger, sending a 50BMG round barreling toward the welx.

The welx hunkered down and hissed, as if it were laughing.

"Damn it," Coyote spat, clamping his arms around a tree trunk. *"We're about to get hit. Everybody hold on!"*

Green magic fanned from the beast's jaws and blasted through the forest in a flash fire. The trees started rattling, shaking off the snipers like fleas. Nethers shouted a curse. Throwing his rifle, he toppled from his tree and struck the snow with a thud; Narwood shielded his face with his hands, grunting as sticks impaled through them and into his gasmask; Coyote tumbled backward, grappling, and braced himself on a branch.

"Go, Hessia!" he yelled. *"Now!"*

Hessia darted from her log, dropping the Isolation Spell so she could raise new magic. She tore off her gasmask as she reached the glade: magic dove from her mouth, spearing into the welx's forelimbs. The beast buckled, but only for a moment, before sending a wall of rocks hurtling toward her.

"Drop, Hessia!" Coyote shouted.

She flattened against the snow and the rocks grazed her spine.

Coyote scanned the trees, panting. *"Call in."*

"I'm alive," Hessia groaned.

Snofrid felt a tremor under her feet. Stumbling, she supported herself against the dome; thoughts of pain spattered across her awareness, stretching her focus. Narwood was dead. Two others were injured. With a bout of panic, she jacked into Coyote's perspective. *"Something's heading toward the glade,"* she warned.

Coyote dropped from his tree. *"What is it?"*

"It's round two," Rhode cut in, reloading his rifle. *"Things are about to get violent."*

A dunespike ripped through the trees and landed beside the boulder, uprooting ice chunks with its paws. Snofrid let out a startled cry, thinking the beast was going to tear through the dome. Instead, the dunespike bit into the welx's neck and dragged it away from the Alchemy Sphere. Snofrid saw and heard frenzy in Hadrian's mind. *"Slaughter it. Rip it to pieces. Kill it."*

The welx twisted, slashing Hadrian's neck with its claws. Blood sprayed the snow, but Hadrian's scales took the brunt of the hit. Snarling, he slammed the welx into the ground and butted it again and again with his horns, puncturing a large hole through its ribcage.

"Vortigern, headshot!" Hadrian growled.

"Calculating distance," Rhode said, peering through his scope. *"Got him, Commander."*

Snofrid heard a dull crack. She backed up, blinking, and hopped to Rhode's viewpoint. All the mud-tusque nests were waking, splaying greedily as they slurped up the bloody snow. *"The nests are active,"* she warned, her voice shaky. *"Watch your feet."*

A mud-tusque mouth, as wide as five men, stretched open beside Hadrian and sucked the welx's hind legs into its throat. With a startled yelp, the beast tore at the ground. Small hooks shot from the mud-tusque's mouth, latching onto the welx's legs and yanked it down farther.

"Bull's-eye," Rhode cheered, pounding his fist on his rifle. *"There's no way the bastard is getting out of that."*

Hadrian seized the advantage. He attacked without mercy, chewing through the welx's hide until its ribs gleamed white in the sunlight. The welx's snout twisted as it tried to wriggle free, its eye sacs flaring. Hadrian targeted its legs and shredded the muscle and bone, freeing it from the mud-tusque's jowls. Then, rising up on his hind legs, he thundered his paws against its back and cracked its spine. Snofrid's eyes enlarged as the welx's body collapsed, limp and stunned. It was paralyzed.

"Whohoo!" Rhode exclaimed. *"Tell me that really just happened!"* He slid from his perch and bolted toward the glade. *"I'm going to be famous. FAMOUS. Nethers, where the hell are you? We need to celebrate. Oh man, we can finally take that trip to Cabo."*

"Everyone regroup at the glade," Coyote ordered. He was coasting down

a ravine slope, shoving a magazine into an assault rifle.

"On our way," Kuzmic said as he lifted a fallen tree off another Draculaslayer's leg.

Snofrid caught ahold of the dome's ceiling lever and yanked; the walls lowered, unveiling a field of red. She stepped over the lip of the dome, still panting, and hopped through the thicket of nests. Gaper fowl swarmed the welx's wounds, screeching as they stripped off flesh; Hadrian stood over the heaving body, now in his man form, with a battle axe in one hand and a khopesh sword in the other. She could hardly believe the sight. The welx was down. Most of them were alive. They could finally signal the Sky-Legion to attack.

"Can he still raise magic?" she asked, stopping at a distance from the welx.

"Not after this much blood loss," Hadrian told her.

She inched closer, gaining courage, and gazed at the beast's six eyes. Blood spilled from gashes in its skull, streaming across the rips in its snout; even so mangled, it betrayed little sign that it was in pain.

"Maybe you should just kill him," she suggested.

Hadrian's tone was disapproving. "A quick death would be merciful. Wolba deserves none." He unclipped a bottled spell from his belt and popped the cap. Green light beamed into the sky, signaling the Sky-Legion. "Lord Pim will ensure that the humans are occupied while we deal with Wolba."

Snofrid stared at the green light as it spread above the city. Her spirits soared with the magic, and, for the first time since the quarantine, she felt herself truly smile.

"We're about the have the biggest family reunion of all time," Rhode called. He skidded to a halt at the edge of the glade, his eyes bright and his skin flushed. "Not so mighty now, are you Wolba?" He laughed, nudging the welx with his boot. "What do you think? My name is going to go down in history as the guy who finally nabbed you. I bet that makes you want to be me, doesn't it?" The welx snapped at his boot and he skittered back, laughing. "I'll take that as a yes."

In minutes, Hessia and seven Dracuslayers had reported to the clearing, some with severe injuries. Kuzmic, a bull-necked boy with black clipper cut, glared at the Fail Floor suspiciously. "Why the hell didn't the floor collapse?" he demanded. "We checked and double checked it. There's no reason it could've malfunctioned—unless someone rigged it."

"Maybe you should have a chat with Hessia," Rhode suggested, drawing a longsword from his back holster. "Ask her why she's all words and no brain."

"My magic was flawless," Hessia asserted, her tone hot. She backed away from Rhode's sword, her eyes mistrustful. "It failed because *someone else* slipped up."

"Everyone quiet," Hadrian ordered. He looked over the Dracuslayers faces. "I want a death count. Where is Nethers?"

Coyote shook his head, wiping blood from his cheek. "I don't know. He exited the bug dial pool a few minutes ago, but I didn't see him get hit."

"I saw him fall from his perch," Snofrid told Hadrian. "I don't think he landed well. He might need help."

"That sounds like Nethers," Rhode snorted. "He's always checking out before everyone else."

"Kuzmic." Hadrian waved a claw. "Find him. Darling, too."

As Kuzmic ran off, Rhode set his hands on his hips. "So. How should we kill it?"

"Slowly and painfully," Hadrian decreed. He aimed his khopesh at the welx. "Nox Wolba, you've been sentenced to death for treason by the five Lords."

The welx cocked its head up and its snout curled back. Snofrid swore it was smiling. Choking and gurgling, it wheezed out a sequence of throaty sounds.

Rhode kicked its hide. "Sorry, Wolba. Didn't catch that. I don't speak dying welx."

Hadrian held eye contact with the beast, the creases on his face deepening. He concentrated intently, as if party to some kind of unheard communication. "He said we should run."

"*Commander,*" Kuzmic alerted through the bug dials. "*Nethers was shot. Darling too.*"

Rhode's head snapped up. "Dragonshit! Nethers wasn't shot!"

"*Verify that it was unfriendly fire,*" Hadrian ordered.

A dark feeling slunk through Snofrid, and she swept the trees for hostile snipers. "I think we should kill it," she advised. "Right now."

"Good plan," Coyote agreed.

Rhode darted into the trees, panting and whipping back branches with both hands. Snofrid heard his thoughts, as if they were her own. "*Nethers, you bastard! You're not allowed to die! What the hell am I going to tell Fern?*"

"*Unfriendly,*" Kuzmic finally reported. "*Both were hit at point-blank range.*"

Hadrian tapped a point on his tailbone armor, activating his Swoegar. "We're going to be taken out by All-Steam Hunters," he announced. "Before I give any of you permission to die, we finish this job."

Daringly Dared

Fear incapacitated Snofrid at the thought that she was going to be shot. It brought on the ripest, hottest panic she'd ever experienced. The wind seemed to die, languidly batting at the leaves; the frozen blood stains were more brilliant looking; and her muffled breathing buzzed loudly in her ears. Her emotions surged, high on a thrilling terror that focused each of her bug dial perspectives with crystal-clear resolution.

"It's a pincher ambush," a Dracuslayer burst out. *"Everybody take cover!"*

Snofrid saw three Dracuslayers scatter as shells peppered the air, Hessia dove behind a tree, Hadrian charged the welx, and the remaining Dracuslayers flopped onto their stomachs.

Snofrid threw herself into the snow, instinctively cradling her head. One soldier's perspective faded, then another's, before she'd even begun to clamber for cover. A well-aimed bullet grazed Hadrian's neck; he cupped the spurting wound and went down in a burst of shrapnel as a tree disintegrated beside him.

"Black Tree down!" a Dracuslayer shouted, high-crawling into the dome. *"All units respond to Bourkan!"*

Coyote, cracking his lightning whips, sent webs of anvil-crawler lightning scuttling across the glade, fracturing the Fail Floor. "Out!" he roared. "Everyone get out!"

Grenades exploded on the tree line, spitting clouds of black smoke. Snofrid screamed. She rolled away from the discharge and struck her back on the boulder. A grunt tore from her throat as she slumped onto her back with pain swelling in her shoulder. Shells zoomed above her; branches shattered and cries rang out all across the glade.

"Who got hit?" a Dracuslayer demanded. *"Who the hell is in command?"*

"Grypher is down!"

"Leave him! We have to move, now! Go. Go. Go." A Dracuslayer skidded behind a tree, his mind a blur of adrenaline. Turning around, he took aim at the welx with steady hands. *"I've got a clear shot. Taking him out."* A bullet sped at his face, puncturing his gasmask, and he checked out of the bug dial pool.

Still scrambling across the glade, Snofrid's mind ground out thoughts: *Who's still alive? What do we do? Is the welx dead?* She spotted a rifle through the smoke and leopard-crawled toward it. *"Where is everyone?"* she screamed. *"Is the welx alive?"*

Shrapnel blasted from the tree trunks. Something fiery slashed through her cheek, lodging in the roof of her mouth. There was no pain, only numbness. But then it came—as if her jawbone had been steeped in sulphuric acid. She collapsed with a shriek. Clutching her face, she choked on pieces of bark and bone. Dark spots blurred her vision. Blood poured over her tongue, warm, thick and creeping from the corners of her mouth. That she could still move her head gave her a second of relief.

"Where the hell are they?" a Dracuslayer coughed. *"I can't see through the smoke."*

"We're taking mad return fire, over here. We need cover!"

A third Dracuslayer jumped to his feet and stumbled into the glade. *"They have us pinned down! We have to take out Wolba now."* He raced through the smoke, gun blazing.

Snofrid convulsed as her face healed. A cold death wind ripped through her body, from her brain to her lungs, all the way down to her floppy legs. Under the few remaining perspectives, she saw an army of All-Steam Hunters in white flak jackets converging upon the glade; some broke out of snowdrifts with rifles; others climbed out of the Fail Floor, spraying fire from flame throwers; and still more dropped from the trees, shedding Concealing Spells. They opened fire with machine pistols. Dracuslayers dove for cover, their bodies jolting as they were pelted with bullets.

"I'm h-hit," a Dracuslayer wheezed, cupping his stomach with bloody hands.

Another Dracuslayer's armor was enrobed with fire. He dragged himself toward the welx, leaving a flaming trail of charred flesh behind him. Just as he propped up his rifle, a bullet ripped through his neck and his head smacked against the snow.

One by one, Snofrid watched the viewpoints fade. Flames were everywhere, fanning through the pandemonium like a hurricane wind. She could see nothing in the smoke but blue whips slashing through the air, shooting bolts of positive electricity in deafening cracks.

Slowly, the pain in her face vanished, leaving her throat more parched than cracked mud. Through flare-ups and flying shells, she dragged herself behind the boulder, heaving and choking on smoke. Her eyepieces had fogged over, but she was able to discern that Hessia had run off. She blinked, using all her strength to tap into the Seer's vision stream; an iron wall had been erected around her mind. *"Rhode,"* she panted. *"Rhode, where are you? Are you alive?"*

No reply.

Snofrid scooted her back to the boulder, shaking violently. Still coughing, she tapped on Coyote's perspective. He resisted at first, but then allowed her to enter. *"Coyote,"* she cried. *"Did you get the welx?"*

He replied, but not to her. "Go get the healer. She's behind the rock."

Snofrid panicked at the sound of approaching footsteps. She made a move to run, but two Hunters grabbed her by the arms and yanked her to her feet. Bucking wildly, she tried to twist out of their grip. *"Is someone alive?"* she screamed. *"Is anyone alive!"*

One of the soldiers rammed his rifle into her spine. Snofrid arched her back at a bolt of pain.

"Struggle, and I'll shoot you as many times as you can heal," he warned.

Her knees buckled and she sagged like a leaf in the Hunter's arms. *"Is anyone alive?"* she wheezed.

"Over here," Hadrian panted.

"Hadrian?" Hope bubbled inside her, giving her thoughts clarity. *"Where are you?"*

"Close."

She went limp and allowed the Hunters to haul her into the middle of the glade. The plowed snow was scattered with shells and adorned with dead Dracuslayers.

Near the tree line, Hessia stood behind Hadrian, her hands clamped around his neck. Blood seeped through her fingers; he stood tall, as if the scorching paralysis of her magic didn't hurt him. Hessia's collar lay at her feet and her mutilated face beamed with a victorious smile.

Approximately thirty All-Steam Hunters enclosed the site, their rifles trained on Hadrian; some cheered, shooting dragon-ale fire from their masks, while others pumped the dead with extra bullets. Their grey helmets were shaped like hyena heads, but they were crested with six horns—three on each side. The welx lay in a pond of bloody slush, laughing amid the slaughter; Nethers, Darling and Kuzmic were combing the glade, checking the bodies of the fallen Dracuslayers.

Snofrid did a double-take, her mouth trembling. Nethers and Darling were supposed to be dead. She had no idea what was going on. But then a realization hit her, fast and brutal, like an uppercut to the stomach. *"They're All-Steam Hunters."*

"This is what happens when little men drink too much poison." Hadrian's bloodshot gaze teetered toward her face. *"They start to hallucinate power."*

Snofrid choked out a reply. *"It doesn't look like a hallucination to me. We're outnumbered and you can't even move."*

"Watch me." He wiggled his claw.

She didn't find the jest humorous. *"If they find the portal, it's over."*

"They won't find it."

"You can't promise that." Her tone was bitter, but his bitterness was more potent. She could sense his mounting rage. He hadn't even suspected that there had been traitors in his ranks; for someone who claimed to never trust anyone on their word, he'd trusted these Dracuslayers on exactly that.

The Hunters stopped at a distance from the welx and began shackling her wrists over her stomach. Breathing hard, her eyes combed the bodies, desperate to find one of the Dracuslayers still alive. Most had been hit in the head; the others had been decapitated by Coyote's lightning whips. There was no one—no one left but her and Hadrian.

Hadrian's mind flinched. *"Feeling sorry for yourself is the first mark of failure. Don't stain my mind with it."*

"They were YOUR men!" she shouted. *"You should've seen this coming!"*

"Instead of casting blame, think about how you're going to survive."

She felt a prick of shame. *"I'm not wearing bug dials, but you are, so you can get help. Call Lycidius."*

Hadrian refused. *"The welx will be dead in a few minutes and it would take my brother an hour to get here."*

"Not on his Steelrunner."

"Twenty minutes, then." Hadrian's mind aura was obstinate. *"But it's still too long."*

"It might be," she granted, wrestling her shackles in frustration. *"But for ONCE, admit that you need help."* Even as she spoke, she scarcely expected him to comply. Dracuslayers were trained to complete missions without reinforcements, so calling his brother for help would indirectly be admitting failure. But she had to try. *"Please call him."*

Hadrian settled his sights on the welx, muttering a curse. *"Send me an image of his location."*

Snofrid concentrated on their designated corner in the Alley, then channeled the image into Hadrian's thought stream. *"He should be in that corner."*

"He's not in the corner," Hadrian reported.

"He's not—" She paused in confusion. *"Then where is he?"*

Coyote had just finished reconnoitering the site and soaked his sweaty hair with a water canteen. Dirt and blood sullied his pallid robes and streaked his cheeks and gloves. The way he carried himself, with his shoulders thrown back and his torso tall, radiated pride. Wrenching up his mask, he spit into the snow and waved his rifle at Hadrian. "Nethers. Relieve the Commander of his bug dials."

Nethers jogged to Hadrian's side and stripped the electrodes off his temples. As Nethers stuffed the bug dials into his harness, Hadrian bared his teeth at him. Nethers gave him a middle-finger salute and the other Hunters busted into whistles and laughter.

"How does it feel to be dominated, Commander?" a Hunter goaded.

"I bet you're wishing you didn't butcher your father about now," another called, lobbing a snowball at Hadrian's back. "He would've ended your complete failure with a headshot by now."

Coyote picked up Hadrian's khopesh from the snow. He strode toward the welx, spinning the blade around in his hand. "Keep Hadrian restrained," he told Hessia.

"He won't take one step," she promised.

Hadrian craned his head toward the Seer. "I'm going to drag you all the way down to the twenty-third level of the Under Dungeons," he growled.

She hissed a laugh. "That's exactly where you'll be, *master*, when we frame you for being an All-Steam Hunter."

"No one will choose the word of a slave over a Commander."

She squeezed his neck until his claws twitched. "I'm no slave. Not anymore." Her voice morphed into a terrible yelp. "I think it's time *you* kneel! It's time you see what it's like to be shamed."

"Wrong!" he roared. "Only slaves kneel!" Hadrian rocked back, ramming his tailbone armor into Hessia's chest. She let out a shocked screech; blood squirted from her chest as he ripped his tailbone armor from her sternum. Sinking to her knees, she clawed at her chest with a gurgle.

Snofrid watched Hadrian charge the welx with thundering anticipation. Shots zoomed through the glade, rebounding off his Swoegar. He was going to make it. *"Go!"* she yelled. *"Go. You're almost there."*

"Bring him down," Coyote shouted, racing toward Hadrian. "Bring him down!"

A dozen Hunters tackled Hadrian. Hadrian stumbled but held, continuing with the Hunters hanging off him, his back bowing under the weight of nine men. He took five steps, before he went down roaring in a pile of rolling, wrestling bodies. Arms and legs tangled together; boots struck gasmasks; grunts, shouts and curses filled the clearing.

"Get up," Snofrid urged, leaning forward. *"Get up. Just ten feet!"*

Coyote staggered from the heap of bodies, cradling his shoulder. "Darling, put him down! Use the tranquilizer."

Snofrid finally spied Hadrian in the commotion. Her shackles rattled as she screamed for him to hurry. Bowing his head, he butted a Hunter in the back with his bull horns, spearing his shoulder blades. The man crumpled onto a mud-tusque nest. Hadrian powered to his feet. He seized a second Hunter by the arm and leg and heaved him upward. With a howl, he brought the man down over his knee, snapping his spine, and tore the rifle from his dying hands.

"Shoot the welx," Snofrid cried. *"Do it now!"*

"Hit him," Coyote roared, moving to shield the welx. "Put him down NOW."

Hadrian shot down a row of hunters, clearing a path to the welx. From cover, Darling fired a tranquilizer dart into his neck. Hadrian slapped a claw to his neck, ripped out the dart, and then stumbled sideways. With a grimace, he swung into a tree, careened, and then collapsed onto his side.

"Damn it," Snofrid panted, struggling against her restraints. *"Damn it!"*

Coyote looked at the bodies of the dead Hunters with fisted hands. Frenzy danced in his eyes. "Bastard!" Running to Hadrian, he kicked his head again and again, shouting, "Bastard!"

Nethers joined him, using the butt of his rifle. "You're fortunate so many Governors want to kill you!" he spat. "Otherwise, every man here would gladly do it."

"And every woman," a cool voice asserted. "But he's not down: a tranquilizer won't subdue his dunespike for long."

Snofrid's arm hairs stuck up at the austerity of the voice. She cautiously turned around. At the edge of the glade, the Hunters had taken a knee, heads bowed before the mightiest woman Snofrid had ever beheld.

She emerged from their ranks with a strong, mechanical stride befitting a warrior. A flock of beautiful Necromancers traced her steps like a pair of living wings; no men were among the party. Grotesque feather headdresses strung with beads of bone crested the women's heads—they were *Vanquishers*, rare female warriors who subdued enemies with their bare hands.

Snofrid noted that the chief woman flaunted a mask-less face, one that held every gaze; Silver beast scales overlapped the flesh from the left side of her face, all the way down to her left foot. Her lips were painted red, so vibrantly that they gave Snofrid the thought that she'd drunk from a trough of blood. Spiraled goat horns straddled the sides of her head and coal black hair fell to her thighs, tangled in the protractile claws on her left hand.

For a moment, the woman's eyes found Snofrid. It was startling, because the woman didn't move her head—her eyes simply slid toward Snofrid, their whites glinting in the sunlight. As Snofrid endured her stare, she grew increasingly afraid. A cold shadow stretched over her mind, seemingly reaching down and touching her very soul. Trembling, she took a small step back. "Who is she?"

"Jekel Necrosis," one of the Hunters replied. "She was Invidia's Chief Adviser on Armador. Which means you bow to her." He pulled Snofrid to her knees.

Jekel continued on her path toward Hadrian, as if it were the most important one she'd ever walked. She deactivated his Swoegar suit and then drew a curved Shotel sword from her back holster.

"A man without pride is not a man," she announced. "So what will this man be when I take his Halo?" Letting out a shrill war cry, she hacked off his arm from the elbow down, severing his Halo from the rest of his body.

Snofrid winced as blood oozed from his bicep. He didn't move, didn't even know that he'd been ruined; and he probably wouldn't know until the

Hunters had escaped. For the first time, she feared for him. Not only for losing his Halo, but for the shame he would receive when he reported the failed mission to his Lord.

"Remove the Halo, Dracuslayer Bourkan," Jekel said, handing him the severed arm.

Coyote whipped a bowie knife from his harness. Taking Hadrian's bloody arm, he ripped the raptor claw from its palm; the sparkling silver power-source was fading. Coyote scalped off the Halo and then handed it to Jekel. Snofrid's stomach lurched. She looked away, thinking that she was going to empty her stomach.

Jekel dangled the Halo over the welx's jaws and said, "Show me the portal, Wolba, or I'll make you suffer as no man has ever suffered."

The welx clamped its jaws shut with a laugh.

"So be it," she said, and turned to Coyote. "Take his teeth."

Coyote used the pommel of the khopesh to break the welx's teeth. The Hunters gathered around to watch, cheering and battering the beast with their rifles until it yelped; two of them broke from the crowd to scorch the mud-tusque nests with flame throwers, while one of Jekel's Vanquishers administered medical aid to Hessia.

Coyote shoved the Halo down the welx's throat and Snofrid's strength threatened to abandon her. She knelt stock-still, zapped into a panicked stupor. Images of Armador streamed before her eyes, all burning in the breath of blackchant. Why someone would want to free Invidia she couldn't even fathom. Earth would bow under her power, just like Armador had bowed. Invidia wouldn't be merciful. She'd put both human and Inborn civilizations in chains. And nothing—no weapon or soldier—would be strong enough to challenge her.

Her mind was so numb she almost didn't register the feathery sensation unfurling across it. Her vision divided; on one side, she saw the welx being force-fed the Halo, and on the other, she saw a sniper barrel jutting from the opening of a hollow log. Two small white hands covered the barrel with leaves as a voice said, *"It looks like I missed absolutely nothing."*

Snofrid lifted her head. *"Rhode?"*

"Who else would it be? Everyone else is either dead or a traitor."

She wrested back the hope that was trying to spill through her. *"I tried to call you before. Why didn't you answer?"*

"I needed to confirm that you weren't pro-Invidia like Nethers and all the rest of those bastards."

"What about you?" Snofrid checked. *"How can I trust you when you're Coyote's half-brother?"*

"If I was a dirty traitor, I'd be out there and not over here, girl." He scraped up some frozen mud, softened it in his palm and then rubbed it on his mask. *"And even if I was a traitor, I would never have trusted Jekel Necrosis. She's famous for hating men. All men, even the Lords and the Governors. The only people she likes are her Vanquishers and Invidia. Bourkan should be watching his back."*

Snofrid had had the same thought. Jekel would choose her allegiance to Invidia over every person here. *"Why is her face like that? Is she half Skinwalker?"*

"She wishes," Rhode scoffed. *"She broke a Covenant Spell a while back. Being ugly is her punishment."* He slipped on a pair of ear defenders. *"Okay, girl. Since you're anti-Invidia, I'm going to use you—for whatever it's worth."*

Snofrid had never been so eager to work with Rhode. *"I was going to say the same about you."*

"You're the one in handcuffs, girl. Since the Commander is out and the Coyote is a double-agent, I'm in command now." He dipped a finger in the snow and scrubbed dirt from his eyepieces. Then he peered through his scope, zooming in on the crowd of Hunters. *"I only have a butt shot on Wolba, and his butt is armored, so I'm going to need you to blow him up with the Coyote's acid grenade."*

Snofrid spotted the grenade swinging from Coyote's belt. *"How am I supposed to get it? My hands are shackled and he's over fifteen feet away."*

"Patience, girl." Rhode placed his mil dots on Coyote. *"I'm going to herd the Coyote to your position. You'll probably only have one chance to swipe the grenade, so don't miss."*

"Don't worry." She unfolded her hands, her shackles clanking. *"There's no way I'll miss."*

Rhode cast a brief look at Hadrian stretched out in the snow. *"They're going to try to frame the Commander as an All-Steam Hunter as soon as they get the portal coordinates. After you blow up Wolba, you need to hit the woods. We're witnesses, so they're going to want us dead. We can't let that happen."*

Snofrid had already deduced this much. *"I know. But we're going to need backup after. The Commander's brother is in the city. Is there any way you can contact him with your bug dials?"*

"Yeah, but wait a minute." Rhode snorted. *"How do you know Cid the Insidious?"*

"He's my Shadow."

Rhode switched on his phone and pulled up a bucket list.

"What are you doing?" she said.

"It's none of your business, girl." He put a checkmark beside the goal—fight beside Cid the Insidious—and then went on. *"Okay. Stream me a picture of Cid's location."*

Snofrid, praying Lycidius was somewhere in the Alley, recollected all the rooms inside and channeled them to the boy's mind. *"He should be in one of those. But hurry. The welx just ate its last Halo."*

She waited in a bout of sweating, counting seconds that felt far too long. Over by the welx, Coyote twirled his khopesh impatiently. Silver light glowed from the beast's throat as it swallowed Hadrian's power-source. The Hunters, also impatient, kicked it harder, and shouted for it to digest faster.

Jekel stepped on the welx's neck, forcing its head into the snow. "If you weren't such a coward, Wolba, we might have allowed you to live. You would've spent your life buried in a box, and, since life seems to be all you desire, I'm sure it would've been sufficient."

"Okay." Rhode clicked back into Snofrid's mind. *"Cid's en route. He's packing a Hematic and something called a Steelrunner."*

"The Hematic is my brother, Desya."

"Whatever." Rhode pinched an eye shut. *"Get focused. I'm moving the Coyote right now."*

"Okay." She slid one foot out in front, preparing to sprint. *"Ready when you are."*

A shot fired, striking the snow at Coyote's feet. The Hunters dispersed to the edges of the glade while Coyote leapt out of the line of fire, landing a few feet from Snofrid. Lunging forward, she broke from her two guards and rammed him. He spun around and elbowed her in the windpipe and brought his knee up to her gut. The air fled her lungs. Choking, she staggered back into the arms of the Hunters.

"Tell me you didn't just utterly fail," Rhode exclaimed.

She coughed, straining for air. *"I didn't utterly fail."*

Rhode checked Coyote's empty belt. *"Okay, okay. But that's just the first step, girl. Never celebrate until the fight is over."*

"Yeah, right," she wheezed. *"You were the one cheering twenty minutes ago."*

Coyote, now ducking behind the boulder, sent five Hunters into the forest. "Kill the shooter."

"No," Jekel intervened. "Your men have proved their worthlessness one time too many." She summoned two of her Vanquishers and ordered them to kill Rhode.

"Never going to happen," Rhode laughed, shifting his scope on a Hunter. *"No one can find me with this muzzle brake."*

As the Vanquishers dashed into the trees, swinging their hook swords, Jekel put two more on Snofrid. "Don't let her move again."

"Yes, Mistress."

Snofrid felt like a dwarf in comparison to the two women that moved toward her. The male Hunters restraining her pedaled back as the Vanquishers placed their large hands on her shoulders. Right away, she started to dread the moment when she'd make her next move.

"We need to hurry," she said to Rhode, seeing that the welx had finished feeding. *"As long as the welx is alive, the coordinates will be readable. Clear me a path and I'll toss the grenade."*

"Not so fast." Rhode looked up, and a tree branch fell over his face. *"Even with my sharp shooting, chances are, you're going to get shot."* He adjusted the branch, fitting it back on his head. *"The hard part is going to be getting away. If you get nabbed again, I'm not going to save you."*

She nodded, fingering the pin of the grenade in her sleeve. Her blood was rushing so fast, she felt lightheaded. Somewhere in the back of her mind, she registered that she was about to destroy the *only* way back to Armador. This weighed her down with the strongest guilt she'd ever felt. How many families would she separate for all time? How many people would be abandoned to a life of slavery because of what she was about to do? Yes, she knew destroying all ties to the portal was her only choice, but it still felt wrong. It still felt like a crime.

Duty over fear, she told herself. It was the single thought that kept her from dropping the grenade. *"Make the shot,"* she said.

"Calculating distance," Rhode announced. *"The Vanquisher on your left is about to give up wearing tall heels."* He pulled the trigger, sending a bullet flying at the woman's ankle. The ankle blew apart as the bullet struck, and the woman toppled over, hissing.

"Now," Rhode ordered, firing a shot at the other Vanquisher's hand. *"Throw it now."*

Snofrid's adrenaline heaved as she pulled the clip. Dropping to her knees, she skidded across the ice and chucked the grenade through the welx's gaping ribcage.

"She just threw a live one!" Nethers gasped. He bolted out from behind his tree cover. "Get it out. Get it out!"

A dozen hunters stampeded the welx, knocking into one another. They slid to a halt and stuck their arms in the welx's ribcage, sorting through its innards in search of the grenade.

"Where the hell is it?" Coyote said shakily. "Where the hell is it?"

Snofrid felt the Vanquisher who'd taken a hand-shot seize her by the shoulders with her uninjured hand. The woman's cold fingers squeezed her nape, before threads of icy-hot pain stunned her skull. *"Rhode, get her off me!"*

"I don't have a clear shot. Move," Rhode urged. *"Move, or you're going to get melted."*

Snofrid couldn't move under the Vanquisher's grip. Welts formed on her skin, bubbling into blisters.

"My bullet took her hand clean off," Rhode yelled, *"Punch the wound."*

Snofrid started panting hard, so hard she began to hyperventilate. She wasn't going to be beaten. Not again.

"Run!"

An intense current of resistance built inside of her, sucking the energy from every part of her body, and filtering it to her core. She shuddered, feeling like she was going to explode. And she did. The current yawned in her chest. It flared out down her arms and pooled in her wrists, jerking her spine in a whiplash motion. The shackles jangled as she was lifted upright. She splayed her hands out in front of her, screaming, before an eruption of energy bloomed around her. A white shield spilled from her hands and wrapped her in an impenetrable sphere. The Vanquisher was thrust backward; she struck a tree and was skewered on a branch.

Rhode rose to his knees. *"Whoa. Where is that coming from?"*

"I-I don't know," Snofrid gasped, maintaining the shield in place. An instant later, a crack erupted in the glade and the welx exploded.

"Bull's-eye!" Rhode cheered.

Snofrid stared, wide-eyed, as Hunters were thrown into the tree line; a great spot of red marked where the welx had been while bits of beast flesh and innards rained down about the glade. Jekel let out a furious roar; Coyote scrambled to his knees, desperately scraping the blood into a puddle, hoping to see the coordinates; Nethers and Darling were beside him, motionless with despair. The Hunters and Vanquishers recovered and charged Snofrid with their weapons drawn.

"You better hold that deflection shield in place," Rhode advised. *"Drop it and you're going to be decorating the forest."*

Snofrid broke into a cold sweat as the Hunters cordoned her off. Bullets rained down on her shield, each one sapping a portion of her strength. They ricocheted off her shield's surface, and, like boomerangs, returned to the men who'd fired them, wounding, and even killing them. Tears of exhaustion and fear spilled from her eyes. She willed herself to sustain the power, but her body felt drained; she might've collapsed from fatigue, if her body wasn't repeatedly regenerating itself.

"Cease fire," Jekel ordered. She strode away from the welx's remains, shoving her Shotel blade in her scabbard, and vomited a pillar of magic at Snofrid's shield. Green and vicious, it issued from her open mouth like a molten tornado. Snofrid's arms quaked, threatening to snap as if they were corn stalks.

"Rhode," she cried. *"I don't think I can hold it."*

"Think like that and you won't," he said. *"Just focus, and tell yourself you can do it, girl."*

Snofrid summoned all her strength. She gritted her teeth and splayed her hands wider, until the shackles bit into her wrists.

"That's it," Rhode encouraged, banging a fist on his rifle. *"Keep doing that."*

Tilting her head upward, she stared at the blinding shell of energy sizzling around her. A rush of hope flowed through her, reinforcing her endurance. Jekel's magic continued to rage across the shield, zigzagging through the cracks, seeking a way inside. Digging her heels in the snow, Snofrid wrenched her hands farther apart, breaking her shackles; the shield expanded and rippled across the glade. Hunters staggered back, toppling over, scattering like straw in a strong wind.

Jekel's magic veered sideways into the forest and set the trees aflame. With a snarl, she snapped her teeth shut, breaking the flow.

"Whohoo!" Rhode cheered in excitement. *"You totally owned her!"*

"Pack up," Jekel growled. "We need to be at the aircraft before the Legion attacks." She wiped spittle from her chin, her beast eye fluttering wildly. "Five of you will remain. As soon as the girl releases the shield, bury her alive."

"It will be done, mistress."

Five Hunters situated themselves at the tree line with rifles. A giant Hunter, roughly six foot seven, grasped Hadrian's ankles and dragged him from the glade, leaving a streak of blood in the snow; Coyote, Nethers and Darling gathered up chunks of the welx and stuffed them into leather rucksacks; the Vanquishers took formation behind Jekel while other Hunters helped the wounded to their feet.

"Where is the shooter?" Jekel demanded, scanning the trees. "We can't leave until both witnesses are accounted for."

"Then you'll never leave," Rhode chuckled. *"And when I run out of bullets, Cid the Insidious will dominate you all."*

"I'll find him," Coyote assured. Tossing his rucksack to Nethers, he jogged into the trees.

Snofrid watched after him with a nervous feeling. Coyote had excellent hearing to have been able to detect laser wire. *"Rhode, maybe you should change your position."*

"Bourkan can't find me," he guaranteed, patting the muzzle of his rifle. *"This muzzle brake is designed to keep the shooter's location hidden."*

"Still, it might be a good idea to move."

Rhode sighed. *"Girls. They always worry. That's why only a few make good soldiers."*

Peripherally, Snofrid noticed Jekel staring at her. The woman's eyes were slanted again, baring the whites.

"Why do you look so pleased?" Jekel inquired. "There are other ways to locate the portal."

Snofrid saw her bluff as clearly as if it were dressed in red. "If there are other ways, then you shouldn't look so disappointed."

"Your stunt here was a setback that I didn't intend, but revolutions are never simple." Jekel's voice grew lighter, more optimistic. "Unrest is growing in our kind like a sickness. Within ten years, the unrest will drive them to attack the Lord Office. The Lords *will* fall. It's only a question of time."

"You'll free yourselves from five tyrants, only to enslave yourselves to one," Snofrid pointed out. "You think Invidia will give you some kind of utopian existence, but how is that possible when all her power is capable of is destruction?"

Jekel's beast eye glinted. Her voice latched into Snofrid's mind, reverberating as a harsh whisper. *"Yes, Invidia will destroy,"* she granted. *"But it will be Inborn men. In Invidia's new world, men will serve womankind."* Her twisted eyes swept across the lines of male Hunters. *"They'll be kept alive for only one purpose: breeding."*

Rhode snorted. *"This lady's brain is in her foot if she thinks that's Invidia's plan."*

Snofrid didn't have time to respond: she noticed the Coyote making a break for Rhode's hideout. *"Rhode, watch out,"* she warned.

"Clam down, girl," Rhode said, taking aim at Coyote. *"I've got him at point-blank range."*

Coyote, still tearing toward Rhode, cracked one of his lighting whips. The whip sent out a burst of heat, melting Rhode's bullet like a flake of snow.

"Shit." Rhode threw his rifle and darted into the trees, panting loudly, shedding branches from his forest suit.

When Rhode glanced over his shoulder, Snofrid saw Coyote unwinding a Longxu hook from his belt and panicked. *"Run, Rhode! He can hit you at ten meters."*

Coyote swung the Longxu rope in a wide arc, sending the hook hurtling toward Rhode's feet; it coiled around his ankles and then jerked tight. Rhode stumbled, tried to brace his fall, and then crashed into the snow.

Snofrid's heart staggered. *"Oh my hell."* She took a step forward, nearly releasing her deflection shield. *"Get up, Rhode. Get up!"*

Rhode flipped onto his back, groaning. His jaw clenched in anger, and he shouted, "You'll regret this, Bourkan!"

Coyote aimed his rifle at the boy's chest with a quiet laugh. "Not likely."

Rhode propped himself on his elbows, his eyes watering. "ALL turncoats get their due."

"This isn't a video game, Vortigern." Coyote stepped on the boy's chest, slamming him into the ground. "In the real world, fairness doesn't exist. If it did, the Five Lords would be corpses, Inborns would be free from the oppression of the Lord Office, and we'd all return home."

Rhode tried to wrestle Coyote's boot off him, and tears sprang from his eyes. "Armador stopped being our home the minute we left."

"Wrong," Coyote corrected. "Armador stopped being *your* home the minute you cozied up to earth. We don't belong here; we never will." He cocked his rifle. "But it sounds like you'll be happy to die here."

Coyote fired two shots into the boy's chest. Rhode slumped onto his back with his legs bent under him and his eyes wide open.

Snofrid screamed. Her body jerked upright in horror before a violent rage ripped through her, all the way to the marrow of her bones. Everything around her diminished, so that all she could make out were grey spots clouding over Rhode's vision. Before it faded, Coyote tossed the rope to the ground and said, "Shooter down. All units move out."

Deadlocked

Snofrid hated Coyote. She wanted to kill him, along with everyone who'd betrayed her. She was panting hard, her face flaming hot with panic, as she supported her deflection shield. Sobbing and choking, she engaged the impulse to release the deflection shield and check if Rhode was still alive; but five Hunters prowled outside the glade like hyenas waiting to feed.

Sweat trickled into her eyes as she scanned the forest in search of Lycidius and Desya. All she saw were the gnarled shadows of trees reaching across the smooth snow; every now and then, a squirrel scampered across a branch, racking up her hopes for a few seconds, before leaving them to shatter.

"You can't hold that shield much longer," a Hunter hollered. He'd taken a break from digging a deep pit where he intended to bury her alive. "If you're smart, you'll lower it now. Do it and I'll let you keep a few fingers."

"That won't work on me," Snofrid called. His intimidation tactics were as apparent as the smut stains on his trousers. "Take my fingers and they'll grow back."

The Hunter was shorter than the other four, but had a stalky build. Each time he turned his head to speak to his comrades, she caught a glimpse of his reddish-brown faux hawk, tangled in his gasmask straps, and the flexing cords in his neck.

"If they grow back, there will be more to take off," he pointed out. He flung his shovel to the ground. "Let us in, or wait for us to come in there and drag you out. Either way, you're going to suffer."

"I'm not letting you in."

"Think about it this way. The longer you hold that up, the deeper the hole gets."

She looked off into the trees, unable to stomach the sight of him. All Dracuslayer training was the same. *Stress and pressure.* He'd hammer her with both until she gave into fear. Lycidius and Desya would arrive any moment and she only had to sustain her power until they did. "Then you're going to have to dig to the core of the earth, because I'm not taking it down."

He sneered. Cracking his knuckles, he started circling the shield, breathing slow through his gasmask filter. "When a man doesn't see his work pay off, he looks for someone to blame. I'm really going to enjoy torturing you before you go under ten tons of dirt."

Snofrid felt vulnerable as he strolled behind her. "If you really had a Plan B like your Mistress Jekel said, then you shouldn't be so upset."

"It doesn't change what I sacrificed, or how many people put down their lives to guarantee that this day happened." He stopped on her left side. "But an earth-lover like you wouldn't know anything about sacrifice."

Snofrid detected a growing resentment in his tone but didn't care if she pushed him.

"That's the problem with plans," he said. "They rarely go the way you intend. The best way to get what you want is to impulsively go for it. The expectations are lower."

"Set your sights low and you'll never get anywhere," she assured.

"A smart strategist moves incrementally—one step at a time." He gave the shield a quick run over. "Bullets can't get through this, but since you're shivering, it looks like something can." He tapped the corner of his hyena mask. "And it looks like a bit of shrapnel tore up your filter real good."

Snofrid's resilience took a blow. She hadn't even known that she could raise deflection shields until thirty minutes ago, so she was totally ignorant when it came to their capabilities. "I can block out whatever I decide," she told him. "Blow something in here and I'll send it back your way."

"Let's do a test round," he decided, and held up a hand. "Riskel. Smoke grenade."

One of the Hunters rifled a green cylinder grenade from his rucksack and pitched it to his comrade. Catching it, the Hunter yanked out the pin. He dropped the grenade and smoke rose around his feet, fanning into the shield.

Snofrid coughed the instant the smoke penetrated her filter. It rolled all around her, seeping through the shredded rubber of her mask and pouring into her lungs. Taking a wider stance, she tried to will the smoke back, but she only choked harder.

The Hunter continued walking, now with a lighter step. "Have you ever seen fruit desiccate in a dehydrator?"

Snofrid started wheezing. Her throat was so dry she could hardly intake air.

"Phosphorus pentoxide dries up the throat similarly," he told her. "Let's see how long you can inhale it."

She refused to break now. Drawing oxygen through her nose, she steadied her airflow with long, labored breaths. Fluid glazed over her eyes and her tendons pulled tight from the pressure. She was going to drop the shield if she didn't get out of the smoke. Her arms trembled. *"Don't let it fall,"* she urged herself. *"Five more minutes."* At a sudden sneeze, her shoulders hunched and the shield vanished like a popped bubble. It only took a second for her to register what had happened, and then another to run. Propelled by fear, she dashed toward the tree line until a pair of hands gripped her shoulders and towed her backward.

She kicked her captor's shins with frantic desperation. There was NO way she was going to be taken prisoner again.

"Snofrid, stop. Calm down." The hands slid to her waist, tightening to keep her in place. "It's Desya."

She straightened up, still shaking. "Dez…" His gasmask appeared in the clearing smoke, and above it, his soft brown eyes. Whirling, she threw her arms around him. "Dez!"

"It's okay, Sno," he said, folding her in his arms. "You're safe now."

"I'm sorry."

His grip tightened. "I was pissed coming over here, but now I really don't care what happened. Just calm down. I'm not mad."

She couldn't find any calmness. Her blood was surging, her brain communicating nothing but the urgency to explain herself. "I'm sorry," she said again, burying her face in his jacket. "I'm sorry."

At the sound of crunching snow, she lifted her head to see over his shoulder. Lycidius was dragging the Hunter toward the hole by his jacket collar. Blood spattered the front of the Hunter's flak jacket where his throat had been torn open, but his boots twitched, signaling that he was still alive. Lycidius threw him down at the edge of the hole and tore off his own gasmask.

"You just dug your own grave," he said. He stretched his mouth open, baring his teeth, and then roared until fire raged from his throat. The man burst into flames and crumbled into the hole in a cloud of smoke.

Snofrid closed her eyes, bracing herself for his reaction. Desya let her down and she ran to Lycidius. He grabbed her face and drew her against him. There was always that one person who was impossible to hide emotions from—who intensified everything until self-control moved out of reach. For her, Lycidius was that person. She couldn't bottle up her sadness or her rage and fear. For a moment, he did comfort her, made her feel like nothing existed outside of the small space they occupied. Her painful emotions melted into a sedating warmth that touched every part of her body. With each muffled sob, her body shook and Lycidius's hold readjusted to keep her secure; but all his efforts fizzled out when his confusion became too overwhelming.

"What happened?" he finally said, cupping her face. "Some little punk contacted me and talked my ear off, then left a P.S. about you being held hostage. Why are there dead Dracuslayers everywhere? And what was that shield you were holding?" He jerked his head at the pile of mush that had once been the welx. "And *what* the hell died over there?"

"I'll tell you everything," she promised. "But we have to get out of here, Lycidius. It's not safe."

"Cid," Desya called, jogging toward them. "I want to know what happened too, but she's right. We need to leave before the Sky-Legion flies in. We can figure this all out when we get to the Underground."

Lycidius said nothing. He took Snofrid's arm and led her toward the tree line. She started to ask about Jazara's whereabouts, but an emergency siren blared across the city, drowning out her words. She aimed her sights skyward, searching for signs of the Sky-Legion. Through the aquamarine bolts of electricity, she saw little more than snow clouds.

"The Sky-Legion's been spotted," Desya realized, stepping back to gain a broader scope of the sky. "Take her to the Underground, Cid. I need to go."

"Wait." Snofrid craned towards Desya. "You're not coming?"

"I will," he promised. "But when the Legion gets in here, the Chancellor's gonna be the first target. I need to find Parisa and get her out."

"No," Snofrid objected. She wrestled free of Lycidius and seized his arm. "No. Dez, please don't go."

"I can't leave her to die. The Sky-Legion will kill her, Sno. They'll *torture* her."

Snofrid's self-control almost splintered. She'd practically sold herself to ensure his safety, and now he was risking his life for someone that had left them to die. For someone who'd *abandoned* him. "What if you can't get her?" Snofrid demanded, her voice cracking. "What if she doesn't even let you see her, Dez?"

"She *will*. But if not, then at least I tried."

"Please don't do this," Snofrid begged. "Dez, I can't lose you, too."

Lycidius stepped between them. "We need to go," he said to Snofrid. "My Steelrunner is parked a half-mile off."

"Wait." She gave Desya a last pleading look. "Desya. *Please*, come with us."

He scraped his hands down his gasmask and, for a moment, she thought he might reconsider. But then he turned abruptly and ran from the glade. "I can't, Snofrid," he called. "I'm sorry. I'll be back before the shield goes down."

Out of the Underground

Flight hanger 400 of the Hollowstone Underground was already swarming with Inborn refugees when Lycidius landed his Steelrunner. From the pillion, Snofrid could see teams of crewmen hauling luggage into the cargo bays of aircrafts. Hundreds of passengers, young and old, stood in zigzagging lines across the warehouse, each clasping their ticket as they anxiously waited to board. Snofrid's fear left her. The more she looked about the hangar, the more a homesick sense filled her. This was where she'd first met Lycidius and she remembered the space as if it were a part of her—the marble floor that smelled of antiseptics, the neat rows of gunships and aircrafts, the frosted electrical fixtures, and the buzz of the radiator system. As she had the first day she'd come here, she felt hopeful. Even though the hangar was cold and vast, it reminded her of all the carefree optimism she'd had back then.

"Jazara's waiting by the ship," Lycidius said, stepping off the

Steelrunner. He lifted off his gasmask and then proceeded to unstrap Rhode's body from the back of the pillion. "I'm going to load up my Steelrunner, this body, and all the luggage, and then we'll talk."

Snofrid stared at Rhode, rolled up in her white parka, and misery crawled into her heart. He hadn't deserved to die, especially like this—by the betrayal of his own half-brother. She wanted to tell Lycidius everything but knew it would set off a chain of events she'd have no power or influence to control. He'd go after Hadrian and she'd be obligated to release him from his Shadow position right now.

"Which ship are we taking?" she asked, dismounting the pillion.

"The *TS Infineon*. It's the black one by the doors." Lycidius nodded toward a ducted-fan, twin-rotor gunship grounded near the hangar's entrance. The roof of the fuselage had been painted with a large handprint; each finger on the handprint was color-coordinated to one of the five formal Inborn species—blue, green, red, rose and white. It would communicate to the Sky-Legion that they were friendlies.

"The captain is an old contact," Lycidius said, hoisting Rhode's body into his arms. "He used to be a Dracuslayer in the forties. Tell the crewmen you're with me and they'll let you board early."

She gave Rhode one last glance, then picked up her satchel. "I'll see you in there."

"Wait, Snofrid. My brother told me about the Covenant Spell," he said. "I understand you couldn't tell me the truth, and I'm not angry."

She pressed her forehead to his shoulder. "Thank you."

The crowds leading to the gunship were thick and Snofrid was forced to nudge people from her path. Outside the cargo bay, she found Jazara waiting with a pink checkered backpack slung over her shoulder and bangles jingling on her wrists; her bicycle and three suitcases were being loaded onto the ship under her watchful eye. Snofrid loosed an easy breath at the sight of her. When she flagged her down with a wave, Jazara gasped loudly. Charging forward, she flung her arms around Snofrid.

"Just because I'm hugging you, doesn't mean I forgive you," Jazara huffed. "I'm still mad."

"I know. You have a right to be mad."

"We thought you got blown up in the bombs," she went on. "And then we thought you were found out. After that, we thought you got lost. And then we didn't know what to think."

"I can't imagine what I put you through. I'm sorry."

Jazara's tone softened. "Well, I'm not *that* mad anymore. It's just...I was scared you were hurt."

"I would've thought the same thing if it had been you," Snofrid said. She took the girl's hand and hurried toward the fuselage ramp. "I'll tell you everything as soon as we get to the Earth Square Fortress."

"You'd better."

While they waited in line to board, Snofrid inspected the gunship. This was the ship that would carry her from Hollowstone forever. It looked sturdy enough, but she was aware that it would need to fly out of the city without being shot down by human anti-aircraft weapons. This didn't trouble her so much on her own account; it hadn't escaped her that everyone in the world she loved would be onboard.

After the crewmen had granted them entry, they strode up the ramp into the fuselage. "Is Dez with Lycidius?" Jazara asked, as they climbed a staircase to the highest level of the ship.

"No," Snofrid replied, noting the girl's concern. "He's doing something important in the city, but he'll be here before we takeoff."

"What important thing?"

"He's picking up one of his friends. I'm not sure yet, but she might come with us to Earth Square."

Jazara's eyes puffed up with suspicion. "Dez didn't tell me we were bringing anyone else. Which friend is it?"

"I don't think you've met her," Snofrid said, avoiding eye contact. "But I'm sure he'll introduce you later."

"He'd better. I thought I knew all his friends, but now I find out he's keeping secret ones." She frowned, staring dismally at the glass floor. "He promised me he'd never keep secrets."

On the main seating deck, Snofrid took a window seat behind Jazara and shrugged from her soiled coat. A blizzard of thoughts swirled about in her head, tossing her this way and then that, until she felt stretched thin; but it was Rhode that left her feeling hollow. A similar feeling came to her each time a person she knew died, as if a piece of the universe had been chipped off. The world felt emptier, leading her to wonder where those pieces might go after they were broken off. Humans and Inborns alike believed in plenty of afterlives. Although she'd tried when she was younger, she'd never been able to put her faith in a paradise; largely, because she feared that if one existed, she might not be allowed to enter. As she'd been locked out of society all her life, it seemed fitting that all other places would do the same.

Exhaustion set in like a harsh cold, but for a while she couldn't fall asleep. The realization that she was blowing off Atlas made her feel restless. It had occurred to her on the flight over that she was going to skip out on her part of their bargain—even after he'd upheld his. She gave herself confidence with the idea that he was probably taking the fastest jet out of the city to escape the Sky-Legion.

With this thought reassuring her, she fell asleep. She dreamed of Ryuki, and of their old house on Quintree Quay. Daylight shone through the whole dream, making the world seem perfect and free of sadness. When she opened her eyes, it was dark and Lycidius was gently shaking her awake. Through her grogginess, she observed a clear change in him. He was sitting coolly in his jackal-head bomber jacket, with his legs stretched out, and a rifle over his knees. "How long was I out?" she asked.

"A while. It's 2:00 a.m. on Saturday."

Her gaze jumped across the deck in search of Desya. The seats were packed with passengers, some asleep, others talking on their phones, and quite a few holding one another for comfort. "Where's Desya?"

"On his way over. He found Parisa a few hours ago, but with all the riots and traffic, it could take them a few more hours."

"The Chancellor just let her leave?"

"The Chancellor doesn't know," he muttered. "She left him, just like Desya."

Snofrid suddenly worried about Desya getting arrested. But she doubted the Chancellor's men would be able to locate them in the mass hysteria.

She spotted Jazara talking to some younger children a few rows down and took advantage of the privacy. "I'll tell you what we were doing," she finally said, forcing herself to look Lycidius in the eye. "Me and your brother."

"Go ahead, Snofrid."

She took a moment to map out her story before relaying it from start to finish—including the details of her Covenant with Hadrian, how they'd been betrayed during the hunt, and how Rhode had helped her bring down Nox Wolba. Lycidius maintained an almost inscrutable expression throughout. His face paled at each mention of Hadrian, and he chewed his barbell tensely when she spoke of Wolba. She found it more difficult than she'd anticipated to tell him that the All-Steam Hunters had taken Hadrian with them and added that she understood if he wanted to go after him. She even admitted the side-deal she'd made with Hadrian in which she'd agreed to free him from his duties as her Shadow in exchange for a pardon for her and Desya.

Lycidius's answer to all of this surprised her.

"I can't help Hadrian right now," he said, his knuckles white on his rifle. "At first, I thought the Coyote was crazy for trying to frame Hadrian as an All-Steam Hunter. But now I'm thinking differently. It might work if one of the Lords or even just a few Governors back him up."

"Why would anyone do that?"

"Hadrian has even more enemies than his father did. So if the Coyote gets the support he needs, Hadrian will be put on trial in the Empyrean City. But you're a credible witness; even better, they think you've been dealt with. If this all plays out right, you could get Hadrian exonerated."

Snofrid would do this for Lycidius in a heartbeat. But there was a problem. "If I testify in the Governor's Court, it might not mean much. I'm still a halfbreed, Lycidius. Hadrian promised to make sure I was pardoned, but in his situation, he can't exactly help me anymore.

"It doesn't matter. You can still testify legally and the Governor's Court won't be able to do a damn thing about it."

"Is that what you want me to do?"

"If Hadrian's defense calls for witnesses, then yes."

Snofrid nodded, trying to hide how afraid she felt. "When would it happen?"

Lycidius broke off to give a nosy onlooker a warning glare. When the person turned away, he tilted his head closer, his breath warming her ear. "I don't know," he whispered. "Our trials aren't like human trials. Things move fast. If you're called on to testify, it's going to happen soon."

"How soon?"

"A few weeks." Lycidius rubbed his temples. "There's something else. If you do this, you'll need to go into witness protection until the trial. We'd have to put Earth Square on hold until then."

She sat back, needing a moment to process. Just a few hours ago she'd believed that she'd be free, that all her problems would vanish with the death of the welx. Now, more daunting matters were tumbling in around her, suffocating her with their immensity. If she testified in the Governor's Court, she'd be directly blocking the agendas of some very powerful Inborns. Once again, she was faced with a choice that frightened her to the depths of her being—the kind of choice that could have serious repercussions for her family.

"Are you really planning on releasing me?" Lycidius asked softly.

She checked his cloudy eye, which was glinting even in the gloomy lighting; for the first time, Rima looked hopeful. A sore lump swelled in her throat. "I promised your brother I would."

"Do you *want* to release me, Snofrid?"

"No. But I've kept you from the Inborn Army long enough, Lycidius. And, like you said, if somehow all of this plays out right, then Desya and I will both be pardoned. We could be together without breaking our laws— and you wouldn't be shamed."

He eyed her hand, as if wanting to hold it. "Getting relieved of my position isn't something that can happen overnight. I need to contact your uncle, Lord Alcander, and five other people before anything can be done."

A sudden tremor under the gunship made Snofrid clasp her seatbelt. "What is that?"

Lycidius lifted his eyes to the ceiling. "It's magic. The Sky-Legion has been trying to breach the energy shield for the past five hours."

"Is it safe for Desya to be out there?"

"Yes. But if he doesn't get here in an hour, I'll go and get him."

"Dez is here!" Jazara announced. She was running down the aisle toward them, her cheeks rosy with excitement. "And he brought his friend, too."

Snofrid got to her feet. "I'm coming."

"One minute, Snofrid." Lycidius leaned over her path, blocking her exit. "That shield you raised..."

She touched her Halo reflexively. "I don't know where it came from. I was going to ask you if I've ever raised one before."

"No." He checked her Halo curiously. "Not that I've seen."

"Hurry up!" Jazara hollered. "Dez is coming up the stairs."

"Let's go," she urged, stepping over his legs.

Snofrid jogged down the aisle with Lycidius on her tail. That Desya was safe put down the last of her immediate worries. She found him pinned at the top of the staircase, being interrogated by Jazara about the Sky-Legion; Parisa was below him, looking uncomfortable. A gold beaded face veil screened all but her upturned brown eyes, which retreated to the floor as Snofrid arrived; the red peplum dress she was wearing stressed a conspicuous bump in her belly.

The shock hit Snofrid like a blast of frozen air. In a flash, her gaze darted to Desya. His face looked battered by humiliation and anger, which Jazara didn't seem to pick up on; the rims of his eyes were bloodshot, his chest rose and fell in an erratic breathing rhythm, and she could see the indentations of his fangs behind his lips.

"That better not be the Chancellor's kid," Lycidius said through gritted teeth.

Snofrid tried to hope the same thing, but the discomfort in Parisa's face obliterated it. "If it is, the Leathertongue's will come looking for her," she realized. "It will be dangerous to have her here."

"That's why she's not going to stay." Lycidius guided Desya past Jazara and farther down the steps. Once they were a safe distance, he said, "Whose baby is that?"

"Whose do you think?"

"Don't be so sure. Your wife gives a lot and leaves more hanging."

Desya rammed his forehead into Lycidius's nose, so hard that blood jetted out. Before Snofrid could react, Lycidius struck back. He smashed his elbow against Desya's windpipe, restricting his airflow. Desya collapsed on the handrail, clutching his neck and wheezing.

"Stop!" Jazara flung herself over Desya and screamed at Lycidius, "Don't hurt him, you stupid head!"

Snofrid raced down the steps and grabbed Lycidius's arm. "Lycidius, stop. Don't you *dare* hit him again!"

Desya propped himself up. Rage drained his face ashen white as he shoved past them all. At the top of the steps, Parisa reached out to him. "Wait, Desya. Where do I go?"

He stared at her as if she were muck on his boot soles. "I don't give a damn anymore." He strode onto the seating deck.

While Jazara scrambled after him, Snofrid gaped at Lycidius. "You *hit* him."

Lycidius turned to Parisa. "Get out of here. Now."

"No," Snofrid cut in. She climbed the steps and called to Parisa, "Go find a seat. You can fly out with us, but you're on your own as soon as we land."

Snofrid left both Parisa and Lycidius on the stairs. She passed Jazara, who was sulking in her seat, and hurried into the chair beside Desya. He stared grimly at the tarnished chain in his hand; his wedding band was clipped to one end.

"I'm sorry, I should never have gone after her," he said. "I'm done with her. For good this time. As soon as we're out of here, I'm going to reenlist."

"Desya, stop," Snofrid urged. "You can't make this kind of a decision when you're like this."

"When I'm like *this*?" Resentment bled into the question. "I've been like *this* since both of my families died. Since my baby died, and since Neko was murdered." His voice grew louder, hovering on feverish. "I'm never *not* going to be like this, Snofrid. I don't have anything left."

"You have *me*, Dez."

A tear dripped onto his jeans. He brought a fist over his mouth to force in a sob.

Snofrid sat silently while the breathy sounds of his crying pounded nails into her heart. She strained to say something to comfort him, to convince him that everything would turn out all right; but each idea she came up with felt weightless with the realization that he'd suffered more than her by far.

"I need to walk," he said, moving to stand.

"Wait, Dez." She picked up the ring. "You don't want this?"

"I told you, Sno. I'm *done*."

As he disappeared down the aisle, Snofrid stared at the tarnished wedding band. For as long as she'd known him, he'd put his faith in something, whether it was his family, friends, or love. The despair he was feeling now had destroyed that faith. If the ring had meant anything to him, it was hope, and she refused to let him live without it. She tucked the chain into her pocket.

The deck appeared darker as she reclaimed her seat. Parisa had found a spot alone in the back where she was cupping her baby bump and blinking back tears; Jazara was curled up on her seat, her face buried in her arms. Outside of the grief, Snofrid was grateful to see Lycidius talking to Desya near the staircase; the heat between them had been replaced by somber nods and words in Russian.

Wiping her eyes, she turned to the gunship next to theirs. Through the window, she noticed a little girl with blond curls watching her and clasping a stuffed polar bear. The girl smiled before facing her mother, who was reading her a picture book. Snofrid swallowed hard. She didn't want to see her family ripped apart, which was what had been gradually happening since Ryuki's death. Both Lycidius and Desya had hurt her at times, but she knew she'd willingly bear the pain rather than lose them completely.

Lycidius hurried into their seat row and touched her shoulders. "I'm sorry," he said, his expression guilty. "I swear I didn't mean to hit him, Snofrid. It was reflex."

She nodded. "It's okay, Lycidius. I know."

"Attention passengers," the captain's voice announced over the loud speaker. "The shield is down and we've been given the go-ahead to fly out. Fasten your seatbelts and everybody hope we don't get shot down."

Snofrid stayed close to Lycidius. She hardly heard the wave of restless murmurs that passed over the seating deck. She scarcely even noticed when the gunship rocketed out of the hangar, across the Underground, and into the sky. Her mind was submerged in a desperate prayer to Ryuki. If he was in a heaven, she asked him to use his power to help them escape the city alive.

"It's okay," Lycidius told her, as if sensing her worry. "We have an escort." He motioned to the window.

At first she saw nothing until a flapping wing caught her eye. Two half-creature-half-machine dragons weaved in and out of the fog, bearing giant riders in cobalt armor; their facial armor plated only their foreheads and cheeks, and fur-lined cloaks flapped off their tanzanite beaded pauldrons. They seemed to be racing. One pulled ahead, streaking by their window; she could've sworn he winked at her.

"Who are they?" she asked.

"Contacts from my old unit. I called them a few hours ago on the transmission globe. They'll make sure we get out of the city without taking a hit."

She leaned closer to the window, and her breath quickened at the sight of flames bourgeoning all across the city.

Above, the grey storm clouds churned with a multitude of screeching dragons. Hundreds of thousands of them. Some swirled in tornado motions or flew in wedge formations, and others swan-dived into the city, spraying red fumes from their jaws; more hovered in flight, ruffling their wings and stretching their long, scaly necks as their riders closed in around

Hollowstone, casting a menacing shadow over the skyscrapers. It was impossible to see the streets amidst the commotion of flare-ups, wings, bodies and blood. Explosions collapsed gangways, which tumbled downward into the trees in flurries of sparks, and flames swarmed across houses, melting the metal into iridescent goo. As the fire raged, it superheated, so that buildings and bridges combusted from a distance; the wind propelled burning debris at a blistering speed, setting fleeing transports and civilians ablaze. Snofrid saw fighter planes, drones and attack helicopters flying out to meet the Sky-Legion, firing missiles into the ranks; everywhere, the bloodcurdling echo of explosions shocked the air.

She tightened her seatbelt when the gunship started to shudder. Passengers gripped the sides of their chairs.

"We're experiencing some minor turbulence," the captain announced calmly. "No cause to be alarmed. But in case of an emergency evacuation, parachutes are stored under the seats."

Snofrid huffed. "That's not very comfort—"

All her fear subsided when Lycidius squeezed her hand.

For the next few minutes, she kept her eyes on the window, holding her breath while the gunship flew over the city barrier. Everyone was silent, as if they too were marking the moment. They soared over the forest on the other side and Snofrid spotted the first rays of dawn on the horizon. In her heart, she thanked Ryuki.

Then she breathed freely.

VERDICT DAY

COMING IN 2017

Dear Reader,

In case you weren't already aware, T.S. Pettibone is a pen name. Our real names are Brittany and Nicole and we're identical twins. We just wanted to take a moment to thank you from the bottom of our hearts for reading Hatred Day. This story has become very dear to us over the past nine years that we've spent writing it, and we sincerely hope that it's become dear to you as well.

As you know, nothing helps a book gain traction more than positive reviews and word-of-mouth recommendations. So, if you've enjoyed Hatred Day, we would be deeply grateful if you took the time to leave a short review where you bought it, and if you recommended this book to your family and friends. Every single review and recommendation is a massive contribution to the success of this story. Once again, we're so thrilled you chose Hatred Day and hope you are excited to read the second installment in the Hatred Day Series, Verdict Day, coming in 2017.

Warmly,
T.S. Pettibone

Acknowledgements

First, and most notably, we owe thanks to our wonderful parents whose encouragement, guidance and support is the sole reason we are able to share this book with the world. Mom, thank you for reading and re-reading every draft we ever wrote, for always being there for us and for daring us to chase our dreams. And dad, thank you for sending us to writing classes, for teaching us to always aim high and for believing in us. We love you both.

To our editor, Matthew Zepf, for his eagle eye and brutal honesty. You are not only an extraordinary editor, but an extraordinary friend.

To our sister, Isabella, for her brilliant suggestions on plot and character.

To our secretary, Juliette Frelon, who was our first fan and will therefore remain the most special.

To Eric Egan, Jacqueline Garcia, Melissa Ranftl, Jeannie Freed and Hannah Phillips, for supporting us.

And thank you, lastly, to the readers of Hatred Day. We hope you are as excited to keep reading as we are to keep writing because the story has just begun…

T.S. PETTIBONE are identical twins with non-identical personalities. They live in California with their dog. For a glossary of terms and an in-depth look at the world of *Hatred Day*, visit tspettibone.com

www.facebook.com/tspettibone
@tspettibone

CPSIA information can be obtained at www.ICGtesting.com
Printed in the USA
LVOW08s2155180816

500936LV00010B/1006/P